D0064932

C 5-09

ALSO BY CATHY HOLTON

The Secret Lives of the Kudzu Debutantes

Revenge of the Kudzu Debutantes

BEACH TRIP

Cathy Holton

BEACH TRIP

A NOVEL

BALLANTINE BOOKS | NEW YORK

Beach Trip is a work of fiction. Names, characters, places,
and incidents are the products of the author's imagination
or are used fictitiously. Any resemblance to actual events, locales,
or persons, living or dead, is entirely coincidental.

Copyright © 2009 by Cathy Holton

All rights reserved.

Published in the United States by Ballantine Books, an imprint
of The Random House Publishing Group, a division of
Random House, Inc., New York.

BALLANTINE and colophon are registered trademarks
of Random House, Inc.

Permissions TK

ISBN 978–0-345–50599–6

Printed in the United States of America on acid-free paper

www.ballantinebooks.com

2 4 6 8 9 7 5 3 1

FIRST EDITION

Book design by Laurie Jewell

FOR MY PARENTS

In youth we learn; in age we understand.

— MARIE VON EBNER-ESCHENBACH

ACKNOWLEDGMENTS

Many thanks to Kate Collins, Kelli Fillingim, and all the folks at Ballantine for their editorial assistance and support; to Karen and the girls of the Thursday Night Out Club for helping to plant the seeds of this novel; to Kristin Lindstrom for her unfailing encouragement and advice; and to Mark, my truest reader and companion.

SPRING OF
1982

Lola was engaged to Briggs Furman, so her roommates were stunned the evening she came home and told them she was in love with a boy named Lonnie. They sat around in various poses of disbelief and concern, watching Lola and Lonnie, who stood, arms entwined, in the middle of the living room. Lola had leaves in her hair. This was six weeks before they were all set to graduate from college and go their separate ways into the wide world, and no one had suspected Lola of a secret love affair. Least of all Briggs.

Mel was the first to recover. "Lola, what are you doing?" she said.

Lola laughed and reached up and kissed Lonnie on the ear. Small and pretty, she had the face of a Botticelli angel. "That's Mel," she said, pointing. "And that's Sara and Anne Louise."

Sara and Anne Louise raised their hands mechanically.

Lonnie said, "How you doing?" He was pleasant-looking enough, with blue-gray eyes and light blond hair pulled back in a ponytail; still, he did not look like the kind of boy a daughter of the former governor of Alabama might bring home.

"Briggs has called ten times looking for you," Mel said flatly. From the first time they met freshman year, Mel had thought of Lola as the little sister she never had. There was something childlike about Lola, something fragile that made Mel want to protect her.

Lola seemed unconcerned that Briggs had called. She seemed unconcerned by anything but Lonnie, standing there and staring up at him with a look of absolute devotion on her face. She had never looked so happy, or so vulnerable. "I don't care," she said gaily. "I don't care about Briggs."

"Well, maybe you should tell him that."

"I tried. He won't listen."

Mel stood up abruptly. "Lola, can I talk to you?"

"No," Lola said. She dragged Lonnie off to the kitchen and a few minutes later they could hear them giggling and rummaging through the cabinets.

"Fuck," Mel said. "Now what do we do?"

"Why do we have to do anything?" Anne Louise asked irritably. She was sitting on the sofa, bundled in a heavy blanket even though it was May. She had grown so thin her round, pretty face seemed almost skeletal, the skin pulled tightly across her jaw and cheekbones. Anne Louise had always been difficult, but over the last few weeks she had become nearly unbearable. "It's her life. Let her marry whom she chooses."

"Are you kidding?" Mel said. "The guy's a high-school dropout! He's a maintenance man. What do you think Maureen's going to say about that?" Maureen was Lola's widowed mother, the Dowager Empress of Alabama, and no one had any doubt what she would say. After all, she had handpicked Briggs Furman based on his impeccable pedigree and social connections.

"Annie's right," Sara said, giving Mel a grave look. "Lola's happy. Leave her alone."

"She's happy now, but will she be happy later when Maureen finds out? Because you know Maureen's not about to let her only child run off with a barely employed maintenance man."

"She won't know about it until it's too late to stop it."

"But what about later? What about when she cuts Lola off without a dime? She's used to privilege and money. Can you imagine Lola clipping coupons or living on a budget, scraping along to make ends meet on a teacher's salary? And what about Briggs?"

No one said anything. Sara combed her long brown hair with her fingers. "What about him?" she asked finally.

"What's he going to say? What's he going to *do*?"

No one wanted to think about what Briggs might do. A former prep school quarterback, Briggs had wide shoulders and a violent temper.

"You heard Lola. She's not planning on telling him anything until after graduation. Until after she and Lonnie elope."

"And you think this elopement is a good idea?"

Sara shrugged. "It's what she wants. She's in love."

Mel made a disparaging sound. "Love?" she said. "Love doesn't put groceries on the table. It doesn't put Pampers on the baby." Mel had recently ended her own tragic love affair and now she was a cynic. The day after graduation, she was heading to New York to become a writer.

"I hope you're not suggesting what I think you're suggesting," Sara said evenly.

"I'm not suggesting anything," Mel snapped. Not that a marriage to Briggs Furman would be a love match either, at least not on Lola's part. Still, Briggs was from Lola's social class and he would know how to take care of her. Which is what Lola needed, Mel was convinced. Someone to take care of her.

"Because it's Lola's life and we have to let her live it."

"Yes, Sara, I know that."

"Twenty years from now," Annie said, looking thin and melancholy, "I don't want to be sitting around regretting the past. I don't want to be sitting around thinking about what I should have done."

Mel gave her a heavy look. "Twenty years from now, none of us will remember any of this."

There was a sudden sound of traffic in the street. Mel got up quickly and went to the window. In the kitchen, something crashed against the floor, followed quickly by Lola's sharp yelp of laughter.

Mel stood at the window, her shoulders rigid against the fading light. "Oh, my God," she said. "It's Briggs."

2005

Chapter 1

~~~~~~~~~~~~~

The phone rang but it was Mel, and Sara had no intention of talking to Mel. She relaxed and sank deeper into the steaming water of the bath. Candles flickered on the side of the tub. Pachelbel's "Canon" played softly in the background. Mel had called twice before and Sara hadn't answered either time. They had grown up together in tiny Howard's Mill, Tennessee, and had once been as close as sisters, but that was long ago. They still exchanged Christmas cards and the occasional e-mail, but they hadn't actually spoken for nearly twelve years, not since Sara's daughter Nicky was born.

Besides, Sara knew why Mel was calling.

Lola had reached her two days ago and in her drawling Alabama accent had invited her for a beach trip. "At my new beach cottage! For a week! No husbands or kids! Just the four of us together again for the first time since college. Annie says she'll go. Mel says she'll go if you do." Lola had sounded even more spaced out than usual. She kept referring to her beach house as a "cottage" when everyone knew it was a beachfront palace on exclusive Whale Head Island in North

Carolina. Lola's husband, Briggs, had made a fortune by investing in a lit-tle start-up called the Home Shopping Channel.

"I'll think about it," Sara had said, knowing full well that she had no in-tention of going. She hadn't even bothered mentioning it to Tom, al-though she was sure he'd tell her to go ahead, he'd take care of the kids.

The phone rang again. Sara sighed and checked the caller ID. It was an unknown cell number and she frowned, knowing that sometimes Nicky forgot her cell phone and used a friend's to call home. She hesitated and then sat up to answer it.

"Okay, fly, why are you ducking my calls?" Mel asked. *Fly.* It was one of the nicknames they'd made up for each other as kids. A fly was someone who ate shit and bothered people.

"I'm not, fly."

"Liar."

Sara sank down into the tub, flicking the stream of water with her toes. It didn't matter how many years had passed, it didn't matter how much heartache and disappointment had passed between them, she would always feel like she was ten years old when she talked to Mel. "I haven't talked to you in nearly twelve years and the first thing you do is call me a liar."

"Why is that?" Mel said, lapsing into a Southern accent. "That we haven't talked in twelve years, I mean."

"Because you never call me."

"You never call me."

"Well, I guess we're even then." Sara turned the faucet down to a trickle and sank deeper into the steaming water.

"Hey, I was at the last reunion Lola planned," Mel said. "The trip to London. The one you never showed up for."

This was meant to make her feel guilty so Sara ignored it. She could hear loud music in the background, some kind of blues standard. "It's a lit-tle early for happy hour, isn't it?"

"It's never too early for happy hour. You used to know that. Before you became a Republican. Before you became a Volvo-driving soccer mom."

"I would have called you back. Eventually. And don't call me a soccer mom."

"I suppose you'll use them as an excuse to not go on the beach trip. The hubby and kids, I mean." Mel's voice had an edge to it despite her attempt at good humor.

"No, it's not them," Sara said quickly. "It's just, I'm really busy at work. I've got a big case coming up." Which was another lie, of course. The partnership had broken up last year and most of her former partners had ended up at various law firms around Atlanta. Sara, though, had decided to drop back to part-time and had taken a job as a child advocate for the Fulton County court system.

"That's funny," Mel said. "Lola said you'd left the firm and dropped back to part-time."

Damn Lola. You never could be sure what she actually picked up when you talked to her. Was it all in one ear and out the other, or did something actually stick? Apparently, Sara's news about becoming a part-time lawyer had stuck.

"How's the new book coming along?" Sara asked.

"Don't change the subject." Mel had written a series of novels about a tough-talking Staten Island private investigator named Flynn Mendez. "Did you read the last one, *I'll Sleep When You're Dead*?"

"Actually, I don't read your novels anymore. I got tired of seeing myself as the villain."

"Now you're being paranoid."

"Okay, sure."

"Maybe you have a guilty conscience."

Sara pretended she hadn't heard that last part. Tom's class ended at 3:30 today so he'd be picking Nicky and Adam up at school and taking them out to dinner. It was her day to do whatever she wanted. She could lie in the bathtub until her skin wrinkled or drink herself into a martini-fueled stupor. Or both.

"Let me guess," Mel said. "You're in the bathtub. Mozart is playing on the CD player. There are candles flickering everywhere."

Sara turned off the water. "Actually, Pachelbel is playing," she said. "Mozart comes later."

"Just like in college. Always using up the hot water so nobody else has a chance to shower."

"I don't remember you being all that fond of showers in college."

"Very funny. So come on. Will you go on the beach trip or will you wuss out like always? You know Lola has a boat. Maybe we can do some deep-sea fishing." Her voice held a clear challenge. No one had ever accused Mel of being subtle.

Sara put her head back and stared at the ceiling. "I'll think about it."

"You'll think about it? What's the matter—are you afraid I'll push you overboard?"

"The thought has occurred to me."

Mel laughed. "Water under the bridge," she said.

She was still laughing when she hung up. Outside the window the gray Manhattan skyline rose against a pewter sky. Gray. Everywhere she looked. No wonder depression was rampant in this city. No wonder everyone was in therapy. She went to the kitchen and made herself a shaker of Cosmopolitans, thinking how good it had been to hear Sara's voice. She had a large circle of friends in New York but there was something special about that childhood best friend, that person who'd known you before you could tie your shoes, who'd suffered with you through the awkward agony of adolescence. They were still friends despite the different paths their lives had taken. Despite everything that had happened between them.

The truth of the matter was, Mel was looking forward to the beach trip. It would be nice to head South again, to be in a place where the sun shone most of the time and life moved as slowly as people talked. She hadn't been South since her last book tour, and that had been hurried and hectic except for the week she'd spent with Lola in her rambling mansion in Birmingham. The sun and the surf and the slow-moving lifestyle would be good for her depression. It would be just the thing to lift her out of the funk that always befell her when she was between books and between boyfriends.

It would be good to see her roommates again too, the four of them together for the first time in twenty-three years. Four girls who couldn't have been any more different. Annie, private and reserved, the roommate who'd been most likely to get up in the middle of the night and polish the toaster. And Lola, sweet Lola, who had the bland, pretty face of a doll and a mind to match. Depending on her mood, she could be either charmingly funny or so vague you couldn't understand a word she said.

And Sara would be there this time. Mel had thrown down the gauntlet and Sara had picked it up, just like when they were kids. Mel grinned, thinking about that.

Stevie Ray Vaughan finished playing on the CD player. She glanced at the clock and then poured herself a Cosmopolitan. She had a date tonight with Jed Ford, an editor at *The New Yorker*. She had met him a few weeks ago at a *Black & White* book party at L&M and for a while it had seemed like he might be the man she'd been looking for to fill the void in her love life. But then last night the inevitable had happened, just as it always did when her love life looked like it might be headed for tranquil seas.

She had dreamed of J.T. Radford.

The dream contained one of those orgasms that seemed to go on forever. She spent the whole day thinking about it. It was pathetic that her adult life had been spent vainly trying to recapture the intense sexual relationship she'd once shared with her college boyfriend. The J.T. dreams came less frequently now than they used to, but they still left her with a vague sense of longing and regret and the depressing certainty that whoever the man in her life was right now, he could never be J.T. She wondered if he ever dreamed of her.

But this was fruitless thinking, she knew, and dangerous so close to the beach trip. She would make a conscious effort not to think of him again. What was it she had said to Sara?

Water under the bridge.

Annie was down on her hands and knees cleaning the refrigerator grille with a toothbrush. She had told her housecleaner, Waydean, to do it but Waydean was sick and had sent her daughter, Clovis, instead. Waydean had worked for Annie for nearly fifteen years and she knew the way Annie liked things done, but Clovis was always in a hurry and didn't pay attention to details. And it was the details that mattered most to Annie.

She was down on her knees and elbows with her ass stuck up in the air. She finished the top row of grillwork and then moved on to the second row, trying not to imagine what she must look like in her Ann Taylor suit, Padovan pumps, and rubber gloves, groveling on the floor like a supplicant at the throne of Genghis Khan. She hadn't planned on cleaning the refrigerator grille. She'd come in from a meeting of her garden club and had noticed a line of hairy dust balls, which Clovis had obviously missed, peeking from beneath the edge of the refrigerator. It had been more than Annie could bear. She put her purse down and went to work. She tried not to imagine what her garden club would say if they could see her now. They had given her the black rubber gloves with the faux diamond ring and the frilly polka-dot fringe that she was wearing as a joke, but she imagined that they wouldn't laugh if they could see her now. They would just think it was sad.

Annie flushed and wielded her toothbrush with renewed vigor. Why should she have to apologize for liking her life clean and orderly? Why should she feel guilty for preferring routine and discipline?

She had once overheard one of the younger moms at her sons' school refer to her as *that OCD room mother with the two-by-four stuck up her ass.* And this simply because Annie had sent home notes asking that all mothers send in homemade treats for snack time and not store-bought, cellophane-wrapped treats loaded with preservatives and carcinogenic food dyes. Also nothing with more than five grams of sugar per serving. Or peanut oil. Or any kind of tropical fruit. Or nuts.

You'd have thought she'd asked for the still-beating hearts of their first-born children for all the furor it caused. After that the other moms would watch her nervously when she came into the school. They called her Q-Tip. *Q-Tip's in the house,* they'd say, giggling, or *You better run that by Q-Tip before you hand it out.* Although why they called her Q-Tip, Annie was unsure, unless it was because she had short, prematurely white hair and walked with the ramrod-straight posture Southern girls of her generation had been taught to use. Annie was pretty sure the nickname had a lot to do with that woman who'd first called her an *OCD room mother.*

She got even with her. She had her assigned to the calling-for-pledges committee for the annual school fund-raiser.

Annie finished the second row and started in on the third. Mitchell was home recovering from his fifth kidney stone and she could hear him moving around in the den. The boys had always been sweet when they were sick and she had hovered over them anxiously, but Mitchell's illnesses irritated her beyond words. Especially the kidney stones. There must be something he was eating or drinking, or not eating or drinking, that was causing them. Annie figured anyone else would have gone through that first kidney stone and then figured out some way to keep from getting another one.

She sat back on her heels and looked around the gleaming kitchen. The boys were grown and away at college now, and it was just her and Mitchell rambling around in this big old house, but she wouldn't have traded it for the world. Her dream house. As a girl she'd grown up in a small cottage in East Nashville, long before the area became fashionable with writers, artists, and musicians. On Sunday afternoons she would go for drives in the country with her parents to see the mansions and sprawling estates of the country-and-western stars, and pointing with a chubby finger she would say gravely, "I'm gonna have me a house like that one day." Her parents thought it was cute.

And now here she was. True, the house wasn't as big as their neighbor, Alan Jackson's, and they only had fifty acres instead of several hundred, but there was a pool out back and a guest house, and more bedrooms than she and Mitchell and the boys had ever needed. Not that they were as wealthy as Lola and Briggs Furman, of course, but their Cluck-in-a-Bucket chicken franchise had done pretty well. They had stores all over the southeast, a Cluck-in-a-Bucket empire stretching from Miami to Little Rock, Arkansas.

No, she'd done pretty well in life for an East Nashville girl. And she'd done it by careful planning and by setting her goals out clearly in front of herself. Once she set her sights on something, Annie never wavered. Except for that one transgression her senior year of college, the one she tried never to think about, she had never been a spontaneous person. At twelve she'd been dragged to a Wednesday night fish fry at church and had listened as a blond-haired, blue-eyed fourteen-year-old named Mitchell Stites belted out "Lord, You Are My Fortress in a Time of Trouble." The following Wednesday night, she was waiting in the car when her parents came out to drive to church. "Why, Anne Louise," her mother asked in surprise, "have you found religion?"

"What she's found," her father said, winking, "is Preston Stites's boy."

"The one with the harelip?"

"No. The other one, who sings in the choir."

The next week Annie invited him to come over to listen to music. Their house was small and lacked privacy but Mitchell was from a good, God-fearing family so Annie's mother allowed them to go back to her bedroom and sit with the door open. They each carried a coke and a plate of cookies. Mitchell sat on the floor and looked around in wonder and amazement at her room. Stiffly starched curtains hung in front of the spotless windows. Jefferson Airplane played on the record player.

"How come all your Barbie dolls are still in their boxes?" he asked. She had them neatly categorized by date of purchase and stacked on shelves beside a couple of open-faced fruit crates she had painted pink. Their tiny clothes were ironed and hanging on tiny hangers, arranged by seasons of the year, with the tiny shoes sorted in rows underneath.

"They stay cleaner that way," she said.

He smiled and looked at her in wonder and admiration. "You sure are a funny girl. I don't think I've ever met anyone like you."

"You'll need a coaster for that drink," she said.

Annie finished cleaning the refrigerator grille and then sat back to admire her handiwork, pulling off her rubber gloves. The grille sparkled. You could lick it, not that she would, of course, but it was comforting to know that she could. If she had to.

She could hear Mitchell breathing in the den. With each out breath he wheezed like an old generator. Not that he was in any pain; he'd taken enough OxyContin to bring down an elephant. He just liked the drama of being an invalid.

"Hon?" he called. When she didn't answer he said louder, "Honey, can you make me a sandwich?"

"I'm busy right now. I'm cleaning the kitchen."

"You cleaned the kitchen an hour ago."

"I'm busy."

"Okay," he said cheerfully. "I'll just come in there and make myself a sandwich. I'll just come in there and make my own big mess."

Annie stood up quickly. "I'll get it," she shouted. "Don't you dare come near my clean kitchen." She could feel him smiling from the other room.

Damn. She needed a break. She needed to get away from her life if only for a week. This beach trip would be just the thing. And she was looking forward to seeing Lola, Mel, and Sara again, to being with friends who knew her from before her Q-Tip days. Lola had promised Annie her own bedroom, and Annie had eagerly jumped at the chance. She and Lola had shared a room in London, and Annie had felt like she was babysitting a small child, one who wanted to chat all night, sleep all day, and couldn't keep to a schedule if her life depended on it.

Forget London. This trip would be different. She had bought two new swimsuits and several trashy beach novels, had undergone a bikini wax, and had had herself sprayed with a fake tan.

Anne Louise was ready for anything.

Lola awoke from an Ambien-induced sleep. The room was dark. Her head felt thick and swollen, like it was too heavy for her neck. She would stop taking the sleeping pills no matter what Briggs said. She hated the way they made her feel, comatose and heavy, the way she couldn't dream, as though sleep were a thing to be endured and not a release. She never took sleeping pills when she was with *him.* She never took any of her medication when she was with him. Briggs kept her as drugged up as a Saigon brothel girl but he never made her take anything.

She leaned over and pushed the button beside the bed and the automatic window blinds rose slowly. Bright sunshine flooded the room. She plumped the pillows behind her head and sat up slowly, letting her brain adjust to the new elevation, letting her eyes adjust to the light. Briggs's side of the king-size bed was still rumpled where he had slept. He was an early riser. Early to bed and early to rise. No sleeping pills for Briggs.

There was a slight knock on the door and Rosa entered, carrying a small coffee service on a silver tray.

"Good morning, Meesis Furman," she said, smiling and setting the tray down on a table beside the bed.

"Good morning, Rosa." The girl's aura was lovely, all pink and golden and standing out around her head like a halo, like a painting of some fifteenth-century saint. She had a Madonna's face and an aura to match. "Did you sleep well?"

The girl blushed but her eyes met Lola's steadily. "Yes," she said. "And I lock the door like you tell me to."

"Good." Lola smiled faintly and poured herself a cup of coffee. Briggs had a bad habit of abusing the help, especially those as young and pretty as Rosa, and Lola had given her a can of mace and had the deadbolt changed on her door the day she hired her. She had warned Briggs, too, and he had laughed and said, "What are you implying, my dear?"

Lola had thought it was pretty clear what she was implying.

She lay back on her pillows with the coffee cup and saucer resting on her chest. Rosa went around the bed and began to smooth the sheets where Briggs had slept. "Meester Henry, he looked good," she said.

"Yes," Lola said, thinking of her only son with pleasure. He had come home from Cornell last week and brought with him the girl he planned to marry. Neither one had said a word but she had seen it in their faces, in the way their auras flared and flickered toward each other, drawn like smoke through a window. It had made her feel peaceful knowing that he loved someone else, that he no longer needed her.

She sipped her coffee and watched Rosa work. "You have a lovely aura," she said. Rosa frowned slightly but kept working. She was used to Lola's ways. It was the oxazepam that had first given Lola the ability to see auras, but now she could see them without the drugs. It was how she read people, how she knew whether their characters and intentions were good or bad. She wished she'd been able to do this as a young woman. It would have saved her a lot of heartache.

"Carmen thought she would make a shrimp salad for lunch," Rosa said. "Okay?"

"Yes. Shrimp salad will be fine." Briggs's aura was dark. His whole energy field was dotted with thick black masses like tumors.

"Your husband, did you ever love him?" he'd asked her a few weeks ago. She'd looked up into his face and smiled. "It's complicated," she'd said.

"It shouldn't be."

Thinking of him, she was suddenly cheerful. Too cheerful to contain what she felt. Joy bubbled up from her toes to her fingertips, and she put her coffee cup down and flung open her arms exuberantly, wiggling her fingers. "Oh, Rosa," she cried. "I'm so happy!"

Rosa, who was accustomed to Lola's dramatic mood swings, came around the edge of the bed and hugged her. She patted Lola on the back. "Good," she said.

Lola hugged her fiercely. She was deliriously happy. In another week she would see her friends and everything would be wonderful, the four of them laughing and carrying on like crazy women, like they had in college, together again for one last time.

"Meester Furman, he say he'll be back in a few days. He flew to the island to make sure the house and the boat are ready for your trip."

Lola pulled away. She smoothed her hair off her brow and stared at Rosa. "What?" she asked.

"He say for you not to worry. He say he'll take care of everything. Just like always."

The day, which had seemed so joyous just a few short minutes ago, became suddenly ominous. Shadows moved across the ceiling like rain. Lola put her hand to her face and lay back against the pillows. Rosa rose and tucked the bedclothes around her.

"You want to get up now, Meesis Furman?" Rosa's aura flared around her head like a corona. Lola closed her eyes against its brightness.

"No." The joy had gone, leaving in its place a dull feeling of dread. Lola tried to decide what to do but her head felt heavy. She couldn't think clearly. They had agreed not to use the cell phones for a while. She could leave a message for him at the marina, warning him, but he might not get it for days. Lola turned her face to the window. "I'm tired," she said. She covered her eyes with her hand. "And Rosa?"

"Yes?"

"Push the button for the blinds, will you?"

Chapter 2

~~~~~~~~~

SUNDAY

Sara touched down in Wilmington, North Carolina, around two o'clock and made her way to the only bar in the terminal. Mel's flight had gotten in forty minutes earlier, and Sara figured the bar was the best place to look for her. She was right. She heard Mel's laugh even before she saw her, sitting at the bar with a guy in a dark gray suit.

"There she is!" Mel shouted in greeting, and the businessman turned to look as Sara walked in, pulling her carry-on behind her. Mel hadn't changed at all, damn her. Her hair was shorter and blonder but she still had a figure like a Las Vegas showgirl, all legs and bosom. Sara, aware that she was still carrying postpartum baby weight from twelve years ago, kept her purse strategically in front of her belly as they hugged.

"How was your flight?" Mel said. In the light slanting through the windows Sara could see the lines around Mel's eyes and at the corners of her mouth and she relaxed a bit.

"Not too bad. It's a pretty short jump from Atlanta to Wilmington." She had forgotten how tall Mel was, standing there in her stacked-heel sandals and jeans.

"What time does Annie get in?" Mel said, making room for her at the bar. Sara, Annie, and Mel were all flying into Wilmington, and Lola was sending a car to pick them up at the airport and take them to the ferry landing.

"Around three-twenty, I think."

The man in the gray suit stood and nodded, gathering his bags. He handed Mel a card. "I've got a plane to catch," he said, winking at her. "Call me."

Sara sat down on the stool, pushing her carry-on between her feet. She caught the bartender's eye and ordered a pomegranate martini.

"What do you think?" Mel asked, watching the man in the gray suit walk away. "Married?"

"Definitely."

"Yeah, that's what I thought." Mel smiled at Sara, giving her an appraising look. Sara had been a pretty girl, but she was a lovely woman. She seemed to have come into her own. She had filled out some since college; she was definitely curvier, but on her it looked right. Her hair was still dark and curly, although threaded now with highlights.

Sara, feeling Mel's eyes upon her, glanced at her reflection in the mirror behind the bar, and quickly looked away. "So how are you?" she said. It felt awkward but it was all she could think to say. It had been easier talking to Mel on the phone than it was sitting beside her, face-to-face.

"I'm good. Life is good." Mel smiled and nodded her head, wondering if she sounded convincing. You couldn't just pick up where you left off twenty-three years ago, at least not without a great deal of effort on both their parts. Maybe another drink would help. She raised her glass and nodded at the bartender.

Sara spun a paper coaster on the bar in front of her. "So how's New York?"

Mel smiled. If she told Sara about New York, then she'd have to ask Sara about Atlanta, and neither one was ready for that. "I like what you've done with your hair," she said, putting her hand up and lightly brushing Sara's bangs. "You've added some highlights."

"I had my upper lip waxed, too."

"I had mine lasered. Isn't modern technology wonderful?"

Sara glanced in the bar mirror again, fluffing her hair with her fingers.

She tried not to stare at Mel, who watched her with an amused expression. "Remember in college when we used to slather ourselves in baby oil and lay out in the sun?"

"No. But I do remember how you used to roll your hair around a jumbo orange juice can and then sleep with panty hose wrapped around your head."

Sara shook her head. "I can't believe we were so stupid. I can't believe we're not dead from skin cancer."

The bartender brought their drinks. "You don't still do that, do you?" Mel asked innocently, raising her Cosmopolitan.

"What, slather myself in baby oil and bake in the sun? Of course not."

"No. Wear an orange juice can and panty hose to bed."

Sara eyed her steadily above the edge of her drink. "No," she said.

"Too bad. That was such a good look for you."

They stared at each other and slowly grinned. Mel tapped the edge of her drink to Sara's. "Cheers," she said.

They drank for a while in companionable silence, both happy now that the awkwardness between them seemed to be slipping away. A plane taxied past them on the runway. Far off beyond the distant rim of blue sky, a bank of white clouds drifted slowly. Mel sighed, set her drink down, and touched Sara's arm. "Okay," she said. "Show me the photos of your kids. You never send any photos with your Christmas cards."

There was a reason for that, of course, but Sara said nothing, just leaned over and pulled her wallet out of her purse. She opened it to the school photos of Nicky and Adam.

"Wow," Mel said, taking a photo from her. She flushed slightly, gently removing a smudge from the plastic with one finger. She hadn't expected this. "He's gorgeous. How old is he?"

"Fourteen."

Mel picked up the other photo. "And she looks just like you."

"I know, everyone says that." She had a picture of Tom, hidden behind those of the children, but she didn't take it out, trying to walk the thin line between her own pride and Mel's motherless, single state.

They both sat staring politely into her children's faces and then Sara slid them back into her wallet and put it away. Mel turned around and set her elbows on the bar, sipping her drink. "Lola has a good-looking son," she said after a while.

"Henry? Oh, I know. He looks a little like Briggs did at that age. And he's a good boy, too. He adores his mother. They've always been so close."

Mel smiled slightly, and set her drink down. "She was like a girl when we took that trip to England. Always calling him, *Henry, we're at your favorite place, the tower of London* or *Henry, I got lost on the tube and the Bobbies had to hunt me down.* The two of them always giggling together over some crazy thing she'd done."

"*Did* she get lost on the tube?"

Mel raised one eyebrow. "Repeatedly," she said. "On the tube. In Harrods. Walking along Carnaby Street. You know Lola."

Sara smiled sadly and ran her finger around the top of her glass. "She was always kind of scatterbrained but I swear it's getting worse with age."

"It's that fucking Briggs," Mel said. "He keeps her so medicated."

Sara looked surprised. "Do you think so?"

"I'd bet money on it."

"How do you medicate someone against their will?"

"Who says it's against her will? Remember, she's married to Briggs."

"I thought you liked Briggs."

"Maybe twenty years ago. Not now." Mel stood up, excused herself, and went to the rest room. When she came back she glanced at the clock and said, "What time did you say Annie gets in?"

"Three-twenty, I think. Lola's car is picking us up at three-thirty."

"Okay, that gives us just enough time," Mel said, waving at the bartender.

"Just enough time for what?"

"Just enough time to get loaded before Annie gets here."

Sara laughed and looked around the bar. It was a small airport and there were only a few people, scattered here and there, waiting for their planes. "I love Annie."

"I love Annie, too, but she drives me crazy if I'm sober."

"They have medication these days for obsessive-compulsive disorders."

"She doesn't take it. Trust me, I was with her in London."

"I hope you realize you're getting ready to spend a week with her on a practically deserted island accessible only by boat."

Mel grinned and said, "But I plan on getting liquored up so it won't matter." She picked up her glass, drained it, then set it back on the bar. "Deserted island?" she said. "Accessible only by boat?"

Sara laughed at her expression. "You obviously haven't done your homework." The bartender brought their drinks and Sara sipped her martini before continuing. "Whale Head Island is accessible only by ferry or private boat. It's very exclusive. No cars are allowed on the island, only golf carts or bicycles. Families have been coming there for generations to get away from the stress of modern life. There wasn't even electricity until the nineteen-sixties. There are no condos or hotels, only private houses that are very expensive to rent." She shrugged and crossed her arms on the bar. "It cuts down on the riffraff I guess."

"No riffraff? Who am I going to party with?"

Sara grinned slowly. She picked up her glass and tapped it against Mel's. "I guess that would be me," she said.

Annie called Sara the minute her plane touched down. She could hear giggling in the background, which meant they were probably already sauced. Which meant she'd have a hard time getting them collected and into Lola's car. *Damn.* "Where are you?" she asked.

More giggles. "In the bar." Of course they were. The boat ride to the island would be a long one. Annie hoped this wasn't going to be like London, where she had wound up taking care of everyone. She'd taken care of Mitchell through five kidney stones, and she was pretty much over the whole Florence Nightingale thing.

"Anne Louise!" Mel shouted when she saw her, lifting her glass. Her face was flushed. Sara was leaning against the bar sipping from a wide-mouthed glass. Annie picked her way through the sparse crowd, pulling her bag behind her. "Don't get us banned from the airport," she said, stowing her carry-on and a small cooler under the nearest barstool. "They're pretty strict these days about unruly travelers." Sara stood up and hugged her, and Annie hugged her back.

"Who you calling unruly?" Mel said.

"You've let your hair go white," Sara said, holding her at arm's length.

"I quit coloring it years ago. I got tired of messing with it."

A weary-looking bartender slouched across the bar. He had brown hair pulled back in a ponytail and a moon face covered in freckles. An earring dangled from his left ear. "You ladies might want to get something in your stomachs," he said, slapping a menu down on the bar.

"Just keep the drinks coming," Mel said.

"We really don't have time to eat," Annie said, picking up the menu and giving it back to him. "We're being picked up in five minutes." She pointed at their drinks and held up two fingers, indicating that he should close out the tab. The bartender, looking relieved, turned around and went to ring them up.

"I'm so glad you're here," Sara said, smiling at Annie. "We need someone to keep us in line."

Mel swung her arm around her head like she was twirling a lasso. "Crack that whip," she said.

"Crack it yourself," Annie said. "I'm on vacation."

The car sent to take them to the ferry was a long white Escalade with twelve-spoke wheels. "That car has Briggs written all over it," Mel said as it pulled up in front of the airport. A young man wearing a blue polo shirt and khaki pants opened the driver's door and jumped out. "You must be Mrs. Furman's friends," he said, coming around to take their bags. "I'm Stewart. I'll be your driver today." He grinned and Mel grinned back.

"Where's Mrs. Furman?"

"Oh, she's back at the boat with Captain Mike. They're waiting for you at the ferry landing."

Mel looked at Sara and mouthed *Captain Mike.* Sara shrugged and helped Stewart load her bags into the back of the Escalade.

"Careful with that cooler," Annie said. "It's got deviled eggs in there."

"You brought deviled eggs to the beach?"

"Well, I couldn't just come empty-handed, could I?"

No, of course she couldn't. They were all Southern girls and had been raised to come bearing gifts. What each woman brought said a lot about her personality. Sara brought a beautifully wrapped, lacquered picture frame with a photo of the four of them standing out in front of their college apartment. Mel brought a bottle of Dos Amigos tequila.

Stewart closed the back door. "Are we ready, ladies?"

"I'll ride up front with Stewart," Mel said, quickly climbing into the front seat.

It was a forty-minute drive from the airport to the Whale Head Island Ferry, long enough for Sara and Mel to sober up. They drove down narrow asphalt roads surrounded on both sides by wide flat fields of marsh grass. Late-afternoon sun shimmered across the landscape, and high overhead a hawk soared, circling above the distant tree line. Sara's cell phone rang once but she didn't answer it. It was Tom, calling to see if she'd arrived. She couldn't talk to him here, in front of everyone. A faint feeling of homesickness stirred her bowels. They'd been married for seventeen years, and in all that time had never been apart for more than two nights. She thought of her husband's smile, of her children's sweet faces, and the homesickness swelled to a thick lump in her throat. Away from them she felt only half herself.

Annie, as if reading her mind, asked, "How're Tom and the kids?"

"They're fine. Thanks. And Mitchell? The boys?" Even now, when things got so bad, Sara could not imagine a life without Tom.

"As ornery as ever. The boys have summer jobs, William in Chicago and Carleton out in Colorado."

"We're not going to talk about the husband and kids the whole time we're here, are we?" Mel asked.

The fleeting camaraderie Sara had felt with Mel in the bar seemed false now, a desperate desire to become what they had once been, and could never be again. A product of that age-old elixir of forgetfulness, alcohol. This trip would require a lot of alcohol.

She looked at Mel and thought, *I shouldn't have come.* She thought, *Things will turn out badly.*

The ferry landing was a low, quaint building of weathered gray cypress built to resemble something in a New England port town. It was swarming with tourists and island dwellers who didn't have their own boats and had to ride the ferry with the tourists. There was only one grocery store and three restaurants on the island, so people brought most of their own supplies, loaded into big plastic tubs with locking lids. A long line of shiny SUVs stood outside the landing, their owners unloading plastic tubs, bicycles, and beach gear on to a series of trolleys manned by an army of fresh-faced porters, who rolled the loaded trolleys into the baggage hold of the ferry. Children played in the sun, oblivious to the shouts of their stressed-out parents, who were trying to keep one eye on the luggage and one eye on their children.

Stewart pulled slowly past the long line of SUVs, careful not to hit any of the scurrying pedestrians, and drove several hundred feet along the water's edge to a small marina. The crowds here were thinner and less hectic, as island people loaded supplies onto their boats and called to one another by name.

"Which boat is Lola's?" Sara asked.

"Boat?" Stewart said, chuckling. He lifted one hand and pointed. It was the largest one in the marina, of course, a one-hundred-twelve-foot Hargrave yacht sporting the name *Miss Behavin'.*

"I love that name," Mel said.

April, the girl hired to make beds and cook, stood out front holding an empty trolley. She was tanned and pretty, and had the confident air of a young woman in her twenties. Behind her was another trolley loaded with groceries. She introduced herself to the women, then went to help Stewart load the luggage.

"Where's Lola?" Annie asked, shielding her eyes with her hand and squinting at the *Miss Behavin'.* But Lola had already seen them and was running across the deck and the gangway toward the dock. She looked like a girl, with her hair loose about her shoulders and her feet bare. She was wearing a pair of white capris, a sleeveless shirt, and dark-rimmed sunglasses.

"My God, you look like a movie star," Mel called to her.

She threw her arms around Mel and then hugged each one of them, laughing. Even Annie got caught up in her exuberance and smiled shyly. "I brought deviled eggs," she said.

Out in the water the crowded ferry gave two sharp whistle blows, then pulled slowly away from the dock. People sat up top or below in the covered cabin, their faces pressed eagerly to the glass. Seagulls followed noisily in the wake of the huge ship.

Lola waved at the passing ferry like she was hailing a taxi.

"Is that yacht really yours?" Sara asked, watching as the *Miss Behavin'* rolled lightly in the ferry's wake.

"It's not mine," Lola said. "It's Briggs's."

"The eggs are in the cooler," Annie said. "But we should probably get them into the refrigerator."

"Will you shut up about the damn deviled eggs?" Mel said.

Annie ignored her. She had learned long ago to ignore Mel. She turned her head slightly and watched as the ferry moved slowly toward the open sound. "I make mine with fresh chives," she added, getting the last word in.

"Come on," Lola said before Mel could reply, putting her arm around Annie and pulling her gently toward the boat. "I'll introduce you to Captain Mike."

He was climbing down the steps to the deck when they boarded. "Welcome aboard," he said, taking off a baseball cap that read, WHAT WOULD

ELVIS DO? He ran his fingers through his sun-bleached hair. Mel guessed he was somewhere between thirty-five and forty, not really handsome, but attractive in a faded-athlete kind of way. He called Lola *Mrs. Furman,* very proper, very correct. She called him *Captain* or just plain *Mike.* He had a self-assured air that Mel found vaguely annoying. He shook hands with everyone and then went to help April with the groceries. She smiled at him and he grinned and gave the trolley a playful tug. *So that's how it is,* Mel thought, watching the two of them together.

The ride to the island took only fifteen minutes. Sunlight sparkled on the choppy water of the sound. In the distance, past two narrow spits of land that curved inward like pincers, the sea was a wide blue haze. Lola, Mel, Sara, and Annie sat out on the aft deck, where it was too windy to talk, their hair whipping around their faces. April was in the galley and Captain Mike was up on the flying bridge. Mel wanted to ask Lola about him but it was hard to talk with the noise of the engines and the roar of the wind in their ears. She was pretty sure Briggs had planted Captain Mike and April to keep an eye on Lola. They were probably paid to send detailed reports to Briggs every night; after London, he wasn't about to trust Lola with her crazy girlfriends unchaperoned.

Mel wasn't sure how Lola had stood it all these years, being married to Briggs Furman. He was as jealous and controlling as Lola's mother had been, ruling Lola's life with an iron fist. Still, Mel thought, watching the way the wind caught Lola's hair, the way the sun slanted across her smooth, pretty face, Lola looked better than she had in years. She seemed animated and confident. She definitely looked better than she had in London a few years ago, where she had wandered about as numb and bewildered as a lost child.

The boat sped over the blue waves, past dolphins swimming in precise formation, past a buoy that rocked and dipped with their passing. Ahead they could see the island in the distance, with its lighthouse, Old Baldy, rising from the interior like a giant chess piece. A sailboat passed in front of them, its sails straining with the wind. As they approached the island, Captain Mike cut the engines, and the yacht slowed to a crawl as they entered the harbor.

The whole island had been built to resemble a sleepy New England fishing village. Tall gray-shingled cottages and storefronts clustered around the marina. Behind the village, to the north and west, the marsh glimmered between banks of tall grass, while the interior of the island sur-

rounding Old Baldy was covered in a maritime forest of live oak, saw palmetto, yaupon, and wax myrtle. To the south and east stretched miles and
miles of uncrowded beaches. And everywhere, sitting up on the dune
ridges, clustered in small enclaves beneath the spreading live oaks, and
along the quiet marshes, were the weathered cedar-shingled houses, their
tall roofs and mullioned windows glittering in the sun.

"Oh, my God, it's beautiful," Sara said.

"Yes, it is," Lola said. "I've enjoyed it so much."

There was something in her tone that made Annie ask, "Are you getting
ready to sell it?" Mitchell had promised her a beach house years ago, but
somehow they'd never gotten around to buying one.

"Oh, no," Lola said quickly. "It's just, well . . . it is beautiful, isn't it?"

"Like something from another century," Sara said.

"Where are all the nightclubs?" Mel said.

Lola laughed. "No nightclubs, I'm afraid. Everything pretty much
closes down at ten o'clock."

They pulled slowly into a slip not far from where the ferry was unloading its crowd of happy tourists. A long line of trolleys connected together
and pulled by a motorized cart stood waiting to whisk them to their rented
houses. Each trolley bore the name of the house where its occupants would
be staying, and the porters, sweating now in the heat, hurriedly loaded the
luggage from the ferry onto the appropriate trolleys. Tired parents climbed
on board to wait and watch with weary smiles as their excited children
pointed out boats, bicycles, turtles, and seagulls.

Captain Mike helped the women disembark, then followed them up
the dock to the landing. "You go ahead and take the smaller golf cart, Mrs.
Furman," he said. "April and I will come along later with the luggage."

Everywhere they looked there were golf carts, traveling like gypsy cara-
vans along narrow asphalt roads, parked in front of the storefronts with
their electrical cords tethered to rows of electrical outlets.

Lola's golf cart was a custom-built unit made to resemble a Mercedes.
Lola, noting their expressions, said apologetically, "It wasn't my idea.
Briggs had it specially built." She disengaged the electrical cord and
climbed in and Mel climbed in beside her. Annie and Sara sat behind
them, facing backward. Lola slammed the lever into reverse and quickly
pulled out into the road. She pushed the lever to the right and took off
with a sudden lurching motion that caused the women to grab for the
nearest canopy frame.

Briggs had also had the electric motor modified so that the cart, which normally had a cruising speed of eight mph, now clipped along at a frightening speed of twenty-five mph. Lola laughed and talked the whole time, waving her hands and turning around to talk to Annie and Sara in a way that made Mel nervous.

"Damn it, Lola, let me drive," she said, but Lola just laughed and kept talking about Henry and his new girlfriend. They sped along a narrow winding road that led from the village to the interior of the island. There were only two major roads, Blackbeard's Wynd, which ran down the middle of the island through the maritime forest, and Stede Bonnet's Wynd, which ran along the beachfront.

"Most of the roads are named for pirates," Lola called gaily as they passed a slower-moving cart. She lifted her hand and waved. The people in the cart waved back.

Ahead Mel could see the intersection where Blackbeard and Stede Bonnet split off from each other. She looked nervously at Lola. "Which way are we going?" she said. Lola showed no signs of slowing down. She was still talking about Henry's new girlfriend, whom she adored.

"Damn it Lola, slow down," Mel said, thumping the bottom of the cart with her foot like she was pumping an imaginary brake.

Lola said, "Her name's Layla. Isn't that a lovely name?" She turned around to smile at Annie and Sara. "Her dad named her after that song by—oh, what is that guy's name?"

"Eric Clapton," Sara said. "Watch the road, Lola."

"I think I might be getting sick," Annie said.

"Eric Clapton!" Lola said, turning again to smile at Sara. "I love Eric Clapton."

"I really shouldn't be riding backward," Annie said.

They were almost to the intersection now and Mel clamped her foot down against the floor of the cart and put one arm out in front of her, grabbing the canopy frame with the other. At the last minute, Lola took a sharp right onto Stede Bonnet and the cart tipped up on to two wheels. Without thinking Sara swung her leg out like a rudder. Beside her, Annie hissed like a scalded cat. Lola spun the wheel and leaned against Mel, and the cart righted itself. "They'll get married in Michigan," she said, her face dreamy and tender with thoughts of Henry. They were out from beneath the trees now and cruising along the beach road in the bright sunlight. A strong wind buffeted the cart. To their left rose a series of terraced dunes covered in steep-roofed houses. To their right stretched the Atlantic Ocean, its blue waters sparkling in the sun.

"She's from Ann Arbor, Michigan," Lola said. "Can you believe Henry's marrying a Yankee?"

Mel slowly unclenched her fingers from the canopy frame. She took a deep breath and said, "Pull over, Lola, so I can drive before you kill us."

"I'd really like to see my kids again, Lola, if you don't mind," Sara said.

"Does anyone have a Dramamine?" Annie asked.

Lola put her head back and laughed her musical little laugh. "Y'all are funny," she said.

Lola's house sat by itself on top of a long sandy ridge that overlooked the sea. A weathered sign beside the gatepost read, WILD DUNES. The house had been built to look like it had stood for a hundred and fifty years, like a Newport palace, but with all the modern amenities, tall windows that faced the sea, soaring ceilings, an open floor plan, and hardwood floors. They walked around the house in awe, exclaiming over its elaborate features. "There are five bedrooms upstairs with their own baths, so help yourselves to whichever one suits you," Lola said. "My bedroom is down here on the main floor." She took them through the master suite that ran across the back of the house, complete with a wet bar, built-in flat-screen TV, and French doors opening onto a private deck facing the sea. The house was angled slightly on top of the dune, so that most rooms had a view of the ocean.

"Where do Captain Mike and April sleep?" Mel said. They were standing in Lola's bedroom in front of the massive king-size bed.

"Out back in the two-bedroom crofter," Lola said.

"Crofter?"

"It's kind of like a guesthouse."

"Oh."

They looked through the French doors and saw a tall-roofed shed covered in weathered siding. It was about fifty feet beyond Lola's private deck, connected to the main house by a boardwalk. A small deck stretched across the front of the crofter, its rails covered in some kind of twisting vine. Two white rocking chairs sat at one end, facing out to sea.

"Together?" Mel said.

"What?" Lola asked, her smile fading.

"Captain Mike and April. Do they sleep together?"

Lola stared through the French doors at the crofter and the distant rim of blue sea. "Oh, I don't think so," she said.

They decided to skip dinner that first night in favor of appetizers and mojitos. They sat on the porch at a table overlooking the ocean, watching as the sun sank slowly behind the clouds and the water deepened to a dark metallic gray. The evening was soft and balmy, with a constant breeze blowing in from the sea. In the middle of the table, a thick candle sputtered beneath a hurricane glass. Scattered around it were half-eaten trays of crab dip, shrimp toast, baked brie, and Annie's deviled eggs. White-capped waves glimmered in the moonlight, and overhead in the great dark dome of the sky, stars flickered and fell.

"Annie, tell us a Mitchell story," Mel said. There was a slight shuffling of chairs as the women settled back to make themselves comfortable. It hadn't taken them long to fall back into their routine of friendship.

Annie hesitated, looking out at the moonlit sea. She shook her head slowly. "That man," she said finally, which is the way she began every Mitchell story. Over the years, Mel had collected Mitchell stories and had even used a few in her novels, which was perplexing to Annie. It was as if Mel thought being married to her made Mitchell some kind of martyr. In London she'd made the mistake of telling Mel about a beach trip that she and Mitchell had taken several years ago with some business acquaintances. Mitchell had complained steadily of a pain in his abdomen and Annie had insisted it was nothing more than a bad case of indigestion. On the third day, while she was out walking the beach, one of the other wives had driven Mitchell to the emergency room. Even then, Annie had refused to admit that it was anything more than a case of bad oysters, right up to the moment they wheeled Mitchell into the operating room for an emergency appendectomy.

"You know he's home recovering from a kidney stone," Annie said.

"Another one?"

"My God, how many does that make?"

"Five."

"Poor thing," Lola said.

Annie looked at her darkly. "Well, the other day I came home from the grocery store and he was standing in my kitchen looking pretty proud of himself. He was holding something in his hands and when I asked him what it was he held up this container and said, "My kidney stone. They saved it for me." That's when I noticed that he had it in one of my Tupper-ware containers."

"Oh, no."

"Please tell me you didn't bring the deviled eggs in a Tupperware con-tainer."

"No," Annie said. "I threw it out. I'll never buy Tupperware again."

A long line of white-capped waves thundered in from the sea, crashing against the beach. One of the French doors opened and April came out carrying another shaker of mojitos. Light spilled across the porch from the opened door.

"If you don't need me anymore tonight," she said to Lola. "I think I'll go to bed."

"Yes, yes, go ahead," Lola said, rising to hug her. A moth the size of a hummingbird hovered around the candle.

"What time will you want breakfast?"

Lola looked around the table as if waiting for the others to answer. She seemed uncomfortable giving directions to Briggs's servants.

"Oh, I don't know," Mel said. She looked at April and shrugged. "How about noon?"

"I'll be up by ten," Sara said. "I like to walk the beach before it gets too hot."

"It depends on how well I sleep," Annie said. "I'm usually up around eight o'clock. But if I'm away from home I don't always sleep too well, so it may be earlier."

"Ten it is," April said. She said good night and walked back inside, clos-ing the door behind her. They watched her cross the kitchen and disappear down the back hallway.

"Let's play a game," Mel said, raising her drink above her head. Her glass caught the candlelight, reflecting like a jewel.

The others groaned and looked at one another across the table. Mel had always been partial to games.

Mel, undiscouraged by their reaction, said, "Each woman writes down on a slip of paper something she wants to do this week and then we bury the notes in a little box in the sand under the edge of the porch. At the end of the week, we'll dig up the notes and anything that hasn't been accom-plished will have to be done before we leave the island."

"Why don't we just go around in a circle and *say* what we want to do?" Sara said.

"Because that's not the same thing. If we write it down secretly we'll be bolder in our ambitions."

"So you're saying it has to be something bold?"

"Yes. Something outside your comfort zone." Mel looked around the table at their distrustful faces. "Come on, girls, how long's it been since we got together and did something crazy? Twenty-three years?" She looked so young in the flickering candlelight and, gazing at her, Sara couldn't help but feel a sudden catch in her throat, a lingering sadness at the unpredictability of life.

"I don't know what you mean," Annie said. "Is this like Truth or Dare?"

Lola got up to go into the house. She came back a few minutes later carrying a small box, a piece of paper, and four pens. She tore the paper into four strips and passed the pens around.

"Just write something down," Mel said. "Something you'd like to do if you had the nerve. And, Annie, don't write *clean the baseboards.*"

"You're funny," Annie said. She was remembering a long-ago game of Truth or Dare when Mel had made her stand on her head in a mini-skirt in front of the Honk 'n' Holler convenience store while a long line of traffic passed slowly in the street. "I can tell you right now I'm not standing on my head."

Sara was remembering her own version of the Truth or Dare incident. "I'm not taking my clothes off," she said to Mel. "I want that understood up front."

"Y'all are kind of missing the whole point of this little exercise. The point is to stretch out, get a little outside your comfort zone. Do something slightly crazy."

Lola looked up from writing. Her eyes were wide and blue, and her shimmering hair curved over her cheek like a wing. "Does it have to be legal?" she asked.

They all laughed nervously, looking at one another across the table. You never knew with Lola.

They finished their notes and Lola collected them in the little box. Then she tripped down the steps and disappeared under the edge of the porch. A few minutes later she was back, slapping the sand off her hands and prancing up the steps like a gymnast.

Mel lifted her drink in a toast. The other three followed suit. "Here's to the good old days," she said.

"That weren't always so good," Sara said.

FALL OF
1981

Chapter 3

~~~~~~~~~~~

Mel awoke to the sound of the vacuum cleaner. It was Saturday morning, house-cleaning day, and Annie was up early. Mel groaned and rolled over in bed, pulling the covers up around her ears. J.T. was already awake. He sat up on one elbow and grinned at her, his hair falling around his face.

"I see your crazy roommate is up," he said.

"She's an early riser."

With his dark brown hair and green eyes he was beautiful, although he didn't appear to know this, which was a good thing. It annoyed Mel that some men could look so good in the morning, without any effort, while she always looked haggard and puffy-eyed. "I'm hungry," he said, nuzzling her neck.

"Me, too. Let's go down to the Waffle House and get a big stack of pancakes. "

He grinned and flipped her over on her back. "I had something else in mind," he said.

When they awoke again, the house was quiet. Bright sunlight slanted through the room. The trees outside were a brilliant red and yellow, and the air drifting through the opened window was thick with the scent of wood smoke. Mel showered, dressed, and went into the kitchen. Annie was on her knees in the small bathroom off the kitchen, scrubbing the toilet. She had a bandanna tied around her hair and was wearing a pair of rubber gloves. Through the opened screened door Mel could see Sara lying in a lounge chair in a pool of sunlight. Blondie blared from the portable radio beside her.

"Where's Lola?" Mel asked, pouring herself a cup of coffee. J.T. was in the shower and she could hear water running behind the wall.

"She went somewhere with Briggs." Annie stuck the toilet brush in its plastic pail and sat back on her heels. "To the library, I think." She stood up and cleaned the mirror, then the window.

Mel made herself a piece of toast. She leaned against the counter and ate her breakfast, watching Annie thoughtfully. When she had finished she brushed the palms of her hands together and said, "Okay, Mommy Dearest. What are my chores for the day?"

Annie flushed a dull red and gave her a *drop-dead* look. "Don't call me that," she said flatly. "You don't have to help me clean unless you want to."

"Of course I want to," Mel said. "I love to clean on my day off. Really."

"Fine," Annie said. "You can dust the front room. And mop the kitchen floor."

"I'll get J.T. right on it." Mel gave her a snappy, two-finger salute and turning, took her coffee with her out into the yard, the screen door slamming loudly on her heels. A slight breeze stirred the leaves at her feet. The neighbor's dog, a fawn-colored pug, stood at the fence watching her. "What're you reading?" she called to Sara.

Sara put her hand over her eyes and looked up. "*Middlemarch*," she said.

"Oh, God."

"Not really," Sara said, spreading the book on her lap. "I find the secularized morality of George Eliot's novels comforting."

"That's because you're an atheist," Mel said, arranging herself in the other tattered lawn chair. She crossed her feet at the ankles and rested her elbows on the chair arms, holding the steaming coffee up to her face.

"No, I'm not. I'm an agnostic."

Mel thoughtfully sipped her coffee. A jet passed slowly overhead, leaving a faint vapor trail. "The irony, of course, is that Dorothea is a deeply religious woman. Which is one of the problems I have with the novel. Eliot seems to imply that humanitarian change can be brought about by compassion and not by social anarchy."

"Now you sound like a communist." They were both English majors, although Mel had ventured off onto the dangerous and uncharted waters of the creative writing track, while Sara had stuck with literature.

Mel thought about it a moment, then said, "Eliot's characters are all a bunch of cleverly drawn poseurs. They walk around spouting all these highbrow ideas, all this philosophical hyperbole, but no one actually *does* anything. I mean, come on, Dorothea! Have a fling with Ladislaw, leave Casaubon, run off with Lydgate, do *something*."

"You've just admitted that she's a very religious woman. She couldn't do any of those things. Besides, you have to read the novel within its historical context."

"Of course you do. But it's still boring."

"Maybe to someone who likes Raymond Chandler and Cormac Mc-Carthy."

"Hey, at least something happens in their novels. At least the plot *moves*." Mel stretched her legs along the length of the lounger, letting the warmth of the sun envelop her. It was late September and they were enjoying a long, hazy period of Indian summer. The days had been warm and breezy, and in the afternoons the temperature rose into the seventies. Mel could not remember a prettier fall in the four years she had been at Bedford. "I'll miss this place," she said, looking around at the tall trees and the distant rim of mountains rising against the pale blue sky.

"We all will."

Bedford University was one of the oldest and most prestigious liberal arts schools in the Southeast. It was an Episcopal school and the tuition was steep, but Mel came from money and there'd been no doubt, once she was accepted, that she would attend Bedford. Sara's dad was a high school history teacher, and her admission had been a bit more uncertain. She was a good student and she'd managed to win a scholarship that paid for most of her tuition, but she'd had to work a series of part-time jobs to pay for books and living expenses. She never complained but Mel knew it had been tough for her, working to pay her bills and studying to keep her grades up while carrying a full load. Mel had always admired Sara's tenacity, her air of quiet resolve. They had been friends since first grade, since their first year together at Howard's Mill Elementary, a friendship that had continued through high school and now into their fourth year of college.

"Have you thought about what you're going to do when we graduate?" Mel put her head back and stared at the cloudless sky.

"I don't know." Sara closed the book on her lap and watched a yellow cat who was slinking through the rhododendrons like a leopard. The neighbor's dog coughed a warning, pressing its bug-eyed face against the chain-length fence. "I'm thinking about working for a year and then maybe going to law school."

"No shit?" Mel turned her head, resting her cheek on the lounger and shielding her eyes with one hand. She stared at Sara for a moment and then said, "Actually, I can see you as a lawyer, fighting for the underdog."

Sara grimaced and pulled her knees up, avoiding Mel's eyes. She always had the feeling Mel was making fun of her, belittling her in that soft, sarcastic way she had. Mel was one of those friends you put up with, despite the fact that she pushed all your buttons, because she made you laugh. She made you laugh at her, and she made you laugh at yourself. "How about you?" Sara asked, still avoiding her eyes and staring at the cat in the rhododendrons. "Why don't you go to law school, too, and we can partner up to save the world?"

Mel made a dismissive sound. The cat crouched at the edge of the lawn, its tail twitching. "No offense, but I'd rather kill myself than pratice law." She dropped her hand and closed her eyes. After a while, she said sleepily, "I'm heading for New York."

"So you're serious about that?"

"I'm following in the footsteps of Carson McCullers and Dorothy Parker. I'm going to be a writer."

"You mean you're going to wait tables and starve?"

Mel grinned. "Possibly," she said. She knew she wouldn't starve. Even as a child, she had known her life wouldn't be ordinary. While other girls dreamed of becoming brides and ballerinas, she dreamed of being an astronaut, a cowboy, and a fireman. She dreamed of living in a teepee and riding horses across the plains with her Indian sidekick, Tonto.

She had learned early that she could control other children by telling outrageous lies. (*Stories,* her father, Leland, liked to call them, not *lies.*)

Standing in front of a group of her classmates, she was like a snake handler mesmerizing a basket of cobras. She had what, in those days before Ritalin, was called an "active imagination," meaning that she was only a half-hearted student and spent a lot of time gazing out the classroom windows, daydreaming. (The only teacher who ever liked her was Miss Booth, her third-grade teacher. *That child is a creative genius,* she once overheard Miss Booth tell Mrs. Griscom, the lunchroom monitor. *That child is the biggest liar on God's green earth,* Mrs. Griscom replied grimly. *She wouldn't know the truth if it fell out of the sky and clumped her on the head.*)

Mel's imagination was so good it sometimes got her into trouble. She could take a situation and rethink it, taking it apart and reworking it back and forth so that in the end she wouldn't be able to tell the difference between what had really happened and what she imagined had happened. She could convince herself that a thing was true, even if it wasn't. In other words, she could stand there and lie boldly without ever batting an eye or shuffling her feet (a trait that would come in handy later in life).

"Well, you'll have plenty to write about," Sara said. "Your life is like a soap opera."

As if to confirm this, the door swung open behind them and J.T. strolled out into the yard wearing a pair of torn jeans and an old T-shirt. His feet were bare. Sara immediately picked up *Middlemarch* and went back to reading.

"George Eliot?" he asked, leaning his elbows against the back of Mel's lounger and peering down at the novel in Sara's lap. His eyes, in the sunlight, were sea-green.

"Your girlfriend doesn't think much of George," she said, not looking at him.

"What can I say?" he said, fondly ruffling Mel's hair until she hit him. "She's a postmodernist kind of girl."

"Don't make it sound so dirty," Mel said.

"Come on," he said. "Let's grab some beer and head out to Sliding Rock."

Mel shrugged and looked at Sara. "Sliding Rock?" she said.

"I can't. I have a test in my Fugitive Poets class."

"Oh, come on. You can study later. It's a beautiful day and we shouldn't waste it."

Sliding Rock was a local park where the students went to drink beer and slide down a waterfall that cascaded over a wide, flat rock. Bedford was out in the middle of the wilderness, an hour and a half from the nearest city, which happened to be Charlotte. You had to make your own fun.

"I'll buy the beer," J.T. said. He leaned his weight on the back of the lounger so that it tilted slightly and Mel said, "Stop."

Sara read the same sentence over and over again, trying to make it stick.

"I'm not going if Sara won't go," Mel said, trying to pry his fingers off the back of her chair.

Sara colored slightly. "Don't drag me into this," she said.

"Besides," Mel said to J.T. "Annie says you have to mop the kitchen floor."

"I didn't say you had to mop the kitchen floor," Annie shouted through the screen. "I said Mel had to."

J.T. shook Mel's chair. "Let's go."

"No."

"We won't get many more chances like this." He gave her his most charming smile, the one that made women stutter and forget their train of thought.

Mel stared up at him, wondering what would happen between the two of them when she went to New York. She tried not to think too much about the future. She tried to live every day in the present, savoring each experience, knowing she'd use it one day in a novel. "Mop the floor, and we'll go," she promised. "Besides," Mel said, ducking to avoid his hand as he playfully tried to pinch her nose. "You practically live here anyway. You're practically a roommate. You should do chores like the rest of us, shouldn't he, Sara?"

"Sure," Sara said, bending suddenly to collect her things. "If you say so."

Listening to the three of them joke around outside in the yard, Annie sat back on her heels and tried not to feel bitter. She couldn't help it that she liked things clean and orderly but Mel sometimes made her feel like she was some kind of freak because she did. And she didn't really care if Mel mopped the damn kitchen floor or not. She had offered, and Annie had agreed, but the truth was that Annie would rather do it herself. That way, she knew it'd get done right.

She got up and went to get the mop, filling the pail at the kitchen sink. She stood at the window and watched as J.T. put his arms around Mel and picked her up, and poor lovesick Sara quickly gathered her things and tried not to notice. It amazed Annie that Mel didn't seem to know that Sara had a thing for J.T. Or maybe she did know and chose to ignore it.

Watching Sara mope around the yard, Annie was glad she'd settled on Mitchell Stites. Her love for Mitchell was steady and dependable; it was the kind of thing you could build your whole life around. It wasn't the wild, crazy love that Mel and J.T. shared with their endless fights and passionate reconciliations. Nor the sad, yearning kind of love that Sara seemed to feel for J.T. Everyone was always going on and on about passion, but Annie could see how passion might really screw up your life. It might keep you from thinking clearly. It might make you do things you'd regret later.

No, passion was for movie actresses and novel heroines. Annie would settle for safety and security.

She filled the pail with water and floor cleaner and took it to the far corner of the room. She locked the screen door so they'd have to go around and come through the front door. The one thing she couldn't stand was footprints all over her freshly mopped floor. Mel and J.T. were sitting in one of the lawn chairs now looking out at the distant mountains. J.T. was sitting behind Mel with his arms wrapped around her, and she had her head resting on his chest. Sara was nowhere in sight.

Annie dipped the mop into the pail. She wrung it out and began mopping with long, even strokes. It didn't take her long to fall into a rhythm. It was almost like a Zen meditation, mopping, and one that made her feel calm and peaceful. After a while, she lost track of the time, glancing periodically at the clock as she worked. Mitchell was supposed to call her at two o'clock. He called her every Saturday at precisely two o'clock and every Wednesday night at precisely eight o'clock. It was a routine they had established when Annie first went away to college and one from which they never deviated. Mitchell hadn't gone to college. He had gone to work in his father's Cluck-in-a-Bucket store immediately after high school graduation, but Annie had felt that a college education was important. She was majoring in anthropology with a minor in business, the idea being that whatever she learned might be applicable later when she and Mitchell took over his father's store. That was the plan. Graduation and then marriage at twenty-two, two children by twenty-five, a house in the suburbs by twenty-eight. It was all going like clockwork.

She was almost to the sink now and she stood up to take a break, crossing her arms across the top of the mop and staring out the window. An errant breeze blew through the screen, warm and balmy. J.T. and Mel were making out in the lawn chair and Annie watched for a moment, feeling faintly repulsed and yet curious, too.

Sex. She just didn't get it. She had spent her entire freshman year listening to Mel, Sara, Lola, and the rest of the girls on her dorm floor talking about sex, and finally she just couldn't take it anymore. She had to know for herself what it was like. When Mitchell showed up at school her sophomore year for Homecoming Weekend, she was ready. She had gone down to Planned Parenthood and gotten on the pill two weeks before, and they had given her a box of condoms to use until the pill became effective. They were sitting in Mitchell's pickup truck out at Edwards Point when she told him. The ridge below them was bathed in moonlight. An owl flew overhead, its great wings flapping soundlessly.

Mitchell stared at her, his face a mixture of shock and outrage. "What do you mean, you want to have sex?" he said.

"I mean, it's time," she said, handing him the box that might have contained maybe two hundred condoms. "I'm ready. Let's do it."

Mitchell stared down at the box and then up at her. His mouth hung open. A vein pulsed in his temple like an emergency flasher. "But you're a *good girl,*" he said finally. "Good girls don't have sex until *after* marriage."

Annie didn't see what the big deal was. They'd been dating for nearly six years, and for the last two, Mitchell had been relentlessly trying to coax her into taking off her clothes. "Look," she said, beginning to get annoyed. "You've been after me for years to do it and now I'm ready, so what's the big deal?"

Mitchell tossed the box of condoms on the seat between them. He put his hands on the steering wheel, then took them off again. He looked like a man whose orderly view of the world had been suddenly and inexplicably dismantled. "But that's my job!" he cried. "I'm a man and I'm *supposed* to try to get you into bed!"

"And I'm a woman. What's my job?"

"To resist," he snapped. "Your job is to resist."

Annie looked at him in astonishment. She put her hand out to him but he shrank into the corner. "You're being ridiculous," she said. She crossed her arms over her chest and chewed her lower lip, watching him through lowered lids. She wondered if other girls had this much trouble losing their virginity. She wondered if Briggs Furman or J.T. Radford had put up this much of a fight. "I want sex," she said finally, pushing the box toward him. "And I want it now."

Mitchell put his hands on the steering wheel again and stared through the window. When his breathing had slowed, he said glumly, "I can't just perform at the drop of a hat. You can't just turn to a guy and tell him you want sex and expect him to perform like a trained monkey."

"Why not?"

"Because it doesn't work that way!"

"Oh, for crying out loud," she said, taking off her shirt.

After that, things went a bit more predictably. Still, when it was over, she had to ask herself, *What's the big deal?* It wasn't anything like the girls on her dorm floor had described. And even later, when it got a little better, or at least a little easier, she sometimes had to ask herself, *Is there something wrong with me? I just don't get it.*

And she still didn't get it, although Mitchell seemed to enjoy it and she guessed she should take some pleasure in that. Looking through the window at J.T. and Mel sprawled on the lawn chair, she realized that Mel obviously did enjoy it. She wondered what that must feel like.

It probably felt like that slight, trembling sensation she got in the lower part of her abdomen whenever Professor Ballard walked into the classroom. Annie picked up the mop and went back to work.

Best not to think about that.

Briggs dropped Lola off at the library and she went up the wide steps and waited just inside the front doors. When she was sure he had driven away, she opened the doors, tripped down the steps, and ran around back to the administration building, where Lonnie Lumpkin was working.

She had met Lonnie several weeks ago at the Duck Pond. Lonnie was a local boy who worked as a maintenance man on the campus and he liked to take his lunch breaks down by the pond, feeding the ducks. The Duck Pond was a secluded little park on the outskirts of the campus, surrounded by benches, tall trees, and war memorials to dead alumni stretching back to the Mexican War of 1846. It was too far from the quad to be used by most students, and Lola liked to go there to be alone and think. She had noticed Lonnie several times before she ever spoke to him. He seemed to come the same time every day. He wore a uniform and a cap with the school crest emblazoned on the front that he would take off and lay beside him on the bench. His hair was blond and he wore it in a ponytail. He was tall but thin and his hands were long and slender like a concert pianist's. She noticed that he would feed the ducks with pieces of his own sandwich, breaking off larger and larger bits until, on some days, there was little left for himself.

On the day they first spoke, he was squatting at the edge of the pond trying to coax one of the ducks to take a crust of bread from his hand. He had done this on several occasions, and one of the bolder ducks, a mallard with a beautiful green head, had come close to taking it. This day the duck waddled up on the bank and fixed Lonnie with a bright, beady eye. Then slowly, stealthily, it stretched out its neck and with a sudden movement like a snake striking, took the crust and flapped back to the water.

"You're the first one I've ever seen do that. They don't trust most people," Lola said in amazement.

He grinned at her, still squatting at the water's edge with his arms on his knees. "He knows I'm pretty harmless," he said. He stood up and dusted off his pants, pulling his cap out of his back pocket. His uniform was obviously made for someone much shorter. His socks were sucked down into his shoes and she could see his bony ankles under the edge of the upturned cuffs.

He held on to the brim of the cap and said shyly, "I'm Lonnie."

"Lola." She smiled and went back to reading.

Over the next few weeks she got to know him as their meetings at the Duck Pond became more frequent. Lola was not one to strike up conversations with strangers but there was something about Lonnie that put her at ease. Like the ducks, she trusted him. He had a kind heart. She could see that. They talked about many things but never about the fact that Lola was engaged to another man. She didn't say much about Briggs at all other than to admit that she had a steady boyfriend she'd dated since her junior year of high school. Her mother, Maureen, always introduced Briggs as "Lola's fiancé," holding his arm greedily and smiling like a woman who knows she's snagged the most eligible man around. It was Maureen who, on being first introduced to Briggs, had decided that come hell or high water, he would be her future son-in-law. His grandfather had been a state senator from Mississippi, and Lola's father and grandfather had been governors of Alabama. To Maureen, it had seemed a match made in heaven. Lola, an only child long accustomed to compliance with her mother's wishes, had not put up much of a fight. She liked Briggs well enough.

But that was before she met Lonnie. Now she noticed things about

Briggs that she didn't like. Like the way his thick knuckles were covered in dark hair and the way his skin smelled like rusty iron when he sweated. And he had a bad temper. He was a big man, a former prep school quarterback, and when angered he would shout and clench his fists. Lola would feel her stomach tighten, not because she was afraid of him but because she didn't like being around angry people. They upset her. They caused little disturbances in the air around them, vibrations that rolled through the atmosphere like shock waves following a detonated bomb.

Still, as her mother so often pointed out, he was from a good family, he was blond and good-looking, and he was an ATO to boot. And Briggs was a Southern gentleman to the very core of his being. Most of the time he treated her like a princess, like a glass figure on a pedestal. So she should have felt guilty about deceiving him on this bright fall day as she left the library and hurried around the corner toward the administration building. But Lola wasn't thinking about Briggs at all. She was thinking about Lonnie.

He was up on a ladder painting the second-story soffits. She stood for a moment with one hand on her hip and the other shading her eyes as she looked up at him. It took him a few minutes to realize she was there, but when he did, he grinned slowly and stopped painting.

"Hey, girl," he said.

"Hey, Lonnie."

He climbed down the ladder, holding the paint can and brush carefully in one hand. His overalls were covered in paint splatters. "What'd you bring me for lunch?"

Lola got so caught up in looking at him that for a moment she couldn't think of anything to say. He had an earring in one ear and the tattoo of a dragon on his right forearm, and he was just about the most exotic-looking boy Lola had ever seen.

"Sorry?" she said.

He grinned slowly, his gray eyes kind but lively. "Just kidding," he said.

She smiled and moved away so he could step off the ladder. "Do you have to work all day?"

"No. I get off at noon." He took a rag out of his pocket and began to clean his hands with paint thinner. When he'd finished he stuck the rag back in his pocket. "Why?"

She wasn't quite sure what to say, so she asked, "Do you like working here?"

He shrugged. "It's a job. It pays the bills until the music thing takes off." He was a musician, the lead guitarist in a heavy metal band called the Lords of Ruin. They played at various small clubs around town. He had invited her on a number of occasions to come hear them, but so far she had declined. She knew that if she saw him up on a stage with a guitar strapped to his chest it would be all over. Her life as she knew it, as her mother had planned it, would be over.

"My boyfriend might be able to help you out," she said, noting the way his eyes turned from gray to pale blue depending on the light.

He arched one eyebrow. "Your boyfriend?" They spoke of Briggs now as if he was some kind of private joke between them.

"His frat's having a party. They need a band to play."

His smile widened. A dimple appeared deep in one cheek and Lola fought a sudden urge to kiss him. "We don't play many frat parties," he said.

When Sara got back from her walk, Mel and J.T. had already left for Sliding Rock. She felt relief wash over her, followed swiftly by a feeling of dejection as she climbed the front porch steps and went upstairs to her bedroom to lie down. The house smelled of disinfectant and citrus cleaner. She could hear Annie moving around in her bedroom. Lola must still be at the library.

Sara lay on the bed with her ankles crossed and her hands behind her head, staring at the ceiling. The window was open, and a sultry breeze blew through the room, flapping the edge of her Led Zeppelin poster that had come loose at one corner. Faintly in the distance, a leaf blower hummed.

She wasn't sure she could last another year. She had made it through three years already and that had been torture enough, but this year, when she was a senior, when she should have been enjoying her last year of college before heading out into the big world, Sara wasn't sure she could stand the anguish. She fantasized about taking her clothes out of the closet and throwing them into her suitcase; she imagined tearing her posters off the walls and heading for home.

But what would she tell her parents? That she was in love with the same boy Mel loved? That she couldn't stand the strain anymore of trying to pretend that she didn't feel what she felt?

She had never been in love before, and she was unprepared for the ruthless misery of the emotion. There was no relief, even in her dreams, from the dull constant grief that afflicted her like an abscess. She had had other boyfriends. She had been popular enough in high school and had dated a steady stream of boys. But she had never felt more than a mild attachment to any of them. She had watched her friends contend with disappointment and heartache, and she had asked them, *What's the big deal? Leave him. If he doesn't love you, then stop mooning after him and just leave.* It had seemed so simple.

And then she met J. T. Radford and everything changed.

It was during her first weeks at Bedford. She and Mel had come up to school together in Mel's car while Sara's parents followed behind, and after three weeks at Bedford they had begun to settle in. Mount Clemmons was beautiful, a rambling village of Victorian cottages clustered around the tall redbrick Gothic buildings of the campus. The overall effect was that of an English boarding school set down in the wilds of North Carolina. Mel and Sara were suitemates in Nordan Hall along with an amiable girl from Alabama named Lola, and a not-so-amiable girl from Nashville named Anne Louise. Nordan was the dorm closest to the woods, the one easiest to sneak out of after curfew, a fact it did not take Mel and Sara long to discover. On their third weekend on campus, they heard about a bonfire down by the lake and decided to go. Lola and Anne Louise were less enthusiastic.

"You'll get caught," Anne Louise said, sitting on the edge of Mel's bed watching them dress. She had her hair wrapped around big curlers. Her face was covered with green paste. She looked like the Wicked Witch of the West from *The Wizard of Oz,* only without the hat and the long black dress. "You'll get caught and then you'll get expelled."

"The only way we'll get caught," Mel said, looking pointedly at Anne Louise, "is if someone rats us out."

Anne Louise, under her covering of green paste, managed to look offended. "Well, don't look at me," she said.

"This is so exciting," Lola said, clapping her hands and gliding into the room in a floor-length nightgown. They had been here three weeks and Sara had not seen Lola wear the same nightgown twice. *Where does she keep them all?* Sara had asked Mel, who replied, *I think she wears them once and then throws them out. The girl's dad was governor of Alabama. She can afford plenty of nightgowns.*

"Why don't you come with us, Lola?" Mel asked. "It'll be fun."

Lola looked tempted but then frowned and shook her head. "I better not," she said. "Y'all might get in trouble." Lola had gone to an exclusive all-girl prep school and she still had the naive respect for authority engendered in such places. Four years with Mel and Sara would eventually cure her of that.

"They can't expel all of us," Sara said reasonably. "It's going to be a big party. They'd have to expel half the school."

Mel gave her a high five. "Good thinking," she said. She turned to Lola and Anne Louise. "Come on, girls. Take a walk on the wild side. Live a little."

In the end Lola and Anne Louise were not convinced, so it was Mel and Sara who ran barefoot through the wet grass toward the woods, giggling and shoving each other. Moonlight dappled the tall trees and fell in silver swells across the wide lawn. When they reached the woods, they sat down and put their shoes on, then followed a narrow twisting trail down a sloping embankment toward the river. All around them, mountain ridges wreathed in fog rose into the evening sky. Frogs sang in the swampy bottoms. The girls followed the trail through thick stands of mountain laurel, around boulders that glistened in the moonlight like the backs of slumbering beasts.

"How much farther?" Sara asked. "Are you sure you know where you're going?"

Ahead they could hear distant music. Light flickered among the tree trunks, and as they got closer, it flared into a wide vista of dancing firelight. The trail ended on a low ridge. Standing there looking down a steep sandy embankment to the river, they could see a huge bonfire roaring on the beach, surrounded by a crowd of moving figures. Several cars were parked on the beach. Someone had opened the doors of one of the cars and "L. A. Woman" blared from the radio.

Mel and Sara stood up on the ridge for a while and watched the party.

"I don't know about this," Sara said. "I don't see anyone I know."

"We're freshmen," Mel reminded her. "We don't know anybody. That's the whole point of being here."

"Do you think it's safe?" Sara said, but Mel had already started down the embankment, her feet kicking up little clumps of sand. Sara stood for a moment listening to the eerie stillness behind her and then started down. She figured the chances of being abducted or assaulted were less likely in front of a crowded bonfire than standing alone on a moonlit ridge.

Once she got to the beach, however, she began to rethink this. Several boys had already noticed Mel, and by the time Sara reached the beach, they had come forward to greet them. There were girls, scattered here and there, but it was mostly a male crowd, which made Sara uncomfortable. It wasn't that she didn't like boys. She did. It's just that, unlike most of the girls she knew, she wasn't planning her whole life around catching one. Boys were okay alone but in groups they tended to be rude and nasty. They tended to treat girls like *things* that existed solely for their own pleasure.

"Hey, do you want a beer?" one of the boys asked them, holding up a plastic cup. They had set up a keg in the back of a pickup truck and were taking turns shooting a stream of foamy beer into an endless supply of clear plastic cups.

"Sure," Mel said.

"No, thanks," Sara said.

Maybe it was because she'd grown up with younger brothers. She'd grown up with stained underwear scattered across the bathroom floor, with pinup girls and Matchbox cars, and with bedrooms that smelled faintly of dirty socks and old cheese. Boys were predictable. Sara knew male code intimately; it was not a hard code to crack.

"So you girls go to Bedford?"

"That's right," Mel said.

Sara stood at the fringe of boys surrounding Mel and tried not to feel self-conscious. She stuck her fingers into the pockets of her jeans and stared at a couple of guys who had broken into an impromptu wrestling match. A crowd gathered quickly to egg them on.

"That dickwad Jemison," one of the boys said to Mel. "He took state last year and thinks he's tough shit."

"My dad watches the WWF," Mel said. "I hate wrestling."

Sara tried to catch Mel's eye but Mel was obviously ignoring her. When Mel had asked her earlier if she wanted to go to a bonfire, Sara had pictured something a little more sedate, with maybe a few cheerleaders and several clean-cut members of the football team gathered around singing school songs. She hadn't imagined the raucous, long-haired dopers she saw congregated here. Not an athlete among them, she thought, looking around the crowd, unless you counted sprinting from the law as a track-and-field event. (Except, of course, Jemison, the all-state wrestler, who now had his opponent pinned up against the tire of one of the cars.)

"Hey, assholes, watch out for my car!" someone shouted above the blare of the music.

The air was thick with the sweet, acrid aroma of grass. Sara watched a doobie make its way slowly around Mel's circle of admirers. "Toke?" the boy next to Sara asked, offering her the joint.

"No, thanks," Sara said.

"Sure," Mel said, reaching for it.

Sara had partied in high school; everyone in Howard's Mill drank, even the Baptist minister (surreptitiously, of course, and never in front of his own flock. He drove to Nashville to booze it up). But Sara didn't like to lose control of herself, and she didn't like the taste of alcohol, so usually two beers were enough for her. After that she took care of everyone else who didn't seem to know when to stop, Mel included, holding their hair while they were sick, making sure they didn't pass out in dangerous places, making sure she was the one who drove everyone home. She never did drugs. She'd gotten used to her role as designated driver in high school but it wasn't something she'd wanted to carry over into college life.

"If you get shit faced," she said to Mel, "how're you planning on getting back to the dorm? I can't drive you and I sure as hell can't carry you."

"She can spend the night here," one of the boys, a big red-faced guy named Darrel, said. The others snorted and showed their teeth like a troop of chimpanzees.

"Good luck explaining that to the R.A.," Sara said, ignoring them. Mel took another hit and giggled.

It wasn't that Sara minded having a boyfriend, although certainly not one like these idiots, she thought, looking disparagingly around the circle at their red hairy faces. Her last boyfriend, Heath, had been the high school quarterback and he'd been nice enough. (The rumor was that he'd gone out with Sara to get back at the cheerleader who'd dumped him; he'd figured the best revenge was dating a "smart" girl.) Heath was good-looking and clean, and he smelled of Old Spice and shaving cream. He'd picked her out of the yearbook because Sara was photogenic and took a good picture, and he thought she'd looked "pretty" and "nice." (She didn't mind about the revenge rumor.) He was nice, too, and the things they did together were nice (some were downright enjoyable), but despite his being good-looking and charming and popular, she still didn't trust him completely. She still couldn't give herself to him. Heath didn't handle rejection well. He pouted and sulked and became overbearing and obsessive. He couldn't seem to comprehend that she didn't want what other girls wanted: marriage out of high school and three children by twenty-five. He couldn't seem to see the big picture as she so patiently explained it to him.

When she broke up with him, he'd shouted, "You can't break up with me! I'm the quarterback!," which Sara thought was childish and pathetic, really. But by then she'd become enamored of Faye Dunaway's character in *Chinatown* (*I don't get tough with anyone, Mr. Gittes. My lawyer does.*) and saw herself ten years into the future, a powerful woman navigating the treacherous male-dominated waters of corporate law like a sharp-toothed barracuda.

"Hey, who's this?" Jemison, the all-state wrestler, had appeared out of nowhere, shirtless and pumped up like a silverback gorilla. His hair stood up wildly around his head. He leered at Mel and sauntered over. "Who's this foxy girl?" he asked. Mel rolled her eyes and glanced at Sara, who gave her a quick *let's go* look.

He slung one meaty arm across her shoulders and Mel quickly pushed it off, saying, "Take a shower, why don't you?"

He laughed loudly. His beady eyes narrowed as he looked around the circle. "I like her," he said. He noticed Sara then, and stuck his plastic cup out to her. "Have a drink," he said.

"I don't drink." Sara looped her fingers around Mel's belt in the back and gave a little tug to get her moving.

"She doesn't drink, Jemison," one of the boys said. "We already tried."

"Yeah, Jemison, she doesn't smoke either," another one chattered, hopping from foot to foot and waving his long arms.

"Huh," Jemison said, squinting at Sara. "She doesn't drink and she doesn't smoke. What does she do?" The others chuckled and looked around nervously. Jemison leaned in so close Sara could smell his sour breath, and growled, "Are you a narc?"

"Leave my friend alone," Mel said.

"I'll get to you in a minute."

Sara stepped back. State champion or not, she figured they could outrun him as long as he didn't take to the trees. As if guessing her intent, he put one hairy arm out to stop her but before he could grab hold of her shoulder a voice rang out across the clearing. "Leave her alone!" It was a voice of authority, deep and masculine, and Jemison stopped, his arm hanging midair. The crowd parted and they could see him now, a lone boy sitting in the back of a pickup truck, one knee drawn up and one arm resting casually across the top.

The world stopped suddenly, or at least it did for Sara; everything became blurry and grainy, like a film in slow motion. The boy in the back of the truck seemed lit by a strange phosphorescence. Or maybe it was just a moonbeam, trained on him like a spotlight. The image made Sara dizzy. She felt like she'd been hit over the head and covered by something dark and heavy. He raised his hand and beckoned to them and Sara began to move toward him like a sleepwalker.

"Sorry, Radford," Jemison shouted, stepping back, and the spell was suddenly broken. The crowd began to shift and disperse. Jim Morrison sang "Don't You Love Her Madly?" and Jemison raised his hand and said again, "Sorry man, I didn't know they were with you," and turning, slunk off into the night.

John Thomas Radford. He was a third-year English lit student from Charlotte, North Carolina, and, climbing up into the bed of the truck beside him, Sara felt like she'd known him all her life. Mel sat down on the other side of him and later, when they got cold, he took off his jeans jacket and put it around Sara and made one of the other boys give his jacket to Mel. His hair was long and straight and fell just below his ears. He seemed lit by some kind of strange incandescence. Even in the shadows cast by the dancing fire, Sara knew his eyes were green, knew he had a small scar at the outside corner of his right eye, knew his lower lip was full and round, knew what it would feel like to kiss him. She had never, until this moment, believed in love at first sight.

A low-lying band of fog drifted off the river. Stars twinkled above the ridgetops.

"Your friend sure is quiet," he said to Mel.

The moon was low in the sky and the fire had burned to embers by the time they decided it was time to go. The crowd had gradually broken up, slipping through the trees like wraiths, and the clearing was filled now with a cold gray light. J.T. nudged Mel with his shoulder. "Y'all better get back to the dorm before you get caught and put on restriction."

"Spoken like someone who knows how that works."

He laughed and jumped down from the bed of the truck, putting his arms up to help them. He held Mel a few seconds longer, Sara noticed, and she smiled slyly up at him and said, "What's your girlfriend going to say about you hanging out all night with a couple of strange women?"

He let her go. "What girlfriend?" he said.

Sara made a move to return his jacket to him but he said, "No, you keep it until we get back to the dorm. I'll walk you home. Two pretty girls like you shouldn't be out alone in the woods at night." It was a corny thing to say, of course, and normally they would have protested. But neither one wanted to let him go so they said nothing and followed him across the clearing.

"Where are you going?" Mel said, pointing at the sandy embankment they had run down. "We came this way."

"Next time take the trail," he said, pointing, and they could see the dim outline of a narrow trail rising from the beach and crisscrossing the ridge, several hundred feet from the embankment. "You're less likely to fall if you take the trail."

"Who says there'll be a next time?" Mel asked.

He stood there in the violet light, grinning at her. "Oh, I think you'll be back," he said.

Sara led the way. The trail was steeper than it looked from the beach, and was covered in trailing vines that caught at their legs and feet. They were halfway up the ridge when Mel fell. Sara heard her go down like a sack of potatoes hitting a dirt floor. J.T. leaned over, picked Mel up, and set her on her feet, but she winced slightly and said, "Shit. I think I twisted my ankle." He bent over to check her leg. In the sky above his shoulder, the faint rim of moon hung like a silver coin. He prodded her ankle gently with his fingers. Mel looked at Sara and grinned, her teeth gleaming in the darkness. "Ouch," she said.

It was a good thing J.T. stood between them, because if he hadn't, Sara would have pitched Mel over the edge. All this over a boy. But not just any boy. As if to remind her of this he looked up, his face slightly luminous.

"I'd better carry you," he said to Mel and swooped her up in his arms. She made a faint squeak, like a small rodent being squeezed. Sara headed up the trail, trying not to hear Mel's giggles and the soft grunting noises J.T. made as he climbed.

"You're a lot stronger than you look."

"You're a lot heavier than you look."

Down on the beach someone was starting the vehicles. Headlights clicked on, sweeping the beach. Sara picked her way up the trail, hearing Mel's soft little cries like a knife turning beneath her heart. Almost to the crest, they stopped so J.T. could put her down and catch his breath. He stood there, tall and broad-shouldered against the fading stars, and quoted,

"When the stars threw down their spears,
And water'd heaven with their tears,
Did he smile his work to see?
Did he who made the Lamb make thee?"

Mel said, "I hope you're not comparing me to a tiger. Because that's not very flattering."

"Who says I'm comparing you to anything?" he said, grinning at her. "Who says it's about you at all?"

"I like Blake all right," she said, putting her head back to him. "But Yeats! Now there's a poet."

Sara swung around and plodded up the trail, trying to put as much distance as possible between her and them. A faint violet light bathed the eastern sky. Their voices became fainter. If they knew she was leaving them behind, they didn't seem to care.

2005

Chapter 4

~~~~~~~~~

MONDAY

Their first morning at the beach they awoke to a breakfast of seafood crepes and fresh fruit. April, it seemed, was working her way through culinary school and had a notebook full of recipes she was dying to try out. She disappeared soon after they had gathered around the enormous breakfast bar, and reappeared a short while later dressed in a swimsuit and carrying a towel.

"Just leave the dishes in the sink," she told Lola. "I'll get to them when I get back."

"Don't worry about us," Lola said. She was standing in a bright slash of sunlight looking sweet and cheerful, her thick-lensed glasses glinting in the sun.

April went out the French doors on to the deck and they watched her walk along the boardwalk and disappear over the dunes. A few minutes later she reappeared, a tiny figure moving across the wide expanse of beach. Captain Mike, Mel noted, was nowhere to be seen.

The women took their time eating breakfast, enjoying the opportunity to be lazy. They were all still dressed in their pajamas. Lola wore a pair of red silk pajamas that looked comfortable and expensive, but seemed strangely out of place with her heavy-rimmed glasses. Annie wore a nightgown with matching robe and slippers. Mel had on a camisole and sleep shorts covered in yellow ducks, and Sara wore a pair of sweat pants and a Carolina Law T-shirt.

"Let's stay in our jammies all day," Sara said. "This is the most fun I've had in ages."

"You don't get out much, do you," Mel said.

The kitchen and breakfast bar overlooked the cavernous great room and when they had finished eating they took their coffee into the great room and sat across from one another on two long sofas positioned on either side of the stone fireplace, Mel and Annie on one sofa and Sara and Lola on the other, their feet stretched out and resting on the big glass coffee table. Beyond the wall of soaring windows overlooking the beach, the Atlantic glittered in the sun. A blue haze hung over the distant horizon.

Mel looked critically at her long legs stretched out on the table. "I need to get some sun on these bad boys," she said, turning them this way and that. They were perfect legs and anyone looking at them could see that.

"Do what I do and go down to one of those places where they spray the tan on," Annie said, lifting her nightgown so they could see her own heavier, rather splotchy legs.

Lola picked up a controller and punched a button, and the flat-screen TV slid out from behind a painting on the chimney breast. She scrolled aimlessly through a series of channels, stopping briefly on one of those entertainment shows that spread gossip about Hollywood stars.

"This show is good," Sara said.

Mel picked up a magazine and thumbed through it slowly. "Since when do you have time to sit around watching daytime TV?"

"I told you I was only working part-time right now." Adam was settling into his third new school and she'd quit to spend more time with him, but Sara didn't want to go into all of that. She picked up a magazine too. "Is this the Bedford alumni magazine?"

"Briggs gets those," Lola said quickly.

Sara looked at Mel and Annie. "Do y'all get the alumni magazine?"

"I get it but I never read it," Mel said.

"I don't get it," Annie said. "Or if I do, Mitchell throws it away before I see it."

"They must have lost my address." Sara yawned and tossed the magazine on the table, where it opened to the center page, a glossy roundup of Bedford grads, past and present. Annie turned it around with her toes. "Hey," she said, pointing at a photo of a bride and her much-older groom, "didn't we go to school with that guy?"

Mel leaned over and peered at the photo. "Oh yeah," she said "Bart. Sara used to date him."

"I never dated a Bart," Sara said.

"Sure you did."

"Well, okay, maybe once." She shuddered at the memory, and Lola smiled brightly and said, "Sara's never loved anyone but Tom."

There was a moment of silence, broken only by the gurgling of the coffee pot in the kitchen. Annie picked up the magazine and peered at the photograph. "Wow," she said, holding it to Mel, "he must have robbed the cradle. She looks twenty years younger."

"Trophy wife," Mel said. "I hope he drops dead of a heart attack on his honeymoon. It would serve him right."

Annie swiveled her head around to Mel. "As I recall, you like younger men yourself. What was the name of that bartender in London, the one with the curly hair?"

"Let's not go there," Mel said.

"Oh, let's do," Sara said. "I don't think I've heard that story."

"Well, I think it's sweet," Lola said, obviously not following the conversation. "I think it's sweet that Sara's still in love with her own husband." She tilted her head and gazed pensively at the TV. From time to time an air of melancholy drifted across her face, seeping through the cracks of her happy facade like smoke.

"Lola, you're a hopeless romantic," Annie said.

"Am I?" She seemed surprised by this.

Mel looked up and then went back to glancing at the magazine.

"Besides," Sara said to Mel, trying to change the subject. "As I recall, it was you who had the thing for Bart."

"I never had a thing for him. I just slept with him."

"Yes, I remember."

Mel closed the magazine abruptly. She sat very still, watching Sara. "Do you really want to stroll down memory lane? Do you really want to go there?"

"I'll stroll if you will," Sara said.

"I thought we were talking about Bart and his child bride," Annie said nervously.

"We are," Mel said quietly. Her eyes were brown and steady.

Sara colored and turned her face to the TV. Outside the windows a gull hung motionless, riding the currents. Lola held a pillow against her chest as if she was cradling a child. Through the windows behind her the sea shimmered, a long line of whitecapped waves.

Annie took the alumni magazine from Mel and tossed it on the table. "If we're going down to the Beach Club pool, we'd better get going," she said, rising. "If we wait any longer all the good chairs will be taken."

As children, Sara and Mel had been as different as two girls could be. Howard's Mill in the 1960s and '70s was a small but prosperous village of twenty-five thousand people clustered along the banks of the Tennessee River. Sara's father taught history out at the high school, and they lived in a modest three-bedroom brick ranch house in a neighborhood of other modest three-bedroom brick ranch houses. Sara had two younger brothers and a pretty mother who stayed home to cook and clean just like June Cleaver, only on a tighter budget.

Mel's father owned the town's only car dealership, and she lived out from town in a big columned house with a boot-shaped swimming pool out back. Mel's mother, Juanita, was Leland Barclay's second wife and was rumored to have been his housekeeper and, as if that wasn't scandalous enough, Mel's older half-brother, Junior, was the town's first heroin addict. He had dropped out of high school and gone out to Haight-Ashbury for the Summer of Love, where he took Timothy Leary's advice to "Turn On, Tune In, and Drop Out" to heart. He was eleven years older than Mel, and by the time she was twelve he was back home in Howard's Mill living in the pool house, working in Leland's Ford dealership, and trying unsuccessfully to go straight. Mel and Sara used to go out to the pool house to find him sleeping with his eyes open, the Doors or Jimi Hendrix blasting on the stereo.

Sara liked going out to Mel's house. There was always something to do, with the boot-shaped swimming pool and the playroom crammed with every toy imaginable, and the mini-bikes out in the barn. Mel's mother was a small shy woman with a Guatemalan accent who stayed mostly in her room, scurrying down the back stairs to fix meals and then scurrying back up them before Leland Barclay came in to eat. Mel's daddy, Leland, was loud and brash, and he had a big red nose and a belly that hung over his belt like a feed sack. He wore cowboy boots and a belt buckle with his initials on the front, and he liked to brag that he'd been born in West Texas, *out where the men were tough as the calluses on a barfly's elbows* ("He should know," Mel liked to say).

Sara also liked driving out to the country club in Leland's big Cadillac Coupe de Ville with Leland at the wheel and her and Mel jumping around in the backseat to "Itchycoo Park" or "Take the Last Train to Clarkesville." The Howard's Mill Country Club was nothing more than a small brick building with a nine-hole golf course and a concrete swimming pool surrounded by a chain-link fence. There were probably only a thousand members (who didn't include Sara's parents), but it was the closest thing to upscale that Howard's Mill had to offer.

Everyone in town gossiped about the Barclays; long before spoiled blonde heiresses and bad blond rock stars became the norm, the Barclays were local celebrities whose every move was noted and commented on. Sara liked being part of the Barclay inner circle. She liked ordering cokes at the bar and signing Leland's name. She liked that all the staff knew to put her chili cheese fries on the Barclay tab. It was magical the way anything you could possibly want would suddenly appear and all you had to do was sign for it. Being rich was like finding a genie in a bottle. The older she got, the more time Sara spent with Mel's family. Her secret wish was that the Barclays would offer to adopt her and then she and Mel could truly be sisters.

She especially loved to eat dinner at Mel's house. Eating dinner at Mel's house was like waiting for a fight to break out in the stands of a Friday night football game between Howard's Mill and Suck Creek. You never knew who was going to throw the first punch but you knew it was just a matter of time before everyone joined in. It wasn't that way at Sara's house. At Sara's house everyone waited their turn to speak. They didn't scream or shout or talk over one another or start eating before grace was said. That was considered bad manners, and Sara's mother wouldn't have tolerated it. If there was one biscuit left on the plate, and you wanted it, you'd ask politely if you could have it and if no one else did, it was yours. At Mel's house, if there was one biscuit left on the plate, there was sure to be a fight to the death between Leland and Junior. She'd actually witnessed Junior throw a fork at his father one night over a lone biscuit and Leland had counterattacked by hoisting his glass of Old Crow at his son's head. Sometimes, just for family solidarity, Mel would join in, too.

One rainy Friday evening not long after the start of eighth grade, Sara came home with Mel to spend the night. They'd been friends since first grade and by now Sara was accustomed to the mayhem of the Barclay household. On this particular evening Juanita had made fried chicken, squash casserole, mashed potatoes, and biscuits, and not long after setting the steaming food on the table, she had disappeared up the back stairs. Mel and Sara washed their hands and sat down at the table. There was never any evening prayer given at the Barclay table; you just started in helping your plate. A few minutes later Leland came in, followed shortly thereafter by Junior, who looked like a younger, longer-haired version of Leland only without the red nose and the beer gut.

The evening went pleasantly enough at first, with Sara and Mel chattering on about the homecoming dance, Leland sitting in uncharacteristic silence at one end of the table and Junior at the other. Leland sat hunched over his plate with his elbows on the table and his head lowered like a junkyard dog guarding a ham bone. From time to time he would sip from the tumbler of Old Crow at his elbow, watching his son over the edge of his glass with red-rimmed eyes. Junior just sat there looking sickly and skinny, and picked at his food.

"Eat your food, boy, don't play with it," Leland said suddenly, pointing at Junior with his fork. He'd given the boy every advantage and Junior had disappointed him in every way imaginable; he was bad at sports, he couldn't hit the side of a barn with a scattergun, and he had absolutely no gumption or goals in life. Worse, he couldn't hold his liquor (Leland lumped all narcotics in with alcohol) whereas Leland could down half a quart of Old Crow in one sitting and never show the effects.

"I don't need you telling me how to eat," Junior said in a surly voice.

Mel kept on talking about the homecoming dance but Sara turned her attention to the dueling Barclays. She thought it was cool the way they could just say what they were thinking, right out in the open with no restraints. At her house, saying what you thought was considered bad manners. She had never heard her parents argue. If they disagreed over something, they didn't speak to each other, sometimes for days. Sara and her brothers would walk around on tiptoes, aware of an undercurrent of tension and a brooding silence that wafted through their house and into their dreams like a sinister presence. When the prescribed amount of silence had been carried out, as if on a signal, her parents started talking to each other again and everything went on as civilized and sedately as before. The source of the disagreement was never mentioned.

"You don't like the chicken, we can get the girl's ma (here he pointed at the backstairs with his fork) to make you something else. Cookin's the one thing she's still good at."

Junior picked up a drumstick and stuffed it into his mouth. Mel gave Leland a baleful stare. She didn't like hearing her mother abused in her presence. "She's good at a lot of things," she said.

"Not the things that matter," Leland said, lifting his tumbler.

"How do you know what she's good at? You never even talk to her."

"It's hard to talk to someone who's shut up in her room all day."

"No one wants to be around you, you smelly old goat."

Leland grimaced and set his drink down. "Now, Sister, this don't concern you. It's between me and the boy here." Leland liked to give Junior pep talks about getting his life back on track. *Sling it against the wall, son, and see if it sticks* was one of his favorites. Or sometimes, *Run it up the flagpole and see if anyone salutes*. And if that didn't work he might weigh in with, *If the fish ain't biting, boy, change the bait*. This was back in 1973, long before anyone in Howard's Mill had heard of rehab.

"Stop calling me boy," Junior said, his mouth full of fried chicken.

"Well, you sure as hell ain't a man," Leland said.

Junior scowled and started packing his cheeks with mashed potatoes. "Fuck you, old man," he said.

Sara snorted and glanced at Mel and then down at her plate. She tried to imagine what her mother would say if she heard someone use the F-word at the table. She'd probably say, *Just because you have money doesn't mean you have class*. She'd also say, *Don't ever set foot in the Barclay house again*.

"Why don't you just leave him alone?" Mel said to Leland. She stared at her father with a dangerous expression on her face. "Can't you see he's sick?"

"He ain't sick," Leland said, slapping the table with his hand so that the silverware rattled. "Ain't nothing wrong with that boy a little hard work won't cure." He lifted his tumbler and took a long pull. When he set it down again, the glass was empty. "Anybody can swim into a whirlpool, boy," he said. "It's coming out that counts." He coughed, sucked his teeth, and nodded sagely at Junior over these pearls of wisdom.

"Nobody cares what you say," Mel said. "Nobody cares what you think."

Leland ignored Mel, pointing one long hairy finger at Junior. "It's all them bad habits you picked up out there in Chicky Butte, California or wherever the hell you were."

"Well, it sure as hell wasn't Nosepick, Tennessee," Junior said, talking through a mouthful of fried chicken and mashed potatoes. "Thank God for that. Thank God I didn't wind up down in Numbnut, Texas with all the other greasers and shitkickers."

"If you had, you might a learned something, by God."

Sara giggled over *Nosepick* and *Numbnut,* but Mel just sat there with her eyes moving from one to the other like the steady swinging of a pendulum clock.

Junior, who'd been busy stuffing more mashed potatoes, fried chicken, and squash casserole into his mouth, suddenly went limp. It was his best defense against his father. His passive-aggressive slumping drove Leland wild.

"Sit up there, boy!" Leland roared, slamming his fist against the table so the silverware jumped and the glasses rattled. "Don't be such a candy ass!" But Junior sat slumped like a possum in the headlights of an oncoming car, his cheeks stuffed full of mashed potatoes and a thin strand of drool hanging from his bottom lip. Seeing his only son like that was a kick in the gut for Leland, partially because he looked just like Leland sitting there slump-shouldered and defeated, and Leland didn't like to see himself like that. He sucked in slowly but before he could say anything else, Mel said, "You're a mean, vicious old goat and I hate you."

Leland chuckled and pushed himself away from the table. He got up to pour himself another tumbler of Old Crow. When he sat back down, he pointed at Mel and said proudly, "If you had half the spunk that girl's got, you'd be a man. She don't let nobody get the best of her!"

Mel would later say it was her dysfunctional childhood that had turned her into a writer but Sara figured it was more the material advantages she'd had that had done that (Leland supported Mel for years in between book contracts and husbands). Mel always put down her family's social standing like it was no big deal. She was always going on about how she still had relatives who lived in trailer parks and Leland was nothing but an uneducated redneck who'd made his wealth dishonestly, but the truth of the matter was, money was money. And having it was better than not having it. Sara didn't like to admit that she might be jealous of Mel but the truth was, if she'd had Mel's advantages, there was no telling how much easier her life might have been.

• • •

It was almost one o'clock by the time they showered, dressed, and arrived at the Beach Club. The pool was not quite Olympic-size, but it was large and surrounded by a stamped concrete deck bordered on three sides by a tall wrought-iron fence and palm trees, and on the fourth by a large open bar. The pool was one of only three on the island and it was crowded with young mothers and their young children.

"Not a good-looking man in sight," Mel said, dejectedly setting her beach bag down on a poolside lounger. They quickly commandeered two other loungers but had to walk around the pool to find a fourth. Toddlers wearing water wings and soggy swim diapers were everywhere, scampering beneath their feet, scurrying between the pool and the fence like trapped rodents.

"Is that even sanitary?" Mel said, watching one child in a droopy swimsuit who had stopped at the end of the lounger to stare at her.

"Oh, isn't she adorable?" Lola said.

Mel grimaced and the child stuck one grimy fist into her mouth and tottered off.

"The swim diaper keeps the larger things—contained," Sara said, thinking how it was only yesterday that she had outfitted her own children with water wings and swim diapers and watched them splash joyously in the water. Now they were twelve and fourteen, and had entered that stage of surly adolescence that made them difficult to be around. Or at least Nicky had. Adam's surliness, of course, went much deeper than adolescence and wasn't really his fault at all.

"They usually keep the chlorine levels pretty high," Annie said.

"Well, I don't care how high the chlorine levels are, I'm not getting in the water." Mel took her cover-up off and leaned back against the lounger. Her figure was good but her skin was pale. She didn't get a whole lot of sun in New York.

"Look at you in your white bikini," Sara said flatly.

"It matches my skin."

"I haven't worn a bikini since college," Annie said wistfully. "Not since Carleton was born."

"I have a couple but I don't wear them in public," Lola said. "Only on the boat."

"Why not?" Mel said, flipping her sunglasses up on her head and looking around at her friends. "You look great. All of you look great."

Annie shook her head slowly and patted her stomach. "Stretch marks," she said.

"Oh, who cares?"

"It just doesn't seem right wearing a bikini," Sara said, putting her knees up. She kept her towel bunched around her waist to hide her post-pregnancy bump. She'd always been self-conscious about her figure, even when she was twenty-two and it was perfect. "It seems kind of pathetic, like you're trying too hard to hang on to your youth. You hit forty and there are some things you should just automatically put away. Things like black eyeliner, belly-button rings, and bikinis."

"Okay, Hester Prynne, you've made your point. I don't agree with you, of course, but I get it."

Sara tossed a flip-flop at Mel.

"Besides," Mel said. "Who among us has a belly-button ring?"

Annie and Sara looked sharply at Lola. She giggled and raised the top of her tankini to reveal a gleaming metal ring lying against her taut belly.

"Lola, you slut!" Mel leaned over to get a better look. "What happened to our demure little governor's daughter? What happened to our sweet little homecoming queen?"

"She grew up," Lola said.

The music playing on the PA system was a slow repetitive jazz number, like a tamped-down Chuck Mangione, as staid and innocuous as elevator music. After about twenty minutes, Mel had had all she could take.

"For crying out loud, play some real music," she said loudly. She sat up and adjusted the back of her lounger, looking around. "This shit is putting me to sleep. What do you think, Lola? Led Zeppelin? Steppenwolf?"

"Free Bird," Lola shouted.

A group of young mothers sitting to their right stopped talking to stare at them.

Mel raised her hand for the cocktail waitress and ordered a round of espresso martinis.

"I can't drink caffeine after twelve o'clock or I'll be up all night," Sara said.

"That's the idea," Mel said.

"Caffeine gives me the shakes," Annie said.

"The vodka offsets the caffeine. Trust me."

Lola pulled her tankini down over her belly-button ring. "I'll drink it," she said.

Chapter 5

~~~~~~~~~

Her mother always said Lola was a good little girl. Maureen liked to forget about Lola's little mistakes and, later on, her one Big Mistake, as if they never really happened at all.

"She's an angel," Maureen told her cronies in the Junior League. "Why, if she was a boy I'd have to call her Little Jesus," she bragged to her fellow members of the United Daughters of the Confederacy at their annual Mother-Daughter Tea.

Lola was four at the time. She smiled prettily and stuck two plump fingers into her mouth. She sucked steadily and smiled whenever anyone looked her way. She was dressed in a pink raw silk dress with lace ballerina sleeves and a pink satin sash tied around her waist. She sat on a high-backed chair with her chubby legs stuck straight out in front of her, both tiny feet covered in white anklet socks and a pair of shiny white patent-leather Mary Janes.

"If the good Lord saw fit to bless us with only one child," her mother said, sighing, "thank goodness it was a sweet one."

"An absolute angel," Mrs. Logsdon cooed, leaning over to touch one of Lola's bright curls. Maureen made the curls herself, brushing and coaxing each one around her fingertip while Savannah stood in the background of the mirror and watched. Savannah used to brush Lola's hair before her mother decided it was a job only she could handle. Lola loved Savannah. She loved her wide soft lap and the cut-onion smell of her underarms and her warm gentle hands. On days when Lola wasn't shopping or attending Mother-Daughter Teas with Maureen, she was following Savannah around the house like a little puppy. Lola's daddy was gone most of the time, "traveling" her mother always said with a strange look on her face, and it was just the three of them rattling around in the big old house with the wide sloping lawn and the swimming pool out back shaped like a teardrop.

"I just wouldn't know what to do if I had a big old nasty boy," Maureen said to Celia Shanks, the mother of four strapping sons. "Boy children are always so much trouble."

"Well, the only thing that can make a *man* is a boy," Celia cooed in response.

"As if making a man is a *good* thing," Maureen snapped.

Lola sucked her fingers and smiled so deeply her dimples showed. She had learned long ago that if she smiled and acted sweet and obedient she could do pretty much whatever she wanted to do. Other children might gnash their teeth and kick their feet and throw temper tantrums to get what they wanted, but Lola knew this behavior only tended to aggravate adults. She had learned this not long after she first learned to wear big girl panties, but Charlotte Hampton had never learned it at all.

Charlotte was stout and had red hair and freckles. She was an only child, like Lola. Their mothers had gone to school together at Agnes Scott in Atlanta, and they were always giggling and calling each other "Scotties." Mrs. Hampton was a small, frail woman with faded blue eyes and an expression of permanent bewilderment. She idolized her daughter but seemed incapable of handling her. When Charlotte didn't get what she wanted she would roll around on the floor flailing her chubby arms and legs and screaming in a shrill, piercing voice. If this didn't work she would hold her breath until her face turned purple and Mrs. Hampton would scream for the nanny or Mr. Hampton and plead with her recumbent child to "please take a breath for Mommy's sake, darling."

Lola was terrified of Charlotte, who would often pinch her or slap her when they were alone. Maureen and Mrs. Hampton were constantly arranging play dates for the two girls. Lola would cry and cling to Savannah and beg not to be sent to Charlotte's house, but Maureen would have none of that. She was determined that Lola and Charlotte would grow up to be good, good friends just like she and Mrs. Hampton. Once a Scottie, always a Scottie.

On a dreary February morning not long after the Mother-Daughter Tea, Mrs. Hampton sent a car to pick Lola up. Savannah bundled the sniffling child into her Rothschild coat and placed her into the backseat of the long black Lincoln Continental. Maureen stood at the front door with a serene expression on her face, her hands clasped in front of her.

As she leaned over to kiss Lola good-bye, Savannah pressed a small bag of candy into her tiny hand. "Offer that stout chile some of this candy and maybe she won't be so mean to you, baby," she said.

Charlotte was waiting for her upstairs in her bedroom when she arrived. Lola allowed Mrs. Hampton to take off her coat and then followed her up the winding staircase like a condemned felon on her way to the gallows.

Mrs. Hampton stopped at Charlotte's door and knocked timidly. "Precious? Your little friend is here." There was no answer so she swung the door open and stepped inside.

Charlotte was sitting cross-legged on the bed, roughly combing one of her dolls' hair with long violent strokes. The doll seemed to look at Lola with an expression of abject misery on her shiny plastic face. *Help me,* she seemed to plead silently. Lola, trembling, stepped behind Mrs. Hampton and wrapped her fingers in the woman's skirt.

"I want cake," Charlotte said. She sat with her neck thrust forward and her shoulders rounded up under her ears, glaring at her mother and Lola.

Mrs. Hampton laughed nervously. "Now, darling, you know what the doctor said about sweets." She unwrapped Lola's fingers from her skirt and gave her a gentle push into the room.

Charlotte stopped brushing. She squinted her eyes and pushed out her lower lip. "I want cake."

Mrs. Hampton's little hands fluttered around her face like a flock of panicked starlings. "Oh, look, sweetness, at the lovely dress Lola has on! Would you like me to take you shopping later? Would you like mommy to buy you a pretty new dress just like the one your little friend has on?"

"Cake," Charlotte said.

"Let me check with Beatrice and see what she has in the kitchen," Mrs. Hampton said brightly. She went out, swiftly closing the door behind her.

Lola would have followed her but Charlotte's eyes had shifted to her now and held her, spellbound, like a mouse hypnotized by a snake.

"Sit over there," she said pointing with the brush and indicating a small wooden chair in the corner, "until I finish with Esmerelda's hair."

"Okay," Lola said, sitting down.

She resumed her terrible grooming of the doll, tearing out great clumps of silky hair that clung to the bristles of the brush like the fur of slaughtered animals. The sound was not unlike that of a plant having its roots ripped from heavy soil. Lola could feel each stroke in the pit of her stomach. Charlotte stuck the tip of her pink tongue between her large teeth as she worked. After a minute she stopped and looked slyly at Lola. "You wanna see something?" she asked and before Lola could answer she had pushed Esmerelda facedown in her lap and pulled down her panties. Several small black craters speckled the doll's glistening buttocks.

"She's been very naughty," Charlotte said. "She had to be punished."

"Here," Lola said, pulling the bag of candy from her pocket and holding it out to Charlotte.

Without a word the girl slid down from the bed and crossed the room. She snatched the bag from Lola and ripped it open, pouring a handful of jelly beans into her sweaty palm and then tossing them one by one into her mouth. She chewed slowly, her eyes narrowed and her cheeks plumped. "Next time bring chocolate," she said.

"Okay," Lola said.

Charlotte poked through the bag with a chubby finger, pulling out the black jelly beans. She closed them up in a tight fist and then held her hand out to Lola, opening the fingers slowly to reveal a black mass like a lump of coal in the palm of her hand.

"Eat this," Charlotte said.

"No, thank you," Lola said politely. "I don't like licorice."

"Eat it."

"Okay," Lola said.

Later they played Bad Barbie, and when Charlotte had tired of this they went on to Mean Librarian, Bad Orphanage, Evil Schoolteacher, and Queen and Slave. In all the games Charlotte was the stern authority figure and Lola her willing minion. During Queen and Slave Charlotte tied Lola's hands together with a belt and led her around the sprawling room, stopping finally at a small half-door under the eaves. The door had a sliding bolt and led to a long dark crawl space filled with discarded toys and doll furniture. Lola knew it well because the last time she had come to play, Charlotte had locked her inside the claustrophobic space for nearly an hour.

"Okay, slave," Charlotte said, sliding the bolt back so that the door swung open on creaky hinges. "Time for you to go to the dungeon."

Lola took a step back. "No," she said.

Charlotte gave the belt a little jerk. "Bad slaves go to the dungeon," she said.

"No." Lola's heart leapt up into her throat. She could feel it beating there, flittering around in circles like a bird with a broken wing.

"Get in, slave."

"I don't want to."

"Now."

"What's that?" Lola said, pointing with her chin.

Charlotte leaned over with her pudgy hands resting on her dimpled knees, and stared into the darkness. "What?" she said. "I don't see anything."

Lola shoved her into the space and slammed the door, holding it closed with her shoulder until she had managed to free her hands and slide the bolt into place.

When Mrs. Hampton came up later carrying two slices of cake on a little silver tray, Lola was sitting on the bed softly crooning to Esmerelda. She had bathed her and dressed her and gently smoothed her torn hair off her face.

"Where's Charlotte?" Mrs. Hampton said vaguely, looking around the airy room.

The racket from the crawl space, which had long ago ceased, began again with a furious staccato of hands and feet, followed by a loud, piercing wail.

"Oh, my God," Mrs. Hampton cried, dropping the tray. "My poor baby!"

All the way home Lola sat with her face pressed against the car window. Rain fell in sheets, drumming against the roof of the car and filling the streets with a rushing torrent of gray water. They passed through Hueytown, past rows and rows of little cookie-cutter houses with the lights just coming on and families sitting down to dinner. They passed a house where an old woman in an apron stood looking out at the rain and another where a large family, illuminated behind a plate-glass window like actors on a movie screen, gathered around a long table. The father sat at one end, the mother at the other, and the children were lined up in between. They seemed happy and complete behind their illuminated window, and Lola wondered what it would be like to grow up in a little house no larger than a stable with a father at one end of the table and a mother at the other. If she had been older, she would have told the driver to stop. But she was still a child, vacuous and ignorant, so she said nothing, watching the family until they were nothing more than a twinkling in the darkness behind a curtain of steadily falling rain.

Her mother was standing on the portico when the car pulled up in the circular drive. The headlights illuminated her grim face and the dazzling whiteness of the large columns she stood between. Savannah hurried down the steps beneath an umbrella and opened the door for her, saying nothing but taking Lola's hand and giving her a little squeeze of encouragement. They went up the wide steps together and followed Maureen into the house.

Maureen switched on a table lamp. A circle of light sprang up around her, glistening on the dark wood floors. She thought of her friends in the UDC and the Junior League snickering behind their hands when they heard what Lola had done to Charlotte Hampton. She thought of Amanda Logsdon and Celia Shanks giggling and rolling their eyes. She leaned over and struck Lola twice on the back of her thighs with an open hand. The child made no sound but Savannah moaned deep in her throat as if Maureen had struck her instead.

"Go to your room," Maureen said. "There'll be no supper for you. You've misbehaved in a home where you were a guest, and I'm very, very disappointed in you."

Later, fearing she had been too hard on the child, Maureen climbed the stairs with a peanut butter sandwich and a glass of milk on a tray. Savannah had bathed Lola and dressed her in a clean nightgown, and the two were snuggled on Lola's bed, reading *Winnie-the-Pooh*. The rain had stopped but an occasional rumble of thunder rattled the windows. Maureen set the tray down on a bedside table. "I'll finish the story," she said to Savannah.

The child sat stiffly beside her while she read, slowly chewing her sandwich. When Maureen had finished, she stroked Lola's cheek softly and said, "Do you understand why Mommy was so angry earlier?" When she didn't answer, Maureen laid her down on the bed and pulled the covers to her chin. "I'll expect you to call Mrs. Hampton and Charlotte in the morning and apologize for your behavior," she said. "Do you understand? Is there something you have to say?"

Her mother's face was soft in the lamplight. Her voice was gentle. Lola thought of the family in the little house shut up behind their plate-glass window and she began to talk, slowly at first, hesitantly, but then with more conviction. She told her mother of the things Charlotte had done to her, of the slaps, bites, bruises she had suffered at Charlotte's hands, of the Indian burns the girl had given her whenever her mother was out of the room.

When she was finished Maureen stared at her for several minutes. Then she rose, vigorously smoothing the covers and fluffing the pillow behind her daughter's head. "Don't be ridiculous," she said, leaning to turn off the lamp. "Louise Hampton is one of my oldest and dearest friends. She and I were Scotties together. You'll call Charlotte tomorrow and apologize and then we'll hear no more of this ridiculous nonsense."

She turned, and without another word she went out, closing the door firmly behind her.

Chapter 6

~~~~~~~~

By two-thirty the women had succumbed to the heat and gone in for a swim. A swollen orange sun hung from a colorless sky. Cicadas sang in the trees. The heat was unusually oppressive for the middle of May. They swam slowly through the tepid water, making their way through the splashing, squirming toddlers, who bobbed across the surface of the water in their swim vests and water wings like so many brightly colored fishing buoys. Their mothers sat along the edges of the pool in twos and threes, dangling their lean brown legs in the water and keeping a wary eye on their undulating offspring.

It was less crowded in the deep end of the pool, although some of the more adventuresome children followed them there, kicking their legs and squirming their bodies like fat tadpoles.

"Jesus," Mel said. "This is ridiculous." They were huddled in a corner with their elbows resting behind them on the lip of the pool and their feet floating up in front of them.

"There's so many of them," Annie said.

"They're all adorable," Lola said.

"I think those floaty devices are the worst things that ever happened to kids," Mel said. "I mean, think about it. When we were kids we *knew* not to go into the water until we could swim. We were afraid of it. We respected its dangers. Nowadays kids are strapped into those things before they're even weaned and dropped into the water. They can't swim. All they can do is bob around helplessly but they lose their fear of the water, and there's the danger." As if to prove her point, a naked baby staggered to the edge of the pool and, without slowing his pace, stepped off into the water. He sank like a stone. The frantic mother ran after him and jumped in, screaming, "Claiborne, Claiborne!" until the water closed over her head. The lifeguard stood up on his chair and blew his whistle sharply but he was unable to dive into the soup of floating toddlers for fear of injuring one. He scurried down the chair and ran to the edge of the pool but by then the mother had surfaced with the baby in her arms. The child seemed oblivious to his near-death encounter. He grinned and blew bubbles while water streamed down his face.

He reminded Annie of Agnes Grace, a girl she'd met while volunteering out at the Baptist Children's Home. Agnes Grace had a similar personality, all fire and vinegar.

"Thank goodness we took that baby swim class at the Club," Claiborne's distracted mother said to the crowd that was quickly gathering. "They taught him to hold his breath underwater." Claiborne squirmed in her arms and tried to get back into the pool.

"See what I mean?" Mel said.

Lola watched the baby fondly. His mother was carrying him away from the pool and he was not happy about that. He waved his arms, kicked his feet, and wailed like a banshee. "Don't y'all miss those days?" Lola said wistfully.

"Sometimes," Sara said.

"Only when I'm drinking," Annie said. She remembered her own boys as toddlers, remembered their squirming brown bodies, the sweet scent of their sun-bleached hair. Other mothers had warned her, *Appreciate these days while you have them. They'll be gone too soon.* And Annie had thought they were crazy—how could anyone find time to appreciate the days when you were always scrambling frantically to keep up with your schedule of feedings, baths, playtime, naps, and more feedings?

"I'd have had a dozen kids if I'd been able to," Lola said, smiling wanly at the retreating Claiborne. She'd suffered a series of tragic miscarriages after Henry's birth and after a while she and Briggs had simply stopped trying. Sara put her arm around Lola and pulled her close.

A few minutes later they climbed out of the pool and went to lie down. The heat spread over the landscape like a shimmering cloud. Palm trees stirred faintly with the breeze. After a while, Mel closed her eyes and dozed off. When she awoke a short time later, Annie had moved to the shade of a nearby umbrella, and Lola was lying on her stomach on the concrete deck, idly flipping through a magazine. Sara had donned a straw hat and was sitting beside her, reading. She looked up when she saw Mel stirring.

"You know you snore," she said.

"I most certainly do not," Mel said.

"Not loud," Lola said. "Not like Briggs."

"Y'all are crazy. I don't snore." She peered over the edge of her glasses at Sara, trying to figure out some way to change the subject. "What's the book?"

"The Known World."

"Still reading the good stuff, I see."

Annie held up a brightly colored paperback so they could see the cover. "I'm reading *Nice Girls Don't Wear Stilettos.* It's about a pair of crime-fighting supermodels who take on an evil fashion designer who's slowly poisoning America's top models so he can replace them with robots and take over the New York fashion world."

Mel stared at her with an expression of disgust and disbelief. "Are you fucking kidding me?" she said. She had written ten moderately successful novels and had somehow thus far (miraculously) managed to stave off the need for a day job, so she figured she had the right to be critical.

"Hey, it's a bestseller. The movie rights have been optioned by Paramount."

"Let me see that."

Annie passed the novel to Mel and she flipped it over, hoping the author's photo would reveal a cleft palate or slightly crossed eyes, but no, the writer was young and beautiful. Very young. "I can tell you right now, no one this attractive ever wrote a novel," Mel said glumly.

"Oh come on, you're attractive," Sara said, reaching for the book. She stared down at the photo. "Damn," she said.

"That's probably not even her," Mel said. "The book was probably written by some desperate ghostwriter who used a supermodel to pose for the author's photo."

"Actually," Annie said, "she *was* a model. The author, I mean. She made millions on the catwalk in Paris and New York and then retired. Writing is just her hobby."

"You mean she writes for fun?" Lola said.

"Well, I don't think she needs the money."

Mel snorted. "She's probably self-published then."

"Random House," Annie said.

"She probably took a lowball advance just to see her name in print."

"Two million," Annie said. "A three-book deal."

Mel gave her a hard look. "Another word out of you and I toss the book in the pool."

"What?" Annie said, quickly shoving the novel into her bag. "I thought you'd be happy. I thought all you writers supported one another."

"Oh, fuck," Mel said. She stared bleakly at a young mother struggling to insert her toddler into a pair of overinflated water wings.

Lola sat up cross-legged on her towel and pulled a thick book out of her beach bag. It showed a large hatchet on the cover, dripping into a pool of congealed blood.

"Oh, my god, Lola," Sara said, "what are you reading?"

"It's a true-crime story. It's about this guy who took an axe and murdered his entire family in upstate New York and then faked his own death so he could spend the next twenty years on the lam."

"On the *lam*?"

"Lola, since when do you read gory crime stories?"

Lola opened the book on her lap and smoothed the pages with one hand. "It's all I ever read."

Sara and Mel exchanged a long look. Sara said, "I don't know, Lola, I guess I never imagined you enjoying a book about cold-blooded killers."

"A belly-button ring and now a murder-and-mayhem fan. What else do we not know about you, Lola?"

Lola giggled suddenly. She clamped her hand over her mouth and made a sound like she was choking. Her face turned bright red all around the edges of her sunglasses.

"Mitchell likes those espionage thrillers," Annie said. "He likes fast cars, big guns, and things that blow up." She frowned slightly, and thumped Lola on the back. "Lola, are you okay?"

"Sorry," Lola said. "I think I swallowed a bug."

• • •

By three-thirty they'd had all the sun they could take. But by then the espresso martinis had kicked in, and they found themselves with an abundance of sudden energy. They decided to stroll over to the croquet field and play a round of croquet.

The croquet field was a wide manicured lawn that stretched from the front of the Beach Club down to the seaside road. Scattered here and there along the edges of the lawn were brightly colored Adirondack chairs, some sporting striped umbrellas.

"This looks like something from an F. Scott Fitzgerald novel," Mel announced, setting her beach bag down on one of the chairs. A family of four was just finishing up a game. The mother wore a long white linen dress and a straw hat and the father a white knit shirt and white slacks. The children were dressed identically to their parents. An elderly couple sat in chairs along the sidelines, calling out encouragement to the players.

The women walked up to the equipment stand to get their mallets and balls and then took a few practice shots on the green. Mel was trying to hit Sara's ball out into the marsh and Sara was trying to trip Mel with her mallet when Annie said, "Hey, is that guy talking to us?" She stood with her hands shielding her eyes, gazing toward the Beach Club.

A stern-faced young man dressed in white was quickly crossing the lawn toward them. "Excuse me!" he shouted, waving his hand. "Excuse me!"

Sara looked around. "I think he's talking to us," she said.

"Lola, do we need a court time to play? Do we have to sign up for this?"

Lola stood there with her legs crossed at the ankle, leaning against her mallet. She shrugged. "I don't know," she said. "I've never played before."

"Excuse me, ladies," the young man said, reaching them. He was tall and angular with a thin blade of a nose that curved over his lips like a beak. His nametag read *A. Lincoln, Assistant Manager.* "You must wear dress whites on the croquet grounds. It's a club rule." He was out of breath and spoke in a nasal whine.

"Dress whites?" Mel said, lifting her cover to reveal her white bikini. "Does this count?"

"No," he said, turning an ugly mottled red color. The young family dressed in white had stopped playing and stood around looking appalled. "Club guests must dress appropriately to play," he continued.

"Mrs. Furman here is not a guest," Mel said. "She's a member."

The young man lifted his chin. His beaked nose quivered slightly. "Mrs. Furman is only an *auxiliary* member," he said. "*Mr.* Furman is the member." The sun slanted across his freshly starched shirt. Behind his head a long line of frayed clouds drifted across the wide blue sky.

There was something of Leland about him, something in his tone and demeanor that instantly made the hair rise along the back of Mel's neck. She rolled her shoulders like a boxer entering the ring and asked, "Are you telling me women are denied membership in the Beach Club?"

He stared at a point just to the right of Mel's left ear. His top lip twitched. "Yes," he said.

"Now you're really pissing me off."

"Mel," Sara said in a low voice, laying her hand on Mel's arm. "We don't want to do anything that'll get Lola in trouble."

Mel looked at Lola, who was holding her mallet with two fingers and swinging it back and forth like a pendulum, her eyes swiveling from side to side. She was smiling as if her mind was far, far away. She seemed unconcerned by the conversation.

"Right," Mel said. She jabbed her thumb at Sara. "This is my lawyer."

"Don't drag me into this."

"Rules are rules," the young manager said.

"Ever hear of the Equal Rights Amendment?"

"This is a private club."

"I don't think that's been ratified yet," Annie said, frowning doubtfully.

"Nor will it be," Mel snapped. "As long as women make up fifty percent of the population but only fifteen percent of Congress."

"Fifteen percent?" Annie said. "That high?"

Mel stared off across the wide flat lawn to the sea. The young family had stopped playing croquet and was sitting now with the grandparents along the sidelines, like spectators at a sporting event. "Okay girls, you heard the Hitler Youth," Mel said. "Collect your mallets. And your balls." She looked at him when she said this. "Y'all wait for me at the golf cart. I'll be right back."

She swung around without another word, and walked across the lawn into the Club.

Mel couldn't bear to be told that she couldn't do something. Especially by a male. It was probably why her love affair with J.T. Radford hadn't worked out. It was most likely the reason she'd been divorced twice and couldn't seem to keep a relationship longer than a few months. She knew it had to do with her childhood, with being Leland Barclay's only daughter. Survival of the fittest was the rule in the Barclay household, as poor Junior, God rest his soul, learned too late. Leland could sniff out weakness the way a sow roots out truffles, and she'd had to grow up strong and stubborn, which in many ways was a good thing; she'd learned to appreciate these traits later when she got sick, when she'd had to make the long, dark journey through the pessimistic health-care system, when she'd had to stand up to doctors and say, *No, I won't do that treatment.* Strength and stubbornness had proved invaluable then.

But a strong will and a stubborn nature were not the best prescriptions for a happy love life, at least not in a woman. Mel sometimes wished she could be more like Sara when it came to love. Soft and yielding. Men dated women like Mel but they married women like Sara, women they could build their whole world around without the worry of emotional instability or betrayal. Maybe if she'd had a better childhood, Mel could have been more like Sara. Maybe if she'd had a mother who wasn't afraid to leave her room or a father who didn't bully his children into submission, she might have been a different person.

Mel wasn't bitter but she often wondered how she might have turned out if she'd had parents like Sara's, George and Lynnette. George was tall and skinny, and wore dark-rimmed glasses and short-sleeved shirts with three pens neatly lined up in the breast pocket. He called his sons *Sport* and he called Sara *Princess,* just like in *Father Knows Best.* Lynette was tall and thin and beautiful, and she looked like Grace Kelly in *Rear Window.* Mel fell madly in love with Sara's mother the first time she ever laid eyes on her. Lynette kept her little house as neat as a pin, she made apple pies from scratch, and she was always asking her children how their days had been just like June Cleaver, Margaret Anderson, and Carol Brady all rolled into one. The first time Lynette's cool blue eyes fell on Mel, it was as if Mel's brain had shriveled inside her skull. This was in first grade and she'd walked home from school with Sara. Mel just stood there looking up into that lovely face with her mouth hanging open while her head, empty now of all gray matter, collapsed like a pierced balloon.

"What's your name?" Lynnette asked, smiling sweetly.

"M-M-Mel." She was horrified to hear her own voice. She'd never stuttered before.

"Well, Mel, we're going to carve a pumpkin. Can you help Sara spread that newspaper out on the kitchen table?"

"Yes, M-M-Mel, help me spread the paper on the table," Sara said, grinning.

Mel had never carved a pumpkin before. She'd never made a pumpkin pie or roasted pumpkin seeds in the oven. The next morning when Leland sent one of the boys from the car lot to pick her up, she didn't want to go home. She wanted to stay forever in that little doll house with the family that was so perfect it was like watching something on a television show.

Sara always said she liked to go to Mel's house because there were no rules there. But Mel liked the rules and routines of Sara's home. She liked holding hands at the table while George Sprague said grace. She liked the way Lynette would tuck them into bed at precisely nine o'clock, no later, no matter what was on TV, stroking their hair off their faces with her cool fingers that smelled of vanilla and oranges.

Years later, when she was in high school and she realized that Lynnette Sprague didn't like her anymore, it had been hard on Mel. She knew it had something to do with the fact that Sara spent too much time at the Barclay house and that Mel drove a brand-new Ford Mustang and didn't have a curfew. She knew it probably had something to do with the fact that Mel was Leland Barclay's daughter and had a reputation for being a party girl, which was unfair; she didn't do any more partying than anyone else in Howard's Mill. Whatever the reason, Mel could feel Lynette's dislike now like a cold hand laid on the back of her neck.

Everyone thought being a Barclay was such a grand thing but no one seemed to realize that money couldn't make up for everything. It couldn't make up for love that was doled out conditionally or for a father who thought life was nothing more than his own personal game of King of the Castle.

Inside the tall doors of the Beach Club, it was as hushed and cool as a mausoleum. A wide, high-ceilinged lobby overlooked the golf course. Large overstuffed sofas and chairs were scattered around the room, and a massive reception desk stretched along one wall. Mel went up to the desk and found what she was looking for, a business card holder filled with cards for *A. Lincoln, Assistant Manager.* She took about twenty of the cards and went along the wide hallway to the Surfside Restaurant. The massive doors were flung open but the restaurant was empty except for a few uniformed employees who scurried around carrying linens and tableware. A sullen-looking young woman in a white blouse and a long black skirt stood at the hostess stand scanning the reservation list.

"Excuse me," she said, as Mel walked past. "We're not open yet. And you can't come in here dressed in beach attire."

"Boy, this place isn't very big, is it?" Mel said, glancing around the room.

The woman looked her over carefully. "May I help you?" she said in a tone indicating that she would rather have a root canal.

"I'd like to make a reservation for seven o'clock."

The woman didn't even bother to check the list. "I'm sorry," she said. "We're booked. Tonight is Casino Night. Reservations fill up early."

"Oh, that's too bad." Mel leaned over the desk and peered at the list. It was indeed filled with reservations. *Good.* She gave the woman her most brilliant smile. "Who's the manager on duty tonight?" she asked sweetly.

The woman sighed. She put her head down and checked the list. "That would be Mr. Lincoln," she said.

Mel nodded and put two fingers to her forehead in a kind of casual salute. "Okay then," she said. "Have a nice evening."

She went out into the lobby, sat down at one of the tables, and wrote on the back of all the business cards, *Free Dinner for Two! Kids Eat Free! 7:00 Seating at the Surfside compliments of A. Lincoln.* Then she went down to the pool and passed the cards out to young mothers she picked out of the crowd. "Tonight only," she said. "Be there by seven and bring the kids. Ask for Mr. Lincoln if you have any trouble getting seated. He'll be happy to help you out."

Sara, Annie, and Lola turned in their croquet equipment and walked back to the parking lot to wait for Mel. The golf cart was parked in the shade of a laurel oak. To their left, far off in the hazy distance, the sea shimmered in the sunlight. "What do you think she's doing in there?" Annie asked nervously, looking up at the imposing facade of the Whale Head Beach Club.

"I don't know," Sara said. "But it's probably not good."

"I'm not paying for anything," Annie said. "I can tell you that right now. Any damage goes on Mel's tab."

Lola stood up beside the golf cart and stretched. She put her hand over her mouth and yawned. "I'll go check on her," she said.

"No, Lola, don't go," Sara said.

"You'll be an accessory," Annie called after her.

Lola waved as she went up the steps into the club. Sara and Annie sat for a while in silence, both feeling drowsy with the heat and the rhythmic chanting of the cicadas. After a while Sara slumped in the seat and closed her eyes. Annie stared out at the distant sea, remembering another beach trip she and Mitchell had taken when the boys were small.

They had driven down to Amelia Island, Florida, and were staying at a condo that overlooked the golf course and the faraway sea. Mitchell had taken the boys up to the village store while Annie lay down in the upstairs bedroom to read. She had opened the sliding doors to the balcony to catch the ocean breezes. The room was cool and quiet but for the whir of the overhead fan. Annie settled down in the big bed and began to read. The novel was the story of a nineteenth-century woman who leaves her husband for another man, a circus performer who promises to show her the wonders of the world and then abandons her, alone and penniless, in New Orleans. She had read a third of the way through the novel when she realized that she would not be able to finish it. The treacherous lover reminded her too much of Paul Ballard. She closed the book and set it down on the bedside table.

She had not thought of him in some time but now, under the spell of the novel, she did, lying back in the big cool bed with one arm over her eyes. It was amazing that after all these years, he still had a hold on her. She was thirty-five years old, too practical to be caught up in the tragic remembrance of a college love affair. And yet, once she had begun thinking of him, she couldn't stop. She had not found him remarkable at first. He was not handsome, at least not in the conventional sense. He was small and wiry with a receding hairline that left too much of his wide forehead exposed. Yet he was witty and clever, and had the air about him of a man who was accustomed to having his way with women, an air that had proved irresistible to her.

Through the opened balcony doors she could hear her husband and sons returning from the store on their bicycles. The boys were giggling and calling to their father, and he was yelling in a clownish voice, "Wait for me, wait for me."

She moved her arm and opened her eyes. Above her the ceiling fan spun endlessly, its golden chain swinging in a wide arc. The front door banged open and then closed again. The boys were coming up the stairs. She could hear them calling to her. Mitchell followed behind them roaring like a lion.

"Mommy, Mommy, he's coming!"

"Daddy's a monster!"

No, he wasn't. That was the problem. It would have been easier if he had been. It would have lessened her guilt somewhat.

When Mel got back to the parking lot, Sara and Annie were dozing on the golf cart but Lola was nowhere in sight.

"Where's Lola?"

Sara sat upright, blinking in the light. She wiped a thin trail of saliva from her lower lip. "We thought she was with you. She kind of wandered into the club after you did."

"Shit." Mel tossed the keys to Sara and sat down in the back. Annie woke up, her cheeks pink from the heat. "Pull up to the front door of the club and I'll go in," Mel said. "Keep the motor running."

"Now you're making me nervous," Sara said.

Mel found Lola sitting at the real estate table watching, entranced, as an eager young associate, not realizing that she already owned one of the largest properties on the island, made the sales pitch of his life. Mel pulled Lola away. She smiled at the salesman and said "Sorry," and allowed Mel to hurry her down the wide corridors. "Where are we going?" Lola said breathlessly. "Did I do something wrong?"

They hurried through the front doors and down the steps, flinging themselves on to the back of the golf cart.

"Step on it," Mel commanded, and they pulled away from the curb, tires squealing, and headed for the open road.

A long ribbon of asphalt road stretched before them, and to their right, beyond the wide expanse of beach, the sea glistened. They passed a cart of merry teenagers who shrieked and waved. Lola laughed and waved back. "So what happened back there?" Sara said over her shoulder to Mel. "You've got that look on your face that you used to get whenever you were getting ready to go up against some male authority figure. Whenever you were getting ready to disobey your father."

Mel told them what she'd done with A. Lincoln's business cards. "Let's see how he likes telling a mob of hungry women and their hyperactive offspring that it's all been a big mistake," she said, grinning.

"You know, you really are devious," Sara said.

"Twenty years of writing detective novels have taught me to think like a criminal."

"Well, you do it very well."

"Thank you."

The endless blue sea stretched beside them. Seagulls swooped and dived above the beach that was slowly disappearing beneath high tide. Far off in the distance storm clouds rode the horizon.

"So where are we going to eat tonight?"

Lola was staring out at the sea but after a minute she realized they were waiting for her to speak and she said, "I told April to take the night off. She and Mike are taking the boat over to Wilmington."

"I think I may have sand in my swimsuit," Annie said.

"I hear the Beach Club has pretty good food."

"I don't know about y'all but I refuse to eat in a place that refuses membership to women. If they won't take me, they can't have my money either," Mel said. "Besides, it's Casino Night. They're booked. Overbooked," she added, grinning.

"I'm chafing pretty bad," Annie said.

"That's really not something we want to hear about," Mel said.

Sara glanced at Mel over her shoulder. "Of course you realize we're now banned from The Whale Head Island Beach Club. If we show up again, one of the surly mothers is sure to recognize you as the woman passing out bogus meal tickets."

Mel shrugged. "So what? I didn't like that place anyway. Too stuffy. Why do we need a fucking kiddie pool when we've got the whole Atlantic Ocean—*capisce?*"

"Sure," Sara said. "I *capisce.*"

"There's the Oyster Bar down on the docks," Lola said hesitantly, still trying to figure out where they could eat dinner.

"That sounds good."

The breeze blowing off the ocean was fierce. Far off in the distance the shrimp boats passed, their nets raised like wings.

"Did you see his nametag? That stuck-up manager's? It read A. LINCOLN."

"Do you think the A's for Abraham?"

"Most likely Adolf," Mel said.

Chapter 7

When the women arrived at the beach house Captain Mike and April were loading up the extra golf cart, getting ready to head down to the marina. Dressed in a blue striped polo shirt and a pair of faded blue jeans and flip-flops, Captain Mike had cleaned up nicely. He was not classically handsome, but he was tall and well built, and his voice was pleasantly deep. Mel had no doubt that other women found him attractive.

"So what's in Wilmington?" she asked casually, stepping off the golf cart.

"The best beer on the east coast," he said. April stood beside him, methodically punching the buttons of her cell phone, looking young and bored and very pretty. "There's a microbrewery down on the waterfront that brews some of the best-tasting, coldest beer around."

"Oh, yeah? Well, thanks for asking us to go."

He grinned and looked at Lola. "Sorry," he said. "Where are my manners? It goes without saying that you ladies are invited to join us if you like."

"No," Lola said, waving her hand for them to go on. "We're having a girls' night."

They stood in the driveway and watched as the golf cart drove off, weaving in and out of sight along the winding beach road. "What's his story?" Mel asked Lola. "He's got ex-military written all over him."

Lola hesitated and then said vaguely, "I think he might have been in the marines. Or Special Forces. Something like that."

"I thought so. Divorced?"

"Widowed." Lola pushed her hair out of her face. She watched as the cart disappeared over a distant rise. "His wife died in a car crash. A few years ago."

They were all quiet for a few minutes, absorbing this.

"Poor guy," Annie said.

"He seems so young," Sara said.

"Are he and April serious or just fuck buddies?" Mel said.

Lola laughed and leaned to pick up her beach bag. "Why don't you ask him?" she said.

"Fuck buddies," Sara said. "Very nice."

"You know what I mean."

"You mean you'd like a chance with him yourself."

"He's not my type."

"Keep your hands off the captain. This is a girls' trip, remember?"

"Even if he *was* my type," Mel said, "I'm the only single girl on this trip so if I choose to hook up with the help, that's my prerogative."

"As long as it doesn't interfere with your bartending duties," Lola said.

"Don't worry," Mel said. "Nothing interferes with that."

It wasn't that Mel had bad luck with men. In fact, if anything her luck was too good. There were always too many men, too many distractions that interfered with whatever relationship she found herself in at that particular moment. She didn't understand women who complained that there weren't any eligible men in Manhattan for women over thirty-five. There were plenty of eligible men if you knew where to look. If you kept your expectations realistic and didn't fall into the same trap she saw so many women in their mid-thirties to mid-forties fall into—the cult of the knight in shining armor, the savior, the pressure of that old maternal clock ticking relentlessly down to destruction. She saw them everywhere, these world-weary women who wore their desperation on their faces: *I want a husband! I want a child! I want them now!* A man could spot them blocks away. They exuded hopelessness like a bad smell.

Mel didn't like children, and she had never looked for a knight in shining armor. She couldn't have cared less if men found her attractive and so, for the most part, they did. It was an old trick, not caring, and one she'd perfected not long after first arriving in New York, a fresh-faced Southern girl come to seek her fame and fortune in the Big Apple.

In those days in the early eighties, the city was dark and dangerous. John Lennon had been shot dead in front of the Dakota in 1980, and a pall still hung over the city. Mel took a nasty little walk-up apartment off West Fifteenth and found a job as a writer for a company that published corporate magazines geared to everything from the travel industry to the thriving real-estate market. She was shuttled back and forth between twenty or so different quarterlies and found herself writing an article on wahoo fishing in Aruba one week and the next an article on buying distressed property in the Poconos. It was tame, predictable work but it paid the bills.

New York was not what she had expected. It was not the exuberant, intellectual world of the Algonquin Round Table, of Robert Benchley, Dorothy Parker, and Robert Sherwood that she had so often imagined. People were brusque and impatient. They didn't like to wait the length of time it took her to speak in her slow Southern drawl and would roll their eyes or snap their gum irritably when she ordered takeout or asked for directions. She missed the South. She missed the slow, unhurried pace of life. And even though at times it had driven her crazy, she missed talking to strangers in line at the grocery store, the Laundromat, the gas station, the dry cleaners, or while waiting for a table at a restaurant. New Yorkers didn't talk to strangers unless it was necessary. They weren't cold but they were wary. Mel missed Lola, married now to Briggs and living in Birmingham, and she missed Annie, married to her childhood sweetheart and living in Nashville. Sara lived and worked in Charlotte, and Mel still talked to her from time to time.

Mel missed the South, she missed her girlhood friends, but mostly she missed J.T.

Their breakup, of course, had been inevitable. Still, there were times, lying in her bed and listening to the rain drum against the windows or waking from a dream with his name on her lips, when she regretted their parting. Then she would rise and go about her business and she would think all day of calling him. Even a year after she first moved to the city, when she had grown accustomed to thinking of herself as a New Yorker and was living with Phil, an editor she worked with, she still thought from time to time of calling J.T.

And then one day, she did.

It was a sunny day in early September when the air was cool and pungent, and the trees in Madison Square Park were glorious with the red and yellow foliage of fall. She had been out walking in the park with Phil and they had come in, their faces red from the cold and the exercise, and he had made them a couple of Irish coffees. He lived in the Flatiron District in a large comfortable apartment not far from the park. They snuggled for a while on the sofa, reading, and then Phil remembered some work back at the office and he rose reluctantly and left. Mel made herself another Irish coffee and sat in an overstuffed chair in front of the long windows, sipping her drink. Below her the city moved at its usual hurried pace. Gray metallic buildings glittered in the bright sunlight, silhouetted against an azure sky. Around the distant skyscrapers hazy clouds drifted like smoke. There was something in the chilly air, some quality of light slanting in through the windows and pooling along the hardwood floors, that reminded her of North Carolina. It was on days like this that she and J.T. might throw their gear into a couple of backpacks and hike the Appalachian Trail down into the Nantahala Forest around Tusquitee Bald. Or maybe the Rim Trail from Huskins Branch to Big Stamp, depending on how much time they had to spend.

She hadn't seen him or talked to him since graduation, but today on this cool September day, lost in her memories, Mel picked up the phone and called him.

The phone rang several times, long enough for her to nearly change her mind. There was a clattering noise as someone picked up the receiver. "Yeah?" he said. He sounded tired, his voice heavy with sleep.

"It's me."

There was a pause and a sound as if he'd put his hand over the receiver. She imagined that there was a woman there. She imagined him rising from the bed and taking the phone into another room where he could talk without fear of discovery. A moment later, he came back on. "Hey," he said.

"Sorry," she said. "Were you sleeping?"

"Yeah."

"This late?"

"Rough night," he said. His voice was cold, impassive. "How're things in the Big Apple?"

"Good. Really good." She was nervous suddenly, desperate to fill up the long silence between them. "I work for a company that produces corporate magazines. I write articles on wahoo fishing and how to take the stains out of concrete."

She had meant it as a joke, something to lighten the tension between them, but he didn't laugh. "What about your novel?" he said.

"I'm working on that, too. In the evenings." Far off in the distance someone was flying a kite in the park. She could see it dancing on the currents between the tall buildings, bobbing against the dark blue sky like a paper boat on a stream. "What about you?" she said.

"I'm teaching. At a boys' school for the moment but I've applied to Tulane and Duke."

"Wow. A boys' school. That must be exciting."

There was a moment of silence, a dull hum on the line that thickened and spread out between them like a plume of roiling smoke. Mel couldn't think of anything else to say.

"Was there a reason for this call?"

"No," she said. "No reason."

"I've got things to do."

"I thought we could be friends," she said, "but I can see now that that won't work."

"This is how you wanted it," he said coldly, and hung up.

She sat there for a long time in front of the windows as the sky darkened and the lights of the city gradually came on.

She was still living with Phil when she met her first husband, Richard. He was a video editor who lived in Phil's building, and their first few meetings on the elevator had been erotic but brief. A smile, a furtive meeting of their eyes, a fleeting touch as she pushed past him and got off on the fourth floor, and he traveled on up to the sixth. By the end of the second week they had spoken, and by the end of the third week he had pushed her roughly up against the wall of the elevator and kissed her before the doors to the fourth floor slid open. After that it was inevitable. The next time they met she didn't bother to push the button for the fourth floor but instead followed him up to the sixth. She allowed him to take her hand and lead her out of the elevator without a word.

There was a scene, of course, when Phil found out. She was still young and naive enough to believe that face-to-face breakups were best, and she had left work early to pack and wait for him to get home. Her explanation was brief and to the point, but as gentle as she could make it. He took it hard, and when there was a knock on the door and Richard appeared to help her move her things, a sudden threat of violence hung heavy in the air. Richard was tall and thin but there was a determined intensity in his dark eyes that kept Phil from throwing the first punch. Richard was not physically imposing but he had the look of a man who would fight hard for what he wanted. And he wanted Mel.

She lost her job at the corporate publishing company—Phil saw to that—but it didn't matter. Richard was Old Money. In addition, he made a good living as a video editor, and she stayed home to write. They married the following year and moved into an Upper East Side brownstone and Mel published her first novel that same year. Four more followed at yearly intervals, and by the time she reached twenty-nine her marriage had settled into the doldrums. Richard had begun to hint desperately of children. But by then she had already met Booker, a documentary filmmaker three years her junior. The sex was incredible. Mel turned thirty, divorced Richard, and moved in with Booker. They married three years later and their marriage survived its endless pattern of violent breakups and passionate reconciliations right up until the time she turned thirty-eight. That was the year she got sick and learned that the vow "in sickness and in health" did not hold true for some people. Booker left her soon after her diagnosis. Not that she blamed him. Her track record was not much better.

Romantics constantly go on and on about their one true soul mate but Mel had learned that there was no such thing. She had had four soul mates, and she was sure there must be others out there just waiting to be found.

That being true, and she knew in her heart that it was, it was odd that after all this time it was still J.T. she dreamed of at night.

Chapter 8

They had dinner down at the Oyster Bar and then drove back along Blackbeard's Wynd through the middle of the maritime forest. Moonlight fell between the arching branches of the live oaks. It lay in silvery pools along the road and washed across thickets of red bay and wax myrtle. Here and there they passed a large house, set back in the trees with its windows twinkling in the darkness. There were no streetlamps or neon lights, and other than the moonlight, the stars, and the patches of light that fell from the occasional house they passed, the road was dark.

"It's kind of spooky," Annie said. She was sitting beside Sara in the rear seat, facing backward. Mel was driving and Lola sat beside her, humming a little song under her breath.

"Can you see where you're going?" Sara asked Mel.

"Barely." The headlights of the golf cart did little to illuminate the road in front of them.

"Maybe you should slow down then."

"Maybe you should drive," Mel said. She relaxed against the seat with one hand on the steering wheel and the other resting in her lap. It was almost like flying, she decided, whirring along in the quiet darkness with the night breeze on her face. *This is how an owl must feel gliding above a moonlit field.*

"Is that a fox?" Annie asked, pointing, and they slowed down to look.

It *was* a fox, a slight, fragile-looking creature the size of a miniature collie staring back at them from the shadows of the forest. It disappeared without a sound in the underbrush. Mel clamped her foot down on the pedal and they sped on, past the old lighthouse standing in a moonlit clearing, past the small cedar-shingled post office and the interdenominational church with its white steeple and tall arched windows reflecting the moonlight.

"What do y'all say we go back to the house and play a game of Clinker?" Mel asked.

"I'm not up for any drinking games tonight," Sara said.

"Me either," Annie said.

Lola raised her hand like she was answering a question in class. "I'll play," she said.

"You're on vacation," Mel said to Sara. "Live a little."

"I'm not sure my liver can take a week with you."

"Oh come on, Sprague, never underestimate your capacity for binge drinking."

"I'm not Sprague anymore."

Mel stared at her in the rearview mirror. "No, you're not."

They broke from beneath the arching trees. To their left, the wide flat marsh glimmered in the moonlight. To their right, a series of distant dunes covered in sea oats stretched to the sea.

"Take a right at the next corner," Lola said. "It'll take us to the seaside road."

Lola's house was beautiful in the moonlight, perched across a wide dune with the light from the tall windows spilling across the sand. Captain Mike and April had not yet returned. Mel pulled the golf cart carefully into the two-cart garage beneath the crofter and plugged the electrical cord into the wall. They walked up the steps to the boardwalk. Ahead of them, beyond the sea oat–covered dunes, the white-capped Atlantic slumbered in the moonlight.

"Look at that view," Sara said. They stood for a moment, quietly watching, and then walked across the veranda into the house.

While the others went upstairs to put on their jammies, Mel made a carafe of espresso martinis. Regardless of what they had said earlier, Mel was confident in her bartending abilities. *If you make them, they will drink.* She poured herself a glass and then sat down at the bar to wait. A few minutes later Lola came out of the bedroom wearing a pair of blue silk pajamas. She crossed to the armoire, took out a couple of decks of playing cards, and set them down on the glass coffee table.

"Here you are, my darling," Mel said, handing her a martini.

Lola took the glass and sipped carefully. "Yummy," she said.

When Sara came down a short time later, she noticed the carafe of martinis on the bar and said flatly, "I told you I'm not drinking. My liver's still compromised from last night."

"We're on vacation," Mel said. "You have to drink."

"We're not kids anymore, Mel. You can't tell me what to do. You can't make me do things I don't want to do."

Mel responded with a derogatory snort. She knew she was bossy and self-absorbed. She'd been told she was enough times in her life: by her father, by her college roommates, by her successive lovers and husbands, by her friends in New York. But they all forgave her for it, because she was entertaining. Mel knew how to tell a good story.

"I'll have April make us up some wheatgrass shakes with milk thistle," Lola said, as if that settled everything, "and then you don't have to worry about your liver."

Annie, who'd just come in, said, "As delicious as that sounds, Lola, I think I'll pass."

Lola raised one delicate eyebrow. "We could take some zeolites," she said.

Mel said, "Zeolites?"

"Crystals," Lola said. "Volcanic crystals that take the toxins out of your body." She reached up into a cabinet and took out a large plastic bottle. "All the Hollywood stars take them," she said, holding the bottle out to Annie.

Annie sighed and looked at Sara. "Oh, all right," she said.

"That settles it then." Mel poured two more fresh glasses and handed them around. "Here," she said. "Drink your toxins."

After a couple of hands of Clinker they were feeling pretty festive. All thoughts of an early bedtime disappeared soon after Mel shuffled the deck and poured the second round of martinis. It was her turn again so she dealt the cards facedown to everyone. "One-two-three," she said and everyone flipped over a card. Mel turned over a four of hearts and Annie turned over a four of clubs. "Clinker!" Mel shouted and slapped her hand down on the table.

"Damn," Annie said.

"You lose," Mel said. "Drink up."

Annie sipped her martini. She wasn't drunk—she knew enough to pace herself—but she was pleasantly buzzed. She had once written a college paper on the Mazatec people in Mexico and their use of the hallucinogenic psilocybin mushrooms in religious rituals. And while alcoholic beverages didn't usually qualify as "hallucinogens," the way Mel mixed them did. She knew from experience that Mel's concoctions could make you forget yourself. They could make you do things you'd regret later.

"No fair," she said to Mel. "You've lived in New York too long. You talk faster than the rest of us."

"You mean I *think* faster than the rest of you."

Sara shuffled the cards. "You react better under the influence of alcohol than the rest of us," she said. "Gee, I wonder why."

"I can't help it if I can hold my liquor and you can't," Mel said, tossing a peanut at Sara. The next round went on for several minutes until Lola and Annie both turned over Jacks.

"Clinker!" Annie shouted, slapping the table.

Lola giggled. "I'm supposed to say something, aren't I?" she said, and downed her martini.

"That's right, Lola, you're supposed to say Clinker. Before Annie does. And slap the table."

"I just hope I don't go home from this trip an alcoholic," Annie said, grimacing and gathering up the cards.

"Oh, come on," Mel said. "How often do you drink at home?"

"Hardly at all. Well, I mean we might have a glass of wine if Mitchell and I go out to dinner. And he drinks beer, of course, but I don't like the taste of it."

"See? You're not going to become an alcoholic just by drinking to excess once every twenty years."

"We only drink on the weekends," Sara said. "And then it's only wine or beer. No hard liquor."

"Bully for you," Mel said.

"Isn't anyone going to ask me how often I drink?" Lola asked. Annie stopped dealing and everyone waited patiently for Lola to continue. "Every day," she said. "We have cocktails on the patio by the pool and Briggs tells me all about his day, how many deals he closed, how much money he made, what he shot on the golf course."

No one said anything. Annie went back to dealing.

Sara lost the next round. "This is getting pretty boring," she said, draining her martini.

Mel poured her another one. "We can play something else," she said.

"You're so competitive," Sara said. "Why don't we just relax and sip our drinks and watch TV?"

"Chug the Jug?" Mel said. "Polish Poker?"

"Didn't we use to play Polish Poker in college?" Annie asked.

"Shit-faced Driver?" Mel said. "Suck and Roll? You Blink You Drink?"

"It says a lot about you that you still remember those games," Sara said.

"Hey, Annie, remember that party senior year at Whitey Fogo's? The one where you and Mitchell had broken up and you came with Mule Gebhardt and got so drunk?"

"I never broke up with Mitchell."

"Really?"

"I never dated Mule Gebhardt."

"Sure you did."

"Okay. Once."

Lola giggled. "I remember Mule," she said. "He was sweet."

"I think you're remembering someone else," Sara said. "Mule was anything but sweet."

Lola frowned slightly and cocked her head like a small, bright-eyed bird. "Why did they call him that?" she asked, gathering up her cards. "Mule wasn't his real name, was it?"

"The other guys on the football team gave him that nickname," Mel said. "It's because his pecker hung down like a mule's. They also used to call him Donkey Dick."

Lola's eyes grew round. She put her hand to her mouth and giggled. "Oh, my," she said. "Wouldn't that be painful?"

Mel grinned. "You mean for his girlfriend?"

"Only if it was true," Sara said.

"Well, Annie, was it?"

"Shut up, Mel." She had lied when she said she didn't remember that night. She remembered it clearly, right up to the moment she had let Mule take off her T-shirt. She had wished then that Paul could see her, that he might be watching jealously from some dark corner of the room. But then she had seen the bulge in Mule's jeans and she had known she couldn't go through with it no matter how badly she wanted to get back at Paul Ballard.

"You were so drunk you got up on a table and sang the school fight song."

"I don't remember," Annie said.

"What were we drinking that night?" Sara asked.

"Tequila," Mel said.

"Oh, yeah. That rotgut stuff that Whitey brought back from Mexico with the grub in the bottom."

"And Annie got the worm," Mel said.

"I don't remember," Annie said.

"Those were some wild times."

"I guess," Annie said.

Mel gave her a wary look. She leaned over to pour her another drink. "What happened to you senior year? You kind of went crazy there for a while."

Annie held her drink up to the light like she was examining a precious stone. "Wild oats," she said. "I was sowing them. Right before I settled down to being a good wife and mother, and a God-fearing Republican."

Chapter 9

~~~~~~~~~

Three days after they met him at the bonfire, J.T. called and asked Mel out. Sara had been expecting this—she had steeled herself to accept it—but when the call came she found herself unable to stay in the room with Mel. She took her backpack and went downstairs to the quad. It was a cool evening in early October and the maples along the edges of the lawn shimmered like firelight. Students sat in groups around the quad, clustered beneath tall streetlamps, talking quietly. Here and there a cigarette glowed in the darkness.

Sara had come down with the idea of studying but now that she was here she didn't even bother to open her backpack. She walked to the shadows at the edge of the quad and sat down on an empty bench, listening as someone strummed a guitar and began to sing softly "Fire and Rain." James Taylor suited her mood. She put her head back and stared at the stars, listening.

She had seen him twice on campus but he hadn't seen her. She'd made sure of that, ducking behind a laurel bush, lurking in the doorway of the science building until he passed. Both times she had felt cowardly, ashamed, but she couldn't face him. Not yet anyway. Not while there was a chance that she might stammer or sweat profusely or knock something over. She needed time to work on her routine of cool detachment. She practiced in front of the mirror in their room when Mel was out. *Don't I know you?* she would say, waving one hand airily in front of her face and making her expression vague. *You look familiar to me. What was your name again?*

Across the quad the guitarist had moved on to "Bartender's Blues." Sara sighed and put her feet up on the bench, wrapping her arms around her knees. Mel would be excited about the date. She'd only mentioned him a couple of times since the bonfire but both times a delicate flush had appeared on her cheeks, and her eyes had shone with a subtle light. Sara guessed that he probably had that effect on a lot of women. She had hoped that despite what he had said that night on the beach he was already committed to someone else. That he had a girlfriend. That way she and Mel could pine together. They could form a sisterhood of unrequited love. She had hoped it was true, and yet deep in her heart she had known it was not. She had known he would call and it would be Mel he asked for.

And she, of course, would have to be happy for Mel. That's what good friends did. They supported one another no matter what the cost. No matter how painful.

She lay down on the bench with her hands behind her head, gazing up at the stars. The evening air was sharp and smelled of dead leaves and wet grass. Pegasus stared down at her and above him Perseus shone in all his splendor. When they were girls she and Mel had learned the names of all the constellations. They had checked out books from the library and took turns spending the night in each other's backyards, spraying themselves with insect repellent and huddling in lawn chairs while all around them fireflies glowed and shooting stars streaked across the sky.

Sara looked up at Pegasus and tried not to think about Mel laughing and talking on the phone with J.T. All around the quad, dormitories towered against the evening sky, their windows making little cheerful squares of light. She thought, *It could have been me he called.* She tried to imagine what that might feel like. She tried to imagine him coming toward her in the darkness, crossing the quad with long, purposeful strides. Heathcliff striding across the moors toward Cathy. Darcy searching in the moonlight for Elizabeth Bennet. *Fuck. I read too much,* she thought.

She stood up suddenly, hoisting her backpack across one shoulder, and began to walk swiftly around the perimeter of the quad. The guitarist had stopped playing. He was loading his guitar into a case as she walked past, her backpack thumping against her hip. A couple of Goth kids dressed like Nancy Spungen and Sid Vicious came toward her, holding hands in the darkness. She thought, *I don't care if I ever see him again.* She thought, *He means nothing to me.*

"Hey," someone said behind her. She kept walking, her legs trembling as if she had run a marathon. Her breath fogged the air around her face. The moon, shrouded in clouds, rose above the turrets of Amsterdam Hall.

"Hey!" The voice was louder, more insistent. She stopped walking and swung around.

"Oh," she said. "It's you."

He stepped forward into the light. "Sorry," he said, as if he found her expression amusing. "Sorry to disappoint you." He was dressed in a corduroy jacket and a pair of ragged jeans, his hair shaggy around his ears.

"I'm not disappointed," she said without thinking, and her face flared with heat. She put her head down and began to walk again.

He fell into step beside her. "Where are you going?"

"Nowhere. I'm just walking."

"I called your roommate."

"I know."

"We have a date Friday night."

"Cool."

"She said for me to come over. She said you were watching *One Flew Over the Cuckoo's Nest.*"

"Well, if she said that then I guess we are."

They walked for a while in silence until they came to the front of Nordan Hall. He brushed her arm lightly as they went up the steps, her backpack bumping against her hip. He opened the double doors and she stepped inside, blinking for a moment under the fluorescent lights. Her face was numb from the cold. She signed him in at the front desk and they walked down the narrow corridor and stood waiting together for the elevator. He was even better-looking than she remembered, tall and broadchested. She stood looking at her reflection in the elevator doors, trying to remember if she had put on any lipstick.

"I like your hair," he said. "It's curly."

She put her hand up self-consciously and touched it. "It does that when I don't straighten it," she said.

The elevator door opened and two girls got off. They looked at J.T. and giggled. He put his hand out to keep the door from closing and she slipped through in front of him and punched the button for her floor. The door lumbered close and they began to rise slowly.

The elevator smelled of alcohol and cigarettes. She tried to think of something clever to say. "You know there's a twelve o'clock curfew," she said. It was the best she could do.

He looked at her curiously. His eyes were a deep green flecked with streaks of gold. "I won't stay long," he said. "I promise."

Later, after he'd gone, Mel tossed a pillow across the room and struck her in the back. Sara was lying on her bed, facing the wall, pretending to sleep. "I know you're not asleep," Mel said.

Sara rolled over and flung the pillow back. Mel caught it, looking at her with a thoughtful expression. "You were kind of quiet tonight."

"Was I?"

"Don't you like him? Don't you want me to go out with him?" She sounded uneasy, as if she was afraid Sara would say no. Overhead, the light flickered. Faintly, down the hall, the Eagles were singing "I Can't Tell You Why."

"Don't be stupid. Go out with whomever you want to."

"It's not worth ruining a friendship over."

Sara pulled the covers to her chin and turned again to the wall. "Nothing's worth that," she said.

Chapter 10

~~~~~~~~~~

Their second morning at the beach, they rose late. Mel came into the great room to find Sara and Annie propped on one sofa staring, bleary-eyed, out at the ocean. Lola sat across from them, playfully rolling a tennis ball from one hand to the other. Mel took one look at Annie and Sara and laughed.

"Shut up," Sara said glumly.

They'd stayed up past midnight playing Clinker and had heard Captain Mike and April come in around one-thirty. Mel had slept with her window open and had awakened later to the sound of muffled giggling coming from the crofter.

Annie sipped her orange juice despondently. She had her robe buttoned to the neck and her slippers, resting on the coffee table, looked like they had been freshly laundered. "The next time you offer me an espresso martini, remind me to stick needles in my eyes," she said, fixing Mel with a baleful stare. There were creases in her left cheek where she'd slept facedown and comatose for the last three hours.

"Why?" Mel said.

"Because that's how it felt at three o'clock this morning when I couldn't sleep, lying there staring up at the ceiling."

Mel leaned her elbows on the breakfast bar and raised one eyebrow at Lola, who was counting softly under her breath as she rolled the ball back and forth. She looked none the worse for the espresso martini binge. In fact, she looked rested and relaxed, as if she hadn't a care in the world. "So you're telling me the drinks kept you up?" she asked Annie innocently.

"We don't have your stamina," Sara said morosely.

Mel stood up and went to the cabinet to take down a coffee mug. "Well, I'll tell you what kept me up last night—listening to what went on out there in that crofter. Damn, Lola, you've got to do something about your horny help."

Lola stopped tossing the tennis ball. "What do you mean?" she said, staring at her blankly.

"I mean, tell Captain Mike and April to keep it down out there."

"You're just jealous," Sara said.

"That's right. Jealous as hell." Mel didn't like to think how long it'd been since she'd had a steady boyfriend. She poured herself a cup of coffee. A tray of bagels sat on the breakfast bar surrounded by various cream cheese spreads and a platter of fresh fruit. She toasted an onion bagel, plopped it on a plate, spread a thick layer of cream cheese across the top, and carried the bagel and coffee with her to rejoin the others. "April must be sleeping in," she said. "No doubt she's resting up after last night." She made a wry face, plopping down on the sofa next to Lola.

Sara picked up the remote and turned on the TV. She scrolled aimlessly through the channels. "If there's anything in particular anyone wants to see, just let me know." No one said anything so she offered the remote to Annie. Annie shook her head.

"No thanks," she said. "I don't watch much television."

"If you don't watch television, what do you do with your spare time?" Mel asked, resting her coffee cup on her chest.

Annie yawned and stuck her feet up on the glass coffee table. "I clean my house. I shop. I do laundry and make meals for my family. I volunteer at the Baptist Children's Home. I'm a member of the Federation of Republican Women," she added, looking steadily at Mel. She'd been a Republican all her life, although she'd begun to question a party that supported a failed war and the National Rifle Association while cutting 300,000 slots for poor children's after-school tutoring. She'd begun to question a party that supported strident militarism in a foreign land while denying the scourge of poverty at home.

Mel groaned and chewed her bagel. Sara had stopped on a talk show that featured two women sitting on a raised stage. Lola stared at the television screen, her eyes narrowed slightly. She stopped tossing the ball. "That's strange," she said.

"What's strange?"

"Their auras look kind of subdued under the klieg lights."

Mel and Sara exchanged a long look across the coffee table. Annie flushed a dull red and tried to change the subject. "Why are they wearing pajamas?" she asked.

"They're hosting a pajama fashion show."

"Hey, those look a little like the ones you have on, Lola." They all turned to look at her. She was wearing a pair of cotton pajamas in a zebra-skin print with red piping.

"Do you ever wear the same pajamas twice?" Sara asked.

"Sure," Lola said. "Just not two days in a row. I like the feel of clean clothes against my skin."

"I like to wear mine until the stains set," Mel said, taking another bite of bagel.

"That may explain your love life," Sara said.

Lola and Annie laughed in a guarded way but Mel just sat there chewing her bagel. Her eyes, in the slanting light of the tall windows, were a pale golden brown. "There's nothing wrong with my love life," she said, chewing in a slow, deliberate manner.

She and Sara locked eyes. They were interrupted by the sudden insistent ringing of Sara's cell phone. She slid it out of her pocket and held it out in front of her, smiling when she saw that it was Tom. "Hey, you," she said, rising. She went quickly through the French doors and out on to the porch, closing the doors carefully behind her. The sun was so bright she blinked, shading her eyes with her hand.

"How's it going?" Tom said. The sound of his voice, deep and pleasant, made her heart swell suddenly in her chest. She could feel it, heavy and dangling like a ripe fruit. Sara never looked at other men. She never imagined what it would be like to sleep with them. From the moment she first laid eyes on Tom, she knew she would never love anyone else.

"It's going great," she said. "How're things at home?"

"Well, let's see. Nicky spent the weekend with Grace Franklin out at the lake. Her class is taking an end-of-the-year field trip to Six Flags today so I had to get her to school early."

"Did she use sunscreen before she left?"

"I made her lather up pretty good. And she took the bottle with her so hopefully she'll use it later. And let's see, what else? Oh, yeah, she likes Caleb Knox."

"Caleb? I thought she liked Chris Kirby."

"That was last week. This week it's Caleb. He's asked her to the movies Friday night."

"Well, just make sure you drive them and pick them up."

"It's already taken care of. The arrangements are made."

A couple pushing a baby stroller passed slowly along the beach. A waverunner cruised by, shooting out a plume of spray in its wake.

"How's Adam?" Their conversations always came back to Adam. All her life, she had thought, *If I am good, good things will happen to me,* but now she knew the error of that premise. It wasn't about being good at all. It was about fate, the unpredictability of genetic code.

"I took him to that appointment with Dr. Eberhardt." He stopped and cleared his throat and tried again. "I took him to that appointment with Dr. Eberhardt and I think he's going to be able to help. I really do, honey. I know it's too early to get our hopes up—we've been down this road before—but I've got a good feeling about this. About his protocol."

Despite her usual pessimism, Sara felt her spirits rise. *Hope is a wondrous thing,* she thought. "Did he talk much about medication?"

"Yes, but a lot of it is behavior modification. You'll see when you get home. He gave me reams of information to read."

He talked for a while about what he had learned and Sara found herself drifting, lulled by the sound of his voice, the warmth of the sun, and the rhythmic breaking of the surf along the beach. Her husband could make anything sound possible, and she was grateful to him for that. It was Tom who had sustained her through the guilt and bitterness that had followed Adam's diagnosis. He never wavered in his devotion to her or the children. When so many marriages would have splintered under the strain, theirs did not.

"I talk too much," he said finally, laughing. "How are things with you?"

"Good. We're having a good time."

"Everything okay with you and Mel?"

"Yes, fine. Why?"

"I miss you," he said. "It's hard to sleep when you're not here."

"I miss you, too." He was a good father. A good husband. She'd done the right thing marrying him. It was the one thing in her life that she could have no regrets over.

Seagulls floated above the beach, tiny specks in the deep blue sky. Out past the breakers and the sandbars, the sea was calm and placid. Mel sat on the sofa and watched Sara through the French doors, wishing there was someone to call her, someone she could get excited about, but there was no one, not even Jed Ford, the editor from *The New Yorker.* That had ended before it had even begun. She wished sometimes that she could be more like Sara, one of those people whose moral compass always pointed due north. Once set on the path, Sara did not deviate. It was disheartening to flounder through life while Sara seemed always to make the right choices at the right times.

"I haven't watched this much television since I was home sick with the flu," Annie said, stretching her face in a wide yawn.

"I can make us a wheatgrass shake," Lola said in her little-girl voice. "If you're feeling sick."

Annie grimaced and put one hand on her stomach. "No thanks, Lola. Maybe later."

They turned their attention to the television screen. A commercial advertising an antidepressant came on, showing a sad, limp-haired woman locked in a bedroom. Mel picked up a magazine and began to thumb through it aimlessly. After a while Sara opened the French doors and came back in. Her face was pink from the sun.

"Everything okay with hubby and the kids?" Mel said, glancing up from the magazine. "Everything still perfect in suburbia?"

Sara, on her way out of the room, said nothing.

Chapter 11

~~~~~~~~

Mel went out with J. T. Radford despite the fact that Sara liked him. (They both knew that was true.) If Sara had asked her not to, Mel would have honored her request. At least she would have initially honored it. Before she fell for him, as she did eventually. Before she became addicted to the sex.

The truth was, she and Sara had always been competitive—as close as sisters but like sisters, always striving against each other, always looking for the advantage. As children they had competed for track ribbons and spelling trophies. Sara had always been a better student than Mel, and during their junior year of high school, when Sara had confided to Mel that she wanted to forgo the University of Tennessee in favor of Bedford, a private college "much harder to get into unless you have a four-point grade point average," Mel had known instantly and irrevocably what school she wanted to attend. She had never even heard of Bedford until Sara mentioned it, but now she was determined that that was where she would go. "It's not that easy to get into," Sara said, as if she already regretted sharing her dream with Mel. "Even if your daddy is rich. You've got to have something besides money to get into Bedford."

Mel didn't believe there was anything money couldn't buy your way into, but to hedge her bets she ran that year for president of the senior class against a boy named Cyrus Clapp. Despite his unfortunate name, Cyrus was handsome and popular, and had served in the student council, the Beta Club, and the National Honor Society for most of his previous three years. He was considered a shoo-in. But Mel had written a speech so smart and funny that it was still being talked about years later, a speech that began with the quote: *I may not know much, but I know the difference between chicken shit and chicken salad.* She won in a landslide vote. The presidency and her father's begrudging donation of a new wing to the fine arts building were enough to overcome her grade point deficiency, and when the offer from Bedford finally came, it was with a great deal of self-satisfaction that she told Sara. Even their admission to college, it seemed, had become a competition of sorts.

So it was only natural, Mel realized later, that they should fall for the same boy. It was surprising that this had not happened before, although they had always had very different tastes in men. Mel liked hers a little rough around the edges and Sara preferred hers quiet and studious, boys she could easily control who were crazier about her than she was about them. Which made it all the more remarkable that Sara had even given J.T. Radford a second look.

Mel had noticed him that first night in the woods as they came down the embankment toward the bonfire, sitting in the back of a pickup truck with the firelight shining on his hair. She had noted the way he sat curiously watching her, his shoulders slumped and resting against the side of the truck and his legs stretched in front of him, crossed carelessly at the ankles. But it wasn't until he spoke, shouting at Jemison to leave them alone, and Sara started moving toward him like a sleepwalker, that Mel had looked at him with any real interest.

Later, as they climbed the ridge in the moonlight and Mel pretended to twist her ankle so he would have to carry her, she had seen the look on Sara's face. She had been intrigued. It was like a game. A game Mel knew she could win. And that first night, when he came over to watch a movie in their room and Sara was so quiet, Mel told herself it wouldn't last. She thought, *I'll go out with him once and that's all. Just to prove I can.* He was nice enough, good-looking and funny, but no guy was worth breaking up a friendship over.

After the movie in their room, Mel walked him out.

"I don't think your roommate likes me very much," he said as they stepped onto the elevator.

"What makes you say that?" Mel said. She liked him well enough but he had a quiet cockiness that she found instantly suspect. You could tell he was one of those guys women always find charming, and he knew it.

"Well, let's see," he said, leaning against the elevator wall. He grinned. A tiny scar curved below his right eyebrow like a piece of white thread. "She doesn't say two words to me all evening. And on the way up here she reminds me that there's a curfew."

"There *is* a curfew."

His grin faded slowly. "Yeah, I know that. But I hadn't even gotten off the elevator before she was reminding me that it was time to go." She didn't say anything and he looked at his feet silently as the elevator made its lumbering descent.

When they reached the ground floor, the door slid open. She stepped out and he followed her down the hallway to the front desk. The monitor behind the desk looked up at them suspiciously, then went back to reading. J.T. leaned over to sign himself out. All along the brightly lit corridor the fluorescent lights flickered and hummed. "Walk me out?" he said, and Mel shrugged and nodded at the monitor.

"The doors will lock behind you," she warned, without looking up.

"That's okay, I've got my card," Mel said.

She followed him out onto the porch. The quad was deserted. Frost shimmered on the moonlit grass. He took her hand and led her down the steps, and she followed him without a word. In the shadow of the portico he pulled her smoothly into his arms and kissed her.

Up until that kiss she could have stopped at any time. She could have sent him packing without so much as a backward glance and spent her whole life without ever thinking of him again. But the kiss changed all that.

When he let her go, she stood there swaying in the moonlight. There was a strange humming sound in her head, low-pitched and rhythmic. She put her hand up to her ear and said, "What's that noise?"

He looked around the moonlit quad. "What noise?"

"That noise. Like water running in a sink. Like a flood through a sluice gate, like . . ." She stopped. The sound she was hearing was her own pulse pounding in her temples.

He grinned. "Are you cold?" he said.

"No." She stood there like a narcoleptic on the verge of a seizure. In the sky beyond his shoulder, Perseus raised his shining bow. Or was it Orion who carried the bow? Mel couldn't remember. Her head felt dense and thick. "I don't know," she said. "I guess," she said.

He opened his jacket as if to envelop her but she shook her head and stepped back. "I promise I won't kiss you," he said, and dropped his arms.

Pink Floyd drifted from an open window. After a moment, she stirred and said, "I should probably go in."

He stood there looking at her with his hands pushed deep into the pockets of his jeans. "I'll see you Friday night then. Friday at eight. I'll call you tomorrow." He backed away and grinned and walked off whistling in the moonlight.

She watched him go. Far off in the darkness a car door slammed. The moon sailed over the turrets of Amsterdam Hall, shining fitfully behind a line of swiftly moving clouds. The sound in her head gradually subsided. It had started out as a game and now everything had changed.

She hoped Sara would understand.

Chapter 12

~~~~~~~~~~

They spent the whole morning lounging in the great room, too lazy and hungover to do anything else. When April came in around noon to check on their plans for dinner, they were still stretched out on the sofas in their pajamas. April looked tired and hungover herself, as if she hadn't slept well, and it was no wonder, Mel thought dismally, remembering the sounds she had heard coming from the crofter in the wee hours of the morning.

"I can go by the market and pick up some fresh shrimp," April said. She was wearing a tiny bikini and a pair of flip-flops with a towel draped around her narrow shoulders. "I can make shrimp scampi."

They all agreed that that sounded wonderful.

"I'll go to the market as soon as I get back from the beach." She gathered her things and walked out the door, and they watched her through the long glass windows as she crossed the boardwalk and disappeared behind the dunes.

"Isn't she lovely?" Lola said cheerfully. "Isn't she sweet?"

"Sweet," Mel said.

"She spends way too much time in the sun," Annie said, staring ominously at the sunlight sparkling along the water. "She'll have skin cancer before she's fifty."

Mel sighed, stood up, and walked over to the French doors, leaning against the glass and peering down at the beach. She watched April, curious whether she might be meeting Captain Mike on the beach. She appeared a few minutes later, a distant figure walking slowly. She was alone. Captain Mike apparently kept the hours of a vampire.

"So what does he do all day?" she asked, turning from the glass.

Lola frowned slightly and looked up. She was still wearing her glasses, and her eyes behind the thick lenses were wide and blue. "Who?" she asked.

"Captain Mike." Mel went back to the sofa and slumped down with her feet resting on the edge and her knees stuck up in the air.

Lola smoothed the front of her zebra-skin pajamas with her hands. "He fishes," she said. "Or works on the boat. But mostly he fishes."

" I thought maybe he slept all day."

"Oh, no." She plucked at the red piping along her sleeve like she was picking lint from a sweater. "He leaves the house every morning at six-thirty to go fishing."

Sara, who had sat for some time in a dazed state of suspended animation, picked up the TV remote and began to scroll aimlessly through the channels.

"Stop there," Annie said, pointing at the TV. A women's college basketball game was in full swing.

Sara yawned. "I played basketball in high school," she said in a sleepy voice.

Mel folded her long legs under her. "All I can say is thank God for Title IX. Twenty-five years ago, only one in twenty-seven high school girls played sports; now it's one in three."

Annie flashed Mel an ominous look. Mel was getting ready to go off on some tirade—you could see it in her face—getting ready to monopolize the conversation like she always did when she felt that she had a point to make. The only thing Annie knew about Title IX was what she'd heard years ago at a Women of God convention speech given by Phyllis Schlafly, entitled "Real Women Don't Cry Over Title IX," most of which she couldn't even remember.

"Well, you know," Annie said, waving her hand in a breezy manner, "if sixty percent of college graduates are women, then who are they going to marry?"

The truth of the matter was, Annie had lost faith in Phyllis Schlafly years ago, not long after she read an article by Schlafly contending that married woman cannot be raped by their husbands because, by the act of marriage, they consent to sexual intercourse forever. It was right about then that she began thinking of Schlafly as an idiot. Not that she was going to admit this to Mel, of course. It was too much fun watching her face bloat and her eyes bulge.

"What in the hell are you talking about?" Mel said.

The truth was, had they not been college roommates, she and Mel would never have been friends. Not that they had been friends in the beginning, of course. Mel was loud and flamboyant, and Annie was an only child used to having her own way. Their dislike of each other had been immediate and mutual. It was not until halfway through their freshman year, when they got drunk one night over a bottle of tequila, that they developed any kind of camaraderie. *A friendship founded in the devil's drink cannot stand*, Reverend Reeves always said, but like so much else that he espoused, Annie had found this, too, to be wrong.

"There won't be enough male college grads to go around," Annie said. She wished now that she hadn't begun this argument. She could see from Mel's face that it was going to be a violent one.

Mel tapped two fingers against her forehead like she was trying to ward off a migraine. "Okay, I'm trying to follow this. Are we talking about marriage? And what does that have to do with Title IX?"

"Title IX ensures that there'll be more female college grads in the future than male ones. It will affect marriage in this country by turning out more female grads than male ones."

"Who says female college grads have to marry male college grads? Who says they have to marry anyone? Marriage is an archaic ritual."

"That coming from someone who's been down the aisle twice," Sara said.

"See. I have experience. I know what I'm talking about."

"Would anyone like another cup of coffee?" Lola asked. "How about some lunch?"

"I like the Rose Bowl," Annie said. "Mitchell always watches it and so do I. I like the parades, and all the floats made with flower petals."

At this, even Lola stopped trying to push refreshments and gave Annie her full attention. Mel breathed slowly through her mouth. She narrowed her eyes and said, "What in the hell does all this have to do with Title IX?"

"Well, Title IX is forcing colleges to close down football teams because feminists don't want money going to male sports teams, and before long there won't be any teams left to play in the Rose Bowl."

"That's the most ridiculous thing I've ever heard. Where did you hear that?"

Annie hesitated before playing her trump card. "Phyllis Schlafly."

Mel's jaw sagged. One eye stuttered like a bad circuit. "Phyllis Schlafly?" she said, looking first at Sara and then at Lola. "Phyllis Schlafly?"

"Now, Mel," Lola said.

Despite her resolve not to, Annie smiled. She couldn't help it. Mel's expression was just too funny. Lola, relieved, began to giggle.

"You bitch," Mel said.

Annie rounded her shoulders up under her ears and showed her teeth in a wide grin.

"I think she had you going there," Sara said.

"Explain to me again why we're friends," Mel said.

"Because I'm a patient and forgiving person," Annie said.

The day was hot and humid, and the surf, frothing along the sandy beach, was the color of oatmeal. A haze hung over the landscape. Even the bees seemed lethargic, moving lazily among the potted geraniums on the deck. Inside the house, the women sprawled on the sofas watching the basketball game. When it went to a commercial break, Sara picked up the remote and began channel-surfing again. She stopped on a local channel that showed a couple getting married on the beach.

"I always wanted a beach wedding," Lola said.

"Too late for that," Mel said.

"What?" Lola stirred and looked at Mel. "Oh, right," she said.

"I have this friend in New York," Mel said. "And when her daughter got married, to a plastic surgeon by the way, the bridesmaids' gifts were a series of Restylane injections from the groom. Can you believe that?"

"I can believe it," Sara said flatly.

"This girl at our church was supposed to get married last March," Annie said. "She invited six hundred people. She had *fourteen* bridesmaids and fourteen groomsmen."

"My God, it must have cost a fortune," Sara said.

"That's outrageous," Mel said. "Who would plan a wedding that big?"

"It gets better," Annie said. "So the day of the big event dawns and everyone shows up. Everyone but the bride, that is."

"Oh no," Sara said. "She didn't leave him standing at the altar, did she?"

Annie grimaced and nodded her head. "In front of six hundred people."

"And twenty-eight bridesmaids and groomsmen," Mel said. "It's almost comical."

"Who could leave their groom at the altar after all that fuss?" Sara asked.

"Who could do something like that?" Annie said.

"Actually," Lola said quietly, "I don't find it hard to imagine at all."

Chapter 13

~~~~~~~~

Lola had tried to leave Briggs once, three years into her marriage, not long after Henry was born. Her despair, in those days, was like something heavy laid across her shoulders. She couldn't breathe with the weight of it. And so, on a rainy morning in early fall, she arose, packed her suitcase and the baby's diaper bag, and left.

Henry was colicky, and when Lola parked her car at the Kool Breeze Motel he woke up in his car seat and began to wail. She leaned over the seat and talked soothingly to him, stroking his brow and trying to get him to take his pacifier, but he arched his sturdy little back and kicked his sturdy little legs and screamed with rage. He reminded her of Briggs when he did that, red-faced and screaming, leaving her panicked and dazed, with the sensation of being struck repeatedly about the head and shoulders. After a minute she climbed out of the car, went around, and opened the back passenger door, struggling with the child seat restraints until she freed him.

The minute she picked him up, Henry stopped crying. He always did. Her mother said that she spoiled him, that a child needed discipline and routine and not pampering, but Lola ignored Maureen's advice. When Henry cried, she picked him up. Unlike most of the rest of their social set she rarely left him with nurses or nannies or babysitters, and she never left him with Maureen. At night, when she heard his first few whimpers on the baby monitor, she would rise with relief from the big bed and pad down the long dark hallway to the nursery. She would pick him up and nuzzle her face against his soft neck, losing herself in the smell of curdled milk and talcum powder. Sometimes he didn't wake at all, falling back into a heavy slumber against her shoulder. She would croon to him softly and then lie down beside him on the narrow nursery bed, watching in wonder as his small chest, illuminated by the soft glow of the nursery light, rose and fell rhythmically.

Briggs, still a relative newlywed, protested. "If I didn't know better, I'd say Lola had this baby just to get out of sleeping with me," he'd complain to a roomful of cocktail party guests, and everyone but Lola would shout with laughter.

The baby hiccupped and Lola patted his back softly. It had begun to rain, large heavy drops that splattered the top of the car and the pavement and then began to fall more steadily, like a curtain being slowly drawn. Lola pulled the baby's hood over his face, and turning, ran toward a door marked *Office*.

The small lobby was overheated and crowded with shabby furniture. It smelled of cat and unwashed linoleum. A large dirty window framed the parking lot, the rain-soaked street, and the neon lights that were just beginning to come on against the darkening sky. Lola stood for a moment staring out at the curtain of falling rain and wondering if she was doing the right thing. But if she went anywhere else Briggs would find her. He would know to look for her at the Renaissance or the Hilton or the boutique high-rise hotels of Five Points South. He would never think to look for her in a place like this.

A woman with long red fingernails came through a swinging door in the back. "Can I help you?" she said, eyeing Lola and the baby suspiciously. She glanced out the window at the parking lot, where Lola's expensive foreign car sat gleaming in the rain.

"Yes. I need a room."

"Thirty-six dollars a day," the woman said in the hoarse phlegmatic voice of a chain-smoker. Her black hair hugged her head like a helmet. She poked one finger up under the edge and scratched reflectively as she squinted at Henry. "Does that baby sleep the night?" she said.

"Yes," Lola lied. Henry blinked in the bright lights and peered curiously around the room from beneath the hood of his jacket. His eyes fixed on the surly desk clerk. He smiled suddenly, brilliantly, and two deep dimples appeared in his fat cheeks.

The clerk was not moved. "My other clients don't wanna hear no baby crying all day and night," she said, grimacing to show a line of crooked yellow teeth.

Lola didn't like to think about who her other "clients" might be. The Kool Breeze Motel had the cheap, seedy look of an establishment popular with working girls and hourly guests. "He's a good baby," she said, re-arranging Henry in her arms. "I'll need the room for several days. Can I pay you in cash?"

She parked as close to the front of the low squat building as she could and then, picking Henry up and slinging the diaper bag over her shoulder, she made an awkward dash for room number twelve. A narrow porch skirted the front of the building and Lola stopped beneath the overhang in front of the door, fumbling with the key while Henry sucked his pacifier and looked out over her shoulder at the sheeting rain. After a few tries Lola managed to get the door open.

The room was cold and musty and smelled of damp socks. A lumpy double bed covered in a yellow bedspread stood in the middle of the room between two side tables bolted to the wall. A lamp crowded one of the tables and on the other a large metallic box sat beneath a sign that read VIBRA-KING VIBRATING BED! LET US MASSAGE YOUR WORRIES AWAY! 25¢ FOR FIFTEEN MINUTES! Above the bed hung a faded print of an English countryside complete with a thatched-roof cottage and a flock of grazing sheep. Across from the bed was a small closet covered by a grimy curtain, and beyond that was a door leading into a bathroom not much larger than the closet.

Lola stood looking despondently around the room. Henry had grown heavy in her arms and she needed to set him down but she didn't want him to touch anything. Beyond the plate-glass window, framed on either side by a pair of threadbare drapes, the rain fell steadily. Lola took Henry's baby blanket out of the diaper bag and spread it across the bed. Then she lay him down on the blanket on his back and piled pillows around him. He couldn't roll over yet but he was getting close. She gave him one of his soft rattlers and he grasped the toy and shook it, making little spastic jerking movements with his arms and legs. Lola leaned and turned on the table lamp and then sat beside him on the bed looking out at the rain.

She wasn't even sure how she had found this sad place. The memory of it had come to her in a moment of quiet clarity in the midst of the panic she had felt when she decided once and for all to leave Briggs. An old memory, dreamlike and grainy around the edges, had shimmered into her consciousness and it wasn't until now, sitting in the lamplit room and looking out at the curtain of falling rain, that she remembered why. She had come here as a child. She had come here with Maureen looking for her father.

Lola pulled her sweater closer about her, determined not to dredge up the ghosts of her past. But there was something about her situation, her flight from a loveless marriage, the damp dimly lit room, the rain drumming against the roof and shimmering like a veil across the neon-lit street, that summoned those ghosts. She couldn't help herself. It was only natural, she supposed, when she had finally done to Briggs what her father had so often done to Maureen, that they should reappear. She was, after all, her father's daughter.

Big Jim Rutherford. Even now she smiled when she thought of him. You couldn't help but like him no matter what his faults. A large handsome man, a politician who charmed people into voting for him by making them laugh, he had lived an unfettered existence right up until the last six months of his life. Then a lingering death, shut up in the big empty house with only morphine and Maureen for company. Lola had been away at school. "Your mother was a saint," people said at the funeral. "She cared for your father right up until the very end." They shook their heads reverently at this image of sacrificial love. But Lola had a different image, one born of many years spent as silent witness to her parents' matrimonial Armageddon, an image of her father dying slowly, inexorably before the silent and unforgiving Maureen, shut away from the genial world he had loved, her prisoner at long last.

I want something better for my son, she thought, stirring herself. She reached and slid her Daytimer out of her purse. She dialed Sara's number and left a message for her on the answering machine, leaving the number of the motel and asking her not to call the house. "I don't want Briggs to know where I am," she said, and hung up. She had left a note on the kitchen table. By now he would have read it.

It was hard to say when she first fell out of love with Briggs Furman. Or whether she had ever really loved him to begin with. They had both attended boarding schools in the mountains of Tennessee, he at an all-boys' school called Cavendish and she at an all-girls' school called St. Anne's. The schools were separated by twenty miles of rolling tree-lined highway, but the boys of Cavendish were often bused to St. Anne's for dances and social mixers, and the girls were bused to Cavendish for sporting events and dances. A Cavendish–St. Anne's match was considered very stylish, and many a St. Anne's girl went off to Ivy League colleges in the east only to settle down after graduation with a Cavendish boy. So it was perhaps inevitable that Lola Rutherford, one of St. Anne's most popular cheerleaders, and Briggs Furman, Cavendish's starting quarterback, should meet and eventually date.

Lola liked him well enough at the beginning. He was polite and tall with a sturdy muscular body that would eventually run to fat but that in his youth looked like an image found on a Grecian urn. He was blond and square-jawed with piercing blue eyes. The girls at St. Anne's were crazy for him. When he came over for mixers they would follow him around in clumps, giggling and blushing and hanging on his every word.

Lola was sitting in the quad in her Mat Maid uniform the day she first spoke with him. The term *cheerleader* was considered gauche and vulgar, so at St. Anne's they were called Mat Maids. The uniforms and the activities were the same but the titles were different, as befitted a twenty-six-thousand-dollar-a-year boarding school. The Mat Maids were chosen for their popularity and their beauty of face and perfection of figure, and Lola had already served on the squad for two years on that bright fall day.

He was crossing the quad in front of a phalanx of giggling girls, walking with that peculiar swagger known only to rock stars and high school quarterbacks. Lola was sitting on the steps of Baylor Hall, her head buried in a copy of Wordsworth. They were ten feet from each other when Briggs stopped his admiring horde, and, throwing up one hand in greeting to Lola, said, "There's my girl."

Lola, still caught up in daffodils fluttering in the breeze, lifted her face, smiled dreamily, then went back to reading.

A small ripple went through the group of girls. Briggs squared his shoulders and tried again. "I thought Mat Maids only read in class," he said. "Never out of class."

A nervous twitter went through his fan club. Lola raised her face again and fixed him with a blank stare. Her eyes were wide and innocent as a kitten's. "Do I know you?" she asked sweetly.

It was silly, she realized later. Of course she knew him. He had dated half the Mat Maids and most of the tennis team. But she had been caught up in Wordsworth, her mind floating free as a wandering cloud, and she had not been able to focus on the boy standing in front of her.

The humiliation he suffered at her hands seemed to awaken in Briggs the first faint stirrings of love. A girl had never treated him that way before. He had always been the sun, and they had been the planets circling endlessly in the glow of his magnificence. But this girl showed little aptitude for circling. She seemed made for straight lines and geometric angles. He called that night and asked her out.

They dated for several months before Maureen found out. By then Lola had already decided to break it off with him. She had decided one night after dinner, when they had ridden the bus together into town to see a movie and had stopped by a local restaurant for a meal. They were sitting at a booth in a brightly lit hamburger joint and all around them was the bustle and banter of the town kids as they greeted one another loudly and hopped from booth to booth. "Stairway to Heaven" played in the background. Lola was looking into Briggs's handsome face and trying to block out the noise and confusion around her, trying to concentrate on what he was saying when it suddenly occurred to her that she was bored. Desperately, terminally bored. She was more interested in what was going on in the booths around her than she was in listening to what he had to say. She thought, *All he ever talks about is himself. I could never love someone like him.*

But when Maureen drove up for Parents' Day she fell immediately for the charming and handsome Briggs. She was like one of his little giggling groupies, hanging on his every word, blushing when his blue eyes rested too long on her. Between the two of them, Lola could hardly get a word in, sitting quietly in the backseat of the car or at the dinner table while they gossiped about people they knew or droned on endlessly about fashion and style and exotic locales. By the time she left, Maureen was as infatuated as a starstruck schoolgirl and Lola decided it would be easier to just go along with it all. She would break up with him over summer vacation.

But Maureen and Briggs's mother had different plans. They got together for day trips and cocktails several times before school was out, and each planned a series of summer "visits" for "the children" complete with cotillions, ice-cream parties, and barbecues. Lola saw more of Briggs that summer than she had all school year. She decided to wait and break up with him in the fall, once they returned to boarding school. But then his mother got sick, and by the time she died the following summer, Lola had already fallen into the inertia of their relationship. Besides, she couldn't break up with a boy whose mother had just died.

By senior year they were like an old married couple that has learned to ignore each other's faults in exchange for the comfort and stability that comes with custom and routine. Lola felt a certain faint affection for him, although she didn't think it was love. He was from the same social class and upbringing as she was, they were both Episcopalian, they shared many of the same friends, and they knew many of the same people.

Many couples she knew had married and started families with less affection and compatibility between them than she and Briggs shared. Her own parents had done it. And although their marriage hadn't turned out well, it had endured long past the impetuous marriages her schoolmates' parents seemed to jump in and out of every six or seven years. Some of her friends had two and three sets of stepparents. The fact that someone would leave a marriage just because they weren't *happy* seemed alien to Lola. It seemed cowardly. Her own parents had done battle for nearly thirty years and neither one had flinched or weakened until the very end.

Her own parents had survived a thirty-year marriage and yet here she was turning tail and running after only three years.

Lola got up and went into the bathroom to bathe her face with a wet washcloth. Henry fretted the moment she disappeared, turning his eyes to follow her, but when she came back he brightened and thrust his arms and legs out like a turtle rolled on its back. She leaned over and nuzzled his neck until he giggled and grasped her hair with his fat fists. After a moment she rolled him over on his stomach, patting his back gently as he practiced lifting himself with his arms.

She wasn't leaving Briggs because she expected to find happiness anywhere else. She had given up on happiness the day Lonnie Lumpkin was wheeled out of her life. She did not expect to find it again. What she wanted was a quiet simple life, a cottage on the beach where she and Henry could spend their days basking in the sun and swimming in the sea.

Briggs's loud, exuberant ways, his fierce temper, and his constant craving for her wore her out. He was, at the root of it all, an unhappy man. And he wanted everyone around him to share his unhappiness.

The phone rang shrilly, startling her out of her reverie. She leaned over and picked it up, putting one hand on Henry's back to keep him from rolling off the bed. "Sara," she said. "Thank God."

"Why are you doing this?" Briggs asked in a heavy voice.

She was quiet for a moment listening to the sound of the rain. "How did you find me?"

"Your mother."

Of course. Maureen had known where to look with an instinct born of thirty years of looking for her own wayward husband. Lola had been foolish to come here; she saw that now.

"Why are you doing this?" Briggs repeated and his voice, which had been flat and expressionless, rose slightly in pitch. "Didn't I give you everything a woman could possibly want?"

"Those are just things."

"Things!" he said harshly. "Just things!"

"I don't want to talk about this right now. I need time to think."

"I loved you through all of that . . ."

"I know. I know."

"You bitch."

"Don't."

"Through all that bullshit with that fucking house painter. Do you know how humiliating that was for me? Do you know how it felt knowing everyone was laughing at me?"

"I know. I'm sorry."

"You cunt."

"I wish you didn't love me. Then it wouldn't be so hard." She could hear him breathing. Outside the window the rain had subsided. Clouds of mist swirled around the streetlamps.

"There better not be anybody else," he said in a quiet voice.

"There's no one else."

"It better not be that fucking yard boy."

"Hush. It's no one."

"Because if it is, I'll kill him."

She knew he would. He was capable of murder. She had learned by now to handle his rages. She had learned to speak quietly, to show no fear. "It's me," she said soothingly. "There's nothing wrong with you. It's me. I need a different life. I need a simple life. I don't need the money. I don't want it. You can have it."

There was a humming sound on the line like a phone left off the hook. When he spoke his voice was bitter. "You don't want the money? Have you ever lived without it, you spoiled bitch?"

"No, but I . . ."

"What?"

"I can get a job."

He laughed. "You? Get a job? Doing what?"

"I can live with my mother."

"No," he said. "You can't. She won't support you. She'll put you out."

Her face, in the mirror, turned pale. She knew he was right. Her mother wouldn't support her in any divorce action. She'd be furious with Lola for the scandal, for the airing in public of family dirty linen. She'd take Briggs's side like she'd always done, like she'd taken the side of the masochistic Charlotte Hampton all those years ago. Once a Scottie, always a Scottie. "All I want is a quiet life," Lola said. The dimly lit room, which before had seemed only dirty and threadbare, now surrounded her like something sinister. She could feel it closing over her like the lid of a box. "All I want is my son," she said.

"*Your* son." And then, as if he had finally realized what he needed to say to break her, he added harshly, "*My* son. And don't think I'll just let you walk out of my life with him. If you go, he stays. You may not prize money but I have a lot of it, and without your mother's support you have nothing. And in case you don't know, Lola, it's the partner with the most money who winds up with the best deal in a custody arrangement."

She began to cry softly. Henry tried to turn his head to see her, bobbing up and down on his elbows. He put his face down on the blanket and began to fret. Lola sobbed into one hand and patted him with the other. Now that she was crying, Briggs's anger seemed to have dissipated.

"Come home," he said in a weary voice.

"No."

"Come home," he said. "Don't make me come get you."

Chapter 14

~~~~~~~~~~

That afternoon they jumped into the golf cart and headed down to the village stores to do some shopping. Mel drove and Sara sat beside her. Lola and Annie sat in the back. The sun was directly overhead, and when they broke from the cover of the overhanging trees it was like opening the door of a furnace, the heat prickling their arms and faces. A narrow strip of asphalt stretched in front of them, bound on one side by scrub pine and laurel oak and on the other by the slumbering marsh. Out past the yellow spartina grass the green waters of the tidal creeks glimmered faintly.

"Are we sure we want to go shopping in this heat?" Sara asked. She wore a black tank top, a pair of white cropped pants, and a straw hat trimmed with a black ribbon. She looked like someone out of *Hamptons* magazine. "We should be lying on the beach."

"We won't be long," Mel said. "Everything closes down at five so we don't have a lot of time to get to the shops. We wasted all morning just lying around the house."

From the back, Annie snorted. "Whose fault is that?" Across the marsh, a lone heron rose into the sun-bleached sky, dragging its legs behind it.

Mel said, "Hey, I can't help it if y'all are lightweights. Don't blame me."

"You were the one making the martinis," Sara said.

"You were the one who wanted to play Clinker," Annie said.

Mel made a dismissive gesture with one hand. "No one twisted your arms," she reminded them. "No one put a gun to your temples and forced you to drink."

"Well, I can tell you right now, I'm not drinking tonight," Sara said.

"Me either," Annie said.

"I'll drink," Lola said.

Ahead the tunnel of live oaks began. They drove from the glaring sunlight into a cool green shade that closed around them like water. Beards of Spanish moss hung from the branches of the trees. Cicadas whirred in the shadows. They passed a cart with floats and boogie boards tied to its roof, ambling along the road. A father in flip-flops and board shorts sat in the backseat beside a curly-haired girl of eight or nine. A mother in a pink swimsuit drove the cart and, tucked beside her on the front seat, a sleepy child sat sucking his thumb. Lola waved as they drove past and the boy lifted his hand and waved listlessly.

"Henry used to love the beach," Lola said, gazing fondly at the boy. "We had a place at Gulf Shores when he was little, and he and I used to stay down there for most of the summer. Briggs would fly down when he could. He used to scream and kick his feet whenever I'd make him come in from the beach."

"Who, Briggs or Henry?" Mel said.

"His hair was so blond," Lola said wistfully, her eyes fixed on the disappearing child. "He used to squat at the edge of the sand and dig holes with his little shovel. And when the water rolled up and filled in the hole he would get so mad and stomp his little feet and throw his little shovel in the surf and then I'd have to go in and get it."

"How did a child with such a bad temper grow up to be so normal?" Annie asked earnestly. She glanced at Lola and colored slightly. She hadn't meant to say that out loud. Sometimes her mouth worked before her mind had a chance to shut it down. Annie loved her own children but she hadn't spoiled them. Once, on a trip through Birmingham, they had met Lola's family at a fast food restaurant. Annie's sons had sat quietly and politely at the table but Henry, on learning that he already had the toy being offered in the Happy Meal box, had insisted on going to a different restaurant to get another toy. When his mother refused, he had a screaming fit that culminated with Briggs throwing the boy over his shoulder and carrying him out. The whole time Henry had stretched his arms toward his mother, and with a tearful face, screamed, "I'm your only little boy! I'm your only little boy!" Lola stood it for as long as she could and then hurried out after them.

"You never know how they'll turn out," Sara said, thinking how sweet and docile Adam had been as a child. He would play by himself for hours, alone in his own little world. That was before he'd come to realize that he wasn't like other kids. The knowledge had made him surly and short-tempered. Or maybe it was just adolescence; Sara didn't know.

Lola smiled dreamily and continued with her daydreams of Henry. "Soon he'll be a daddy with a son of his own," she murmured. Caught up in her memories, Lola gave no indication that she'd heard a word anyone else had said and Annie was glad of that.

"Do you really think he's old enough to be getting married?" Mel asked. "What is he, twenty-one? Twenty-two?"

"I was twenty-two," Annie said, "and so was Lola."

"And I was twenty-four," Mel said, "and that was way too young."

Sara said nothing. She'd married at twenty-eight, two years after finishing law school. By then she and Tom had been dating, off and on, for three years and had been living together for two.

A soft snuffling sound made Mel glance over her shoulder. "Lola, are you crying?"

Lola smiled apologetically and dabbed her cheeks with the backs of her hands. "One day you're standing on the beach with your child," she sobbed, "and the next it's your child standing there with his own son. Where does the time go?" Annie took a Kleenex out of her purse and gave it to Lola, and she took it and blew her nose softly.

It occurred suddenly to Mel that Lola was lonely. And Mel knew a thing or two about loneliness, although with her it was a condition she had chosen. Her career as a writer made a solitary life necessary but it was a choice she'd never really regretted. Well, most of the time, anyway. But with Lola the loneliness was forced, and that was different. Briggs had his money, Mel had her writing, Sara and Annie had their own families, but all Lola had ever had was Henry. And now Henry had found someone else.

"Lola, you and I need to see more of each other," Mel said suddenly.

She put her chin up and stared at Lola in the rearview mirror. Sara put her hand out as if to take the wheel but Mel pushed it away. "Why don't you come up to New York in the fall? We can do the museums, take in a few shows, shop until Briggs cuts you off, and eat in a different restaurant every meal."

The cart whirred through the cool green tunnel of the maritime forest. Insects floated in the still blue air. Lola sniffed and stuck her nose in the Kleenex. "That would be nice," she said, blowing gently.

The village was bustling with noontime shoppers and diners who crowded the island's only two restaurants, Sophie's Seafood and the Oyster Bar. Both restaurants fronted the harbor and faced each other at right angles. Sandwiched in between was the marina, and across the harbor was the ferry dock, where the big ferries ran every thirty minutes between the island and the mainland, carrying happy or depressed tourists (depending on whether they were just beginning their vacation or going home). Clustered along the perimeter of the harbor stood tall, cedar-shingled houses and shops weathered to a soft gray. The boats in the marina bobbed gently on the tide, their canvas rigging snapping in the steady breeze that blew in from the sound and the open sea beyond. Golf carts trundled along the narrow roadways, and children played on the village green under the watchful eyes of their parents, who sat on the deck outside Sophie's sipping frozen margaritas out of wide-mouthed glasses.

Mel pulled the cart into an open bay in front of the cluster of village shops. She got out and plugged the cart into an outlet while the others stood up and stretched.

"Where should we start?" Sara asked, yawning. The sun was hot but the breeze was pleasant and fragrant with the scent of cape jasmine and fried fish.

"There's a really cute dress shop over there," Lola said, pointing. She seemed happy again, which was just like Lola, sad one moment and cheerful the next. "And right next to it is a store that sells little gifts and collectibles for the home."

"I need to go in there first," Mel said, pointing to the Village Market, an upscale grocery store that also sold beach products, cosmetics, and various drugstore items. The building was small and gray-shingled, and looked like an old-fashioned country store complete with a bay window and some type of trailing, pink-blossomed vine running across the facade and up into the eaves. A series of stone steps led from the sidewalk up to the front door. Mel put her arm around Lola's shoulders and they went up the steps together. A little bell tinkled as they walked in. The room was cool and musty with the scent of cinnamon and cloves. Wide planked floors gleamed beneath the overhead lights, and rows of tall shelves ran from the front of the store to the back. A bored-looking youth lounged across a counter reading a magazine. Behind his right shoulder hung a Boar's Head meat sign. "Can I help you?" he said in a thick Ukrainian accent. A good portion of Ukraine seemed to be congregated here on this small North Carolina island. Fresh-faced waitresses, shopgirls, and deckhands all spoke with Ukrainian accents.

"Do you carry Corona?" Mel asked.

"Corona?" he said, looking puzzled.

"It's a beer."

"Oh. All beer is in cooler in back. You must be twenty-one to buy." He grinned at Mel. She grinned back, a slow, lazy smile that showed her dimples to their best advantage.

"Oh, please," Sara said.

She followed Mel back to the coolers, wondering what she was up to. Mel had that look on her face that she always had right before she did something wrong. Sara had spent most of her childhood anticipating that look. "Why are you buying beer?" she asked suspiciously. She was the oldest child in her family, and she had been raised to be the responsible one. It was a hard habit to break.

"It's for tonight. I'm pulling out the big guns."

"Big guns?"

"Corona," Mel said, lifting a six-pack from the cooler.

"I told you I'm not drinking."

"I'm not drinking either," Annie said, appearing behind Sara like a disconsolate ghost. She had bought a kite for Agnes Grace, the girl she visited out at the Baptist Children's Home, and was trying, unsuccessfully, to slide it into a plastic bag.

Mel ignored them both. "Where's Lola?" she asked.

"I'm over here!" They heard her delicate little laugh one aisle over, followed by the sound of something metallic hitting the floor.

Mel checked her reflection in the glass-fronted cooler. "Since we're not going out tonight, I thought I'd make something really special," she said, fluffing her hair with her fingers.

"No," Annie said belligerently.

"What?" Sara asked, unable to stop herself.

"Margaronas."

"Margaronas?" Annie and Sara exchanged puzzled looks.

Mel continued on down the aisle toward the frozen foods. "Since we're not going out. Since we won't be doing any driving. When I serve them at home, I make everyone spend the night. A couple of pitchers of Margaronas and you're out for the count. These things are deadly. Hey, do either one of you have a heart condition?"

"Not that I know of," Annie said, looking worried. "But I haven't had a physical in a couple of years."

"You'll probably be all right then." Mel stopped in front of the frozen foods and scanned the frosty shelves.

"Assuming I was going to drink tonight, which I'm *not*," Sara said, "what exactly is a Margarona?"

"Okay," Mel said, opening the freezer door and reaching in to grab a family-size can of frozen limeade. She shut the door and held the can up. "You put the frozen limeade in the bottom of a pitcher. Then you fill the empty can with tequila."

Sara looked stunned. "Are you kidding me?" she said. "You fill that big can with tequila? That's crazy."

"Right," Mel said. "Blend the tequila and the limeade. Then you pour in two Coronas, stir gently, and serve."

"That sounds vile," Annie said.

"Nectar of the gods," Mel said, turning and wandering slowly down the aisle. They found Lola on the next aisle, standing in front of a magazine display. "Don't read any more of those trashy magazines," Mel told her. "They'll rot your brain."

Lola was thumbing through one of the more lurid rags. She looked up, puzzled, and asked earnestly, "Do y'all think Tom Cruise is gay?"

"Yes," Mel said.

"Who cares?" Sara asked.

Annie was quiet. Like so much else in her life, she was still wrestling with the concept of homosexuality. Reverend Reeves maintained that it was a sin but Annie had begun to question that, too. Her friend Louise Ledford had a son named Roy who'd changed his name to Roi and moved to Chicago to open a bed-and-breakfast with his "friend" Mikhail. Even as a small child, Roi had been different. While other boys played Nintendo or paintball or drove their four-wheelers through the park, Roi had contented himself with giving his mother facials. He also did her makeup and dressed her so that when she went out of the house, she looked like a million bucks. (*I love your purse,* he'd told Annie once at a church function, *but next time try a Baguette.*) Everyone knew Roi was "funny" even before he changed his name and danced the Dance of the Seven Veils at the eighth-grade talent show.

Still, Annie couldn't see any real harm in Roi. It wasn't like he was a serial killer or an alcoholic or a drug addict. And he was sweet to his mother; he called her twice a week and never forgot her birthday, sending her designer dresses and Fendi bags so that she always looked like a fashion plate at the Women of God meetings.

Lola closed the magazine and put it back on the shelf, and they followed Mel down the aisle to a small cosmetics display.

Mel stopped, picked up a box of Miss Clairol, and began to read the back. "Hey, I know," she said. "Let's get drunk and give ourselves makeovers."

"Oh, now, that sounds like a good idea," Sara said.

"At the very least, let's dye Annie's hair." She held up the box of Miss Clairol and grinned.

Annie gave her a steady sullen look. "No one touches my hair," she said.

"Oh, come on, live a little."

"No," Annie said, wishing she could give in to spontaneity but knowing it was impossible. She felt brittle sometimes, as if she was slowly ossifying beneath her flesh, but she had never been a spontaneous person, with the exception of that brief, heady period twenty-three years ago.

And look how well that had turned out.

Chapter 15

~~~~~~~~~~~

Annie had not been a good mother. Age and experience had taught her this. She had been a competent mother. Her sons never went without clean clothes or a good meal or expensive medical or dental care. They were provided with all the material possessions a late-twentieth-century child could possibly want. They attended church and good private schools and had grown up in a stable, conservative, two-parent family. They had been raised in the structured environment so often touted by educators and television child psychologists. And that's where Annie had gone wrong.

She had lived her life, their lives, by schedules. Most mothers kept dry erase or bulletin boards hanging in the kitchen by the phone but Annie's schedules had taken up the entire back of the pantry door. Six sheets of neatly typed and numbered pages taped up like Martin Luther's *Ninety-Five Theses* nailed to the door of the *Schlosskirche*. And the schedules had an almost religious significance for Annie; they were studied by her faithfully every morning, followed with unswerving devotion every day, and were the last things she consulted every evening before laying her weary head down upon her goose-down pillow. Meal schedules, nap schedules, doctors' appointments, reading enrichment, fun with mathematics, supervised television viewing, art lessons, soccer lessons, and piano lessons were all listed and sublisted in outline form down to the most trivial of details. Even playtime was scheduled. An anthropologist studying child-rearing customs and preadolescent development in the late twentieth century could see the whole of her children's sad and dreary childhoods outlined on the back of her pantry door.

The problem with scheduling, Annie now realized, was that in your rush to meet the deadlines set forth in front of you in black and white, you missed the more important things. Things like lazy summer afternoons spent lying in a hammock reading, or fishing for crawdads in the creek, or water gun fights on the lawn, or impromptu games of tag or blind man's bluff or Hi-Ho Cherry O! Annie never *played* with her sons. She wasn't that kind of mother. Lola had once told her that she and Henry had built an entire castle out of refrigerator boxes they painted and taped together, cutting out doors and windows with serrated knives. (*Serrated knives!*) The idea of wild-child Henry Furman wielding a sharp and dangerous instrument had been enough to fill Annie with a sense of doom and impending disaster. *What had Lola been thinking?*

She repeated the story that night for Mitchell as they got ready for bed. "What was Lola thinking?" she said sharply. "Henry could have stabbed himself in the heart! He could have put out an eye!"

"Now, honey, boys need to be boys," Mitchell said and something in his tone made Annie think he was criticizing her.

"Yes, well, boys given sharp instruments to play with are often *dead* boys!" she said, astonished at her own outburst. Why should she care that Lola gave her son knives to play with? Or that she played with him at all?

"Oh, now, Henry's a good boy," Mitchell said, as if to confirm her suspicions that she was being unreasonable.

She gave him an indignant look. "I never said he wasn't."

"Now, honey, don't go getting your shorts in a knot," Mitchell said, reaching for her. "And speaking of shorts, why don't you put on that little black lace bikini thing I bought you for Valentine's Day?"

Now that she was older she could see it. Henry Furman *was* a good boy. He'd turned out fine, despite the fact that he'd never been on a schedule his entire childhood. Despite the fact that Lola had let him go to bed whenever or wherever he wanted to, just dropping wherever he was when he got tired, on the sofa in the den, at the foot of Lola's bed, on the floor in the upstairs hallway. Annie had been appalled at Lola's lack of routine and had on more than one occasion offered to help her make up a schedule.

"A schedule?" Lola had laughed in her silvery little voice. "Oh, Henry wouldn't like that at all."

And now Lola had had the last laugh, although she wasn't laughing, of course; there wasn't a mean bone in her frail little body, and Annie was left with the feeling that she had cheated her boys out of something important in their childhoods.

Not that they blamed her, of course. They were always calling her and teasing her about one little thing or another. William, the eldest, had gone off to UVA first, and Annie had worried that he wasn't being fed right in the school cafeteria. When he called she would always ask him, "What'd you have for dinner?"

The first time he said, "filet mignon au poivre" and the second "trout amandine," but it wasn't until he said, "oysters Rockefeller" that she began to get suspicious. But by then she'd already bragged to the women in her garden club about the gourmet meals served in the UVA cafeteria. When Carleton went off to Duke two years later, he'd done the same thing.

"What'd you have for dinner?"

"Lobster with truffle butter."

It had been a big joke among the three of them, William, Carleton, and Mitchell (because he'd been in on it, of course) and now whenever they were home they teased Annie about how her home-cooked meals didn't come close to the gourmet fare they were accustomed to at college.

She was proud of them, proud of the tall, sturdy young men they had grown up to be. And despite her constant interference in their lives and fretting over them (what was it some pundit had called her generation—helicopter parents?) they still managed to come across as contented and well-adjusted young men.

Still, if Annie had it to do all over again, she'd throw away the schedules and spend each day just enjoying it as it came. She'd ride bikes, and play board games, and build castles in the backyard out of refrigerator boxes and she wouldn't listen to anyone who tried to tell her how to be a better mom. She wouldn't listen to pastors or television child psychologists or well-meaning but misinformed neighbors who tried to give her parenting advice.

When William was four years old she'd let a neighbor convince her to paint his thumb with Mavala to break him of his thumb-sucking habit. And when he'd started kindergarten and was still sleeping at night with a blanket she'd let that same neighbor, who had read every child-rearing book ever written and therefore considered herself an expert, advise her to tie the "bankie" to helium balloons and let William release them into the sky in a kind of symbolic goodbye-to-babyhood ritual. With this in mind, Annie had gathered the neighborhood children for a festive affair complete with streamers, party games, and ice-cream cake, and had allowed the stoic but trembling William to "free" his bankie before the assembled guests. Unfortunately, the balloons carrying the blanket became entangled in the top of a tall pecan tree, where they exploded one by one like firecrackers to the accompanying screams of the watching children. The tethered bankie, rather than continuing its symbolic ascent, became snagged in the branches at the top of the tree, where it hung forlornly above the yard for several weeks like a rotting corpse dangling from a gallows. Every time William went outside he would look up into the branches of the tree and scream. Annie finally paid a tree service to come into the yard with a crane to take it down.

Given that experience she should have known better than to listen to this same neighbor, who advised her that, according to a new book written by the eminent child psychologist Dr. Ernest Witherspoon, a toddler could now be potty trained in less than one day. Dr. Witherspoon's technique involved locking the child and mother in a bathroom together for twelve hours. The trauma of this experience was so great that Annie came into Carleton's room several weeks later to find him squatting in a corner, furtively reaching into his pants to pinch off pieces of a giant turd that he rolled into pellets the size of BBs and dropped surreptitiously into the heating register.

Both her sons had managed to survive her mothering, although there were times when Annie wondered how. With the clear-sighted advantage of age and experience, she was now able to see how woefully inadequate she had truly been. Although William and Carleton seemed mentally healthy now she was sure the failures of her parenting would come to light years from now during some long, gloomy period of middle-aged psychotherapy.

With any luck at all, it would happen long after she was dead.

Chapter 16

~~~~~~~~~~

Mel was serious about the Margaronas. It was close to four o'clock by the time they got back from their shopping spree in the village, and she set about making up a pitcher of something she promised "would take the edge off."

"What edge?" Sara said. "I haven't felt this relaxed in years." And it was true. She hadn't even wanted to come on this trip and now after only two days she was feeling better than she had in a long time. Maybe it was the lack of routine, maybe it was the sun or the food or the friendship, or sitting around in their pajamas until one o'clock talking about everything and nothing at all. Maybe it was the alcohol. Whatever it was, it felt better than a one-hour deep-tissue massage. She had come to the island dreading an altercation and instead she had found fun and companionship. It made her feel guilty about Tom. When she got home she would insist that he take a boys' trip somewhere with a group of his friends. Not that he had that many friends. Neither one of them had done much socializing since Adam's diagnosis.

Annie, always ready to be a spoilsport, said, "I didn't think we were drinking tonight." They were standing at the breakfast bar watching Mel mix the drinks. Behind her, at the sink, April deveined shrimp.

"No one's forcing you to drink, señorita," Mel said, pouring a Margarona and handing it to Lola. She poured Sara one. "I can put salt on the rim if you like."

Sara hesitated and then took it. "This isn't going to take the enamel off my teeth, is it?"

"I make no guarantees one way or the other. I take no legal responsibility for what may occur," Mel said, lifting her glass. "Cheers."

They tapped their glasses and drank slowly.

"Yow-sa," Lola said, her eyes shining merrily.

Sara looked pleasantly surprised. "Not bad," she said. "You hardly taste the tequila."

"I told you," Mel said.

"Okay, okay, pour me one," Annie said glumly. It was no use being a teetotaler when everyone else seemed willing to drink themselves into a stupor. If she stayed sober she'd just have to be the responsible one later on and she was tired of that role.

Mel poured another glass and they drank steadily for a while, watching April work. By the time Mel got up to pour a second round, Annie and Sara were slouched against the breakfast bar and Lola was sitting upright with two bright spots of color on her cheeks. Mel held the pitcher up. "More toxins, Bimbette?" she said to Sara.

"Sure, Homeslice, fill it up."

Annie asked, "What's a Bimbette?" and held her glass up for a refill.

"It's a slutty girl."

"Oh, thank you very much," Sara said.

"One who isn't too smart. You know, an airhead, a ditz, a space cadet." She smirked at Sara and made a vague gesture with her glass.

"The English always say 'silly cow,'" Sara said, ignoring her. She loved English literature and English movies. Beneath her East Tennessee exterior beat the heart of a true Anglophile.

"Or silly wanker," Mel said.

"That bartender at the Black Friar Pub in London used to say that," Lola said. "Silly wanker."

"Yes," Annie said. "But what does it mean?"

"I think it's a masturbatory term," Mel said.

"Oh, well, then, you should know," Sara said.

April finished deveining the shrimp and started mincing the garlic. Mel held the pitcher up and said, "Hey, do you want a Margarona?"

April, who'd watched her mix the drinks earlier, said, "No thanks. I need to stay sober to cook."

"How unfortunate for you but probably best for us," Mel said, happily pouring herself another drink. She paused and said to April, "How about your better half?"

The girl glanced at her over one shoulder. "Who?" she asked.

"The Captain."

"Oh." She shrugged. "Maybe," she said. "I guess," she said.

"He's probably back from the marina by now," Mel said. "I'll go ask him."

"I'll go with you," Sara said in a loud singsong voice. She and Mel exchanged glances across the bar. Mel poured another Margarona and Sara followed her out the kitchen door onto the porch. As they walked along the boardwalk to the crofter, Mel said, "If I didn't know better, I'd say you didn't trust me alone with Captain Mike."

"I'm just looking out for April."

"April doesn't need looking out for. She's a big girl."

"She doesn't know you. She doesn't know how tricky and cunning you can be."

"People who live in glass houses," Mel said, "shouldn't throw stones."

Captain Mike was in the garage under the crofter listening to the Foo Fighters. He had on a pair of cut-off shorts and flip-flops, and he was leaning over Briggs's fancy golf cart with his back to them. The seat was pulled up and he was scouring the connections for the six batteries with a wire brush.

"We brought you a present," Mel said, standing in the doorway. She felt a momentary sense of light-headedness, which quickly dissipated. The Margaronas were kicking in.

He stood up and turned around, still holding the wire brush in one hand and a grease-stained rag in the other. His eyes appeared green in some lights and blue in others, but she saw now that they were really gray. Gray as a rifle barrel. Gray as the sea under a storm-lit sky. Another Margarona and she'd be spouting poetry.

"What'd you bring me?" he said.

"Something guaranteed to make you a happy man."

He grinned and said, "That sounds promising."

Mel grinned back. *Damn.* She was beginning to weave on her feet. There was something about his eyes, something mesmerizing that she couldn't shake, something you didn't pick up on at first but that kind of grew on you over time. If you saw a photograph of him you wouldn't think of him as anything special but standing near him was something else entirely.

"It is something special," she said and took a step toward him but it went wrong. She managed to put too much weight on her right foot and lost her balance, slopping his drink over the rim of the glass before she could recover.

He dropped the brush and put his hand out to steady her. "You girls haven't been drinking, have you?" he said, wiping his fingers on the rag.

"It's not too bad," Sara said. "If you slip it slowly."

"*Slip it slowly?*" Mel said.

"Shut up, Mel. You try saying it."

"Sip it slowly, sip it slowly, slip it sowly."

"See?"

"I appreciate the offer," Captain Mike said pointing to a bottle of Sam Adams sitting on the floorboards of the golf cart, "but I'm a beer man myself." He stuck the rag in his back pocket. "Besides, someone needs to stay sober to drive you girls around later on."

"We're not going anywhere tonight," Mel said, and then she thought, *Shut up, stupid. If he wants to drive you around don't argue.* "Well, not for dinner anyway," she added vaguely. "Maybe later."

"A moonlit ride," Sara said and then giggled as if she'd said something funny.

Captain Mike squatted down and stuck his fingers back in among the battery cables. His T-shirt rose in back, exposing the smooth, sleek curve of the latissimus dorsi. His skin was darkly tanned but she could see the rim of pale skin just below his swimsuit line.

"Where's Mrs. Furman?" he said.

"Who?" Sara asked.

"Mrs. Furman? My employer?" he said lightly, without turning around. No doubt Briggs would be calling tonight to collect any information he'd managed to gather on Lola. Mel immediately went back to not liking him. Captain Mike and April were like some kind of sinister CIA tag team, and Lola was just naive enough to trust both of them. Poor Lola. "She ran off with that young guy at the beach club," Mel said perversely, and then thought, *Why did I say that?*

He turned around and looked at her and then went back to work. "What young guy would that be?"

"The one in the real estate sales office. The good-looking one."

"She's in the kitchen with Annie helping April make dinner," Sara said flatly. She made a face at Mel and sipped her drink.

Mel stared at her, briefly, and then swung her attention back to Captain Mike. She felt foolish now, standing there holding two drinks. "Briggs doesn't know how lucky he is," she said. "Lola could have run off with a dozen men by now, if she'd wanted to." If he was listening to her, he gave no sign of it. He continued to look at the batteries, poking his fingers here and there to check the connections.

She probably should shut up. She was only making it worse for Lola. Briggs would hear about the young real estate salesman and drag Lola home to Birmingham. She should shut up, but there was something in the set of Captain Mike's well-muscled back, in his reserved silence that drove her to say, "She could have run off in college, you know, with some guy named Lonnie." Sara shot her a warning look. Mel thought again, *Why did I say that?* It was hard being ignored by a man as good-looking as Captain Mike. She wondered how old he was. She was guessing thirty-six or thirty-seven although it was hard to tell with a man who still had a full head of hair and shoulders like a high school running back. But April couldn't be more than twenty-four or twenty-five, not with that body she had, and that meant a twelve- or thirteen-year age difference, which was pretty considerable when you thought about it. Pretty unfair, too, for women in Mel's age bracket. "It's a whole new world out there," she lied, lifting her drink. "Women get to run off with younger men now, too. "

He gave her a curious look, and then went back to work.

"Maybe," Sara said. "If you're a Hollywood actress."

"I once dated a guy who was twenty-two years younger than me," Mel bragged, which was another lie; she hadn't dated him, she'd only slept with him. The sex had been great but later, eating dinner at a little dive down in the West Village, he'd said things like *Dude, that sex was off the hook!* and

Damn, Skippy, I was all up in that shit. That shit was tight! and she'd had to fight a sudden urge to lean over, tuck his napkin under his chin, and cut his meat into little squares.

"I don't think you should be bragging about your pedophilic tendencies," Sara said rather cynically.

Mel turned her head slowly and gave her a long look. Sara wasn't making things easy for her, which was extremely hypocritical of her, and if Mel thought about it long enough, might make her really mad. Mad enough to slap the shit out of her. Mad enough to *tell the Mofo to step off,* as her twenty-two-year-old lover would have said.

Despite the Margaronas, Mel decided not to go there.

By the time Captain Mike came in for dinner an hour later, the party was in full swing. Lola, Annie, Sara and Mel were sitting around the farmhouse table laughing about the time Kevin Adler, aka Sweaty Kevin, superglued his face to the floor during a Sluts and Geeks Party. Half-emptied plates of shrimp scampi and Caesar salad littered the table. Their third pitcher of Margaronas rested in the center like a trophy, like the America's Cup of Binge Drinking. April leaned against the breakfast bar listening to them, shaking her head and smiling ruefully, as if she found it hard to imagine them as crazy teenagers.

Captain Mike came up behind her, handing her a plate, and she took it, rolling her eyes at him. He had showered and changed his shirt, Mel noted, although wearing his hair slicked back from his face was not a good look for him. Some men needed their hair around their faces, and he was one of them. He heaped his plate with the scampi, salad, and bread, and April did the same. Most nights they took their plates back to the crofter porch, where they could sit and enjoy their meals privately.

The women were all talking at once and no one seemed to have noticed Captain Mike but Mel. She smiled at him and raised her glass and he smiled back. She beckoned to him in what she thought was a friendly manner, and opened her mouth to say, *Come! Join us!* but what came out was something that sounded like *Cawsh!*

Lola said, "Y'all stop. My stomach hurts from laughing."

Annie snorted and pointed at Mel. "Cawsh!" she said, flapping her arms like a big black crow. Then she began to giggle.

• • •

After Captain Mike and April left, Mel got up to make another pitcher of Margaronas. Getting from her chair to the kitchen involved a bit of careful planning, and was performed with a hump-shouldered lurching movement, her arms spread out on either side of her like rudders. Behind her, Annie pointed and shouted, *Cawsh! Cawsh!* like a deranged parrot.

When she got back to the table, Sara had cleared a spot in front of her and was busy folding her cloth napkin into some kind of intricate shape. Mel poured another round of Margaronas and sat down. "What are you doing?" she asked Sara.

"Cloth origami," Sara said. "Watch this." She folded the napkin carefully. About halfway through the exercise it became apparent what she was making, at least to Mel, who began to chuckle.

"Is it a swan?" Annie asked.

"It looks a little like that photograph of the Loch Ness monster," Lola said. "The one with the big arching neck and the little bitty head."

Mel snorted and Sara kept folding. The shape rose off the table in front of her, curved and quivering.

"Hey, wait a minute," Annie said. "Where's the swan's beak?"

Mel said, "It's not a swan, Annie."

It wasn't until Sara finished gathering the cloth at the base of the long arched shaft and placed it in a wineglass on the table that Lola and Annie figured it out.

"Oh, my God," Annie said. "It's a talleywhacker."

Lola clapped her hands gaily. "Show me how to make one," she said.

They pushed their plates and silverware back to make room at the table. Each one started with a cloth napkin unfolded flat on the table in front of them while Sara gave them instructions.

"Where'd you learn to do this?" Mel asked, as they began to fold.

"Law school."

"You learned to make penis napkins in law school?"

"I sat next to a girl from Tunnel Hill, Georgia in one of my classes. A former beauty queen."

"You mean like Miss America?" Annie said.

"Miss Tunnel Hill."

"Oh."

"What does that have to do with penis napkins?" Mel asked.

"Her talent was cloth origami," Sara said. "And one day she was just fooling around and came up with it."

"Wow," Lola said, shaking her head in amazement. "I wish I was creative like that."

Mel looked at her a moment and then went back to rolling.

"Did she win?" Annie said.

"Yes, she won. She didn't use the penis fold, of course, she used something else. A swan, I think. Or maybe a turtle."

"Wow," Lola said. She continued to shake her head, her expression gradually changing to one of profound wonderment. "But how would you make a turtle out of a cloth napkin? That would be really hard."

"That would be nearly impossible," Annie agreed. She had always been pretty good at arts and crafts but cloth origami wasn't really a craft—it was more like a skill, like baton twirling or sword swallowing.

Mel snorted and said, "This isn't brain surgery, you know. This isn't quantum physics or figuring out a way to stop cancer cells from multiplying."

Annie ignored her. Mel couldn't even sew a button on her shirt. She had the people at the dry cleaners do it for her. Annie looked at Sara and said earnestly, "If she won Miss Tunnel Hill, why did she stop doing pageants?"

"She said the pageant world was too brutal. She decided to practice law instead."

Lola giggled suddenly and pointed. "Look at Annie's," she said.

The other three napkins were beginning to rise from the table, curved and thick-shafted, but Annie's lay there limp and lifeless. "Why is mine so flat?" she said, looking around at the other three.

"Damn, Annie, it's supposed to look like a penis, not a hair braid."

"I don't think you're rolling it tight enough," Sara said.

"Have you ever even seen a real penis?" Mel said.

"I've seen plenty!" Annie cried, looking indignant. Her neck slowly flushed with color. "I mean, I've seen one, of course," she added unconvincingly.

"Of course."

"If you've only seen one then why are you blushing?"

Annie struggled for a comeback. The Margaronas were definitely beginning to interfere with her ability to think sequentially. Whatever it was she was trying to say was locked up behind door number three, if only she could figure out the combination code. "Buff me, Mel," she said finally.

Lola snorted. Mel said, "*Buff* me?"

"It sounds nicer than that other word I don't like to use."

"Which word would that be, Annie?"

Sara put one finger to her lips. "Leave her alone," she said. Her eyes were pink-rimmed, and her nose was red and shiny. "I think we should respect Annie's right to euphemisms," she said.

"What's a euphemism?" Annie asked.

"Saying talleywhacker instead of penis. Saying buff me instead of fuck off."

After that they settled down and went back to work. Lucinda Williams sang on the stereo. Outside the long windows evening fell. The dunes glimmered along the horizon like fallen snow, and beyond them the sea stretched, black and slick as a mirror.

"You see them on TV," Lola said in a drowsy voice, almost as if she was talking to herself. "At least you do on European TV. And sometimes in magazines. In movies."

"See what?"

"Penises."

The other three stopped rolling and looked at her.

"What kind of movies?" Mel said. "Does Briggs have you watching porno films now?"

"Briggs?" Lola said, and giggled. "No, sillies," she said. The other three watched her with blank expressions. She held her napkin up and waggled it at them. "Look," she said. "My penis has a kink in the middle."

Somewhere around nine o'clock they decided it might be fun to have a bonfire on the beach so Lola called Captain Mike. He came over a few minutes later looking tired and irritable, like a camp counselor dragged out of bed in the middle of the night by a group of unruly campers. His hair stood up on one side of his head, and it was obvious from his peevish expression that he'd been called away from doing something he was clearly enjoying. Mel was pretty sure she knew what it was. April hadn't even bothered to come back and clean up the dinner dishes.

"What is it you girls are up to now?" he said, staring grimly at the origami napkins they had lined up in a row down the middle of the dining room table like an obscene centerpiece. His good humor from earlier in the evening had clearly vanished.

"Were you *sleeping*?" Mel asked, narrowing her eyes above her Margarona glass.

"I was trying," he said.

"It's still early."

"I'm a little behind on my sleep."

Mel thought, *Well, whose fault is that?* Lola colored slightly and said, "We won't keep you."

"Keep me as long as you like."

Sara came out of the bathroom and sat down at the table. Her eyes were swollen and threaded with red veins. She could never hide the fact that she'd been drinking. When they got caught once with a bottle of Jack Daniels out behind Nordan Hall, Mel had tossed the bottle into a hedge and lied like a skillful corporate attorney, but the resident assistant had taken one look at Sara and instantly guessed the truth.

Sara noticed Captain Mike standing over by the breakfast bar and she lifted her glass. "Have a drink with us," she said gaily.

He whistled softly and ran his hand through his hair. "I don't think that's a good idea," he said.

"We were thinking we'd go down on the beach and dance around a bonfire," Mel said. "We were thinking we'd holler and whoop it up like a bunch of crazy women."

"I don't think that's a good idea either," he said, beginning to relax a bit. He leaned against the breakfast bar with his arms crossed over his chest and his legs crossed at the ankles. "You girls can hardly stand, much less dance. One of you might stumble and fall into the fire."

"That's *exactly* what I said," Annie said, looking around the table with a self-satisfied air. She stabbed the air with one finger as if to make a point.

"Then you'll just have to stay and keep an eye on us," Mel said, smiling. She was trying to be seductive but she was drunk and it wasn't working.

He ignored her like he always did, as if she were nothing more than a mild annoyance, a slight disturbance in his wide field of vision. Mel would have liked to slap him. She would have liked to hit him over the head with something heavy. She would have liked to lurch over and throw herself upon him like a drowning woman clinging to a buoy.

He lifted his chin and let his eyes rest on Lola. "I hadn't really planned on babysitting tonight," he said pleasantly.

She colored again and looked at her glass. "Sorry," she said.

The evening sky was clear and filled with a big yellow moon. Annie lay in the sand on her back looking up at the stars. Thirty feet down the beach a fire flickered in the portable fire pit Captain Mike had convinced them to use instead of a bonfire. He had wheeled it down to the beach, loaded it with driftwood, started the fire, and then disappeared into the darkness, where he watched, Annie knew, like a protective disembodied spirit. Like their own personal loa. From time to time he would reappear to load more wood on to the fire. Annie pitied April, alone in her cold bed while her lover tended to the needs of a group of inebriated women who should have known better.

"Hey, Annie, come and join us," Mel called to her from the edge of the fire.

Annie raised her arm and waved. "I'll be there in a minute," she said.

Lola, Mel, and Sara clustered around the pit in low beach chairs, their feet stretched toward the fire. Lola was singing a camp song, and Mel and Sara were trying to join in, stopping every few minutes to argue over who was more tone-deaf. They both were, as far as Annie was concerned. She'd sung in the church choir, so she knew a thing or two about tone deafness.

She put her hands behind her head and stared up at the sky. It was one of the things she liked best about this island, the fact that with no neon lights or high-rise hotels the sky was so clear at night, the stars so visible. You could make your way about the island with little more than the light from the moon and the stars to guide you.

The sky reminded Annie of the camping trips she had taken with Paul Ballard that last year of college. They couldn't go anyplace where someone might see them together so they'd backpacked into the wilderness areas of Shining Rock or Linville Gorge, places so remote and isolated they might go days without seeing signs of human habitation. At night, bone weary and sated, they had lain on their backs under a Carolina moon and lied to each other about the future.

"Hey, Annie, what was the name of that girl who used to pull her hair out? Scooter's girlfriend?"

"Lexie. Lexie Cravens."

"See," Sara said to Mel. "I told you."

"Buff me," Mel said.

Lola sang softly in the background, oblivious to their argument.

Annie's parents had sent her to Bedford because she was an only child and they could, even though it meant a second mortgage on the house and a second job for her father. When the guidance counselor at school showed her a brochure of Bedford, and Annie saw its stone and redbricked facade, built to resemble Oxford, she had known immediately where she wanted to go to college. Even though the tuition was more than her father's annual salary. Even though it was an Episcopal school (she had neglected to mention this to her parents and they, thankfully, had never caught on).

Bedford had opened her eyes in a way nothing else in her life had. She wondered now if that had been such a good thing, if the seeds of her current discontent might not have been sown so many years before in the liberal soil of Bedford.

"Annie! Come on!"

"Tell us a story!"

The sand was warm under Annie's back. She could feel herself sinking in, a few granules at a time like sugar through a sieve, like sand through an hourglass. They had stopped drinking forty minutes ago—it was one of the conditions imposed by Captain Mike before he would agree to build the fire—but Annie was still slightly buzzed from the Margaronas. She was so relaxed she couldn't move, soaking up the sand's heat like a lizard stretched on a desert rock. It was better than Vicodin, this feeling. It was better than Prozac or clonazepam or any of the other antidepressants or anti-anxiety drugs the women in her garden club took to get them through their long dreary days. Annie had never taken any of those drugs. She didn't have to take them to know that what she was feeling now was good enough to bottle. She held her hand up to the sky and spread her fingers so that the stars shone through like threads of light. She could understand why native peoples had thought looking into the night sky was like looking into the face of God. The Shuar tribes in Ecuador used mind-altering native plants to induce religious intoxication. It would appear that Margaronas could be used for the same purpose.

"Anne Louise!" Mel shouted. "Come join us!"

"I'm coming."

It was under a sky such as this that she'd had her first orgasm.

"Are you okay, Annie?"

"Yes."

She stood up slowly, gingerly, and brushed the sand off her back. She walked along the beach toward the dancing light and when she reached the fire, Mel stuck her foot out and pushed an empty beach chair toward her.

"Tell us a story, Annie," she said. "Tell us a story about you and Mitchell that we don't already know."

"Yes, Annie, tell us a story."

"Make something up if you have to."

The moon rose over the sea, snared in a netting of stars. Annie shook her head. "You know all my stories," she said. "There's nothing left to tell."

WINTER OF
1982

Chapter 17

~~~~~~~~~~

Annie had been stalking Professor Ballard for several weeks, although if he was aware of it, he gave no sign. He was, after all, accustomed to the attentions of his female students. Annie, waiting outside his office, had on numerous occasions witnessed a young woman exiting from behind the dark oak-paneled door, her eyes bright and her face flushed with color. Annie made up one fraudulent excuse after another to see him. She had several times shown up for office hours only to find him gone and a note taped to his door that read *Come on in. Back in a minute.* Rather than discouraging her, she found these moments alone in a room where he spent so much of his time exhilarating. She was like a pilgrim on a visit to a holy shrine. The room smelled of mildew, old books, cigarette smoke, and something indistinct but undeniably male. *Sex,* she supposed. (Although Professor Ballard was careful never to copulate with his students in his office—he was far too cautious for that, as she would eventually learn.)

She had taken his class her senior year because she was three English credits short and she had thought the class, entitled *Romantic Litera-ture: Invention and Transformation of Genres from the French Revolution to the Ascension of Queen Victoria,* sounded easy. She wasn't particularly fond of English lit, although she liked grammar well enough. The diagramming of sentences had always been rather fun for her, as rational and deliberate as the lines of an algebraic equation. She had come to that first lecture class prepared to find nothing more than boredom, so she had been unprepared when the small, ordinary-looking professor broke into the opening lines of "La Belle Dame Sans Merci." He had a loud theatrical voice, deep and rather pleasant to the ear, and when he read, "O what can ail thee, knight-at-arms, alone and palely loitering?" there were very few in the crowded lecture hall who didn't sit up and take notice.

Annie sat there stunned and open-eyed while the beautiful words fell around her like fairy dust. By the time he started in on "I met a lady in the meads, Full beautiful—a faery's child," she was leaning forward in her seat, her eyes fixed on the professor as he strode back and forth across the lecture stage like a magician. He was a small, only moderately attractive man, but when he stood in front of them and read "and there I shut her wild wild eyes so kiss'd to sleep," what did it matter? The girls sighed and rested their cheeks against their hands. Byron had been born with a clubfoot and Keats had suffered from tuberculosis but what female heart could resist a poet?

She went home and practiced reading Keats's beautiful lines aloud in her room but there was something flat and uninspired about her delivery. There was something in Professor Ballard's delivery that made the lines exciting, passionate, and Annie could hardly wait for the next class.

When Sara saw her reading *Songs of Innocence and Experience* she asked, "What class are you taking?"

"Romantic Lit with Professor Ballard."

"That old letch. Make sure you don't go into his office without taking a friend along. At the very least, keep the door open."

Annie ignored the rumors about him because she didn't believe they were true and, later, because she didn't *want* to believe they were true. By then it was too late anyway.

Losing her virginity to Mitchell Stites at homecoming of her sophomore year turned out to be, in hindsight, a disaster. Whereas he'd been rather tentative at first, by Thanksgiving break he'd become a bit more enthusiastic, and by Christmas break he was like a ten-year-old with a brand new minibike. By the time she came home for summer vacation she could hardly get him to do anything else. Once he realized Annie was on the Pill and there'd be no repercussions, no squalling babies or homicidal parents to contend with, Mitchell took to sex like flies to roadkill. His words. There was nothing of the romantic poet about Mitchell Stites.

She hadn't realized what a problem the sex thing was until the first semester of her senior year, when she'd begun to moon over Professor Ballard. Having become accustomed to regular sexcapades over the summer, Mitchell saw no reason that he should have to go without once Annie returned to school. So he planned a visit to Bedford every other weekend, a schedule that left Annie exhausted. It wasn't the act itself that tired her out but the masquerade of pretending that she enjoyed it. Which she did, in a way. It was very sweet the way Mitchell was always coming up with ways to keep her interested. "Hey, honey, let's try this one," he'd say, pointing to a well-worn copy of the Kama Sutra he'd picked up in a Memphis porn shop. "It's called the Congress of a Cow."

Despite Mitchell's best efforts, Annie was finding it harder and harder to maintain any enthusiasm for his weekend visits. She began to make excuses for why he shouldn't come: *I've got a big test next week* or *I've got a paper due* or, when all else failed, *I've got my period.* Having become obsessed with Professor Ballard, she couldn't think of Mitchell the same way and she definitely couldn't think of sex the same way. She couldn't think of having it with Mitchell although she had no trouble imagining it with Professor Ballard. The positions of the Kama Sutra, which Mitchell had unsuccessfully tried to introduce her to, filled her imagination as she and Professor Ballard moved through the intricate postures like well-trained acrobats. During class, while studying at the library, when walking across campus, it was all she could think of. Sometimes at night the images drove her from her bed and she would wander the dark house like a ghost, looking for something to clean.

Once during class he said something funny and she laughed loudly, too loudly, drawing his attention. His eyes, dark and liquid, fell on her for a moment, seeking her in the crowd. Returning his gaze, she felt lightheaded and slightly nauseous. After that she began to dress for him (she was pretty and had a small, trim figure) and she would feel his eyes upon her as she entered the lecture hall each Tuesday and Thursday morning. By the first week in October he had learned her name and called upon her often in class, by Halloween he had touched her arm furtively in his office, and by Thanksgiving they were having lunch in some out-of-the-way Mexican restaurant in town and plotting their first rendezvous. It happened so quickly and so effortlessly, Annie was amazed. One minute she was sitting in Professor Ballard's office blushing furiously as his fingers brushed her arm, and the next they were sitting in a public restaurant discussing their attraction for each other as casually as if they were discussing whether to order the El Cid chili or the fiesta tamale pie. A girl more experienced than Annie might have taken his obvious ease at seduction as a warning sign but all she could think about was the way his dark eyes had flashed when he read "Ozymandias" in class.

He had her get a room in some shabby, out-of-the way place called the Cherokee Chief Motor Lodge. She paid cash and called him with the room number. When he came in forty minutes later smelling of aftershave and cigarettes, she was suddenly as shy as a virgin bride. He sat on the foot of the bed and pulled her to him, and she allowed him to undress her like a limp marionette. Now that the moment was here, she was uncertain exactly what she should do. All she ever had to do with Mitchell was lie there.

But Professor Ballard had a few tricks up his sleeve. First he gave her a massage to relax her, and then he kissed her in places that made her blush to think about, and then he did something with his tongue that she had heard about but never actually thought possible (it was). By now she was feeling a whole lot more relaxed and was even beginning to enjoy herself. When he came up for air she bit him lightly on the shoulder and moaned.

"Oh, Professor Ballard," she said.

He slid his hand up between her legs. "I think you better call me Paul," he said.

Chapter 18

~~~~~~~~~~

Breaking up with someone she still loved was turning out to be a whole lot more difficult than Mel had originally thought it would be. She had decided they should break up gradually over senior year so that they would both have time to get used to the fact that they'd be heading off in different directions come June. She had imagined it as a slow, painless process. She had pictured them going on as friends but J.T. was having none of that.

"Don't expect me to be there for you during one of your little moments of crisis," he said bitterly. "It's all or nothing. Either you love me or you don't."

Mel didn't think it was that simple but she wasn't about to be blackmailed. She wasn't sure what he meant by *moments of crisis* but it probably had something to do with her brother, Junior, whom she never talked about and didn't want to think about now. "It's nothing then," she said, and walked off. It was a cold sunny day in mid-January and there were patches of snow everywhere on the frozen ground. She walked home across the campus, down wide, tree-lined streets where children played behind white picket fences. Melting snow-men decorated the lawns like sentries, and here and there Christmas lights still twinkled behind plate-glass windows. The sky was blue and cloudless.

Mel plodded across the frozen ground and tried not to think about J.T. It infuriated her that he could be so unreasonable. She had been hinting at this separation for weeks, warning him that she planned to go off to New York the minute she graduated. And he was finishing up his second year of graduate school and would be looking for a job soon (although not in New York, she hoped). They had been together for three long years and it was time for a break. Not a forever separation, just a break. She had been willing to continue their relationship this last year of school just as before, as long as he understood that she would be leaving for New York in June. But he had misunderstood her, or refused to believe her, and had gone on blithely this morning about them "taking some time off this summer after graduation to backpack around Europe." They had been sitting in the campus coffee shop, The Boot, and Mel had paused with a steaming cup of organic Guatemalan halfway to her lips.

She put the coffee down and folded her arms on the table. "I'm going to New York this summer," she said evenly.

He seemed puzzled at first but then he relaxed and said, "Okay, okay, we'll go to New York."

"Not us. Me."

That had started the argument that had raged all morning and into the afternoon, when Mel finally walked off. They had both missed their morning classes, which neither could afford to do (Mel was taking eigh-teen hours this semester in order to graduate in June), and had sat in The Boot all morning arguing and drinking endless cups of coffee. Finally, at noon, they had risen stiffly and walked to the Duck Pond, where they con-tinued the fight until both sat, drained and weary, on a bench beneath a spreading oak tree. The trees were bare against the winter sky, and the snow here was deeper, drifting in rock crevices and beneath shady stands of mountain laurel. The pond was empty of ducks and vegetation, reflect-ing the landscape in mirror image.

It wasn't that she didn't love him—she did. But you could love someone and still crave distance from them at the same time. At least she could, al-though he seemed to be having trouble with the concept. She had hoped they could behave like eighteenth-century courtiers, distant and polite, but the truth of the matter was, their relationship had always been stormy, filled with violent arguments and bitter recriminations.

It was a wonder it had lasted this long.

They had planned their annual Howl at the Moon Party together but Mel hoped, in light of their recent breakup, that J.T. wouldn't show up. It had been two weeks since their argument at The Boot and he had called twice. The first time Mel refused to talk to him, and the second time she took the call but they argued and she hung up on him. He hadn't called since. Mel hadn't seen him on campus although Sara had run into him at one of the local bars, *Drunk out of his mind,* she'd said, looking at Mel as if she was entirely to blame. Mel had already explained the situation to Sara and she didn't feel like talking about it anymore.

"I just hope he won't show up at the party," she said. They'd originally planned on going as Jack and Wendy Torrance from *The Shining,* and it was too late to come up with another costume. Besides, Lola and Annie were going as the creepy twins from the same movie, dressed in matching blue dresses with white stockings, black Mary Janes, and white bows in their hair. Sara was going as Danny, complete with a pageboy wig, overalls and a Big Wheel tricycle. The party had started out as a Mardi Gras affair and had quickly evolved over the years into a costume party with an occult theme, kind of like a cross between Mardi Gras, Halloween, and the Voodoo Ball.

The day of the party Lola, Annie, Sara, and Mel rose early to decorate and make the food. It was something the four of them had always done together, since freshman year anyway, and there was a great deal of chatter and a generally festive atmosphere as they hung fake spiderwebs and Mardi Gras beads, and draped the dining room in black cloth and Bela Lugosi cutouts. Mel made a pitcher of zombies and they spent the afternoon drinking and baking Witches' Fingers, Spicy Bat Wings, Brain Pâté, Corpse Salsa and Chips, and Green Ghoul Dip. Losing herself in the festivities made it easier for Mel to forget the breakup with J.T., the memory of which closed over her at times like a shroud. She'd be going along happy and contented and suddenly she'd hear his voice in her ear saying, *You'll never find anything like we have,* and she'd know with a clear certainty, like a dead weight in her bowels, that he was right.

So what? Life wasn't about perfection. It wasn't neat and tidy. It was about loss and longing. Emily Brontë had known that when she wrote *Wuthering Heights.* That was how Mel thought of herself and J.T. now, like Cathy and Heathcliff doomed to loneliness, to regret, to forever seeking the return of that one perfect love. It was depressing and romantic and so hopelessly *true.* Mel figured the tragic feeling would engender at least one future novel, maybe not as perfect as *Wuthering Heights,* but compelling nevertheless. Hopefully a *New York Times* bestseller.

"There," Annie said, putting the finishing touches on a plate of deviled eggs that she'd made with olives to simulate eyeballs. She'd used carrot shavings for the eyelashes, and the effect was startling. "Do you think I should make some of those little ghost sandwiches?"

"I think we have enough food," Mel said.

"We never have enough food," Sara said. "We always run out."

It was true. The party had grown over the last few years from a small get-together in a dorm room to an affair with close to one hundred guests. "Well, you know what? Those who want to eat will have to get here early." Mel poured herself another zombie. She was already half-buzzed. Another zombie or two and she wouldn't have to think about J.T. Radford at all.

"You can't invite people and then not have anything for them to eat," Sara told Mel, wiping her fingers on her jeans. She was busy wrapping a brie in a puff pastry that she had decorated with thin strands of dough to look like a spiderweb.

"Sure you can. Besides, half the people who show up aren't even invited."

"Go ahead and make those sandwiches," Sara said to Annie.

They'd been arguing all morning. For days, really, ever since Mel broke up with J.T. and Sara ran into him in the Bulldog Pub. It was just like Sara to take J.T.'s side even though they'd hardly spoken more than a few words to each other in the three years Mel had dated him.

They heard the front screen door slam and a moment later Lola came dancing into the room, dressed in her costume. They'd sent her to the store earlier to pick up a keg and a bag of ice but she came in carrying nothing but a bleached human skull. "Look what I found!" she said, holding it up like a trophy. She looked like a little girl in her black Mary Janes and white stockings with the big bow stuck in her hair.

Annie looked like a little girl, too, only a dangerous one. She was chopping the crusts off a loaf of Sunbeam bread with a meat cleaver. "Careful," she said, putting her elbow up to keep the dancing Lola at bay. "I'm using a sharp instrument here."

Mel took the skull from Lola. It was life-size but made of plastic. "Where'd you get this?"

"One of Briggs's fraternity brothers stole it from the drama department. They did *Hamlet* last spring."

"Stole it?"

Lola frowned. She stuck one finger under the edge of the floppy bow and scratched. "Well, borrowed it," she said. "We can give it back when we're through." She took the skull from Mel and went into the dining room, where she placed it in the center of the table between two tall black candelabras. Mel stood in the doorway, watching her.

"Did you get the ice?"

Lola lifted her shoulders under her ears and put her fingers over her mouth like a little girl who's been bad but knows she's adorable anyway. "Oops," she said.

"Never mind. We'll get someone else to go. Did you get the keg?"

"Briggs is setting it up out back." Lola clapped her hands, having already forgotten about the ice. She looked gleefully around the decorated room and did a little dance on the tips of her shiny patent-leather shoes. "Oh, look at the King Cake!" she said.

"Thank your mom for us, will you?" Mel said. Maureen ordered King Cakes for her friends and family every January from a bakery in New Orleans. Her great-grandfather had been one of the founding members of Comus, and it was her way of keeping family traditions alive. Lola donated her King Cake every year to the party; whoever got the Baby Jesus won a door prize. This year's prize was a quart of vodka.

"You better get ready," Annie said to Mel. She pushed her way through the doorway with the tray of deviled eggs in her hands. "People will start showing up any minute." She set the tray down on the table and stood back to admire her handiwork. Looking at Lola and Annie standing there side by side in their matching dresses and white tights, Mel grinned.

"Hey, girls," she said. "Do your thing."

Lola clasped Annie's hand and they made their faces go blank. In deadpan voices they said in unison, "Danny, come play with us. Come play with us, Danny."

"Okay, now that's just creepy," Mel said.

Lola said, "Not as creepy as J.T. carrying an ax and saying 'Here's Johnny!' " She'd said it without thinking, of course. She leaned over and rearranged a bowl of M&Ms to cover her embarrassment. Mel and J.T. had been a couple for so long it was hard to think of them as anything else.

Mel gave her a wan little smile. The feeling of melancholy she'd carried all day had faded to a dull ache. The zombies helped. She thought suddenly of Junior. The last time she had talked to him he had been calling from a pay phone in Memphis. He was homeless and she could hear him shouting, *Get away from my stuff! Get away from my stuff*! and then the phone went dead. She never talked to him again.

"Maybe I can carry the ax," she said to Lola. Every man she'd ever loved had disappointed her in some way. The trick, she'd learned, was to disappoint them before they had a chance to do it to you. "It might be kind of funny if Danny's mom turns out to be the homicidal maniac." She shouted to Sara in the kitchen, "What do you think, Danny? Should I chase you around with an ax?"

"Sure," Sara said. "I can see you doing that."

Lola had painted two little spots of color on her cheeks but Annie had no need of rouge. Her face had a feverish quality these days; she went everywhere with her eyes glittering and her face flushed with color. Twice Mel had asked her if she was coming down with something, laying a cool hand on her forehead, and both times Annie had jumped as if pierced with a needle and said, "No! Nothing's wrong! I feel fine!"

Mel put it down to problems with her love life. Annie had neglected to tell Mitchell about the party this weekend, she had begun to duck his calls on Wednesday nights, and it was just a matter of time, Mel knew, before she broke up with him for good. Everyone but Annie seemed to see it coming, although exactly what it was that they were feuding over seemed unclear. Mitchell had probably forgotten to roll up the tube of toothpaste correctly when he visited last time. Annie would not be an easy woman to love, and Mel felt sure she'd never find anyone who loved her as completely as Mitchell seemed to.

Sara came into the room carrying what remained of the pitcher of zombies. She passed out plastic cups from the sideboard and poured the drinks. "Cheers," she said, and everyone lifted their glasses. "Here's to our fourth and last Howl at the Moon Party."

"No, don't say that!" Lola cried. "It sounds so final."

"It is final," Sara said. "This time next year we'll all be someplace else."

"Try not to be so fucking pessimistic," Mel said. "You're spoiling my buzz."

Sara sipped her drink and made a face. "Speaking of buzzed," she said. "What's in this?"

"Apricot Brandy, pineapple juice, and rum." Mel held up four fingers. "Four kinds."

"Four kinds of rum?" Lola said. "I did not know that." She looked amazed and happy. The white bow drooped over her ear like a gardenia.

Mel ticked off the rums with her fingers. "Heavy-bodied rum, light Puerto Rican rum, and heavy Puerto Rican rum."

Lola sipped her drink and held it tightly against her chest, licking her lips. "What's the fourth kind?"

Mel grinned and looked around the room. "Red rum," she said.

"Jesus," Sara said.

"You're welcome," Mel said.

Annie, who'd just gotten the reference to *The Shining*, snorted. "Red rum," she said. "That's funny."

Chapter 19

~~~~~~~~

Lately Mel had taken to wearing berets, smoking Tiparillos, and talking in a husky voice like a bad Marlene Dietrich impersonator. Sara knew then that J.T. was hanging by his fingernails. Everyone else had been shocked when Mel called it off but Sara had seen it coming; no one knew Mel the way she did. Not even J.T. Least of all J.T.

Sara supposed it probably had something to do with Mel's brother Junior, who'd OD'd in a flophouse in Memphis in late October. Mel hadn't seen Junior in three years but when she got the news, she shut herself up in her bedroom for two days. When she came out, she wouldn't talk about him at all. But she'd been different since then.

J.T. had been surprised by Mel's vehement refusal to discuss her only brother's tragic death. He seemed bewildered that Mel could close off her emotions so well, could shut her heart away like a magician closing the lid of an intricate Chinese box. This bewilderment would, of course, ultimately be his downfall. You would have had to witness Mel's childhood to know why she did what she did.

"Why won't she talk about it?" J.T. asked a week after Junior died. He and Sara were sitting out on the porch on a rainy evening in early November, long after Mel had stalked into the house, slamming the door behind her. Sara sat on the porch swing, her arms wrapped tightly around her knees, and J.T. sat on the top step, his back against one of the pillars. A golden light fell cheerily from the front windows, slanting across the porch floor and illuminating his face.

"You need to stop pushing her," Sara said. "If she wants to talk about it, she will. Don't try to force her."

He shook his head stubbornly. "It's not healthy," he said. Rain dripped from the eaves and glistened along the asphalt road. From time to time a car would pass, its headlights bright in the swirling fog. "If she doesn't get it off her chest it could make her sick."

"Oh, come on."

"Not now, but later. People who don't express their emotions have higher rates of cancer and heart disease."

She figured this statement had more to do with his hurt feelings than it did with worrying about Mel's health, so she said nothing.

Two weeks later Mel began wearing berets and smoking Tiparillos in preparation for her new literary life in New York, and Sara saw the writing on the wall for J.T. She should have been happy that he was finally going to get a taste of what she had been suffering for the past three years, but she wasn't happy. She was too tenderhearted to enjoy the suffering of others. She had worn her infatuation for him like a hair shirt, secretly and penitently. She had hidden her feelings over the years by dating other boys (although never for very long), sometimes double-dating with Mel and J.T. In all that time they had only had two real conversations. The first time was when J.T. found out Sara was an English major and they had argued over *The Madwoman in the Attic,* with Sara taking the side of Gilbert and Gubar, and J.T. holding with Bloom's more Oedipal interpretation of nineteenth-century literature.

The second time was at a drive-in movie in the spring of Sara's junior year. She and a boy named Bart had double-dated with Mel and J.T. for a showing of *Barry Lyndon.* It was intermission and Mel and Bart had gone to use the rest rooms. Sara was snuggled down in the backseat of J.T.'s car while he sat in the front, with his arm stretched along the seat between them.

"What do you think of the movie?" he asked her, staring at the screen, which showed a picture of a box of popcorn with facial features and two stick legs. The popcorn had a cloud swelling out of its box-head like a tumor. Inside the cloud it read, *Hot buttered popcorn! Get your hot buttered popcorn now at the concession stand!*

"Excuse me?" She wasn't used to being alone with him and she was nervous.

He turned around and leaned against the door so he could see her more easily. "What do you think of the movie?"

It was a balmy evening in early May. The windows were rolled down and the scent of newly mown grass was in the air. Children played on a rusty swing set erected beneath the wide screen, or ran laughing between the endless rows of automobiles.

"I love Thackeray, but *Vanity Fair* is my favorite novel."

"Okay," he said, smiling as if he found her slightly comical, "but what do you think of the movie?"

She forced herself to look at him. "I think it's interesting the way Kubrick framed his opening shot almost as if it were an eighteenth-century landscape painting. The dueling figures are so small, so insignificant. It's as if the landscape takes precedence over the people."

He tilted his head, listening intently. "And the way he shoots it with the zoom lens makes it feel two-dimensional, almost like an oil painting."

"Yes."

He looked down at his T-shirt, smoothing it across his chest. He was tall, probably six feet two or three, but in the enclosed space of the car he seemed larger. "You know, you're an interesting girl," he said, as if this had never occurred to him before.

She didn't know what to say. She turned her head and studied the brightly lit concession building and the crowd of people standing in line outside the door. Mel and Bart were nowhere to be seen. "What's keeping them?" she said.

"It's funny because in *The Shining* Kubrick likes to use the tracking shot to keep up with the action, but in this movie he seems to prefer the long shot. Everything is so still, so carefully arranged."

"I guess that's what makes Kubrick a genius."

"Right." His hair, straight and lit with strands of gold, framed his face. He pushed it carelessly behind one ear and stretched his arm out again along the back of the seat. She could see strands of red-gold hair glinting there and she wanted to touch it, to stroke his arm like she would a small, soft animal. He said, "Did you see *A Clockwork Orange*?"

She colored slightly and looked away. "I tried to see it but it was too violent. I had to get up and leave in the middle of the 'Singin' in the Rain' rape scene."

He laughed and dropped his hand over the seat, patting her knee in a friendly manner. Her knee jumped of its own accord, as if it were rigged to an electrical current. It was the first time he had ever touched her. He leaned over to fiddle with the radio and Sara pulled her legs up under her, trying to hide her embarrassment. After a moment she said, "It was the same in *The Exorcist*. I put my hands over my eyes and ears and kept them there through most of the movie. My date was so mad he'd paid for a movie I never saw, he made me walk home."

J.T. shook his head. "Nice guy," he said.

"Not really."

He leaned against the door again, his fingers tapping lightly against the top of the seat. His face was turned toward her, half in and half out of the shadows. "So why do you do that?" he said.

"Do what?"

"Go out with guys who aren't good enough for you."

She looked at him to see if he was joking but he seemed serious. She said, "I don't know what you're talking about."

"Yes, you do." He stopped tapping with his fingers and pointed with his thumb at the concession building behind them. "Like that joker Bart."

"He's a nice guy."

"Is he?"

The color deepened in her face. "Maybe I should ask you before I go out with anyone," she said stiffly. "Maybe I should clear it with you first."

He laughed suddenly. "Maybe you should," he said.

They could hear Mel and Bart returning to the car, whooping and laughing in the darkness. Mel threw open the door and the dome lights came on as she slid in beside J.T., pulling the door shut behind her. She looked at him and then at Sara. "What's going on?" she asked.

"Nothing," he said, leaning to peer at the cardboard tray she held in her hands. "What'd you bring me?"

"A chili dog," she said.

Bart slid in beside Sara and shoved a popcorn bag at her. "Here," he said. "We'll share it. And the Coke, too." He was from California, his father was an entertainment lawyer, and he was tall and blond and talked like a Laguna Beach surfer. He was one of Briggs's fraternity brothers and this was their second date. The first had been to a fraternity semiformal in Charlotte, where he'd gotten so drunk that he passed out under a ballroom table and Sara had to spend the night in Briggs and Lola's room.

The movie came back on and J.T. turned up the volume on the little speaker box.

"This movie sucks," Bart said. He slumped down beside Sara on the seat.

"It's pretty slow," Mel agreed. J.T. said nothing, slowly chewing his hot dog.

"I like it," Sara said, shoving an elbow in Bart's ribs to get him to move over. "I think it's a masterpiece."

"I think it's a masterpiece," Bart said in a loud falsetto voice. Mel snorted and glanced at him over her shoulder, and he grinned and squeaked, "A masterpiece!"

"Why don't you shut up so we can hear what's going on?" J.T. said.

"What?"

"You heard me."

Bart stared despondently at the back of J.T.'s head. He wasn't used to being told to shut up. Back at the fraternity house, he was the life of the party.

On the screen Barry was vowing never to fall from the rank of a gentleman again while the narrator informed them that Barry would eventually die alone and penniless. Caught up in the swelling score of Handel's Sarabande in D Minor, Sara sat there sad and bewildered, trying to ignore Bart, who was now halfheartedly attempting to stick his hand down her pants. J.T. was right. She only dated men she knew were beneath her. But why did she do that, why did she constantly sabotage her few chances at romance? The answer, of course, was sitting in the front seat of the car, chewing on a chili dog.

As if reading her thoughts, he turned suddenly and glanced behind him and their eyes met. She was so startled she moved slightly, spilling popcorn all over the seat.

"Smooth move, Ex-Lax," Bart said.

Sara scooped up handfuls of the popcorn and threw them out the opened window. Bart picked up kernels and began to toss them at Sara, and when that didn't get her attention, he leaned over and tried to drop them down the front of her shirt.

"Stop it," Sara said.

"Stop it," Bart mimicked, grinning.

J.T. swung his arm over the seat and clamped his hand on Bart's arm. "Stop," he said.

"Hey, man, take a chill pill," Bart said, pulling himself free. "I'm just having a little fun here."

"I need to go home," Sara said. "I'm not feeling well."

J.T. and Mel stared at each other.

On the way back to the ATO house, Mel and J.T. got into a big argument. Sara put the window down so she wouldn't have to listen. Bart was quiet on the ride home, huddled into his corner on the far side of the backseat, and when they got to the frat house he got out of the car and went inside without another word.

Chapter 20

~~~~~~~~~

Mel was in the kitchen mixing another batch of zombies when the phone rang twice and then stopped. They could hear her shouting, "Who is this? Goddamn it, stop calling this number! I've put a trace on this line and the cops know who you are!" They heard her slam down the phone and then she appeared, red-faced and shaking, in the doorway.

"Was it our obscene caller?" Lola said, all excited that they might have their very own pervert stalking them.

"He's not really an obscene caller because he never says anything," Sara said.

"Who says it's a 'he'?" Annie asked nervously.

"Two rings and then a hang-up. Two rings and then a hang-up. I tell you he's driving me crazy."

"I wonder if we really can put a trace on the line," Sara said.

"No," Annie said quickly. "I don't think they can do that. Not like they do it on TV anyway. It's probably just some old lady who dials the wrong number and then hangs up when she realizes her mistake."

"Well, she's been making the same mistake for about six weeks now," Mel said.

"Hey, did y'all get those Japanese lanterns hung up in the backyard?" Annie asked, pushing past them into the kitchen. The party was about to begin and she could see Briggs and his fraternity brothers through the kitchen window, helping themselves to the keg out back.

The other three followed her into the kitchen. Sara looked at Mel and grimaced. "Oh, shit," she said. "The lanterns."

"I'll help," Lola said, twirling around so her short blue dress stood out around her slender thighs. *She looks better in this dress than I do,* Annie thought despondently, looking down at her own blue dress and black Mary Janes. She was too short to carry this look off, and she wondered now why she'd let the rest of them talk her into it. She was always letting herself be talked into one thing or another that she didn't want to do.

She waited until they had all gone out into the backyard to hang the lanterns and then she went over to the kitchen phone and called him back.

"Hey," Paul said. "I'm staying at a house not too far from you on Decatur Street. Two-oh-one Decatur."

"Whose house?" Annie said.

"A friend. A colleague. He's in London at a conference."

"We're having a party tonight. It's set to start any minute."

"Come on. Just for a little while."

"I can't."

"Please."

"I can't."

"Come on, baby. I miss you."

"I'll be there in five minutes," she said, and hung up.

It was a code they'd worked out. He would call twice and hang up and she'd call him back at his office. She never called him at home. She didn't know whether or not he was married. He'd never said and she'd never asked. But she could guess. His freshly laundered clothes. His unlisted home phone number. Actually she did know—there was no use lying to herself—but she didn't want to think about it. She didn't want to think about him having a wife and children and another life separate from theirs. She didn't want to think about Mitchell waiting faithfully for her back in Howard's Mill, waiting patiently for their life together to begin. It was all too much; the weight of it, the guilt, would crush her if she let it. So she didn't. She told herself she wouldn't think about it today. She'd think about it tomorrow.

She walked along the deserted street, her black Mary Janes clacking on the shining pavement. Evening was falling. In the little houses lining the street, lights were just coming on; families were sitting down to dinner. Annie walked along, peering at the brightly lit windows, calling softly to the dogs who barked behind the picket fences, heralding her passing. This block was more family-oriented, unlike the block where she lived, which was crowded with large Victorian houses rented mostly by students.

Ahead she could see his car parked in the driveway of a small yellow cottage. She stopped to catch her breath, feeling the cold for the first time. She had come without a coat, shouting to Mel in the yard that she had to run over to the campus to pick up something at the library before it closed. She slammed the door before Mel could protest and hurried out the front door, hoping they wouldn't follow her. The party would be in full swing before she got back.

She went up to the front door and knocked, feeling foolish in her little blue dress, wondering what he would say when he saw her. The light from the porch lamp cast a spindly yellow glow, turning her white stockings tan. She heard him moving in the house, saw the front curtain swing slightly, and then the door opened. He was standing just inside, out of the circle of light cast by the lamp. The house behind him was dark.

"Well, look at you," he said, pulling her inside. He closed the door behind her and locked it. "Did you dress up for me?"

"No, silly, for the party," she said, putting her head back to be kissed. He ran his hands up under her dress and then said, breathing heavily against her ear, "Not yet. Let's have a glass of wine first." He took her hand and led her through the darkened house to the kitchen. They bumped into furniture, giggling and jostling each other, and once he said, "Damn, there goes my stiffy." She laughed because that's how it was between them, it was all just one big joke. Nothing serious was ever discussed. When she was with him she was different, she was *Free and Easy Baby.* That's how she thought of herself. No one knew her quite the way he did. No one knew this side of her, this part that wasn't real, this fantasy she had built to make herself more attractive to him. She was funny and slovenly and nothing bothered her, not the unwashed sheets they slept in, not the dirty kitchenettes they cooked in, not the cold or the damp or the mosquitoes they camped among. In the beginning, it was all about the sex. It was still about the sex but now it was about the fantasy, too. The truth was, she liked *Free and Easy Baby* better than she liked herself. She liked that he'd turned her into someone else. It wasn't love, but it was close.

He reached the kitchen and flipped on the switch. The sudden bright light made her shy. She blushed and looked at her Mary Janes, now scuffed and muddy from her walk. "I should have changed," she said.

"No," he said, his eyes passing slowly over her. "I like you like this. I'm surprised we haven't thought of this before." He put his hand on her breast and kissed her again, a long, deep kiss, and then he went to pour the wine. She crossed her legs and leaned against the dishwasher. When he touched her she could feel it in the pit of her stomach like a jolt, a sudden firing of axons and sensory receptors. Until she met him, she hadn't known what an orgasm was. Nothing she had ever been able to do herself, nothing poor Mitchell had been able to accomplish had ever come close to what Paul Ballard was able, so casually yet so skillfully, to do.

Their meetings were always hurried; he was always late for a class or on his way to run an errand. She imagined him calling to his wife as he left, *Do you need anything at the store? I'm going out for milk,* and then rushing to meet her at the Cherokee Motel before stopping at the convenience store on his way home to pick up a carton of milk and a newspaper. Twice they had gone camping. On the first trip he'd gotten sick and they'd spent the weekend miserably huddled in a tent under a steady downpour, and on the second trip he'd called home from a crossroads store in Linville Gorge, and learning of a sick child, he'd packed up the car and driven them home a day early. They always met at seedy motels or in mildewed tents, or several times, in the backseat of his car. They'd never met in a house before, in someone's home, and looking around the cheerful kitchen with its gleaming countertops and glass-fronted cabinets, Annie felt odd. As hard as she tried, she'd never been able to imagine the two of them in a setting like this, engaged in the mindless details of an ordinary life. The truth was, she'd never be able to trust Paul. There'd always be the girls in his classes, the girls like herself, to worry about.

"You're quiet tonight," he said, handing her a glass. He never called her by her name. He always called her *Baby.*

She sipped the wine and stifled a fake yawn. "I'm tired. We've been working on the party all day."

He slid his arm around her and kissed her hair. He smelled of cigarette smoke and aftershave. "You don't have to leave tonight," he murmured against her ear. "We've got the whole place to ourselves."

She looked up at him. "What about you?" she said.

He shrugged. "They're not expecting me" was all he said.

This is wrong, Annie thought, but he was already kissing her.

He took her hand and pulled her into the living room, leaning to switch on a large television. "It's almost time for *Magnum, P.I.,*" he said, nuzzling her neck.

"I have to get back to the party," she said. "Lola and I are going as the creepy twins from *The Shining.*"

He stared at her and then let go of her hand abruptly and walked back into the kitchen to get the bottle of wine. When he came back in he pushed past her and sat down on the sofa, stretching his legs out on the coffee table. He wore a sulky expression now and stared morosely at the flickering television screen. "If you have things to do with your little friends, why don't you run along?" he said.

"It's just that we planned it weeks ago. We do it every year."

"Go ahead, then. I understand."

"Don't be mad." She sat down beside him and threw her arm across his chest, resting her chin on his shoulder.

He ignored her, staring at the screen. "Go on," he said.

"No." She threw her leg over and climbed up on his lap, straddling him so he couldn't see the set. He pretended to have X-ray vision but Annie saw the muscles around his mouth relax. He sipped his wine and looked at her.

She smiled, and when that didn't work she said, "I've been a very naughty girl." She put her wine down and slowly unzipped the back of her dress. She slid off her Mary Janes and stood up and stripped off the white stockings. Then she climbed back up on his lap. He was smiling now, running his free hand up her thigh.

"You're always a very naughty girl," he said, putting his glass down on the table. "That's part of your charm." He grabbed her and rolled her under him on the sofa and she squealed and squirmed the way he liked.

He took his time, aware that he was keeping her from the party. She tried not to think what Mitchell would say if he could see her now. She tried not to think of her parents or her grandparents or the pastor down at the Harvest Hollow Baptist Church. All she could think about was his mouth and the weight of his hands against her skin.

Nothing else mattered.

Chapter 21

Briggs's fraternity brothers were the first to arrive, of course. Mel stood at the kitchen window watching them swarm around the keg like so many yellow jackets around a cider bowl. She said, "Lola, go out there and tell them not to drink all the beer before the party even gets started."

"I'll tell them," Lola said. "But it won't do any good."

"Tell them to go buy their own damn keg."

Lola was almost to the door when she turned and said, "Where's Annie? Where's my creepy twin?"

"Yeah, where is Annie?" Sara said, coming into the kitchen with an empty tray. Their guests had begun to arrive. They could hear loud shouts and whoops from the dining room.

"She went to the library," Mel said.

"Why?" Sara said. She was wearing coveralls and a pageboy wig. The original idea was that she would ride a Big Wheels into the party just like Danny in *The Shining*. But the party was already getting crowded and Sara's Big Wheels was parked on the front porch, so no one really got *The Shining* connection. Most people just seemed to think she was a farmer.

"Maybe she was meeting someone," Lola said innocently, smoothing the front of her dress.

Mel turned around from the window. She cocked her head and stared at Lola. Sara came up on the other side of her so they stood shoulder to shoulder. "What do you mean?"

Lola colored slightly and chewed her lower lip. She raised one eyebrow and shrugged. "I don't know what I mean," she said.

"Do you know something we don't?" Sara asked, narrowing her eyes suspiciously. "Has Annie told you something she hasn't told us?"

"No," Lola said.

Mel was quiet for a moment, considering her answer. "I think she had to pick up something for a class," she said finally. "Something at the library."

Sara nodded as if she found this reasonable. "She wouldn't do that to Mitchell," she added. "Cheat, I mean."

"Yeah." Mel turned again to the window. "Besides, who else besides Mitchell would put up with her?"

Lola hurried out the back door. Mel watched her cross the yard to the keg where Briggs and his rowdy fraternity brothers had taken up their stations. Briggs put one burly arm around Lola and pulled her close. One of the boys gave her a beer. "I hope they don't drain the keg before everyone else gets here," Mel said.

"I better check the table," Sara said. She picked up a couple of bags of chips and went out.

Mel turned and followed her into the crowded dining room, nervously looking around for J.T. She hoped he wouldn't come but there was a chance that he might. It would be just like him to show up and ruin the party.

The room was packed to the rafters, and most of the guests were in costume. She stepped around The Incredible Hulk, said hello to a Pet Rock and a couple of disco dancers, and pushed her way through a group of Symbionese Liberation Army soldiers who, along with Patty Hearst, were laying waste to the dining table.

"Yo," someone said behind her.

It was Bart, the guy Sara had dated, briefly, their junior year. He'd let his hair grow out, and Mel hardly recognized him. She hadn't seen him since

that night at the drive-in when he'd made a pass at her outside the concession building and J.T., as if sensing this, had threatened to kick his ass.

"Bangin' party," he said, smiling down at her. He was better-looking
than she remembered, tanned and blond.

"It's just getting started," Mel said, glancing around the room.

"So where's the keg?" Someone had put the Allman Brothers on the
stereo and "Statesboro Blues" reverberated off the walls.

"It's out back," she shouted. "Hopefully your fraternity brothers haven't
sucked it dry."

He laughed, leaning in close. "No guarantees there," he said. "Do you
want a beer?" He was dressed like a Sandman from *Logan's Run.* All of
Briggs's fraternity brothers had dressed like Sandmen.

Mel lifted her glass and smiled. She liked him better with his hair grown
out. "No thanks," she said, wishing now that she'd worn something a little sexier than her Wendy Torrance costume.

"What's that you're drinking?"

"Zombie. There's a pitcher in the kitchen if you want one."

"Thanks, but I'll start with beer." He leaned over and said, "Don't go
anywhere," and, grinning, pushed his way through the crowd toward the
back door.

Mel watched him go and thought, *Why not?* She wasn't going steady
anymore. She wasn't wearing anyone's brand. She was free to do whatever
she wanted, even if it meant sleeping with the entire ATO house (not that
she would, of course). After all, the more experience she got, the better
writer she'd be. That's what she told herself these days, anyway. She held
her drink above her head and pushed her way through the crowd toward
Sara, who was standing beside Bette Midler, looking nervously down at
the table.

"At this rate we'll run out of food by nine!" Sara shouted.

Mel shrugged. "Oh well," she said. "Hey, do you remember that guy
you dated a few times—Bart?"

"The douche bag? Yeah, I remember. What about him?"

"He's here."

"Great."

"So I take it you never really liked him?"

Sara stared at her for several beats. "Doi," she said.

"Okay," Mel said, moving on. "Just making sure."

• • •

By ten o'clock the party was in full swing. The food was dwindling but the keg was still flowing. Sara made her way through the crowded house and into the backyard, where Briggs and his fraternity brothers were busy doing keg stands and whooping it up. A group of giggling Delta Gammas stood around watching them. Their parties always wound up like this, with the Greek crowd clustered around the keg in the back and the dopers and Goths swarming the front porch. The two groups touched, sporadically, but they never actually mixed. It was one of the most annoying things about Lola dating Briggs Furman, the fact that he and his ATO storm troopers were always crashing their parties. Briggs was a great-looking guy, smart and well connected, but he was a complete asshole and he always treated Lola like she was nine years old. *No, Lola, I don't want you to go out drinking with the girls* or *No, Lola you can't go to that U2 concert* or *Go in the house and change, Lola, I don't like what you're wearing.* Lola was so sweet and kindhearted she'd put up with just about anything, but sometimes Sara wished Lola wasn't so quick to let herself be treated like a doormat. Then again, who was she to talk?

She pushed herself through the giggling Delta Gammas toward Briggs. "Ex-cuse me!," one of the girls said. "The line starts back here."

"Oh, yeah? Well, this is my party so I don't have to stand in line."

"Bogus," the girl said.

The Japanese lanterns shed a festive light, illuminating the bare trees and tall shrubs that ringed the yard. A pale sliver of moon hung from the winter sky. A series of high temperatures the week before had melted most of the snow, which was good because they'd been able to set the keg up in the yard. Usually this time of year, they were forced to set it up on the side porch, a narrow enclosed space running along the side of the house that they used as a laundry room.

Sara tapped Briggs on the shoulder. He and another frat brother were holding one of the Sandmen up by the ankles while he did a handstand on the keg. Another brother stuck the beer nozzle into the Sandman's mouth. Briggs grinned when he saw her and said, "Yo, Sara, you want to get vertical?"

"I am vertical, Briggs."

"Suit yourself." The Sandmen chanted to ten in unison and now the guy on the keg shook his leg and Briggs and the holder dropped him. He spit out the nozzle, stood upright for a moment, then moved sidewise through the crowd before his knees buckled, and he went down. The crowd roared and Briggs motioned for the next contestant to step up.

"Feel free to go buy another keg," Sara said.

"I bought this one," Briggs said.

"No, you didn't. Lola did."

"Same thing." He grinned and made a dismissive gesture with his hand. "Hey, don't spaz out. I already sent a couple of the guys on a beer run."

"Well, I hope you told them to buy plenty. You and your friends aren't the only guests, you know."

"We're the only guests who count."

"I know it's hard, Briggs, but try not to be an asshole."

"Hey, I'm just being myself."

"Exactly."

On her way back to the house, she met Lola crossing the yard with a plate of food in her hands. "Please tell me that's not for your boyfriend," Sara said sharply. "Please tell me you're not waiting on him hand and foot like a servant. Or a perfect little wife."

Lola giggled and glanced at Briggs, who was busy loading another victim onto the keg. "He's busy right now," she said. "I really don't mind. I really don't mind at all." She backed across the lawn as she was talking, holding the plate up in front of her like an offering.

Sara sadly watched her cross the yard. It was obvious that in Lola's little world feminism didn't exist. Despite her expensive liberal education, Lola would always be what she had been born and bred to be; a good Southern Girl. Sara sighed and went into the house to look for Mel (a not-so-good Southern Girl), stopping in the dining room to replenish a big wooden bowl with potato chips. Most of the special food was gone now and they were down to chips and dips. She pushed through the crowd, stopping to talk to a girl dressed like Linda Blair from *The Exorcist*, who was in her Russian Poets class. It took her a while but she finally reached the front door. She peered through the screen and stepped through, the door slamming loudly on her heels.

She couldn't see Mel anywhere. The porch was hazy with marijuana smoke. An overhead light glowed feebly, casting shadows around the edges, where people clustered in groups of twos and threes, sitting on the balustrades or cross-legged on the floor. Someone had pushed a speaker up to the window screen, and the Eagles were singing "Hotel California." The mood here was mellower, less frantic than the keg stands going on out back.

"This bud's for you," a curly-haired boy said, handing her a joint. She took a couple of hits and passed it on. Out in front of the house a guy dressed as Mad Max was pedaling her Big Wheels up and down the sidewalk shouting, *I'll get you, Toecutter!* She turned to go back in, but as she did, something in the shadows at the other end of the porch caught her eye. She stopped suddenly and stood very still, staring. Mel and Bart were sprawled in the porch swing, making out.

She stood there watching them with a kind of sick fascination. The crowd swirled around her like smoke, parting from time to time to reveal Mel, obviously drunk, sprawled across Bart's lap. The whole scene was sickening and false, and made Sara feel mildly dirty, like a voyeur at a peep show. She thought of J.T. Radford drinking himself into a stupor down at the Bulldog. Despite all that had happened between them (or hadn't happened between them), she hoped J.T. wouldn't show up to see this.

Annie appeared suddenly on the porch steps, materializing out of the darkness like a ghost. "Where've you been?" Sara asked, as she came up on the porch.

"At the library." Annie pushed past her. Her cheeks were red with the cold and it looked as if she'd been crying; her eyes were pink and swollen.

"Are you okay?"

Annie swung the door open and stepped inside, letting the screen door slam against her heels. "I don't feel well," she said, avoiding Sara's eyes. "I think I'll go lie down."

Sara watched her disappear up the stairs. Everyone's life seemed to be unraveling. If Sara could have fixed everything, if she could have made everyone happy, she would have. But standing there watching Mel make out with Bart, she realized how destructive it had all become. Unfixable. It was a fight to the death now between Mel and J.T., and there would be no survivors. People would get hurt. People would have to take sides. Sara imagined herself pitching between the two of them like a battered shuttlecock.

She put her hand on the door to go in. And then, as if to remind her just how bad things could get, J.T. showed up.

Lola waited until she was sure Briggs was drunk before taking him the plate of food. She had fixed it earlier in the evening and then hidden it in the back of the refrigerator until later. Around ten o'clock she took out the plate, ground up one of her sleeping tablets, and sprinkled it all over the Spicy Bat Wings, Brain Pâté, and Corpse Salsa.

It was a beautiful evening, one of those evenings that made Lola happy, as if the moon, dangling like a jewel above the horizon, and the stars, glimmering in the dark velvet sky, had been made just for her. Coming down the steps to the backyard, carrying Briggs's plate in her hands like an offering to Hypnos, the god of sleep, Lola could feel her heart fluttering in her throat. In another twenty minutes she would be free. In another twenty minutes she would be wrapped in the arms of her beloved.

She passed Sara, who stopped to hassle her about carrying the plate to Briggs. Lola wanted to giggle, to laugh out loud. She wanted to say, *Don't worry, it's not what you think.* She wanted to tell Sara everything, because Lola was bad with secrets, but she couldn't tell her, not yet anyway, not until everything was settled. Not until she was sure her mother and Briggs wouldn't be able to sabotage her plans.

"Where've you been?" Briggs asked irritably when he saw her. He was sitting on a chair next to the keg, watching as the Delta Gammas did their keg stands. He reached for the plate hungrily, sucking on a chicken leg and scooping large portions of the dip and pâté into his cavernous mouth. Lola looked away. She couldn't bear to watch him eat. She couldn't bear the way his eyes glazed, the way his jaw popped and creaked and his blubbery lips glistened wetly. "Answer me," he said. "Where have you been?"

"In the house," she said. "Helping with the party."

He grunted and kept chewing. She wondered how long until he was out completely. She usually felt sleepy within ten minutes of taking the Halcion but Briggs was built like a bull, and she had counted on it taking at least twenty minutes. She had told Lonnie to pick her up at ten-thirty.

"Whoa, Barnett, watch where you put your hands!" Briggs shouted at the keg spotter, who was trying, unsuccessfully, to keep one of the Delta Gamma's skirts from falling over her head. Lola figured Briggs would get sleepy and pass out in her bed (in which case she'd arrive home early Sunday morning and climb in beside him before he woke up) or he'd pass out and one of his Sandmen would haul him back to the fraternity house. Either way, Lola figured she'd have eight hours of uninterrupted time alone with Lonnie. And given her school schedule, his full-time job and weekend music gigs, and Briggs's constant vigilance, eight hours was an eternity.

Somewhere deep in the house, the Eagles were playing. Briggs held the plate up to Lola. "Any more of those chicken legs?" he asked.

"No, sorry, they went pretty fast."

"Goddamn it, I knew those potheads would scarf down the food before we could get to it," Briggs said, scowling. "I don't know why you invite those losers to your parties anyway."

"They're not losers," Lola said. "They're nice."

"I'll have some more of the chips and dip then," he said, holding the plate out to her. She hesitated and then took it. He slapped her fondly on the ass as she walked off.

"And Lo," he called after her. "For Christ's sake get some clothes on. You'll catch pneumonia out here."

And then she was running, flitting through the night like a bird, her black Mary Janes flying through the frosty grass. She had never felt like this before. She was in love and her heart spun in her chest, true and weightless as an arrow loosed from a bow. It wasn't the deep habitual love she'd felt for Savannah, which was warm and comfortable as an old coat, or the dutiful love she'd felt for her mother and father. It wasn't the slight affection she felt for Briggs, more like an obligation than love, really. It was something new and entirely different, something that opened Lola's heart to a world made suddenly large and generous.

Behind her the noise of the party gradually grew faint. Ahead the cozy streetlamps glowed, haloed by the cold night air. She could see Lonnie waiting for her at the end of the street, parked in his old Chevrolet truck beneath the glow of a lamp. His old Chevrolet truck with the camper in the bed, the place where they made hurried love most of the time, their own little honeymoon suite that smelled of dog and paint thinner and fishing tackle.

He saw her coming and flashed his headlights in greeting. She was laughing when she opened the door and threw herself into his arms.

"Hey, Sunshine," he said, grinning and kissing her. It was the first time she'd ever had a nickname and she loved it, even though he'd named her after one of the squaws in *Little Big Man*. "Damn, your cheeks are cold," he said, rubbing his freshly shaved face against hers.

She giggled. "Which ones?" she said.

"Let me see," he said, slipping his hands down the back of her tights.

He was wearing a pair of jeans and an army jacket, and he looked adorable with his gray eyes flashing fire in the dim lights of the radio dial. He had cut his hair, and it fell now in shaggy curls around his ears. He leaned over and started the truck and she snuggled up next to him on the seat. He threw his arm across her shoulders.

The old truck clattered and whined and pulled away slowly from the curb. "How was the party?" Lonnie asked as they passed the house, lit up now like a Christmas tree with the Clash blasting from the windows. There was some kind of ruckus occurring on the front porch. Lola could see the crowd milling around and several dark figures moving back and forth but she couldn't make out any faces.

"The party was boring," she said.

"Why?"

"Because you weren't there."

He was quiet for a few minutes, and then he said, "What did you tell your boyfriend?"

"He was busy drinking with his friends. I didn't tell him anything. Besides, he's not my boyfriend."

"Does he know that?"

"Not yet. But he will."

Lonnie made a soft derisive sound. "I'm not holding my breath."

"I told you, Lonnie, we'll work it out." She didn't want an argument tonight. They had eight hours together, his mother was out of town visiting her sister, and they had the house to themselves. She didn't want anything to spoil their time together. "I love you," she said earnestly and he looked at her and smiled. It was one of the things she liked best about him, his easygoing nature. Nothing ever bothered him for long. Briggs would stew about some imagined slight for days, planning his revenge, but Lonnie just let it all roll off his back. He was bighearted and gentle and patient. The ducks at the Duck Pond had sensed this about him, and Lola sensed it, too. He would make a good husband and father. Lola liked to imagine their life together: a big house bursting with children, her in the kitchen, and Lonnie coming in from work in the evening in his flannel shirt, carrying his paint bucket like a briefcase. Lonnie playing baseball with the children in the yard while she cooked dinner. It would be a happy life. A good life.

They drove slowly through the center of town, darkened storefronts reflecting the blinking traffic lights. The traffic was sparse; there were few cars on the streets this time of night. They drove past the Episcopal

Church, with its lovely stone tower, and the public library, the bakery where Lonnie's mother worked, and the hardware store. They drove past the feed store and across the humpbacked railroad tracks, and now the houses became smaller, more shabby and run-down than the Victorian cottages near the campus. Here and there they passed a lonely house still lit up with Christmas lights. The area was called Tucker Town, and it was the kind of place where Bedford students were warned not to go at night. Lonnie and his mother lived in a peeling two-bedroom house on the outskirts of Tucker Town. She worked as a cashier at the Piggly Wiggly and as a late-shift worker at the bakery. There was just the two of them; Lonnie's father had disappeared soon after Lonnie's birth.

The first time he brought Lola home, his mother had been there, sitting in the front room with her feet up. She was shy, and she seemed embarrassed by Lola's sudden appearance in her crowded front room. "Oh my, I wasn't expecting company," she said, standing up and looking helplessly around the shabby room strewn with magazines and newspapers. She was a small round woman with a careworn appearance and graying hair. She was younger than Lola's own mother, but she looked older, with her stooped shoulders and tired expression.

"It's not company," Lonnie said, laughing. "It's only Lola."

Mrs. Lumpkin, who'd obviously heard about Lola, smiled and stuck her hand out shyly. "How do you do?" she said. "I'm Lonnie's mama." She was wearing bedroom slippers and an apron that read KLEGHORN'S BAKERY— PUT A LITTLE SOUTH IN YOUR MOUTH.

"Hello," Lola said warmly, taking the small woman's hand in both her own. "I'm Lola." The house was only a little larger than Lola's childhood playhouse, except that the playhouse had been decorated by an interior designer and had sported French wallpaper, and the Lumpkin front room had pine-paneled walls and an ironing board in one corner covered in stacks of threadbare towels. The only attempt at decoration was a series of small plates printed with scenes of the English countryside that hung above the cluttered sofa. Lola found the plates oddly touching. She had a sudden desire to bundle up Lonnie and his mother and carry them home with her, not to Birmingham, of course, not to Maureen's cold palatial mansion, but to something a little nicer and more stylish than what they had now, perhaps a brick ranch house on a large tree-filled lot where they could all live happily ever after.

"See, I told you she wouldn't bite," Lonnie said, and Mrs. Lumpkin blushed and said, "Now, hush." She moved some magazines aside on the sofa and indicated that Lola should sit down. "Are you hungry?" she said. "I've got some pecan pie in the kitchen."

"No, mama, we just ate," Lonnie said.

"Pie would be lovely," Lola said.

Lonnie pulled slowly into the graveled drive and stopped. The little house was dark but for the porch light that glowed feebly above the front door. He leaned and pulled the keys out of the ignition. "Honey, we're home," he said softly.

Lola felt a deep trembling joy. He made it all so easy. Loving him was as easy as stepping off a ledge. It was as easy as swallowing a bottle of Halcion and going to sleep forever. "When does your mother get back?" she asked.

"The day after tomorrow." He put his arm around her and pulled her close. "You can stay all weekend if you like," he said, his mouth against her hair. "You can stay forever."

She sighed and played with a button on his jacket. "I wish I could," she said.

"It's up to you."

Lola put her hand up and tugged at his curls. "We have to be careful," she said. She frowned and stroked his cheek lightly. "We can't make any mistakes or my mother and Briggs will figure out a way to stop us."

Lonnie put his head back and stared at the roof. He sighed and shook his head. "How?" he asked. "You're twenty-two. You're legal."

"You don't know them," Lola said. "You don't know what they're capable of."

"Yeah, I keep hearing that," Lonnie said morosely.

Lola pulled his face to her and kissed him. "It won't be long," she said. "It won't be long. I promise."

They had begun making their plans weeks ago. On a cold snowy day in November, two weeks after they first climbed into the back of Lonnie's truck, they had begun talking marriage. Lonnie had called her that night to tell her he loved her. She was huddled in the upstairs hallway with the phone clamped to her ear while just a few feet away Briggs lay stretched out on her bed watching TV.

"I love you," Lonnie said. "I've never felt this way before."

"Hush," Lola said, trying to keep her voice low. It was all she could do not to jump up and go dancing down the hallway. Tenderness swelled her chest, catching in her throat. "I know," she said to him, and all the longing of her sad childhood was tied up in those two words.

She lay in bed beside Briggs that night and plotted her future.

Now that she'd fallen in love with Lonnie, she knew she'd been fooling herself about Briggs. She would never learn to love him. And he would never learn to love her, either, not in the way she needed to be loved. Briggs's love would always be conditional, there would always be strings attached. It would always contain an element of possession. *My car, my house, my wife.* Briggs knew nothing of sacrifice.

Lola would graduate from college in June, and she would tell no one about Lonnie until then. It would be their little secret until after she received her degree and her teaching certificate. Her marriage to Briggs was planned for September, but she and Lonnie would be married soon after graduation and it would be too late for Briggs and her mother to do anything about it then. Lola would need to work initially while Lonnie finished his GED and started his own painting business. There would be many years of hard work, scrimping, and saving before they had enough to start a family.

Lola had no illusions about what her mother, deprived of her dreams of a family dynasty, would do. There would be no money coming from Maureen, no down payment for a small house, no expensive wedding or baby shower gifts, no educational trust fund for her Lumpkin grandchildren. When she died, Maureen's money would go to her favorite charities. She would remain spiteful and bitter until the very end.

But it didn't matter. Lola and Lonnie would be happy. They would work hard and they would struggle but they would love each other and each new baby, born to an already-crowded house, would be a blessing. They would sit together in the cool of the evenings and watch their children play, and Lola would know she'd made the right decision choosing Lonnie.

Her only guilt came from not telling Mel, Sara, and Annie about her plans. She wanted to tell them but she knew she shouldn't. At least, not yet.

Some secrets were best kept.

J.T. was wearing a plaid shirt, a pair of faded jeans, and carrying an ax, and for a brief moment, Sara thought he was here to kill Mel. But then he grinned, and, lifting the ax, said to Sara, "Honey, I'm home," and she realized he was doing his Jack Torrance impression and the ax was plastic. The feeling of relief that washed over her was fleeting but intense. She rushed forward to greet him, trying to insert herself between him and the swing, trying to drag him into the house before he noticed Mel and Bart.

"I didn't think you'd come," Sara said, tugging on his arm.

"Why wouldn't I?" he said. He watched her with an amused expression, letting her drag him up the steps by the arm. Even in costume, he was the best-looking man in the place, which only reinforced Sara's belief that Mel was crazy, or at least suffering from some sort of delusional post-Junior breakdown.

"The beer's in the back," she said over her shoulder.

He pulled his arm away and took her hand instead, and she pushed her way through the dope smokers, dragging him behind her. His hand fit neatly around her own, and it occurred to her that, other than that time at the drive-in when his fingers had brushed her knee, this was the first time they'd ever touched. A little flutter of excitement, like a pinpoint of light growing brighter, pierced her chest. She'd had ample time since that night to reflect on what had happened between them in the car, to wonder if it had been simply a trick of her imagination. The attraction, that moment of trembling possibility, might have been in her mind only. Surely J.T. had given no sign since then that anything remarkable had happened between them.

She could feel him behind her, could feel the solid bulk of his body as she stopped to open the screen door. He leaned forward and grasped the top of the door with his other hand, holding it open for her. She looked up to thank him, and in that moment his eyes shifted to the right just, as if on cue from some unseen director, the crowd parted. Mel and Bart were suddenly visible, sprawled on the porch swing beneath the softly glowing light.

It all happened in slow motion like a movie, like a bad dream. The Clash sang in the background, "London Calling." J.T.'s face took on an expression of stunned outrage, followed swiftly by a fleeting look of sorrow. The smile faded from his lips and his eyes grew sharp and steady. Mel, feeling their weight upon her, sat up slowly and looked around.

"J.T., don't," Sara said, trying to take his arm again, but he was already striding deliberately toward them. Mel saw him coming and began to shout. The crowd parted like actors in a chorus, and now there were only the three of them on center stage, illuminated by the softly glowing porch light. Bart sat very still, like a man who sees disaster coming but is helpless to stop it. His face was covered in lipstick kisses, and he wore a dazed, bemused expression. He seemed uncertain, for a moment, who J.T. actually was, and by the time he realized and began to stand, it was too late. J.T. swung, and in one smooth, well-timed movement, smashed his fist into Bart's face. Bart sagged at the knees, and went down.

Sara pushed herself through the ring of spectators. Bart lay on his back, groaning. His hand covered his bleeding nose, and he held his fingers up toward the glowing porch light as if surprised by the sight of his own blood.

"Get out, get out," Mel shouted at J.T.

Out in the street, a broken-down truck passed slowly, its muffler rattling.

J.T. leaned above Bart, breathing heavily. "You had that coming," he said, and then, rising, allowed Sara to take his arm and lead him away.

They stopped by J.T.'s house to pick up a bottle of tequila and then they drove to Edwards Point. Sara clutched the passenger door of the 1974 Mercury Marquis and tried not to give way to hysteria as the big car roared and bumped its way steadily up the rutted dirt road to the top of the point. J.T. had been drinking steadily, and as they reached the top, he laid on the horn and howled like a madman. Sara, embarrassed, turned her head and tried to ignore him. She had never been to the top of the point. A long, narrow valley lay below them, sprinkled with the lights of Decaturville and Lebanon Cove. A thin sliver of moon, draped in silvery clouds, hung from the sooty sky.

J.T. turned off the engine but left the radio on. "Are you cold?" he asked.

"No," Sara lied. She had left the house without a jacket, wearing only her overalls and a turtleneck sweater.

"Here." J.T. shrugged out of his coat and gave it to her.

"How will you keep warm?" she asked, taking it from him.

He lifted the bottle. "Tequila," he said, taking a long pull.

It was a bad idea, of course. All of it, drinking and driving, being in a car alone with him on a moonlit ridge. It all spelled disaster; but from the moment J.T. walked into the Howl at the Moon party, Sara hadn't been able to think clearly. She had led him away from the party and then she had followed docilely as he drove her recklessly to the top of Edwards Point.

He held the bottle out to her.

She took the tequila and tilted her head, grimacing at the taste. She wiped her mouth on the back of her hand and gave it back to him.

"There's something different about you," he said.

"Me?"

"Your hair."

Oh god, the pageboy wig. She'd forgotten to take it off. She pulled it off now and shook her hair free.

"That's better," he said.

She ran her fingers through her long dark curls, her scalp prickling with the cold. He continued to stare at her, and to hide her embarrassment, she leaned to fiddle with the radio. "Waiting for a Girl Like You" came on. She changed the station quickly.

"That's a good song," he said, lifting the bottle. "Foreigner."

They sat for a while, neither one speaking, drinking and watching the lights of the valley.

He sighed and leaned his head against the window, looking up at the stars. "Sorry about breaking up your party," he said. The apology struck him as funny and he chuckled and took a long pull from the bottle.

"You don't sound sorry," Sara said.

"I am," he said. He offered her the bottle but she shook her head. He slumped against the seat, staring despondently up at the stars and the sliver of pale moon. The bottle of tequila rested in his lap. He hadn't shaved in several days and his lower face was covered in shadow. With his half-beard, his plaid shirt, and his wildly glittering eyes he looked a little like madman Jack Torrance. "Sorry I didn't pop him in the mouth last year at the drive-in when he was being such an asshole," he said, his voice trailing off.

So she hadn't imagined it. There had been something there, something to do with her. (Or at least she hoped it had something to do with her.) She smiled secretly, turning her head and gazing down at the glittering lights of the valley. "Yeah, well, if anyone needed a curb-stomping it was Bart. The guy's a total douche bag."

He offered her the bottle. Now that she was over the first taste, the tequila wasn't so bad. And it left a warm glow in the pit of her stomach, something to be appreciated on a night like this.

"I always liked you," he said.

"Really?" It was the tequila talking, she knew, but it pleased her anyway.

"You were always so quiet. So self-contained. But I could see you had a good heart. Anyone could see that."

"I'm not as quiet as you think."

"Well, you were always quiet when I was around," he said, and she waited for him to catch the significance of this, but he didn't. He tugged on the tequila. She looked out the window at the row of dark trees standing like a palisade against the moonlit sky. "You have a tender heart," he said, as if realizing he might have offended her. "You're self-contained, but in a good way. Still waters run deep and all that."

"Oh, thank you very much."

"You know what I mean."

"Yes."

"But her." He raised the bottle and motioned vaguely toward the valley below. "She has a mean streak a mile wide running through her. Look at how she acted after her brother's death. Look how she broke up with me without a flicker of emotion, as if the last three years never even happened."

He couldn't understand Mel's self-containment and yet the reality was, Mel wasn't self-contained at all. She was only giving him what she thought he wanted. She was as readable as an open book. A postmodern novel, not a classical one. He said he loved her and yet the truth was, he'd never been able to read her at all.

"She has no heart," he said, handing her the bottle.

"She has a heart," she said. "She just doesn't wear it on her sleeve." She took a long, slow drink, then wiped her mouth and handed him the bottle. "To understand Mel, you have to understand her childhood."

"Bullshit! We all had dysfunctional childhoods! That's just an excuse. You shouldn't make excuses for her."

She wrote her initials on the frosty glass. "That's what friends do," she said.

They sat for a long time on the moonlit ridge, until the cold began to seep up through the soles of Sara's feet into her bones. When she couldn't stand it anymore, she stirred and said, "Do you want me to drive?" She looked behind her at the dark, rutted road. With any luck, she'd drunk just enough to take the edge off her fear and not enough to plunge them over the steep embankment to their deaths.

He gazed at her over the rim of the bottle. "Are we leaving?" He sat slumped against the door where he'd sat for the last fifteen minutes, lost in a profound silence.

"I'm cold."

He sat up suddenly and said, "I'm sorry, baby." He leaned over and started the car so the heater would run. Sara stared frozenly through the windshield, still caught up by the fact that he'd called her *baby*. After a few minutes, he switched off the engine. "Why don't you move over here next to me?" he said, patting the seat beside him.

She didn't know what to say to this, so she said nothing, sitting stiffly in the passenger's seat and staring down at the twinkling lights of the valley. He didn't ask again. Tom Petty and the Heartbreakers were singing "Don't Do Me Like That," and he leaned over and turned the volume up.

She stared at the scattered houselights below, twinkling like diamonds against the valley floor. She pulled the collar of his jacket up around her face and his smell enveloped her, a mix of musk and wood smoke and Old Spice aftershave.

After a while he began to talk about Mel. She sat quietly, looking out at the slumbering landscape while he tried to unburden himself of his love, as if by talking about it he could shed it forever. He droned on and on and she let him talk but gradually a feeling of despair and self-loathing came over her, creeping in like the cold. She was nothing more than a witness to their tragedy and guilt. She could have been anything, a stone, a flower, a blade of grass.

He fell asleep with his head in her lap, and as the moon faded and the first faint glimmerings of morning lit the eastern sky, Sara knew she would hang on until June. She would avoid Mel as much as possible and she would not see J.T. at all. She would hang on until graduation, when she would finally be free to go out into the world and begin a life of her own, far away from this one.

After that, she didn't care if she ever saw J.T. Radford or Mel Barclay again.

2005

Chapter 22

~~~~~~~~~~

The morning after the bonfire on the beach, everyone but Lola awoke with a hangover. She got up around eleven o'clock and went into the kitchen to make a big batch of wheatgrass shakes with milk thistle. She carried the glasses around on a little silver tray to the darkened bedrooms. Sara groaned and pulled the covers over her head, Annie lay on her back snoring at the ceiling, but Mel stirred, and eventually rose and followed Lola downstairs, where she sat on the sofa staring wearily at the sunlit beach. From time to time, she lifted her glass and sipped, grimacing.

"Jesus, this is vile," she said.

"Of course it is," Lola said brightly. "It's good for you." She sat cross-legged at the other end of the sofa in her pink satin pajamas, looking very much like a princess.

"How do you do it?" Mel said, squinting at her. Her eyes hurt. Each time she moved them she felt a piercing pain in her temples. "How do you spend a night abusing Margaronas and then look so fresh and lovely the next morning?"

Lola lifted her glass. She shrugged. "Wheatgrass and milk thistle," she said simply.

Sara came downstairs a few minutes later with a bulky blanket wrapped around her shoulders. Her tangled hair rose over her forehead like a feathered crest, and there were crease marks on her face where she'd slept hard.

Looking at her, Mel laughed. "Good morning, Sunshine," she said.

"Fuck off, Mel." She plopped down on the sofa, pulling her legs up and crossing them under the blanket. "I blame you," she said morosely. "You and your damn Margaronas."

Lola frowned like a schoolteacher and asked, "Where's your milk thistle shake?"

"I threw it up in the toilet, along with everything else in my stomach."

They sat for a few minutes, staring out at the sunlit sea. A lone jogger passed by slowly. Farther down the beach, a line of brightly colored umbrellas sprouted from the sand like poppies.

"We should go to the beach today," Mel said suddenly, as if the thought had just occurred to her.

"We should!" Lola agreed gaily.

Sara groaned and put her head back. She had forgotten how hard it was to keep up with Mel. She was not as young as she used to be. She was older but perhaps less wiser, more rigid in body and spirit. Life and disappointment had done that to her.

"If it makes you feel any better," Mel said, "I threw up, too."

"Really?"

"No, not really. I have an ironclad stomach."

Sara pulled her blanket more tightly around her shoulders. "And an ironclad liver to match," she said sullenly.

Annie joined them an hour later, her white hair standing up on one side of her head like a gull's wing. She slumped down into an overstuffed chair, stretching her legs out along an ottoman. Her slippers were pale and puffy, and made her legs look like toothpicks stuck in a pair of marshmallows.

"You know, you snore like a freight train," Mel said to her.

Annie turned her head and stared at her with red-rimmed eyes. "Look who's talking," she said grimly.

"As God is my witness," Sara said, holding up one hand, "I'll never drink Margaronas again."

"Oh, now, Scarlett, don't go turning this into a challenge," Mel said.

"I'll never drink anything again," Annie agreed sullenly. "At least not on this trip. I'm giving my liver a break."

"We've heard that before."

"This time I mean it."

"Milk thistle is good for your liver," Lola said, sipping her shake.

Annie gave Lola a weary look.

"Y'all are just a bunch of pansies," Mel said, swiveling her head back and forth so that her eyes rolled and wobbled in their sockets like runaway marbles. She was determined to put on a brave front. "The Margaronas weren't that bad."

"Oh, yeah?" Sara said, eyeing her morosely. "Well, just so you know, I think I might have had an out-of-body experience."

Lola stared dreamily out at the horizon. Her eyes were soft and blue. "Don't you just love the astral plane?" she said to no one in particular.

Beyond the tall windows, rolling dunes glittered in the sunlight. Great waves of spartina grass swayed and flattened with the wind. Annie roused herself, staring out at the sea. "The Shuar tribes in Ecuador use mind-altering native plants to induce religious intoxication."

"See, that's what I'm talking about," Mel said. "Margaronas are like a milder form of LSD. We haven't been getting wasted; we've been expanding our consciousness."

Sara made a derogatory sound. "The only thing expanding on this trip is my waistline," she said. She got up and went into the kitchen to make another pot of coffee. When it was ready, she poured herself a cup and leaned across the breakfast bar, sipping gingerly. "Where's April?"

Lola stopped playing with her empty glass. She set it down on the coffee table. "I gave her the morning off," she said.

"It was the least you could do," Sara said, nodding at the display of penis-fold napkins that still stood erect in the center of the dining table. "Considering how late we kept her boyfriend up."

"I don't think she minded too much," Mel said, "judging from the giggling coming from the crofter at three o'clock this morning."

"April? Giggling? I can't picture that," Sara said.

"I can't believe I'm the only one who hears what goes on back there."

"You're the only one who cares what goes on back there."

"Hey, I'm just trying to get some sleep. Between Annie's snoring and April's giggling, I'm a little behind."

Annie flipped her the bird. The gesture was awkward and obviously little used. Mel laughed and yawned, spreading her arms expansively over her head. "Maybe we should stay up all night so y'all can hear what goes on out in the crofter for yourselves."

Lola coughed lightly and stared pensively at the sea. Watching her, Sara felt a momentary sadness settle around her. It felt sometimes as if there was a tragedy hovering over Lola's life, a hint of calamity waiting patiently in the wings.

As if to confirm her feelings, Lola stirred suddenly and asked, "Don't you hate it when you're traveling on the astral plane and your little silver umbilical cord gets all tangled up and you're not sure you can get back into your body?"

The room got quiet. Mel broke the silence first, snorting loudly and looking at the ceiling as she laughed. Lola smiled but looked puzzled. "What?" she asked. "What's so funny?"

"You are," Mel said. She rose and went into the kitchen to pour herself a cup of coffee. Two boys on boogie boards skimmed along the beach followed by an overweight golden retriever who ran with a stiff rolling gait. Mel stretched out beside Sara across the breakfast bar. Annie and Lola were busy talking astral projection and Ecuadorian tribal practices. Mel prodded Sara with her elbow and pointed at Lola with her coffee cup.

"Whatever she's on," Mel said, in a low voice, "I want some."

It took them about an hour to get dressed and gather their gear, so by the time they headed down to the beach the sun was directly overhead. It was a hot sultry day with very little breeze. Cicadas droned in the heavy air. The sun glared off the surface of the dunes, with their wispy mounds of spartina grass, and glittered along the pale green sea. They walked in single file along the weathered boardwalk, Lola in front, followed by Annie in a wide, floppy hat, then Mel, with Sara bringing up the rear. Sara was carrying a beach chair and a brightly striped umbrella, and she could feel sweat trickling down between her shoulder blades and dampening the small of her back. It was silly to be wearing a cover-up in this heat—she could have simply worn her swimsuit like Mel was doing—but Sara was still self-conscious about the bulge of baby fat around her waist. *Not that it was getting any better with this trip,* she thought, scowling at Mel's trim, long-legged figure. Mel was one of those people who could eat and drink whatever she wanted and never put on a pound. And it helped, of course, that she'd never had a child.

The sea rose and fell before them like a giant slumbering beast. A pair of distant pelicans, drawn by a school of bluefish, flattened their wings and dive-bombed into the sparkling water. The beach in front of Lola's house was empty, and as they came over the last dune and clattered down the boardwalk steps to the beach, Sara was glad they didn't have much farther to walk. Her arm was numb from the weight of the chair, and the umbrella strap was cutting into the tender flesh of her shoulder.

Mel had suggested that Captain Mike bring the chairs and umbrellas down to the beach for them but Lola, staring out at the sea, had tipped her head and said in a small voice, "He's not here. He left early this morning for town. He had some errands to run." Then she added brightly, still staring at the distant water, "He thought we might like to take the boat out tomorrow to the Isle of Pines for a picnic." She lifted her little hand like a visor so that it hid her eyes and shielded her face from the merciless sun.

If Mel was disappointed that Captain Mike wasn't here to carry their gear she didn't show it. She shouldered the umbrella and chair at her feet and headed out across the dunes, stopping when they got to the wide beach. The hot sand burned their bare feet. Mel, cursing, picked up her gear and sprinted to the edge of the water with the umbrella bumping across her shoulder like a rifle. Lola, giggling, followed her but Annie simply stopped, took a pair of flip-flops out of her bag, and slid them on to her feet. Sara did the same, and then they picked up their gear and strolled down to where Mel and Lola were busy setting up their beach umbrella. They had plunged it into the sand and were busy rocking it back and forth. When it was deep enough, Lola opened the top and they arranged their chairs, towels, and bags underneath. Sara slid her umbrella out of its plastic sleeve and began her own valiant attempts to sink it into the coarse gray sand. She had to admit, it would have been nice to have Captain Mike here to set up for them.

"Do you need some help?" Mel said.

"No, I've got it." Sara opened the umbrella and arranged her chair and gear on the sand beneath the canopy, leaving room for Annie. "I just wish Captain Mike was here to wait on us hand and foot like he did last night."

"You're preaching to the choir," Mel said.

"You know, he's probably hiding out from you." She shouldn't have said it; she wasn't even sure why she had. Sara had a sudden image of Mike fleeing the island under cover of darkness, trying to put as much distance as possible between himself and Mel.

Mel popped the top on a tube of sunscreen and began to apply it care-fully to her arms and chest. "What are you talking about?"

"Last night. You were hanging all over him."

"I was not."

"Yes, you were, and you don't even remember."

Mel grinned. "Well, I remember some of it," she said. She bent over and rubbed the lotion on her legs. "Besides," she said, looking up at Sara from beneath the screen of her hair. "What difference does it make to you?"

"I'm just looking out for April."

"I told you before. April's a big girl. She can look out for herself."

"She doesn't know how devious and underhanded you can be."

"There's the pot calling the kettle black."

Lola clapped her hands. "Oh, look," she cried. "Dolphins!" They looked where she was pointing and saw several thick gray bodies rolling through the shallow water like wheels. The dolphins passed slowly along the beach, their fins glistening in the sunlight, their gay little snouts lifted playfully. Annie pulled her camera out of her bag and began snapping photos. Lola clapped her hands and jumped up and down on the sand in her striped bikini, with her hair loose and tangled about her shoulders. Looking at her, Sara smiled.

Lola looked good today, childlike and happy, not drugged-out like Mel always claimed she was. Sara was not convinced. Mel had a way of seeing things the way she wanted to see them, regardless of how they really were. She had always been like that.

Sara slumped down in her low-slung beach chair and stretched her legs out in front of her.

Lola stood at the edge of the water with her hand shielding her eyes from the sun, watching as the gray glistening bodies rolled slowly out of sight. There was something slightly melancholy about her small figure outlined against the vast sea and the great arched sky. She was smiling, but a lingering sadness seemed to surface from time to time, passing across her face like a shadow. Her moods seemed to shift as often as the weather, and although she was generally sweet-tempered with a bland and sunny dispo-sition, it was these moments of fleeting darkness that gave Lola her air of vulnerability. She was so childlike in her happiness and despair that you wanted to wrap your arms around her, to keep her safe from the dark thing that seemed to lurk at the edge of her consciousness. Still, Lola's manic mood swings had more to do with temperament, Sara felt, watching her, and less to do with drugs. She had always been vague and scatterbrained, even as a girl.

A few feet away, Annie was trying to wrench something round out of a nylon tote bag.

"What in the hell is that?" Mel said, flinging herself down in her beach chair.

"It's a sunproof cabana," Annie said. "I bought it for the boys when they were babies."

"Sunproof? Doesn't that kind of defeat the whole purpose of lying on the beach?"

Annie gave Mel a stern look. Her sunglasses were old-fashioned and too large for her face. They gave her a slightly menacing, insect-like appearance. "Melanoma is no laughing matter," she said. "UV light reflects off the sand. That's why you'll get a bad burn if you're not careful." She tossed the nylon circle into the air and it sprang open magically into the shape of a small, three-sided tent. Sara got up to help her push the tent stakes into the sand, and when they had finished, Annie took her chair and beach bag and climbed inside the small cave-like interior.

Lola began to walk slowly along the beach, following the trail of the rolling dolphins.

"I hope she's wearing sunscreen," Annie said, poking her head out.

"She's got a pretty good base coat," Mel said, closing her eyes and leaning her head back against her chair. "I've never seen her so tan." She had her chair pulled close to the circle of bright sunlight so that her legs were fully exposed.

"We better ask her," Sara said worriedly. "I don't want her to burn. I don't want Briggs getting as mad at us as he was after the London trip where you lost Lola."

Mel opened her eyes and turned her head to Sara. "It was only for a few hours," she said.

"Only for a few hours? I heard Briggs called the U.S. embassy and Scotland Yard."

"She just kind of wandered off. You know Lola. One minute we're standing there looking at shoes in Harrods and the next minute she's gone. We looked for her everywhere and then called the police. A few hours later I had to call Briggs, and he called Lola's mother."

"Is that old battle-ax still alive?"

"Maureen? She lives less than ten minutes from Lola in Birmingham."

"She must be eighty years old by now."

"What difference does it make? She'll live forever. She's too mean to die." There were few women who frightened Mel, but Maureen Rutherford was one of them.

Sara began to rub lotion over her legs in long, even strokes.

"We eventually found her," Mel said. "She was in some pub in Chelsea drinking warm beer and singing 'God Save the Queen' with the locals."

Sara laughed. "That sounds like her." She finished applying the lotion and put the top back on. She looked at the small figure of Lola disappearing along the beach. If she didn't turn soon, Sara would get up and follow her. "I'm just glad she seems to be doing better coping with her life. I was afraid Henry's leaving to go off to college would send her into some kind of downward spiral. But she seems to be handling all that pretty well."

"I still think her happiness is artificial," Mel said. "I still think it's something out of a bottle."

"Well, you should know."

"Hey, I don't take antidepressants. They kill the creative urge."

"What about alcohol?"

"It doesn't."

"I haven't seen Lola take anything," Sara said, shaking her head doubtfully. "Nothing besides the martinis, Margaronas, and wheatgrass shakes. And we've all taken those. She seems happy to me, for the most part anyway. A little moody, maybe. Ditzy, scatterbrained, but happy."

"I think you're just seeing what you want to see."

"And you're not?"

Mel looked at her. Her eyes, behind the dark sunglasses, were unreadable. "What's that supposed to mean?"

"I mean, we all see things the way we want to see them. It makes us feel better about our own lives. Maybe it's your own unhappiness you're projecting onto Lola's life."

Mel laughed, a sharp, clear laugh. "Please don't psychoanalyze me. Don't even try. I'm very happy with the way my life's turned out."

"So if you had it to do over again, you'd make the same choices?"

"Would you?"

"I asked you first." They had wandered off into dangerous waters, where neither one wanted to be. Sara tried to imagine her life without Tom and the kids. She couldn't picture it. She'd been such a feminist in

college, worse even than Mel was now. How ironic that her whole existence should have come to revolve around one man and two children.
"Sometimes you have to settle for the small things," she said fiercely. "It's
not always fireworks and heart-thumping music."

Mel seemed surprised. "But it *should* be fireworks and heart-thumping
music," she said. "Always. You shouldn't settle for anything less."

"Annie did. And she seems happy."

"Does she?"

"I can hear you," Annie said loudly from inside the cabana. "Please
don't talk about me like I'm not even here."

A lone gull hung motionless above the beach, floating on an updraft. A
few feet away a swarm of fat flies clustered around a dead crab lying on its
back in the sand.

Mel put her arms over her head and yawned. "I'm sweating like a whore
in church," she said. "I'm going in." She stood up and walked a few feet
toward the sea, and then turned to look at Sara. "Are you coming?"

"No." Sara stood up, brushing the sand off her back. "I think I'll walk
along the beach and see if I can find Lola."

"Annie?"

"No."

Mel watched Sara until she was just a small figure in the distance. The
day was bright and sunny but their conversation had left Mel with a slight
chill, a feeling of goose bumps rising along her skin. She turned abruptly
and walked toward the sea.

Her life sometimes felt like a badly written movie script: stunningly vi-
sual but lacking in any real substance.

Chapter 23

~~~~~~~~~~

Sara had dated her husband, briefly, when she first moved to Charlotte after college. Six months later he left Charlotte to teach at a prep school in Virginia and she went on to law school. They did not see or speak to each other for nearly three years, until he returned to Charlotte to teach at the college and they ran into each other unexpectedly at a downtown movie theater. They were both with other dates, and the shock of seeing each other with someone else had been too much for both of them. He called her the next day and they agreed to start over. Fresh. No baggage or history. She was simply Sara and he was simply Tom, and that was all they agreed to know about each other.

It worked better than they might have expected. He had mellowed over the three years, he was less prone to bouts of moody anger, and she had come into her own. Law school had been good for her; it had given her confidence and taught her self-reliance. And somewhere along the way she had realized that she was attractive, although how she could have gotten through high school and college

without knowing that was still a mystery to her. It probably had something to do with the fact that she'd spent the first twenty-two years of her
life being overshadowed by the stunning Melanie Barclay. Mel was married now to some guy named Richard, and was living the life of a bohemian writer in New York. Although she and Sara still spoke on the
phone occasionally (this was shortly before the falling-out that would further strain their friendship over the next twenty years), their lives had
begun to move in two very different directions.

"Why do you want to stay in the South?" Mel had asked her the last
time they spoke.

"Because I'm a Southerner."

"There are other parts of the country, you know."

"Nowhere else I'd want to live."

Sara was living in a condo in Southpark then, but six months after running into Tom at the movie theater, she had moved into his house in the
Myers Park area of Charlotte. The house was small; it had two bedrooms
and one bath, but it had a large fenced yard for Tom's Akita, Max, and a
big oak that spread its branches protectively over the house in the winter
and provided cool shade in the summer. They had very little furniture—
they both still had large school loans to pay off—but they painted the
rooms in deep, rich colors and furnished it with garage sale bargains. Five
days a week Sara rose and drove to work and Tom, if the weather was good,
rode his bicycle along tree-lined streets to the college. Every afternoon she
returned home with a feeling of anticipation fluttering in the pit of her
stomach, knowing that he was waiting there for her. She had never been so
happy.

She had decided not to go to work for a large firm after graduation, opt-
ing instead for a two-man operation in a grubby building not too far from
the courthouse. Schultz and McNair. Mike Schultz was a large, friendly
man with a beer belly and a big red face. He was married to Laura, who
played tennis three days a week and spent the other four shopping. His
partner, Dennis McNair, was a loud, moody Irishman prone to episodes of
heavy drinking. He was from upstate New York, and still talked with the
hard, clipped syllables of his youth, even though he'd come south for college and law school and had lived in North Carolina for nearly thirty years.
His wife, the long-suffering Moira, was a quiet little mouse of a woman,
the exact opposite of her bullheaded, slope-shouldered husband. Mike and
Dennis practiced family law, which was a nice way of saying that they were

divorce attorneys, and under the mounting pressure of Reagan's supply-side economics and the layoffs that followed, business was good. Schultz and McNair needed an associate to help with the overload, and Sara got the job not only because of her law school ranking but also because, as Dennis (speaking of their female clients) so sensitively put it, "the skirts will like having another skirt to spill their guts to."

As it turned out, the skirts did not like spilling their guts to another skirt. It wasn't that Sara wasn't sympathetic; she was. And the clients liked her well enough when they weren't being forced to give her the sordid details of their damaged lives. It's just that no woman who's been replaced by a smart, beautiful, self-assured younger woman wants to open up to a smart, beautiful, self-assured younger woman. It was too painful. Sara reminded the clients too much of the trophy wives their husbands had replaced them with. These were women who'd married soon after graduating from college and never worked outside the home a day in their lives. They'd raised children, kept themselves and their houses in tip-top shape, made dinner every night of the week except Saturday, supported their husbands in their wobbly climb up the treacherous corporate ladder, and yet still managed to be served with divorce papers soon after their last child left for college. Where was the justice in that?

The justice, of course, lay in sucking every last dime out of the faithless bastards who'd left them, a job Schultz and McNair were only too happy to help them with. Occasionally the firm represented a wronged husband, but these were still the golden days of alimony and large property settlements, and most of their clients were women.

It didn't take Sara long to realize that she wasn't suited to the cutthroat world of divorce law. Six months into her new job, she ran into Dennis McNair in the small office kitchen. He was standing at the sink, tossing peanuts into the air and catching them in his mouth. She told him about a particularly brutal meeting she'd just had with a client, a pious fifty-two-year-old Baptist Sunday School teacher who wanted her *husband's balls nailed to the courthouse door.* Her words.

"She's being unreasonable about her alimony requests. The husband's lost his job. He can't pay her alimony if he's drawing unemployment."

Dennis caught his last peanut. "Why not?" he asked, chewing.

"I don't know, Dennis. I'm starting to feel sorry for the guy."

"Don't." Dennis waggled a hairy finger at her. "Whatever you do, don't feel sorry for the opposing party." He rooted around in his breast pocket for his pipe and tobacco pouch, an activity he'd taken up recently to help break his two-pack-a-day cigarette habit. "It's our clients you worry about."

"I know," Sara said, wearily pouring herself another cup of coffee.

"Besides, he's the one who ran off with his secretary," Dennis reminded her, loading his pipe with tobacco. "Don't forget that."

Dennis was himself the product of a broken marriage; his father had abandoned his mother and him when he was just nine, and Sara often had the feeling that he was vindicating himself in some way by going after deadbeat husbands. His mother was still a major influence in his life. She was always telephoning him. He called her, fondly, the Succubus. She lived in a nursing home in Florida, and the office receptionist had strict instructions not to put her through any time except Friday afternoon, a time when no clients were ever scheduled. Telephone conversations between Dennis and his mother always involved a lot of screaming and cursing, and usually culminated in Dennis shouting, *"My God, Mother, what do you want from me?"* and slamming down the phone before she could tell him what she wanted. This was generally followed by an evening of heavy drinking. Since these episodes occurred as regularly as clockwork, the sound of a raving Dennis on a Friday afternoon invariably signaled the office that happy hour was about to begin.

Sara had gone out drinking with Dennis and Mike a few times but she quickly learned that she didn't have their stamina. Even after four years at Bedford, where the favorite pastime was drinking, she couldn't keep up. Their favorite watering hole was a pub just around the corner from the courthouse frequented by attorneys, court clerks, paralegals, and other assorted heavy drinkers. The place was a usual stop for most of the cab companies, and Dennis and Mike would leave their cars parked at the office on Friday afternoons and walk around the corner with their arms around each other's shoulders like two Irish stevedores on their way for a pint. If Sara went she might drive them—she never drank enough to risk a DUI—but if she wasn't careful, she'd get roped into being their designated driver for the evening, which meant that she might not arrive home until the wee hours of the morning. She didn't like being responsible for Dennis; he had a bad habit of drinking until he passed out, and that could be anywhere. Once she had dropped him off at home and Moira had come out the next day to find him asleep in the shrubbery. He had passed out on his way to the front door and fallen off the porch into one of her boxwood hedges.

Tom was pretty understanding about all of this but he didn't like her going out and drinking with Dennis alone. If she called him, he would suggest meeting them at the pub, which was never a good idea because Dennis had a tendency to get belligerent after he had a few whiskey sours under his belt. He had a habit of telling people things they didn't want to hear, especially if he didn't like them, and he didn't like Tom.

"Go ahead," he growled at her, late one night. Mike had gotten up to go to the bathroom and Sara and Dennis were sitting at a tall table near the bar. "Go ahead and go home to your long-haired boyfriend."

"Thanks," Sara said, motioning for the cocktail waitress. "That's a good idea."

"What does a girl like you see in a guy like that anyway?" He had his pipe clenched in his teeth and he was attempting, unsuccessfully, to light it.

"Oh, I don't know. Affection, stability, sobriety. Take your pick."

"My point exactly," he said. "A pussy."

Sara laughed. "Just because he's sensitive to my needs, Dennis, doesn't make him a pussy."

"Those sensitive guys make me sick," Dennis said, his tobacco catching light and flaring. He swung his hand, extinguishing the match, and dropped it in an ashtray. "What is he, a poet?"

"He's an English teacher."

"Same thing."

Smoke curled through the bar like low-lying fog. Sara lifted her hand and motioned again for the waitress. The girl nodded her head wearily, holding a tray of beers above her head and pushing her way through the crowd of revelers like a branch trying to navigate a log jam. Dire Straits was on the stereo, singing "Money for Nothing."

Dennis clenched his teeth, holding his pipe in the side of his mouth. "Women always fall for the damn poets." This coming from a man who had supposedly proposed to his wife by writing "Will You Marry Me" in Day-Glo paint on the back of his underwear. Sara looked at Dennis and saw a decent-looking, middle-aged man who had never had much luck with women.

She supposed it probably had something to do with his mother.

When Mike came back from the bathroom, Sara paid her tab, made sure the two of them had left their car keys back at the office, and left. The bartender knew the drill. He would call a cab when they got too rowdy or when Dennis passed out, whichever came first.

It was a cool, rainy night in early November. Leaves clogged the gutters and rose in piles beside the streets. The rain drumming against the roof was a soothing sound, and Sara turned the radio off and drove in silence, listening to the rhythmic slap of the windshield wipers against the glass.

When she got home, the porch light was off but the lights from the front windows glimmered cheerfully. Tom was waiting for her on the porch. He stood up and walked across the yard to greet her, Max running in circles around him, barking and waving his tail. The rain had died to a misty drizzle that drifted around the streetlamps.

"I was beginning to worry about you," he said, holding her raincoat out to her. It was one of their favorite things to do, walk in the rain.

"I'm sorry. I had to babysit Mike and Dennis."

He kissed her. "I should have known," he said. He didn't like Dennis. He was convinced that Dennis was in love with her.

"I needed their help on the Bagley case and they, of course, refused to talk business anyplace but the pub."

"Of course," he said, and she could tell from the sound of his voice that she should have called him.

They walked across the lawn and into the deserted street. The dog trotted in front of them, weaving back and forth across the empty street to bury his nose in the leaves piled in the gutters.

"Believe me, I wouldn't have gone if I wasn't desperate," she added, feeling guilty that she had been so late and he had waited for her.

"You still haven't settled that case?"

"No."

Amanda Bagley's divorce case had dragged on for three long years now and she was getting desperate for a settlement. Her husband was a wealthy physician and his attorney was a sleazy trickster named Hamp Hudson. They had shown up yesterday for a court date and Hudson, a master of dirty tricks and manipulation, had arrived with his client and promptly begun complaining of chest pains. The judge, who was a fishing buddy of Hudson's, had immediately postponed the case.

When she'd told Mike and Dennis, they'd looked at each other for a moment, and then burst out laughing.

"Chest pains," Mike said. "Why haven't I ever thought of that?"

"Cagey bastard," Dennis said, nodding his head in admiration.

Tom took her hand. They walked through the quiet, rain-swept streets, Tom listening while she droned on and on about the Bagley case. When she finished, they walked for a while in silence. The rain had begun again, falling softly against the pavement. "I'm never getting married," she said.

"Don't say that," Tom said.

"I'm sorry. This job makes me cynical." A car passed slowly along the street and they moved to the side and waited, calling to Max. There was a scent of wood smoke in the air, a sweet pungent odor that reminded her suddenly of Bedford. "Is a happy marriage even possible?" she asked, looking up at him.

He turned her around, tugging gently on the lapels of her rain slicker. "Of course it is." Rain collected in his hair and eyelashes. "Look at my parents. Look at your parents. You just have to choose the right partner."

"Is it really that simple?"

"Yes." Behind his head a streetlamp glowed, wreathed in mist.

She wanted to believe him. She was young. She was in love. Anything was possible. Looking up into his face, haloed by the streetlamp, she had a sudden fleeting glimpse of her future: a handful of golden-haired children, a Colonial house behind a white picket fence, Tom standing in the backyard behind a barbecue grill with a silly hat on his head. It was so perfect that for a moment she could only stand there, staring up at him with a look of faint surprise and astonishment on her face.

Tom, noting her expression, asked, "What's the matter? Is something wrong?"

"Nothing's wrong," she said. "I'm just happy."

"Good," he said, kissing her. "I like you happy."

She knew then that she would have to find another job. She could not believe in love, she could not believe in the possibility and promise of marriage, if every day she was rooting around in the sad debris of other people's ruined lives.

Chapter 24

~~~~~~~~

Mel lay on her back on a rubber float, letting the undulating waves soothe her to a near catatonic state. The sun was hot, and after a while she rolled off the float and submerged herself in the cool green water. She floated there for a minute, like a giant jellyfish, then she shot to the surface, careful to push off with just her toes (she didn't like putting her feet down on the bottom; there was no telling what she might step on). She looped her arms over the edge of the float and hung there with her legs splayed, trying to make herself look less like a seal, a shark's favorite food, and more like some oddly shaped but dangerous sea creature. She had seen a television show on the great white, and although the dogfish and tiger sharks that inhabited the Carolina coastal waters were probably less familiar with the taste of seal, you couldn't be too careful. There was something instinctive in the shape of a seal (or a person lying on a surfboard or a float) bobbing across the surface of the water, some inherent prey memory that seemed to trigger an attack response in the shark brain, regardless of the species.

She could see Annie huddled in her little cabana reading, her feet and legs covered by a towel and her head covered by a big floppy sun hat. Farther down the beach, she could see Sara and Lola, two tiny shapes in the distance, trolling the sand in search of shells. They appeared to be walking back toward the umbrellas, although it was hard to tell from this distance.

Mel closed her eyes and lay her cheek on the warm float, letting the waves lift her like a sea anemone. She could fall asleep, if she wasn't careful, and drift away, out past the sandbar and into the open sea. The tides here were fierce and the sandbars treacherous, and remembering this she opened her eyes suddenly and saw that she had indeed drifted several hundred feet down the beach. Annie's little cabana fluttered in the breeze but Mel had only a side view now, she couldn't see Annie, and Lola and Sara were nothing more than two small specks shimmering in the distance like a mirage.

Something brushed her leg and she startled suddenly and put her feet down. She began to walk toward the beach, fighting the tide as it pulled against her feet and legs. She tried to remember the rule for breaking free of a strong current. *Swim parallel to the shore and then come in when the undertow lessens.* If she had been in deeper water she might have been in trouble. On the beach in front of her two children played with their shovels and pails, watched over by their parents, who studied Mel warily as she rose from the sea, dragging her float behind her. A lone beach house stood behind them, smaller than Lola's but nice, and farther down the beach several other houses built to look like fishing cottages clustered atop the dunes.

When the water was only hip-deep, Mel turned and began to walk back toward Annie's cabana. It was good exercise; the tide was so strong here she could feel her muscles straining with each step. It was no wonder the treacherous waters off this coast were littered with sunken ships.

"The *Queen Anne's Revenge* is out there," Sara had said last night as they sat in front of their false bonfire on the beach. "That's Blackbeard's ship," she added, as if she suspected that Mel knew nothing of pirates or history.

"Yes, Fly, I know that." There were times when Sara irritated her almost to the point of violence. And yet still, even now, she was grateful to her. Until she met Sara, Mel had never had a healthy female relationship. She had never had one with her mother. Juanita had provided for her basic needs, scurrying back and forth between the kitchen and her own room like a small, frightened rodent. But there had been no mother-daughter teas, no volunteer room mother, no Brownie leader. Juanita had never offered and Mel had never asked. Mel sewed her own badges on her Brownie vest and tagged along with Sara and Lynnette or made excuses as to why she couldn't attend the many mother-daughter teas that were so popular in those days in the South.

"Blackbeard was a pirate," Sara said.

"Yes, asshole, I know that. I went to college, too." She loved Sara like a sister and yet there were times when she could have struck her. "I've read a few books in my time."

"Really?"

"Yes, really."

"Good books?"

Mel supposed this was an indictment of her own paltry novels, although if she'd called her on it, Sara would've feigned innocence. Sara had always been snooty about what she read. She was always turning her nose up at what she considered the inferior quality of the commercial bestseller lists, always quoting obscure writers no one had ever heard of. Mel hadn't asked her, but she doubted that Sara had bothered to read her last few novels (not that they were bestsellers, of course). Mel had learned not to be offended by this. She knew that snotty elitism never got you anywhere. It didn't make you a better writer or a better painter or a better artist of any kind. All it did was freeze you up with paranoia and self-doubt. Mel had a friend in New York who'd refused to go to art school. She was self-taught and she had a kind of primitive, "flat" style that was all the rage these days. In the beginning, the critics had ridiculed her because she couldn't paint a human face, her subjects were always in profile, but now she sold her work for huge sums and gave art lessons to graduates of Montserrat and the New York Academy of Art.

When she was in front of Annie's cabana again, Mel stopped walking through the water and went back to floating like an anemone. Annie appeared to be sleeping; her head was tipped forward and her book had fallen open on the sand beside her. Either she was sleeping or she'd had a heart attack. Farther down the beach, the shimmering dots that were Lola and Sara separated into two small shapes as they made their way slowly back to the cabana.

Something bumped Mel again and she clambered up on the float on her stomach. *It was probably nothing,* she told herself. Just a tiny fish more afraid of her than she was of it. Just some poor mollusk churned up by the surf.

Still, she kept her toes out of the water.

Mel was a junior in college when she decided to become a writer. Pat Conroy had come to Bedford to give a reading and Mel's American Lit professor had assigned the reading as extra credit. The class was called "The Vicious Circle: The Effect of the Algonquin Round Table on the Literary Landscape of the 1920s." Mel was hooked from the first Dorothy Parker quote she ever read: "My land is bare of chattering folk; / the clouds are low along the ridges / and sweet's the air with curly smoke / from all my burning bridges." She quickly found a copy of *Enough Rope* in the library and followed it up with Parker's short-story collections, *Laments for the Living, After Such Pleasures,* and *Not So Deep as a Well. Big Blonde* was Mel's favorite short story. She read it over and over again, along with some of Parker's literary criticisms (*"This is not a novel to be tossed aside lightly. It should be thrown with great force."*) She typed up *"I shall stay the way I am because I do not give a damn,"* and hung it above her bed where she could see it every morning when she awoke.

Not that Mel had any illusions of becoming as good a writer as Dorothy Parker. She read very few of the "literary" novels that Sara and J.T. suggested she read. Her taste in novels ran more to Elmore Leonard, Tony Hillerman, P.D. James, and later, Carl Hiassen and James Lee Burke, good writers who knew how to tell a good story without boring their readers to death. Pat Conroy talked a lot about writing from personal experience, and there in the darkened auditorium it suddenly occurred to Mel that she could do this. She could become a writer. *Why not?* She would graduate in another year and a half with a degree in English and a minor in art history, and she had no desire for grad school or teaching or working in some dusty museum or gallery. Or, worse yet, moving back to Howard's Mill and taking over Leland's car dealership, a prospect that filled her with dread not only because Leland was so actively promoting it, but also because she was so seriously considering it. (The money would be good and she would be the boss. It would be better than some grubby nine-to-five office or retail job, where she'd have to work long hours for low pay and answer to a hierarchy of pinheaded bosses.)

There had to be another choice. And so on that soft spring evening in early March, listening as Conroy droned on and on about life and art and truth, his words clanging in Mel's head like a discordant fire alarm, she thought again, *Why not?* Now that she had discovered Dorothy Parker, a normal life was unthinkable.

She'd always known she wasn't like other girls. She'd always known she wouldn't settle. Growing up with Leland and Juanita for parents had done that to her, had taught her that independence was the thing that mattered most, that relying on others was for suckers and losers and women with low self-esteem. Sitting in that darkened auditorium, listening to Conroy talk about being a writer was like stumbling across the Holy Grail. The spotlight illuminating him seemed like a sign from God, like the heavens parting and angels descending on golden wings. (Not that she believed in God, or at least not in a personal god; Jehovah had always seemed too much like Leland for her comfort.) But at that moment it seemed like Fate, or Providence, or the Wheel of Fortune, or whatever you wanted to call it had turned, and she suddenly felt like she was on a path that had been laid out for her since the beginning of time. The voice in her head said, *You will be a writer,* and she was filled with a strange, humming energy, as if she'd grabbed hold of a live wire.

She knew then what the rest of Conroy's audience did not, at least those who would never try to put pen to paper. Writing wasn't about telling the truth at all; it was about rearranging truth, stretching it, and warping it to fit some safe and less-chaotic world of the writer's own making. And Mel had been doing that, in one way or another, all her life.

Being a writer turned out to be harder than she'd thought. Thinking up a story in your head and writing it down on paper were two very different things. Her first novel, begun soon after she moved to New York and went to work for the corporate magazine people, was a rambling, disjointed historical tale of a girl growing up on the banks of the Tennessee River during the time of the Indian removal. It was florid and sentimental, and when Mel reread what she'd written she was filled with disgust. Good prose had a certain rhythm, a beat like that found in music or poetry, but it also had a simplicity of language and style. It was this simplicity that Mel was having a hard time capturing.

She put the unfinished novel in a box under her bed and signed up for a creative writing class at NYU. The professor was a big fan of Flannery O'Connor and Lewis Nordan, and under his careful tutelage Mel wrote her first short story, a darkly humorous tale of an estranged son who shoots his redneck father one night over a hand of poker. The story, entitled "Big Dudley Goes Down," was good enough for her professor to suggest submission to the *Tribeca Review* and for her classmates to eye her henceforth with an expression of deep distrust and envy. "How in the world did you ever get the idea for that story?" one of them asked her sullenly. They thought she was a creative genius, but what they didn't know was that she'd grown up a Barclay.

She could do Southern Gothic in her sleep.

It was her first husband, Richard, who suggested that she stop working for the corporate magazine publisher and devote herself full-time to novel writing. This was before they were married, not long after she left her boss, Phil, and moved in with Richard. Her job with the corporate publisher was no longer a certainty, it would seem, and she began to halfheartedly send out resumes.

"Why don't you stop looking for another crappy job and stay home and write?" Richard asked her. He was a film editor who worked at home, and he saw no reason she shouldn't do the same. It helped that he was independently wealthy. Richard was from an old New York family, the kind that owned real estate all over the city. When one of the older members of the clan died, the deceased's real estate was passed on to one of the younger members. That was how Richard and Mel came to live in a brownstone on the Upper East Side. Uncle Chappy had died and the place was empty.

Richard came from the kind of people who owned real estate all over the city but who never had any cash in their pockets. If they needed money, they had to cash in stocks or set up a meeting with the lawyers who handled the family trust. But Richard made a good living as a film editor and they lived mortgage-free so it didn't matter if Mel brought in any income. Letting Richard take care of her meant Mel didn't have to work, and she didn't have to cash the checks Leland sent her either. Being a starving artist had never appealed to Mel. She was too much of a realist to believe that living without money was anything she'd ever want to try.

She began working on her first Flynn Mendez novel, about an obsessive-compulsive private investigator working out of an office in Spanish Harlem. She finished the novel in a little under a year and began shopping around for an agent. The manuscript was a rough draft and it needed a good agent and a good editor to help with the final polish, but

Mel knew the story was sound. She had a pretty unbiased eye when it came to her own work. The novel might not be taught in American literature classes a hundred years from now, but it would be enjoyed by a respectable number of people, if she could just get it into print. There too, Richard was able to help. His family had a lot of contacts in the entertainment business, and that was how she wound up being represented by Gabe Tobler. A three-book contract with a major New York publishing house followed shortly thereafter. She would say in later interviews that her success as a novelist had involved a good bit of perseverance and luck, but she would always know otherwise. Publishing was no different from the rest of capitalist America; it was all about who you knew.

Mel was grateful to Richard for her success, and maybe that's why she agreed to marry him. Or maybe it was her way of getting even with J.T. Radford, of punishing him for his lack of faith and steadfastness. Whatever the reason, she said yes to Richard six months before the novel was set to launch. They were having dinner at Le Cirque and he had arranged for the dessert course, a chocolate souffle, to contain a diamond engagement ring once worn by his great-great-grandmother. His version of the King Cake that Lola's mother used to have shipped in from New Orleans every January, only instead of the Baby Jesus it contained a perfect two-carat baguette in a platinum setting. What else could Mel say but, "Are you sure?"

They were married on a beach in Barbados, attended by a small number of family and friends. The relationship between Mel and Sara was strained at the time (although they would later try to patch up their differences, or at least gloss over them enough to make communication possible), and she couldn't very well invite Lola and Annie if she couldn't invite Sara. She kept the wedding party small, only a few of Richard's prep school buddies and their wives, and an even smaller number of Richard's family. Three weeks after the ceremony, she sent Leland a note and a picture of them taken at St. Nicholas Abbey. It would have been different if her mother and Junior were still alive, but they weren't, and Mel felt no familial obligation to include Leland in her plans. He wasn't needed.

The bride gave herself away.

Her novel, *Death Grip,* came out to modest reviews and managed to sell briskly through the late spring and summer months, before sales began tapering off in the fall. Gabe Tobler took her out to lunch and explained to her that only seven percent of all the books published ever sell more than one thousand copies, and given that yardstick, her book was a resounding success. He spent a great deal of time explaining market shares and target audiences, and encouraged her to look at the big picture—future success would come through a mysterious process called *building a readership*. Mel, halfway through the second novel and mired in the mid-book doldrums, listened quietly and tried not to feel discouraged. Each successive book would build on the buzz generated by the preceding one, Gabe explained. He drew a diagram on a cocktail napkin, an inverted pyramid showing a long line of dollar signs at the top with little arrows meant to indicate expanding sales.

He was a handsome, earnest young man with brown curly hair and dark eyes, and after a while Mel stopped paying attention to the little dollar signs and began instead to pay attention to Gabe Tobler. She had never noticed before how dark his eyes were. Each time he looked at her she felt a little flutter in the pit of her stomach, followed quickly by a sharp stab of remorse. She was, after all, a married woman. And he was her literary agent. Did other novelists, she wondered, sleep with their literary agents?

Good God, what was wrong with her?

She was bored. That's what was wrong. Writing wasn't as much fun as she had thought it would be; it wasn't glamorous at all. It was being shut up alone in an office the size of a closet for six hours every day while all around her life went on merrily. It was endless revisions and rewrites and days when she sat mind-numbed and weary for hours, unable to put a single sentence down. *Where was the fun in that?*

She had thought she'd be famous by now. That's how she'd pictured it. She had imagined herself giving readings for sold-out crowds and appearing on afternoon television shows, where she would charm the audience with her Southern wit and all-American good looks. She had imagined herself making enough money to never again have to take a penny from her father or her husband, but it wasn't like that at all. Although she was making a decent living, she couldn't have supported herself, at least not in the style to which she'd long been accustomed.

"How's the second novel coming along?" Gabe asked her, motioning for the waiter to bring another gin and tonic.

"Good," Mel said. "I'm two-thirds of the way through."

"Really?" he said. "That's great."

She wondered if he was married. He didn't wear a ring but that didn't mean anything these days. She felt a sudden urge to yawn, and put her hand up to her mouth.

"Do you want another drink?" Gabe said. The waiter appeared and stood with his hands resting lightly along the back of a chair.

"Well, I really shouldn't," Mel said. "I'm working."

Gabe shrugged. "Okay," he said.

"Make it a vodka martini," she told the waiter.

She was bored in her career, and she was bored in her marriage, too. Hadn't she always known marriage wasn't for her? Richard was a homebody. He was happy if they went out once a month. He worked in an office on the first floor of the brownstone and she worked in an office on the second. In the evenings they ordered takeout or went around the corner to a little Burmese restaurant. Most days they stayed in their pajamas. They'd only been married two and a half years but already it felt like an eternity.

"Are you married?" she asked Gabe.

He looked surprised and offended at the same time. "Yes, to Carol. You met Carol—at Birdie Boykin's cocktail party?"

She'd been drunk at Birdie Boykin's cocktail party. She and Richard had argued in the cab on the way over, which meant that she had shouted at him and he had turned his face stonily to the glass and refused to speak.

"Oh, yes." She remembered now. A mousy little woman with big teeth and a matronly bosom. Not the type she would have pictured Gabe with at all. And there were children, too. She remembered two gangly boys with huge feet skulking in a corner of the room, spying on the adults.

"You have two sons?"

"Yes. Michael and Sam." He smiled fondly and she was afraid for a moment that he was going to take photos out of his wallet. Thankfully, the waiter came with their drinks instead. Gabe sipped his and said archly, "Of course, you two are still newlyweds."

Oh, God, were they? How depressing.

"There's plenty of time to think about the pitter-patter of little feet."

"The only pitter-patter you'll hear coming from our house is the sound of my fingers striking a keyboard," Mel said grimly, lifting her drink. *The pitter-patter of little feet? Who said things like that?* Instantly, Mel let go of her desire to sleep with him.

"I don't know about that," Gabe said, shaking his head. He grinned at her playfully over the rim of his highball glass. "Richard always said he wanted a big family. He always said he wanted five children."

All the more reason to leave him now, Mel thought bleakly.

Years later, after her second marriage had failed and illness had forced her to forever give up any dreams of children, she ran into J.T. Radford and his family at the Denver airport. She was coming back from a book festival in Santa Fe. It was December, the airport was crowded with Christmas travelers, and she was alone, waiting for a flight. She saw him coming toward her in the crowded terminal, and in that moment before his face registered completely and she recognized him, she thought, *Now there's an interesting face. A good face.* A young girl sat on his shoulders with her tiny hands clasped under his chin. An older child, a son, pressed against his side, staring straight ahead with a kind of strange fierce concentration. J.T. didn't see her sitting there. As he passed she could hear him singing "We Wish You a Merry Christmas" under his breath. The girl leaned over and looked down at her father, and he looked up at her, and there was a look of such intense happiness and devotion on his face that Mel, watching, felt as if a knife was slowly piercing her heart. A female voice called to the boy. It was the boy's mother, J.T.'s wife, coming along behind, and Mel stirred suddenly and turned her face away so she wouldn't be seen. The moment was too intimate, too raw. It lasted less than a minute, and yet in that instant Mel glimpsed what her life might have been, if only she'd had the courage to marry the right man.

Chapter 25

~~~~~~~~~~

By the time Lola and Sara got back from their walk on the beach, Annie had abandoned her shady cabana for the sun. She lay now on a garish beach towel with her floppy hat covering her face and her pink toes pointed at the sky. Mel lay beside her on her stomach, her chin nestled on one hand while the other held Janet Evanovich's newest novel. She was a big fan, and her work was often compared to Evanovich's, although Flynn Mendez didn't come close to generating the sales Stephanie Plum generated. *Oh well,* she reminded herself. *Rome wasn't built in a day. It takes time to build a readership.*

Sara unrolled her beach towel and lay down on the other side of Mel. "Is anyone besides me hungry?" she asked.

"I could eat," Mel said.

"We could go up to the house and make some sandwiches," Lola said, unrolling her towel on the other side of Annie. She sat down, leaning back on her arms and staring pensively at the sea.

"That sounds good," Mel said lazily, sinking her chin on her fist. "That sounds like a plan."

No one moved. The heat was like a drug, soaking through their skin and filling their limbs with a strange lethargy. The steady pounding of the surf was as deep and constant as a heartbeat. After a while Mel dropped her book and dozed, her chin still resting on her fist. Beneath her floppy hat, Annie snored softly.

"I love the ocean," Lola said in a small voice to no one in particular. Behind her an airplane trailed across the blue sky. "I always wanted to live on the ocean."

Mel awoke with a start. She rolled over on her back and flung one arm over her eyes. "Why don't you?" she said in a sleepy voice.

"Yes, Lola, why don't you live here?" Sara sat up and pulled her knees to her chest. She dug her toes in the warm sand until the tops of her feet were covered. "Now that Henry's grown, why don't you just move here?"

Lola stared wistfully at the sea. "Briggs wouldn't like it," she said.

"Oh, him," Mel said flatly, from beneath her arm.

Annie's snores grew louder and Mel groaned and rolled over on her side. She leaned on one elbow and supported her head with her hand. With the other hand, she sifted sand onto the brim of Annie's hat. Annie awoke with a snort and sat up. She took the hat off and began to beat Mel with it.

"Why doesn't Briggs want to live here?" Sara asked Lola. "It's not like he has a nine-to-five office job he has to stay in Birmingham for. You all could live anywhere you wanted to live."

Lola cupped her hands like shovels and buried her feet up to the ankles. "He likes the golf course in Birmingham," she said. "It's one of his favorite courses."

"Let him stay in Birmingham and you move here," Mel said.

Lola laughed nervously and shook her head. "It's complicated," she said.

"It always is." Mel got up on her knees and leaned over to brush the sand out of her hair. "You snore like an outboard motor," she said to Annie. "How does Mitchell stand it?"

"You should hear *him*," Annie said, putting her hat back on her head. She pressed her left thigh with her thumb to check for sunburn and then rolled over onto her stomach. "Besides, you should talk," she said, glancing up at Mel. "You whistle in your sleep."

"Sleep?" Mel said. "What's that? I don't sleep anymore. Who can sleep with all that racket going on out in the crofter?"

"You're the only one who seems to hear it."

"Well, tonight I'll wake you up. They usually get started around midnight."

"I could make some sandwiches and bring them back down to the beach," Lola said, her cheeks pink with the sun. "If y'all don't want to come up to the house."

"No, Lola, don't do that," Sara said. "We'll all go up in a few minutes."

"I'll make lunch," Annie said, without moving. "I'm used to it."

"What, can't Mitchell make his own sandwich?"

"No. Not without making a big mess anyway. Besides, that's my job."

Mel lay down on her stomach again, propping herself on her elbows. She stared steadily at Annie, her eyes unreadable behind the dark sunglasses. "What do you mean, it's your job?"

"I mean, I take care of inside the house and Mitchell takes care of outside."

"So you break up your chores along gender lines?"

"That's right."

"How very June Cleaver of you."

Annie made a dismissive motion with one hand. "June had it right. She knew there were some things men do better, and some things women do better."

"Oh really? Like what?"

"Like cleaning. Like cooking. I don't want Mitchell in my kitchen and he doesn't want me in his barn. He doesn't want me on his tractor, sweating under the hot sun while I mow acres of lawn. There are some advantages to being the weaker sex."

"The weaker sex?" Mel scoffed. "The weaker sex?" She looked around at the others as if to confirm the ridiculous nature of this statement. "Is that why we produce seventy-five to ninety percent of all the world's agriculture? Is that why we have a higher tolerance for pain, because we're *weaker?*"

"Our brains are smaller. Boys are better at math and science than girls."

Mel stared at Annie, her mouth sagging with disbelief. "Who says?"

"Michael Tillman in *Boys and Girls Learn in Different Ways!*"

Mel took a deep breath and let it out slowly. "Okay, Tillman is a *novel-*

ist with a graduate degree in *creative writing.* Is this the guy you want to get your biological gender information from?"

Annie, seemingly unaffected by this, said, "He did brain scans and stuff. Men's brains are bigger than women's."

"Yes, Annie, and men's bodies are generally bigger than women's. What does that prove? Women score the same as men on intelligence tests."

"Let's change the subject," Sara said.

"Don't tell me you don't want to step in here," Mel said to her. "Because I know you do."

"I deal with conflict resolution in my job. I don't want to deal with it on vacation."

"Way to cop out," Mel said.

Fifty feet offshore a school of bluefish turned the water silver. Sara, watching, thought she saw a dark fin, but when she looked again, it was gone.

"What exactly is your job?" Lola asked Sara sweetly, trying to change the subject. She liked conflict even less than Sara did.

"I'm a guardian ad litem, meaning I represent the rights of a child whose parents are going through a particularly nasty divorce and child-custody battle. These children are at risk for depression, academic decline, behavioral difficulties, and future substance abuse. You would not believe what some parents put their children through."

"You see?" Mel said. "Going back to my earlier argument that marriage is archaic and unnatural."

"I can tell you right now, it's the only situation that makes sense for raising children," Sara said. "No child wants his or her parents to get divorced. And I don't care how amicable parents try to make a divorce, the children suffer."

"I have some friends who did it right," Mel said. "They bought houses a few blocks from each other and they share custody and seem to get along really well."

"Well, I don't know them personally but I'll bet if someone had asked their children, they would have said, *Don't divorce.*"

Annie said, "In our parents' day they were more responsible. No one got divorced until *after* the children were grown. Nowadays people trade spouses as frequently as they trade cars."

"I guess I'd expect you to advocate a return to good old Republican family values," Mel said. "Never mind how damaging these situations were to women, never mind the abuse women had to put up with for generations."

"No one's talking about abuse," Sara said quickly. "That's a different matter entirely."

Annie propped herself up on her elbows and stared at Mel. "How do you know what I'd advocate?" she asked coldly. "Who are you to judge me?"

Her response was so unexpected that no one knew what to say. Even Mel seemed surprised. She smiled ruefully and said, "You're right, Annie. Sorry. I shouldn't have jumped to conclusions like that."

Annie put her head down on her arms.

"Anyway," Sara continued. "I represent the child. I research the current living situation and make recommendations to the court regarding custody and other issues affecting the child."

"Wow, that must be depressing work," Mel said.

"Depressing and rewarding." It was only a part-time job but Sara was tired when she got home in the evenings, and (sometimes) depressed. Tom didn't particularly like the effect the job had on her, but he supported her nevertheless. He listened patiently while she droned on about other people's dreary lives, and never complained. He seemed to know that it helped her deal better with the problems in her own life, that it helped her put it all in perspective. "More than ninety percent of the cases where a guardian ad litem is appointed never go to trial."

"And that's a good thing?"

"Yes. Because it means the parents have agreed to be reasonable and consider the best interests of their children." Sara wrapped her arms tightly around her knees and stared at the sea. Out past the sandbar, a wave runner skimmed the surface of the sea, its engine whining. A gull hung motionless above the beach. "I can tell you one thing, though," Sara continued drowsily. "Tom and I will never divorce. At least not while the children are young."

"I'm glad Mitchell and I stuck it out," Annie said in a muffled voice, her head still buried in her arms. "Although it was hard at times."

"Most worthwhile things are," Sara said.

"I guess I'm supposed to feel guilty for going through two husbands," Mel said flatly. She sat up cross-legged, dusting the sand off her knees with the palms of her hands. "I'm supposed to feel guilty for buying in to the women's movement?"

"No one's talking about the women's movement," Sara said. "I'm talking about commitment."

"Besides," Annie said to Mel, lifting her head again. "It's different for you. You don't have children." Annie was sometimes unintentionally cruel even when she meant to be kind.

"That's right!" Mel said brightly, glancing at Sara, who colored and turned her face away. "I don't have children. I'm too selfish and self-centered to ever have children."

"No one said that," Sara said.

"That's what you're all thinking."

"Are you a mind reader?" Annie said. "Tell me what I'm thinking right now."

"You're thinking, *Gee, I wish I wasn't such an asshole.*"

Sara laughed. Annie said, "Very funny."

Lola, who'd sat quietly through this whole exchange, said mildly, "I'm so glad I only had Henry."

No one thought of the significance of this remark until later.

Despite their decision to go in to lunch, no one moved. They continued to lay in various positions of repose against the warm sand while the sun reached its zenith, and began its slow descent toward the western horizon. The surf had begun to move farther up the beach and, from time to time, a large wave rolled in and lapped hungrily at their toes.

"We could play a couple of sets of tennis," Mel said, her voice drowsy with the heat. "After lunch, I mean."

"Tennis?" Annie moaned. "With this hangover? All I want to do is sleep."

"Come on, the week's half over," Mel said. "We don't have much time left. Let's spend it doing something memorable."

"What's your definition of *memorable*?" Annie asked.

"As long as it doesn't involve alcohol, I'm game," Sara said.

"Speaking of games," Mel said. "I've got one." She ignored the others' groans. "Each of us has to tell something about herself we don't already know. Something shocking."

"This sounds too much like truth or dare," Sara said.

"I don't want to play," Annie said.

"Okay, I'll go first," Mel said. She grinned and looked around slyly. "I slept with the twenty-six-year-old UPS guy. The guy who delivers my packages. It was kind of a spur-of-the-moment thing. I didn't plan it. It just happened. It was October, that magical time of year, and I had ordered a bunch of Halloween costumes from an online store and they all came at once. I opened the door and this gorgeous guy in a uniform was standing on my front stoop. It was the first snowfall of the year. Big wet flakes were falling from the sky like volcanic ash."

"Don't embellish it," Sara said. "Don't do that thing writers do. Don't try and make it sound more romantic than it really was—a lonely forty-five-year-old woman taking advantage of a minimum-wage delivery boy."

Mel laughed in a guarded way. It sounded sad when you put it that way, and truthful. It confirmed the feeling she'd had lately that she'd reached some kind of impasse in her life, an overwhelming place of stagnation and regret, not just in her professional life, but in her personal life, too. Once she had been confident and self-assured, but now she spent a lot of time second-guessing her choices.

"Actually," Annie said, "I think you're wrong about the minimum wage. UPS pays pretty well."

"That's not the point!" Sara snapped.

Out past the breaking surf, a narrow sandbar stretched across the water like a carpet. You could walk along it for nearly half a mile, until the tide came in, and then be swept out to sea.

"Lola? What about you?" Mel asked.

"We might have some of that shrimp scampi left," Lola said, still thinking about lunch. "I could make a shrimp salad."

Mel said, "Okay, Annie, how about you? Give us something we don't know."

"Yeah, Annie," Sara said, relieved to be off the subject of the UPS driver. She didn't want to argue with Mel again. Mel couldn't help it that she was the way she was. She'd never had to think about anyone but herself. She'd never lain awake at night worrying over a sick child. She led a life breathtaking in its freedom and simplicity. "Surprise us."

"Tell us something that'll knock our socks off," Mel said.

Annie thought, *Oh, I could blow your socks clear across the beach.* She said, "The women at my sons' school used to call me Q-Tip."

They all turned to stare at her. She sat huddled on the sand with her hat pulled down over her ears like an hombre in a bad Clint Eastwood movie.

Mel snorted. "See, I told you, you should color your hair."

"What do you care what they think?" Sara said. "They don't sound like the kind of people you'd want to be friends with anyway." She smiled sadly at Annie.

"Poor Annie," Lola said.

Mel wasn't giving up. "Look, I can pick up a box of Miss Clairol at the village store. Then we'll go back to the house and have a cocktail and I'll dye your hair."

"I'm not letting you color my hair," Annie said. "Especially after you've been drinking."

"It'll wash out. We'll go with something bright and sassy."

"Forget it. That was years ago. I never see those women anymore."

"My turn," Lola said, clapping her hands with excitement. She had finally thought of something she could share. "Once I charged ten thousand dollars on my mother's credit card and gave it to the United Negro College Fund. She'd given me her credit card to charge some new furniture. It wasn't too long after Briggs and I got married and we were living in that little house over on Chariton. She told me to get some new furniture and new drapes and she gave me her credit card to pay for everything. They had this ad on TV, you know the one, 'A Mind Is a Terrible Thing to Waste.' And I just thought that was so sad, you know. A wasted mind. So I called the number and donated ten thousand dollars." She was breathless from telling it. She put her hand over her mouth and giggled.

Annie smiled at her in encouragement. Mel patted her knee. Sara thought how girlish Lola seemed, how vague and empty-headed, and yet for a swift, fleeting moment she wondered if it was all an act, if Lola wasn't somehow putting them on.

"Speaking of wasted minds," Mel said. "Let's make up a batch of pomegranate martinis to take with us to tennis."

They had no trouble getting a court time. The tennis courts, under the merciless midafternoon sun, were nearly deserted. They parked the golf cart and walked past the Beach Club, past a wide verandah littered with tables and chairs, where a few hardy souls were getting an early start on happy hour, and along a narrow asphalt trail that threaded its way between a collection of scattered courts.

The air was sultry and still. They walked in single file, Lola in front, followed by Sara and Annie, with Mel bringing up the rear. Palm trees swayed above them, catching what little breeze there was, and in tall stands of sparkleberry and wax myrtle, cicadas droned like buzz saws.

"Jesus," Mel said. "I'm sweating like a plow mule. Whose idea was this anyway?"

"Right," Sara said flatly. "What idiot suggested we play tennis?"

Annie swatted at a mosquito. "Why'd they put us down on the bottom courts?" she asked irritably. Already her tennis panties felt damp. Her thighs were chafed from the long walk from the parking lot. She'd tried to lose a few pounds before the trip, but all she'd managed to lose was an inch from her already-too-small waist. She carried all her weight in her hips and rear end; she was a perfect pear. She had what her mother so cheerfully called *the Jameson thighs,* which meant she could diet and ThighMaster for months and still wind up with saddle bags as flabby as jello sacks.

"It was probably A. Lincoln's doing," Sara said. "A. Lincoln probably figured out that Mel was in our party and put us out here in the wastelands to make up for Casino Night."

Mel looked over her shoulder at the imposing Beach Club. She'd learned from experience never to underestimate an enemy. "Lola, whose name did you make the reservation in?"

"Mine."

"He knows who we are," Sara said. "You gave him your name that day on the croquet greens."

Lola stopped and looked at her. "I did?" She was wearing an apricot-colored tennis skirt and top that showed off her tan, and her trim figure, nicely.

"Mel did."

"He's not going to remember the name," Mel said, motioning for them to go on. "Besides, he doesn't know it was me who pulled the dirty trick on Casino Night."

"He's probably got a pretty good idea," Sara said.

They passed two clay courts where a group of senior citizens was playing. "Good day for tennis," one of the men called and Lola called back gaily, "Wheatgrass is good for sunburn!"

"What'd she say?" one of the old men asked his partner.

Briggs had called during lunch and Lola had gone into her bedroom to take the call. When she came out later she looked like she'd been crying. She seemed all right now. She was prancing along as if she hadn't a care in the world, and smiling, although there was something false and brittle about her smile.

They came to a lagoon crossed by a narrow bridge. An alligator slept in the murky water below. They could seem him clearly in the green depths. "Remind me not to go in after any tennis balls," Mel said.

"That's assuming we're ever going to *play* any tennis," Sara said. "That's assuming we're ever going to *reach* the court." She wasn't looking forward to this. She hadn't played tennis in years, not since Adam was diagnosed and she'd dropped out of the Atlanta Lawn Tennis Association. She'd found then that in the overall scheme of things, tennis just wasn't that important to her. There were so many things that weren't important.

"Number Twenty!" Lola shouted, all excited, pointing to the sign hanging against the backdrop. "This is it!"

The other three went out on the court to warm up while Mel got set up. Tennis was a Very Big Deal to Mel. She and Sara had played sporadically in high school and college, but in the last ten years she'd joined an indoor tennis league and now she played twice a week with a group of highly competitive twenty-something career girls. She took a water bottle and a bag of Twizzlers candy out and laid them on the bench between the courts. She took a sun visor out of her bag and performed a series of brief stretching exercises.

When she was ready, she went out on to the court with the others. They played doubles for a while, switching partners to keep it interesting, and then they walked to the bench to take a water break. The shade here was paltry; a tall palm tree cast a slender shadow across the broiling asphalt. In the cloudless sky a buzzard circled endlessly.

"I wish I had a martini," Mel said, sipping from her water bottle. They had somehow managed to talk her out of the pomegranate martinis.

"You can't be serious," Sara said. They all stood around the bench drinking from their bottles.

"I don't think you're supposed to drink alcohol when you exercise," Annie said. "It dehydrates you. You start drinking in this heat, you're likely to drop dead of a stroke."

Mel took a long pull from her bottle, staring at Sara above the rim. She put the bottle down and wiped her mouth. "Pray that happens, girls," she said. "It's the only way you'll ever beat me."

"Don't flatter yourself," Sara said.

"It's the only way you'd ever beat me in singles," Mel said.

Sara picked up her racket. "Okay smart-ass," she said. "Let's go."

Mel put her bottle away and followed Sara out on to the court. Lola sat

down on the bench, absentmindedly bouncing her racket off the toe of
one shoe. Annie called after Mel and Sara, "It's too hot to play singles. Lola
and I didn't come out here to play singles." She looked at Lola for confir-
mation of this statement, but Lola appeared deep in thought, staring
down at her racket. She looked odd. Her head was tilted as if she was listening to distant music, and her lips moved soundlessly.

Annie turned her attention back to the court, where Mel and Sara stood
facing each other across the net. "If I'd known we were playing singles,"
she said in a sulky voice, "I wouldn't have come." She stood there with her
tennis skirt flaring over her hips like a parachute, feeling hot and sweaty
and fat.

"Just three games," Sara said. "Just long enough for me to whip Mel's
ass so we can get on to other things."

"Hey, I'm trying to serve here," Mel said. "Stop talking."

"Who said you could serve first?"

"Sorry. We'll spin it."

"My mouth tastes like yellow," Lola said unexpectedly.

Sara watched Mel intently. She waved her hand and said, "Go ahead.
Serve." She glanced over at Annie, but Annie was watching Lola with a
strange expression on her face.

"Are you sure?" Mel asked.

"Just do it," Sara said.

Mel bounced the ball slowly. She had a killer first serve, although after
that she was just as likely to hit it into the net. She tossed the ball high and
leaned back.

"Rosa's aura is like a peacock feather," Lola said to no one in particular.

Annie frowned. "Who's Rosa?" she asked.

Mel froze with her arm stretched behind her head. The ball dropped
harmlessly to the ground, bounced several times, and rolled against the
fence. She slowly lowered her arms and sighed, tapping the toe of one shoe
repeatedly with her racket. "Girls, I'm trying to serve here," she said with
exaggerated patience.

"Okay," Lola said. She put her racket up in front of her face. "Sorry,"
she said.

Palm fronds stirred lazily with the breeze. The sun beat down on their
heads.

Mel bounced the ball and looked at Sara. "Ready?" she asked.

Sara got serious again. "Ready."

Mel crouched down in position. She tossed the ball high overhead and leaned back into her serve. Everyone waited, watching quietly.

Lola said, "Mel, can I have a Twizzler?"

The ball dropped to the court. Sara put her hands on her knees and looked at her feet. Over on the bench, Lola began to giggle.

Sara won, two games to one, although they went to deuce every game. Mel flung her racket over the fence into a palmetto thicket and had to go in to retrieve it, and after that they played doubles again, Mel and Annie on one side of the net and Lola and Sara on the other. Lola was a good tennis player. She had the long, pretty strokes that denoted a privileged childhood spent in private tennis lessons. She was fine for the first few games, but after a while she stopped playing and stood there looking at the sky or staring at her racket as the ball whizzed by.

"Lola, are you all right?" Sara asked. She was leaning on her racket, trying to catch her breath. She'd just run across the court trying to hit one of Annie's lobs while Lola stood at the net looking at her feet.

Lola was staring at the bottom of one shoe with a look of amazement on her face. "Look," she said, holding her foot up so they could see it. "There's a hole in my shoe."

Sara was reminded of her earlier impression that Lola was putting them on. "Let's take a water break," she wheezed.

"Fine," Mel said. "It's our serve anyway."

They went over to the bench and sat down. The sun had moved in the sky, and the shade cast by the palm had lengthened, so that now it was almost pleasant sitting there. Mel poured water over the back of her neck. Annie and Sara sipped their water bottles. Lola sat down and took her shoe off.

"Lola, what are you doing?" Mel asked. "We're between games." The score was three to two and they were ahead, so Mel had no intention of stopping now.

"I've got a hole in my shoe," Lola said, holding it up.

"So what? Put it back on."

"Okay."

They watched Lola put her shoe back on. The courts were beginning to fill up again, as the late-afternoon sun died and the cool of evening began to glide across the landscape. Courts Sixteen and Seventeen were full, and everywhere now came the steady pleasant *thock* of tennis balls hitting racket strings. Annie stood watching the foursome on Court Sixteen play. The perspiration she had worked up during the warm-up had long since dissipated. Mel was a maniac on the court—she poached balls left and right—and after a while Annie had been content to simply stand on the baseline and hit an occasional lob, a shot Mel steadfastly refused to use. With Lola focused, it had been an intense match, with them going to deuce for the first three games, but now that Lola had lost interest, Sara was having a hard time of it.

The women on Court Sixteen were probably in their sixties and seventies, and they played at a leisurely pace that Annie could relate to. She liked a slow, unhurried game, which probably helped explain her hips and those troublesome Jameson thighs. She wasn't fat, but she was *matronly*, whereas Mel and Sara had somehow managed to hang on to their college figures and Lola seemed to be mysteriously regressing toward girlhood. Whatever heartbreak Lola was dealing with in her marriage, it hadn't put a wrinkle in her face or a single dimple in her thighs, and there was something to be said for that.

Annie sighed and tugged her skirt down over her hips. She wondered what Paul Ballard would say if he could see her now. Would he recognize her if she passed him on the street with her white hair and Jameson thighs? Surely he would recognize the Jameson thighs. But no, when she'd known him her figure had been trim almost to the point of anorexia. She'd been unable to eat when she first met him, which was one of the ways she'd known she was falling in love: a complete cessation of all desires except for one, a general lack of hunger that gradually grew into troubling symptoms of nausea and malaise.

Watching the women on Court Sixteen, Annie tried to remember if she had ever lost her appetite when she first met Mitchell. But that was more than thirty years ago, shrouded in adolescent dreams and desires, and she couldn't remember the specifics now. The mature Mitchell did not like skinny women. He liked his women to have what he fondly called "a little cushion." Even now she had to be careful not to let him come up behind her when she was bent over cleaning a baseboard or scrubbing mildew off the bathtub grout.

"A penny for your thoughts," Sara said, gently bumping Annie with her racket.

Annie flushed. "What?" she asked.

"I think Annie has a secret," Mel said, leaning back with her bottle resting on her thigh. "I think there's something Annie isn't telling us."

"Those women on Court Sixteen just went to deuce," Annie said. Mel was right. Despite the little stories she told them about Mitchell, she knew how to keep a secret. She knew how to keep it safe. She made a place for it, a little nest under her heart. She carried it around inside her like an egg.

"She doesn't want to tell us anything else because she's afraid you'll put it in one of your damn books," Sara said.

"I don't write about people I know," Mel said.

"Sure you do."

"I thought you didn't read my books."

"I never said that."

"Yes, you did. You said you stopped reading my books because you got tired of seeing yourself as the villain."

"Well, there is that."

"And speaking of stories, you're the only one who didn't play the game on the beach. You didn't think I was going to forget, did you? You're the only one who didn't tell us something about yourself that no one else knows."

Annie plucked at the strings of her racket, glad to have the attention off of herself. "I doubt Sara has anything to confess."

"We all have something to confess," Mel said.

"But not Sara."

Sara looked out at the shady court and said quietly, "I once withheld evidence in a child-abuse case. The mother was guilty as sin of other things, but not what she was being charged with, but I didn't want the child returned to her. So I suppressed the evidence that might have cleared her and the child was placed in foster care." She waited, as if daring anyone to say anything. She wasn't even sure why she'd told them. She'd never told anyone before, not even Tom.

Mel stretched her legs out in front of her and looked at Sara with a curious expression. "So in other words, you played judge and jury."

"Yes."

"You have a bad habit of doing that."

Sara said nothing, turning her head to watch the women on Court Sixteen. A pair of gulls hung motionless above them, their bright beady eyes glittering in the sunlight.

"Couldn't you be disbarred for that?"

"Yes," she said.

Lola stood up suddenly and walked off. "Where are you going?" Mel called. "We're not finished yet."

"I have to tinkle," Lola said over her shoulder, waving at them with her racket. She walked with a jaunty step, the hem of her skirt flouncing and swaying gaily.

They watched her walk across the bridge and stroll up the narrow winding path between the courts. "Shouldn't one of us go with her?" Sara said.

"She's all right," Mel said. "She can't get lost between here and the clubhouse."

Forty-five minutes later, Mel pulled her cell phone out of her bag to check the time. "Well, shit," she said. "I guess we're finished for the day."

"Where do you think she is?" Sara asked, zipping her racket into her bag.

"Who knows."

Annie, who'd finally succumbed to the heat and the boredom by dozing off, yawned and stood up slowly. She groaned and stretched her arms over her head. "I'm so sore," she said. "I won't be able to move tomorrow."

"How can you be sore when you didn't do anything?" Mel asked. She stood up and began to pack her gear.

"I can't help it if you're a poacher. I can't help it if you hardly let me hit anything."

"Hey, we were winning, weren't we?"

"You were ahead one game," Sara reminded them. "That's not exactly winning."

"I'm not playing with you again," Annie told Mel. "If we play tomorrow, I'll be Sara's partner. Or Lola's."

"That's assuming we can find Lola."

"Is it my imagination," Mel asked, "or does Lola seem a bit more addled than usual?"

"More addled," Sara said.

"Definitely more addled," Annie said. "She was fine until Briggs called."

Mel stared ahead at the shadowy path threading its way between the courts. "If Briggs calls again, let me talk to him."

"Maybe I should just unplug the phone," Annie said.

"No, don't do that," Sara said. "There might be an emergency."

Mel said, "I think she's taking something. I think she's heavily medicated."

Sara shook her head. "We don't know that. Besides . . ." she began, and stopped.

"Besides what?" Mel asked.

"Nothing."

Annie swung her bag over her shoulder. "But how do we know if she's taking pills?"

"Easy," Mel said, starting up the path ahead of them. "We ask her."

Lola was up in the clubhouse, trying on a tennis skirt. When they came through the double glass doors, she was standing in front of a three-sided mirror, turning back and forth. She seemed surprised to see them. "What do you think?" she asked, smoothing the tennis skirt with her hands. "Isn't it adorable?"

Mel let her tennis bag slide to her feet. She turned around and walked a few paces, stopping beside a rack of shirts and staring fixedly out the plate-glass window. Sara said patiently, "Lola, we've been waiting for you."

Lola's eyes widened. "You have?"

"Yes. For nearly an hour."

"We were right in the middle of a set," Annie reminded her. "Did you forget?"

From the checkout counter, the salesclerk watched them curiously.

Lola stared at herself in the glass. "You were waiting for me?"

"Don't you remember?"

She studied her reflection intently. She nodded slightly. "Yes," she said. "I think I do." Her eyes clouded for a moment but then brightened again. She twirled around on her toes like a ballerina. "What do you think?" she asked, indicating the skirt.

"We were right in the middle of a game," Annie said. "You and Sara against me and Mel."

"That's right," Lola said, nodding her head emphatically. "Now I remember."

"You went to take a potty break."

Lola smiled brightly at them in the glass. "I remember," she said. "Sorry."

Mel turned around and came back. She leaned in close to Lola, and in a low, fierce voice asked, "Lola, are you taking anything? Pills. I'm talking about pills."

Lola stared at her with a vacant expression. She plucked at the skirt. "This is on sale," she said.

"That's right," the girl at the counter said brightly. "Fifty percent off. Everything in the store."

"Thank you!" Mel said, rounding on the clerk. "We're just looking, okay?" She tugged Lola's arm, pulling her into the back of the store. Sara and Annie followed.

"Let's take her back to the house to interrogate her," Sara said uneasily.

"Good idea."

They watched as Lola, seemingly unconcerned by the conversation, went over and began to pick through a basket of tennis panties. "Whatever has happened, I blame Briggs," Sara said.

"No one's disputing that," Mel said heavily.

"You were the one who wanted her to marry that asshole."

Mel gave her a steady look. "I don't recall telling anyone who they should marry."

"You have a short memory then."

Annie stepped between them. "Let's not do this here," she said.

Chapter 26

~~~~~~~~

Annie and Mitchell were married the September after she graduated from Bedford. She had spent the summer numbly planning her wedding, going through the dreary details like a robot. The ceremony was held at the Harvest Hollow Baptist Church in Nashville. Sara flew in from Charlotte and Mel flew in from New York for the occasion. They were Annie's bridesmaids. Lola was still on her three-month honeymoon, being held hostage by Briggs in Europe, so she wasn't able to come, although she did send a telegram from Dublin, along with a large bouquet of white lilies that managed to look, in Annie's eyes anyway, somewhat funereal.

Annie's new in-laws, Preston and Gladys, had given the newlyweds a week in Gatlinburg, Tennessee as a wedding present. They were simple country folk and saw no reason why a young couple would want to honeymoon in a place that offered more extravagant diversions than Hillbilly Golf or the world-famous Christus Gardens. The gardens featured life-size dioramas from the Life of Christ including, among others, the Garden of Gethsemane, the Last Supper, the Crucifixion, and the Angel at the Tomb. Mitchell was particularly enamored of an ancient coin collection on display that featured the Shekel of Tyre, thought to have been among the thirty pieces of silver paid to Judas. Annie followed him bleakly around the gardens, trying to ignore the piercing blue-eyed stare of the many lifelike Jesuses. Her guilt would later become a small thing, a tiny festering sore covered by layer upon layer of scar tissue. But in those early days of their marriage her guilt was a gaping raw-edged wound that bled through the bandages when she least expected it: as she said her vows to Mitchell at the altar, as she listened while Mitchell shyly introduced her as *my bride,* as she watched while Mitchell, teary-eyed, knelt at the feet of a lifelike Jesus in the Garden of Gethsemane.

Unable to stomach another day, Annie, pleading a headache, sent Mitchell off to the Ripley's Believe It or Not! museum by himself. She lay on the round, crushed-velvet bed staring up at her sullen reflection in the ceiling mirror and listening as his cheerful whistle died slowly along the corridor. Over in the corner, the heart-shaped hot tub bubbled like a cauldron.

She couldn't go on like this. She couldn't go on living like an empty shell, a husk, a snakeskin, frail and papery on a sun-warmed rock. She had to get hold of herself. *What can't be cured must be endured,* her mother liked to say. She was a fountain of good advice these days. *It'll hurt a little bit the first time,* her mother had warned her about her wedding night (not knowing that Annie and Mitchell had been intimate for years). *But after that, you'll get used to it.* (As if getting used to it was the best she could hope for.) *It's a sacred union, blessed by God,* she had continued, before Annie cut her off with a curt motion of her hand. She had wanted to tell her mother that she was no virgin, not by a long shot, but she bit her lip and kept quiet. If her mother had noticed anything strange in Annie's behavior leading up to the ceremony, she had, like Mitchell, put it down to pre-wedding jitters.

Annie sighed and rolled over, facing the windows. The drapes were open, and in the blue sky beyond the window the clouds stood in ridges, like rows of carded wool. She imagined the same bright sky stretching above Bedford. She wondered what Paul Ballard was doing now. She imagined him hurrying across the leaf-strewn campus on his way to class, whistling an aria from *Tosca,* his satchel swinging lightly as he walked.

Annie pulled the crushed-velvet covers over her head so she wouldn't have to look at her reflection in the mirror. The acts that had occurred in this gaudy room had less to do with a sacred union and more to do with a Juarez brothel, Annie thought dejectedly. The only thing missing was a trapeze, and Mitchell would have no doubt booked them into the Trapeze Room if it had been available.

Annie had shut her mind to what she was doing and followed his instructions obediently. *Do this, put that here, roll over;* she'd meekly done as she was told until he'd finally said in exasperation, "Damn, honey, could you show a little enthusiasm?"

"I'm tired," was all she'd said, covering her eyes with one arm.

It was true, she was filled with a strange lethargy these days. Even during the long dreary summer as she'd planned her wedding, there had been days when all she'd wanted to do was sleep. Just throw the covers over her head and sleep. Like Rapunzel in her tower. Like Sleeping Beauty waiting for her prince to come and wake her with a kiss. Only in Annie's case, the prince would never come.

Years later she would see Paul Ballard as a slightly ridiculous figure. A middle-aged man with nothing better to do with his life than seduce naive young women. It was predatory, if you thought about it. What was it, Annie wondered, about her generation that made them such easy marks for men like him? She couldn't imagine any of the young women her sons ran around with putting up with any such nonsense from a professor. The way girls were today, *they* would be the ones doing the seducing, and once the affair was over, you can bet the wife would hear of it. There'd be no sacrificial secrecy, no willingness to play a passive victim. This thought cheered her somewhat. She imagined that Professor Ballard was having a much harder time seducing Generation X. These girls, raised on reality television and MTV, would have seen through his clumsy attempts at seduction and betrayal, just as Annie did once she grew older and wiser. They would not have fallen for something as absurd as a dramatic reading of Keats.

She looked him up once, on the Internet, and discovered that he had retired and was living in Oregon. Still married, no doubt, to the wife who had put up with his constant infidelities all those years. Annie had felt an overwhelming pity for her; it was amazing to her now, and sad, that she had ever felt jealous of the wife, that she had ever wanted to take her place.

Eventually the guilt she felt over him merged with the guilt she felt over that other matter, the one she tried never to think of, and there were many

times, as her marriage to Mitchell endured and the boys grew slowly to
manhood, that she thought about confessing. All of it. She thought about
letting go of the secret that nestled now like a small hard tumor beneath
her heart. But then she would look into Mitchell's bland, guileless face and
she would know she could never tell him. She could never regain her faith
by destroying his.

All of this was, of course, many years in the future. By the time her honeymoon ended, Annie had steeled herself for a life without Paul Ballard.
She was in the beginning stages of recovery. She knew it was only a matter
of time before her frozen core thawed and joy returned to her life, and
until then she was willing to blindly follow her five-year plan. That's what
five-year plans were for. To keep people on the right track when all they really wanted was to veer off into dangerous and uncharted territories.

Their first year of marriage, they lived in a little rental house in East
Nashville, not too far from where Annie had grown up. Every morning
Mitchell rose and went off to work at "the store," as he called the restaurant, while Annie washed the breakfast dishes and began her relentless
cycle of housecleaning. Every day the floors and baseboards were mopped,
the cabinets, countertops, and appliances were scrubbed until they shone,
the walls and trim were wiped clean of fingerprints, the laundry was
washed, folded, and put away. Twice a week the bed linens were changed,
and the carpets were dragged into the yard to be beaten and aired. In between her cleaning, she planned her menus, clipped coupons, and had a
home-cooked meal hot and waiting for Mitchell every evening when he
returned home, weary and discouraged, from the store. Every Wednesday
she bought groceries, driving sometimes to three or four stores to get the
best weekly deals, and on Saturdays she worked in the yard. Caught up in
her busy routine of cooking and cleaning, she had little time to think of
anything else, but sometime during the month of December, while hanging a handmade wreath on the front door, it suddenly occurred to Annie
that something was wrong.

She wasn't pregnant.

Her five-year plan called for two children by the age of twenty-five and,
given this time frame, her window of opportunity was quickly closing.
After all, she had stopped taking the pill two weeks before her honeymoon. And frequent sex, she knew, equaled pregnancy. So she was a bit
distressed on this warm December afternoon when, lifting her arms to

hang the wreath, she felt the warm, gushing sensation that signaled the beginning of her menses.

She went inside to take a hot shower and think about this. True, the frequency of their sex life had declined somewhat since their honeymoon but since Annie had assumed that she was already pregnant by now, that hadn't really bothered her. Mitchell was, she knew, worried about the business. Money was tight; there was only the one Cluck-in-a-Bucket restaurant, and Mitchell's father, Preston, ran it the same way he'd run it for nearly thirty years (i.e., barely turning a profit). To make matters worse, a variety of fast-food chains and upscale eateries had recently flooded Nashville, and the competition was fierce. Nor could they rely anymore on the patronage of their once-plentiful country-and-western star clientele. Whereas Johnny Cash and June Carter Cash might place large orders with Cluck-in-a-Bucket for their family barbecues, young Nashville was more inclined to frequent the trendy eateries along Second Avenue. Mitchell came home most nights looking weary and dejected.

Standing in the shower while the hot water coursed over her, Annie realized that she'd have to take matters into her own hands.

Mitchell had bought her an outfit for their honeymoon, a French maid's costume complete with garter belt, that she'd taken one look at and steadfastly refused to wear. But on this day, after climbing out of the shower, Annie dried her hair, pulled on a pair of her favorite pajamas, and went to check her closet. She found the French maid outfit in the bottom of a box she was saving for the church clothing drive. She had tried to throw the costume away but her frugal nature would not allow it. She'd hidden it in the bottom of the box hoping none of the ladies from church would recognize the other clothing as hers.

Two weeks later, on a soft gray December evening, Annie stood behind the front door in the French maid's outfit, waiting as Mitchell pulled into the driveway. She waited until he had climbed the front stoop, looking more tired and discouraged than usual, before she flicked on the Christmas lights and flung open the front door. Whether it was the shock of the sudden flare of brightly colored bulbs or the sight of his wife dressed in a revealing outfit, the astonished Mitchell took an involuntary step backward, paddle-wheeled his arms, and fell soundlessly off the porch, managing to break his leg in two places.

After that, his leg in a heavy cast, he was confined to home for several weeks. Annie gave him a little silver bell to ring whenever he wanted her, and she continued to wait on him hand and foot in her French maid's costume. She wasn't taking any chances. She figured she had two weeks of fertility and she wasn't letting it go to waste. The cast presented some problems at first, but *where there's a will, there's a way,* as her mother liked to say, and Annie quickly figured out ways around that. She was a vixen, a tramp, a gourmet cook in a French maid's costume. She was every man's dream wife. Mitchell lost his harried look and began to put on weight. His face flushed with color, his hair grew in thicker, and he went around the house on crutches, whistling cheerfully.

His mother, Gladys, shook her head in amazement and said, "Son, if I didn't know better, I'd say you was having the time of your life."

His physician, old Doc Grunewald, said, "Hell, boy, I wish all my patients healed up as quick as you."

His father, Preston, asked anxiously, "When are you coming back to the store?"

By the middle of February, Annie knew she was pregnant. She folded up the French maid's costume and put it away, and when Mitchell complained that she was no fun anymore, Annie reminded him that they had a lot of work to do to get ready for this baby, and he'd best get himself up on those crutches and hobble on back to work.

Despite the year's optimistic beginning, things did not get better down at the Cluck-in-a-Bucket. Mitchell went back to working late. Every morning he left the house with a whistle on his lips and a spring in his step, and every evening he returned home with a little less spring. Annie did what she could to lighten his burden, keeping the house clean and hot food on the table, but her mind was preoccupied with other things, like furnishing the nursery and attending garage sales with her mother to pick up what they could. She also spent long hours poring over names in baby books trying to come up with something suitable.

Despite her minor in business, she was happy to let Mitchell limp along to work each day, blissfully unaware of personal or company financial matters. The pregnancy was easy, and Annie was determined to treat this as a new beginning, a chance to put the past behind her and start again. She was young and naive enough to believe that this was possible.

When she looked out the door one morning in her fifth month of pregnancy to see two uniformed water-meter workers leaning over the grate in her backyard, she went to the screen door and called to them. "Yoo-hoo," she said, waving. "Can I get y'all some coffee?"

They were bent over the drain, struggling to lift the lid. They looked at her, and then at each other. Then they went back to work.

"Okay then," Annie said, still waving, her little hand fluttering at the end of her arm. She had no idea what they were working on, but it looked important.

Later, when she went to turn on the kitchen faucet and nothing came out but a trickle of rust-colored water, the reality of her situation still didn't sink in.

She went to the phone and called the city water board. "I'm so sorry to bother you," she said to the woman who answered the phone, "but there appears to be a problem with my water. Two of your workers were out here this morning and I think they may have accidentally disconnected some- thing when they left." She was careful not to blame the workers.

The woman was quiet for a few moments, then asked Annie for her ad- dress. She put Annie on hold and came back a short time later.

"Your water's been turned off for nonpayment," she said in a jaded voice.

Annie was quiet, trying to figure out what she meant by *nonpayment*. Mitchell had all the bills sent to the store and she never even saw them. "There must be some mistake," she said finally, and then added politely, "What can I do to fix this?"

"Well, you can start by paying your damn bill," the woman said.

Annie called Mitchell. Then she got in her car and drove down to the water board to pay their bill. On the way home, she decided that she was going to have to take matters into her own hands again. Being poor was not working out. Letting Mitchell handle the family finances was not working out. Unless she stepped in and got Mitchell and Preston straight- ened out, her dream of a house in the suburbs by twenty-eight would never see the light of day.

She began going into the restaurant five mornings a week to help with the bookkeeping. Preston had been keeping the books, a job he hated and put off as long as possible. The ledger was a mess, and it took her a while to get it all balanced. Once she had a clear picture of their dismal financial standing, she set about doing something to change it. She called the store's vendors and negotiated reduced pricing for bulk ordering, something Preston had never thought to do. She arranged for a small-business loan to help with their cash flow, then arranged additional discounts with their vendors for on-time payments. She bought a computer to handle all the bookkeeping and inventory tracking. She instigated Family Night Specials and Cluck Bucks, money-saving coupons given to repeat customers. She advertised catering for office parties, graduations, and PTA fund-raisers. By the time her first son, William, was a year old and she was pregnant with her second, the store's profits were up sixty-four percent. When they received one of the letters from a franchising agent that Preston and Mitchell had been ignoring for years, Annie picked up the phone and called the agent.

The rest, as they say, is history.

Chapter 27

THURSDAY

Lola didn't deny taking medication but she didn't actually admit it either. When she came into the great room the morning following their unfinished tennis match, she walked up to Mel and handed her a prescription bottle. "Here," she said. "I know you're worried, but I never take anything at the beach. These are from years ago, before—"

"Before what?"

Lola smiled. She looked better today, happy and rested. She was wearing a pair of blue silk pajamas that matched her eyes, and her corn-silk hair fell prettily about her shoulders. "I would never mix pills with alcohol. Y'all don't have to stop drinking on my account," she added sweetly.

"Hallelujah," Annie said.

"Listen," Mel said, giving Lola a quick hug. "We worry about you, that's all." It was hard not to hug Lola when she stood there looking sweet and contrite. "I know Briggs kind of set you off yesterday, and I'll be happy to talk to him if he calls again."

Lola's eyes widened slightly. She shook her head slowly. "Oh, no," she said. "You can't do that."

"Sure I can."

"If he doesn't talk to me, he'll just keep calling," Lola said, her sunny demeanor clouding slightly.

"Why don't you sit down?" Mel said brightly, steering Lola toward the breakfast bar. Lola sat down on a stool beside Annie, facing the windows. "And I'll make you some breakfast since it appears that April is sleeping on the job." Mel pushed a platter of fruit she had found in the refrigerator toward Lola, determined to change the subject. "I didn't hear Captain Mike and April come in last night," she added. "They weren't here when we went to bed."

Lola yawned and stared at the beach through the tall windows. "They came in late. They missed the last ferry and had to get someone to motor them over."

"Oh," Mel said. "Did you see them?"

Lola yawned again. "They left me a message," she said. "On my cell phone."

"I can make eggs," Sara said, standing at the opened refrigerator. "And there's bacon. Oh, sorry, turkey bacon."

"No thanks," Annie said. "If it's not pork, I don't eat it."

Lola put her cheek in her hand and yawned again. Outside on the beach a crowd of teenagers tossed a Frisbee. A jet made its way slowly across the deep blue sky. "It's a beautiful day," she said.

"What should we do?" Mel asked.

"Captain Mike says he'll take us out on the boat, if we want to go." Lola's cheeks were pink, and there was a faint sprinkling of freckles across her nose. "We can pack a lunch and cruise to the Isle of Pines. He knows a lot about the island."

"I don't know if I'm in the mood for a history lesson," Annie said.

"Sounds lovely," Sara said.

"I'm game," Mel said. She shrugged and poured Lola a cup of coffee. "If no one has any better ideas."

"You're not fooling anyone," Sara said. "You'd love to spend the day with Captain Mike."

"Well, I can tell you right now, I have to stay out of the sun," Annie said in a sullen voice. "I got burned yesterday." She held up her nightgown so they could see her legs.

"How in the hell did you get burned?" Mel said. "You were practically wearing a burka out there."

"It was when I lay down in the sand and fell asleep and you forgot to wake me."

Mel tapped the counter with her fingernails and stared thoughtfully at Annie. "You know, that's not a bad idea. A sun burka. Sold to women like Annie who are afraid of UV rays. We could make it up in a bunch of designer colors and fabrics."

Lola was beginning to catch on. She giggled and said, "Briggs could sell it on the Home Shopping Channel."

"That's right," Mel said. It was good to see Lola acting more like her old self, more like the girl Mel remembered from college. She had forgotten how exhausting it was taking care of Lola. "We'd make a fortune, assuming there are enough anal-retentive women out there like Annie who love the beach but are afraid of the sun."

"Who you calling anal-retentive?" Annie said.

Outside the windows, the Frisbee sailed over the dunes like a flying saucer. One of the boys ran over to get it, his feet kicking up little clumps of sand.

Annie helped herself to the fruit platter. "Does anyone live on that island? What did you call it? The Isle of Pines?"

"No," Lola said. "It's deserted. It isn't very big. They say pirates used to bury their treasure out there. Blackbeard and Gentleman Stede Bonnet. Before that it was home to the Waccamaws."

"Wow, Lola. Do you watch a lot of Discovery Channel?" Sara asked.

Lola put her head back and laughed. "No," she said. "I'm just a good listener."

They were still sitting around the breakfast bar when Captain Mike came in to check on their afternoon schedule. "What, you're not even dressed?" he said with mock surprise. He was wearing a Ramones T-shirt and a pair of baggy knee-length shorts.

"We were waiting for you to come and help us," Mel said.

Captain Mike smiled faintly at Lola. "We probably should plan on being on the water by two o'clock. It'll take about an hour to get to the island." He seemed relaxed and sure of himself in that way that Mel found especially annoying. In her youth, she'd made men nervous, and she still did some men, but Captain Mike seemed completely immune to her charms. "I thought April and I would go ahead and load up the boat and you can follow when you're ready," he said. "As long as it's before two."

Lola leaned her chin on her palm, studying the sunlit beach, a slight smile on her lips. "Okay," she said.

"I'm not showering," Sara said, glancing at the wall clock.

"Thanks for the warning," Mel said.

"I don't have time to shower if we need to be at the boat by two."

"We need to be on the water by two," Captain Mike corrected her. "You need to be at the marina by one forty-five."

Lola stood up. She yawned and raised her arms so high above her head that her belly-button ring showed, glinting in the sunlight. "I'll be right back," she said, padding down the hallway to her room. The door clicked shut behind her.

Captain Mike poured himself a cup of coffee and stood at the breakfast bar observing them skeptically. "Are we clear on the plans, then?" He seemed to suspect that without a little pushing, they would spend the rest of the day lounging in their pajamas.

Mel still hadn't forgiven him for ignoring her earlier. She said, "Where's April?"

He sipped his coffee. Steam curled around his face and his eyes, in the slanting light, were a pale blue. "She had to pick up a few supplies at the grocery store. She's coming by to pick me up later."

"Lola says she's from Wilmington."

"That's right."

"Are you from Wilmington?"

He set his cup down on the counter. It was apparent that he didn't want to talk about himself. "I've lived there," he said, meeting her eyes. "Among other places."

Before she could continue with her line of questioning, the phone rang. Captain Mike picked up his cup and walked over to the long windows where he stood watching the rowdy teenagers playing Frisbee.

Annie looked at the phone, watching the caller ID display light up like a traffic controller's screen. "It's Briggs," she said morosely, staring at the display. Mel and Sara exchanged glances. The phone continued to ring. "Why doesn't Lola answer it?"

"She doesn't answer it because she doesn't know it's ringing," Mel said. "I unplugged the phone in her room last night when we got home."

"She told you not to do that."

"No, she told me she needed to talk to Briggs if he called. She didn't tell me not to unplug the phone."

"You have a rather convenient idea of right and wrong," Sara said.

"I know. I should have been an attorney."

"Well, someone needs to answer the phone," Annie said flatly. She had no intention of doing so. She had probably said no more than ten words to Briggs Furman her entire life. He had always ignored her, as if she were nothing more than a worn piece of furniture, something large and unwieldy that took up space without adding much in the way of beauty or comfort.

The phone stopped ringing. In the sudden silence they could hear the coffee gurgling in the pot.

Over by the windows, Captain Mike said quietly, "He'll just call again." His T-shirt was torn in the back, and a strip of fabric hung down over his hip like a forlorn flag.

"I don't know why he has to call every day," Mel said, staring at Captain Mike, who stood, alert and waiting, as if he was listening to something no one else could hear. She sank down on the sofa and stretched her legs out, pointing at Annie with her coffee cup. "Your husband doesn't call every day," she said. She hesitated, bringing the cup to her lips and then resting it on her chest. "Sara's husband doesn't call every day."

Sara turned abruptly and went to toast a bagel.

Annie stared at the phone. It was true; Mitchell didn't call every day but he called often enough. He had called last night while she was taking a lukewarm bath, trying to soothe her sunburned skin.

"I miss you, honey," he said. He was watching the History Channel; she could hear the guns of Omaha Beach going off in the background, shelling the beachhead. "This big old bed sure is cold without you here to warm it up."

She surprised herself by blushing. "Did you remember to feed the cat?" she said.

"I mean it, honey. It's cold as a brass monkey in a deep freeze without you here."

She smiled suddenly. "And you'll need to give him his hairball pills. They're in the cabinet above the cat food."

"Remember that little bed we used to sleep in when we were first married?"

Annie remembered it, a dark oak Victorian spindle bed passed down from a dead great-aunt. "You'll have to hold his mouth open and force it in," she said.

"Remember all the fun we used to have?"

She smiled again, picturing him in his faded robe and slippers with his dear little bald spot gleaming under the lights. "Or better yet," she said, "roll it up in a little piece of lunch meat and feed it to him."

Outside the windows the bright orange Frisbee sailed over the dunes. Captain Mike finished his coffee. "If you girls don't need me, I'll go get the boat ready," he said, but he seemed in no hurry to go, standing at the window staring pensively down at the wide beach. "I guess there's plenty," he began, but was interrupted by the sudden chirping of a cell phone.

Sara said, "That'll be Briggs trying to reach Lola on her cell."

"Shit." Mel stood up and looked around. "Where's the phone?"

Annie pointed at one of the chairs flanking the fireplace. "In her purse. Over there."

It took Mel a while to find the purse and even longer to find the phone, fumbling around inside the cavernous bag. By the time she'd found it, the phone had stopped ringing.

"You ought to let Mrs. Furman know he called," Captain Mike said, turning his head so they could see his profile.

"I'll handle it," Mel said flatly, thinking suddenly that he really wasn't that attractive, not in profile anyway, not without the full effect of those blue-gray eyes.

"I think you should let Mrs. Furman handle it."

"Captain Mike is right," Sara said. "Let Lola handle it."

They all irritated her. They seemed to imply that she didn't know what she was doing, especially Captain Mike with his stern, self-assured manner, the hint of disapproval in his voice. It wasn't as if she hadn't protected Lola before. She knew what she was doing. Mel ignored the other two and said to Annie, "If he calls again, I'll talk to him."

She hadn't gotten where she was in life by letting other people tell her what to do. She had learned long ago to trust her instincts. They weren't always right, initially, but they always steered her clear of shoals in the long run. Sara and Annie acted as if their lives were so tough, so complicated, but what did either of them really know about hard work and sacrifice?

Annie poured cream into her coffee and stirred it slowly. "What do you think Briggs said to her yesterday that made her cry?"

"Who knows?" Mel said. "Who knows what goes on between two people behind closed doors." Whatever was wrong with her now had nothing to do with her choice of how to live her life. She would never have been happy with Annie's narrow, restrictive life. And despite her fabulous husband, she wouldn't have wanted Sara's life either, with its constant distractions and detours and myriad small sacrifices.

She had chosen to be a writer. She had made the commitment and never wavered. Her life had turned out the way she had planned it, so why did it feel sometimes as if her career was less like the Holy Grail and more like a blindfold tied across her eyes?

"All I know is he's called every day," she said.

As if on cue, the house phone began to ring again. Mel jumped up and answered it. "Briggs," she said curtly. "How are you?"

"Where's my wife?" He sounded furious.

"She's sleeping," she said, lying easily, too easily. She was gripped by a slight sensation of sadness, passing through her belly like a cramp.

"Well, wake her up. I need to talk to her."

"No, I won't wake her. She's tired. Talking to you yesterday made her tired." She stared at Captain Mike, who stood watching the beach with a kind of rapt attention.

Briggs was quiet for a moment. "Don't interfere, Mel. It's none of your business."

"Yes, it is my business. She's my friend."

"She's my wife."

"Look, Briggs, we're on vacation. We're on a *girls'* trip. We've got three days left, and then you'll have Lola all to yourself. We haven't been together in twenty-three years, not all of us anyway, so give us some space. Okay? We'll send her back to you safe and sound in three days, I promise."

"Tell her to call me when she wakes up," he said, and hung up.

Mel clicked off and tossed the phone on the counter. "Asshole," she said. She couldn't believe she and Briggs Furman had ever been allies. This thought brought another slight cramping sensation in her stomach. The guy was a total and indisputable prick. Neither of her husbands had been that bad. Except for Booker's inability to handle misfortune that didn't involve him, except for Richard's cloying need to be Ward Cleaver, her husbands hadn't been bad at all. Most women she knew would have been happy with either one. This knowledge should have cheered her, but instead it only added to the small knot of despondency she felt growing steadily larger in her chest.

Lola walked into the room wearing a white lace minidress and a large floppy hat, looking adorable and happy. "I can't wait to show you the Isle of Pines," she said, her eyes darting over their faces. "It's one of my favorite places."

Mel said flatly, "Your husband called."

Lola's expression changed, a series of emotions passing swiftly across her face: surprise, distress, sadness. "Oh?" she said.

"He said for you to call him back but no one would blame you if you didn't."

Captain Mike turned suddenly and crossed the room to the kitchen, setting his cup down in the sink.

"No," Lola said. "I have to talk to him. He'll just call again if I don't." She picked up her purse and went into her room, closing the door behind her.

Captain Mike waited until the door clicked shut, then said sharply, "Don't forget. Be at the marina by one forty-five." He went out the kitchen door and they watched him through the glass, striding purposefully across the veranda toward the crofter.

"Is it my imagination," Sara said, "or does Captain Mike get more attractive as the week wears on?"

"It's not your imagination," Annie said. "Definitely not."

"You two go on and get dressed," Mel said. "I'll check on Lola."

They took the beach road to the marina. Mel drove with Lola sitting beside her and Sara and Annie in back. A strong wind buffeted the little cart. Sunlight shimmered on the white sand and the distant stretch of sparkling ocean. The narrow road was crowded with golf carts; teenagers with boogie boards strapped to their cart roofs, and families with beach umbrellas strapped to theirs, shuttled back and forth between the beach and the tall houses.

"Why is it so crowded?" Mel asked, pulling to the side so a cart driven by four underage boys could pass them. The boys honked and waved.

"It's almost the weekend," Lola said. She was wearing jeweled sandals on her tiny feet. Her toenails were painted a deep red. With her dark sunglasses and floppy hat she looked like a movie star from the nineteen-forties, like Ingrid Bergman in *Notorious*. "A lot of people from the mainland come over here for the weekend."

"It's still not as crowded as Hilton Head," Sara said, turning her head to gaze at the expanse of sparsely populated beachfront.

"Or Destin," Annie said.

Lola sighed and looked at the sparkling water. "I love the beach," she said. She seemed none the worse for her conversation with Briggs. It must have gone on for some time but when Mel went to check on her, she was happily applying sunscreen to her legs and singing as if she hadn't a care in the world. "It's like seeing the light at the end of the tunnel," she said when Mel stuck her head in the door, and when Mel said, "What?" Lola laughed her gay little laugh and said, "Do you want sunscreen?"

They passed a golf cart decorated with a sign that read JUST MARRIED, parked in the drive of one of the large houses.

Lola sighed. "I always wanted a beach wedding," she said.

"It seems to be very popular these days," Sara said.

"I always wondered how you'd keep the sand out of everything," Annie said. "Out of your veil. Out of your train. It seems like it would be so—messy."

"I got married on the beach," Mel reminded them.

"Which time?" Sara asked brightly.

Mel ignored her. "Maybe Henry and Layla should have a beach wedding," she said to Lola.

"Oh, no." Lola shook her head gravely and put her feet up on the dash, wiggling her toes. "She's from Ann Arbor. They'll have a traditional wedding."

"What does the ring look like?"

"What ring?"

Mel gave her a piercing look. "The engagement ring?"

"There is no engagement ring," Lola said, tugging at one of her sandal straps. "Not yet, anyway."

Sara and Annie swiveled their heads to look at Lola. "I thought you said they were engaged," Sara said.

"Not yet," Lola said, "but they will be." She stopped tugging at her sandal and sat back with her hands resting in her lap.

Sara turned back around. Mel gripped the steering wheel and watched the road. Only Annie continued to stare at Lola over one shoulder. "How do you know?" she asked finally. "How do you know they're getting married?"

Lola smiled sweetly. "I read their auras," she said.

When they arrived at the yacht, April was in the galley and Captain Mike was up on the flybridge checking the trolling valves. Mel stood on the dock with her arms crossed over her chest watching him until he glanced down and noticed her.

"Need some help?" she asked casually, shading her eyes with one hand. She was wearing a bikini and a pair of short shorts that she knew showed off her long legs to good advantage.

"Sure," he said, going back to work. "Why don't you go down to the galley and see if you can help April stow the food?"

That wasn't really what she'd had in mind but she couldn't very well refuse now that she'd offered. She climbed aboard and set her beach bag on one of the aft bench seats and then went into the galley. April was loading groceries into a Sub-Zero undercounter refrigerator and when Mel told her Captain Mike had sent her to help, she seemed annoyed. She was a quiet girl who kept mostly to herself, and Mel had a hard time reading her. Of course, there was always the chance that she had picked up on Mel's flirtatious manner toward the Captain, in which case she wouldn't blame April for being unfriendly, although Mel was surprised to find that she wanted April to like her. She wanted to reassure April that her feelings for Captain Mike were nothing more than an idle distraction, a chance to fill the dull hours until she could figure out some way to get her life back on track. But then she thought better of it and said nothing at all.

"Those canned goods need to go in the lower pantry," April said, pointing at a brown bag on the counter.

They worked for a while in silence, each one efficiently ignoring the other. "You've got enough food here to feed an army," Mel said finally, closing the door of the pantry. She could see Sara out on the dock, talking on her cell phone. She was probably talking to her daughter, who had already called twice this morning to ask her mother's advice about some boy she was seeing. Mel had listened intently to both conversations, wondering what she would have done if the situation had been reversed, and she had been the mother on the phone giving advice. Would she have said things like, *Be careful, you're only twelve.* or *Take it slow, boys can be fickle and you need to concentrate on the things you can control, like schoolwork or finding a hobby?* No, of course not. She would have said something like, *You're only young once, go for it, Nicky!* It was probably best that she was childless.

She flattened the brown bag and folded it against her chest. "So how long have you worked for the Furmans?" she asked April.

"Off and on for four years."

"How about Captain Mike?"

"I don't work for him."

The girl was being purposefully obtuse. Mel smiled wanly and said, "I meant how long has Captain Mike worked for the Furmans?"

April gave her a steady look. "You'll have to ask him," she said.

She was pretty, there was no denying that, with her perfect skin and almond-shaped eyes, but she wasn't exactly *warm*. She wasn't the kind of girl Mel would have pictured Captain Mike with. She wanted to ask her about him, to ask her how they had met, how long they'd been dating but she had the feeling the girl would only shrug and say, *Ask him*. She didn't look like the kind of person who gave away confidences easily.

Mel picked up the empty brown bags scattered around the galley and began to fold them flat. "So you grew up in Wilmington?"

"That's right. My parents still live there, and my little sister." April seemed distracted, checking a handwritten list and ticking things off.

Mel went back to staring at Sara through the window. She watched her animated face and she thought, *What must it be like to have a daughter?* Even if she ever, by some miracle, found the right man, would she really want a child? Not that she needed a man. She could adopt. She could find a surrogate. You didn't need a man these days to have a child (although she wouldn't, of course, broach this subject with Sara). But even if she *could* have a child, would she really want the responsibility of caring for someone who was totally dependent on her, whose every whim must take precedence over her own desires for the next eighteen years?

No, of course not.

She stacked the folded bags on the counter. "I can't imagine working for anyone nicer than Lola," she said.

April stared at her list and didn't look up. "Lola's awesome," she said.

"I've known her since she was just a girl," Mel said. "Since college. We all met in college."

April crossed out an item on the list. "She paid my tuition to culinary school," she said.

"Lola?"

April glanced up from her list, fixing Mel with a studious expression. "She paid my tuition. She paid for my sister's operation. My parents don't have insurance and she paid for it out of her own pocket."

This didn't surprise Mel. Lola's charity was legendary. "Lola's a generous person."

"She's awesome," April repeated.

"Yes. Awesome."

"There's nothing I wouldn't do for her," April said, giving her head a fierce little shake. "Nothing."

Mel wondered if anyone had ever felt that way about her. The mood in the cabin had grown heavy and she said, "Briggs, now he's an asshole but you have to take the bad with the good." She grinned when she said it but April only glanced at her, then went back to the list.

Mel turned her face to the small galley window. "It looks like we're getting ready to shove off," she said. She could feel the engines throbbing beneath her feet.

Out on the dock, Sara clicked off her phone and slid it into her bag. She was smiling.

Mel turned away, gathering the folded bags in her arms. There was a price to be paid for shutting yourself off, and she had paid it.

Sara stood on the dock watching Mel unsuccessfully flirt with Captain Mike and trying not to feel that little flutter of happiness she always felt whenever Mel tried, and failed, at anything. It happened so rarely. The flutter of happiness was followed quickly by a stab of guilt. She was old enough, surely, to have left the competitiveness of girlhood behind her? Apparently not. She watched Mel, looking like a movie goddess sex kitten in her short shorts and T-shirt, set her bag down and disappear through the sliding glass doors into the galley. Apparently there were some things you never got over, no matter how old you were. *I'll have to tell Tom about this,* she thought, but then realized just as quickly that she would not.

She and Annie walked down to the end of the dock to look at the boats. They stood for a while, looking out at the green sparkling water. Seagulls glided above the harbor or perched noisily atop tall masts. A large yacht christened the *Lisa Marie* pulled slowly into port.

Annie, noting the name, said, "Hey, you don't think that's Elvis's boat, do you?"

"Elvis is dead. What would he want with a boat?"

"How do you know he's dead?"

"Have you been drinking?"

"No, really. Think about it. How do you know he didn't fake his own death to get away from the paparazzi? How do you know he isn't out there right now, living the life he always wanted to live, cruising the seas under an assumed identity?"

Sara couldn't think of anything to say to this, so she said nothing. A ferry pulled slowly into the harbor with its load of happy, waving tourists. The big engines throbbed as the boat nosed up along the landing like a nursing calf. Shouting stewards began to frantically unload, pushing heavy carts up the gangways to the baggage station. Annie put her hands on the rail and peered anxiously down at the water. A dead fish floated forlornly on its side. "Do you think we'll go out of sight of land?" she asked.

Sara, noting the concern in her voice, said, "Have you never been on a boat before?"

"Not on the ocean."

"Well, Annie, I'm pretty sure we'll go out of sight of land. Captain Mike says it's about a forty-five-minute trip to the other island." Golf carts trundled gaily around the perimeter of the harbor. On the village green a group of children played tag. Annie, looking down into the water, shivered.

"Will you be all right?" Sara asked, putting one arm around Annie's narrow shoulders.

"Yes." She sniffed, watching a man and a child fly a kite on the village green. The kite was a tiny speck in the sun-bleached sky. "It's silly, I know, but I've always been afraid of dark water."

"You and Natalie Wood," Sara said. She gave Annie a quick squeeze and dropped her arm.

"Very funny," Annie said. "I haven't thought of her in years."

Sara smiled faintly, watching the steady stream of ferry passengers as they disembarked. She had been a junior in college at the time of Natalie's death, still brooding over a boy she couldn't have, and the whole affair had seemed so sordid and sad. Beautiful, childlike Natalie dead at the tragic age of forty-three. Fragile Natalie, floating in the dark water off Catalina Island in her flannel nightgown and knee socks. Rumors had swirled about a lovers' triangle turned deadly, and caught up at the time in her own lovers' triangle, Sara had understood how it might have happened. She still understood how it might have happened. She saw it every day as she struggled with the aftermath of so many failed marriages.

"Don't worry," she said, trying to reassure Annie. "She wasn't wearing a life jacket."

"Is that supposed to make me feel better?" Annie asked morosely.

After her years in family law, Sara was an expert on infidelity. She knew it happened slowly, gradually, over a period of time. In the beginning it was harmless, just a flirtation. A glance, a shared joke, a moment of false camaraderie when you tell yourself it doesn't matter, you're just friends. Good, good friends. It could have happened with Dennis McNair if she'd let it. But she'd seen too much of what followed: the bitterness, the guilt, the loss of self-esteem that infected lives like a sickness. A very modern sickness.

"I'll probably wear a life jacket the whole time I'm on board," Annie said. "I'll probably have Mel make a pitcher of Margaronas."

"That'll take the edge off," Sara said.

Staying true to your marriage vows was easy, she had found, if you were careful. You stayed on the path. You didn't deviate. You didn't listen to your heart when it said, *Step off here. Don't be afraid; it doesn't mean anything.*

"It'll probably also increase my chances of falling overboard," Annie said, grimacing.

"That's true. If you drink we'll have to strap you in."

Not that marriage was easy. Her own had had its fair share of ups and downs. She and Tom had wanted children so desperately, and yet having them had changed everything. The whole dynamic of the marriage went from *What can we do for each other?* to *What can we do for them?* That's what it felt like sometimes, like they were all in the water and drowning, and with her last dying effort she was trying to shove the children to safety. She sometimes thought that by the time they got Adam and Nicky grown, there would be nothing left of her and Tom but two whittled-down twigs, two emaciated husks.

Not that getting Adam grown would bring much relief.

"Where's Lola?" Annie asked, looking around.

"I think she's on the boat."

Not that she or Tom would ever give up one blessed moment of having Adam as their child. When he was born, they had laid him on her chest, and she had looked down into his wrinkled, chalky face and felt a piercing love stab her heart. She knew then that she would never be the same. He was her own tender heart made visible, offered up to the world with all its terrible possibilities. She was shaking from the anesthesia and from the wonder of it all, and when he cried suddenly, it was the sweetest sound she'd ever heard. She cried then, and so did Tom.

"We probably should get on board," Annie said. She had on one of

Lola's wide-brimmed hats, pulled low over her ears. She didn't look like she wanted to get on board. She didn't look like she wanted to go anywhere near the boat.

"Don't worry," Sara said. "You'll be fine. Everything will be fine."

When they walked on to the *Miss Behavin'*, Mel was waiting for them on the aft deck. The twin engines had started and were rumbling at a slow idle. A smell of burning oil and diesel filled the air. Captain Mike stood on the flybridge with one hand shielding his eyes, scanning the marina.

"Where's Lola?" Mel asked, peering behind her.

"What do you mean, where's Lola? I thought she was with you."

"I haven't seen her since we got to the marina," Annie said.

"Did you try her on her cell?" Sara asked.

"She's not answering," Mel said.

April came out of the sliding doors and Captain Mike leaned over the railing so he could peer down at her. "She's not in any of the cabins," she told him. "She's not below." He walked to the helm and turned off the engines.

Annie put her hand to her forehead. "You know, she was talking on the way over here about getting some bottled water. She kept talking about her mouth being dry. I wasn't really paying attention. Maybe she walked back up to the marina store to buy some water."

April and Captain Mike exchanged glances. "I'll go look for her," April said, but Captain Mike said, "No, I'll go." He bounded down the teak stairs to the aft deck, and stepped over the gangway onto the dock.

"I'll go with you," Mel said.

Despite her long legs, she had to hurry to keep up with him. If he appreciated her presence, he gave no sign of it, his eyes scanning the dock and the harbor like a roving searchlight. Looking at him, Mel had a sudden appreciation of how difficult his and April's jobs must be, trying to keep tabs on Lola. It had less to do with spying, she realized now, and more to do with keeping Lola from falling overboard or hurting herself or wandering off with some psychopathic stranger.

"If you lose his wife, Briggs will not be happy," she said, trying to be funny but it was apparent from his expression that she was not. "He's not the kind of guy who'd let something like that slide."

"I thought you liked Mr. Furman," he said tersely, staring at the water.

"Who told you that?"

He said nothing. A couple pushing a stroller was coming along the boardwalk toward them, and he stopped and waited for Mel to step ahead of him, single file. "You know, Lola comes down here to get away from Briggs," she said to him, over her shoulder. "Have you ever thought of that?"

The couple passed and he stepped up beside her again, moving with a long, loping stride. "It's really not my job to wonder why Mrs. Furman comes down here."

"No, but it's your job to report everything she does to Briggs."

He looked at her now, his eyes a steely gray in the slanting light, and she thought, *I wouldn't want to make him angry.* "I don't know you very well," he said slowly. "But you seem like the kind of person who likes to interfere in other people's lives."

"You're right," she said. "You don't know me very well." Ahead she could see the marina store through a forest of ship masts.

The air inside the store was frigid, and as the door swung shut on her heels, Mel felt the goose bumps rise on her arms. It was obviously one of the older structures on the island and had not been recently remodeled; the lighting was dim, and the wooden floors were stained and warped with moisture. Tall shelves sporting cigarettes, sunscreen, and fishing tackle stood on either side of the door, and along the right wall stretched a long row of coolers. The rafters were hung with trophy fish—marlin, swordfish, and yellowfin tuna—and above a door in the back hung a huge hammerhead shark.

Almost immediately they heard Lola's soft laughter. Captain Mike's face relaxed and he let out a slow breath. He stepped ahead of Mel, and she followed him down a narrow aisle that led to the back of the store. Lola was sitting on the checkout counter talking to a boy, who perched precariously in a chair tipped up against the wall on two legs.

Lola smiled when she saw them. Her tinted Oakleys had lightened in the dim interior of the store, and you could see her eyes, blue and innocent, behind the dark frames. "There you are," she said brightly, as if she had been waiting for them all along.

"There *we* are?" Captain Mike said gently.

Mel shouldered her way up beside him. "Lola, why didn't you tell anyone where you were going? We were worried. We've been standing around in the hot sun trying to figure out where in the hell you were and you weren't even answering your cell phone." She hadn't meant to sound so short but she was tired suddenly, and hot, and she needed a drink. And Lola stood there looking so pretty and cool, as if she hadn't a care in the world, that Mel wanted to shout at her, *Do you think you can just run off without telling anyone where you're going?*

"Sorry," Lola said, not looking the least bit sorry. "I left my phone back at the house." Her legs dangled from the edge of the counter, and she swung them back and forth like a double pendulum. She pointed at the tall, dark-haired youth. "This is Hunter. He goes to Duke. He wants to be an architect."

"Hey, how you doing?" Hunter said in a friendly manner.

"Maybe next time you'll tell us if you decide to wander off," Captain Mike said.

"Okay," she said. She nodded her head gravely as if she thought this might be a good idea. "Yes, of course."

Mel stood there breathing heavily, feeling the sweat trickle down her back. Captain Mike pointed to a cooler at Lola's feet. "Is that yours?"

She nodded. "I filled it with bottled water."

"We don't need bottled water," Mel said irritably. "April just stocked the galley with more bottled water than we can ever possibly drink."

"No, not like this," Lola said, scrambling off the counter. "These have the prettiest labels. See?"

She held one up for Mel's inspection. "Let me help you with that," Hunter said, setting the chair down and reaching for the cooler, but Captain Mike said, "No, I got it," and picked it up before the boy could.

Hunter stood. "There's a dance tomorrow night at the Beach Club," he said.

Lola smiled serenely. "Really?" she said.

Captain Mike said, "Mrs. Furman, we need to get back to the boat."

"I was thinking you might like to go," Hunter said.

"How nice," she said.

"She has friends visiting," Mel said sharply.

"Well, hell, bring the friends," he said, grinning at Mel. "The more the merrier."

"The more the merrier," Lola said gaily.

Mel swung around and headed for the door. Behind her, Lola said, "Bye."

"See you later, Lola," Hunter said.

Mel pulled the door open and Captain Mike stepped up beside her, holding it open for them with his back, his hands full with the cooler. He waited until they had stepped through, his eyes fixed on Hunter, and then he turned, letting the door swing shut behind him with a loud bang.

Chapter 28

~~~~~~~~~~

Sara and Tom had only been married a short time when they packed up and moved from Charlotte to Atlanta. She had heard about a job from an old law school classmate who'd landed at a midsized firm on the perimeter, and she was suddenly restless and eager to solidify her new marriage with a change of scenery. Sara interviewed with the firm, and not long thereafter, sat for the Georgia bar. Two months later she gave her notice at Schultz and McNair.

Dennis was hurt and disappointed, although he acted as if he'd been expecting her to leave. "Something went out of you the minute he slid that ring on your finger," he said to her one night over cocktails. "You lost your killer instinct."

"I never had a killer instinct," Sara said. "That was the problem. I wasn't dirty and underhanded enough to make a good divorce attorney. I have too many scruples."

"Oh, thank you very much," Dennis growled.

She laughed and kissed him primly on the cheek. "I mean that in a good way," she said.

Three weeks later, she and Tom rented a U-Haul, packed up their household goods, and headed south. It was mid-April, and the dogwoods and azaleas were in full bloom. Crossing the Chattahoochee River into Roswell, Sara felt as if her life was just beginning. As if everything she'd ever hoped for or dreamed of was coming true. Tom looked at her and smiled and she pushed over next to him on the bench seat and snuggled up under his arm.

"Happy?" he said, kissing her.

"Yes," she said. "Very happy." On the floor, at her feet, Max whined and thumped his tail.

They were traveling up a slight, tree-lined rise toward the square. Roswell was an old town, a suburb just north of Atlanta, and they had chosen to live here because of its proximity to the city and its history and quaintness.

As they topped the rise, they passed the square with its gazebo and memorial to Roswell King. Small shops and cottages stood along the perimeter, which was bounded on one side by a row of tall brick buildings, cotton warehouses originally, from the days when the river barges used to stop at the warehouses and mills, disgorging their loads of baled cotton.

"Just look at this place," Tom said.

"It's perfect," she said.

They turned right past the mill and followed a narrow cobbled street past a collection of stately brick row houses that ran parallel to the river. The buildings had originally been built in the 1840s to house the mill-hands, and had stood for some time empty and dilapidated. They had only recently been remodeled and converted into single-family townhomes. The redbrick buildings, clustered so close to the water's edge, had an air of melancholy about them, a trace of times long past, of lives lived and lost. Sara felt an instant affinity for the place.

"This must be it," Tom said, pulling into the parking lot and turning off the engine. Cicadas sang in the trees. The heavily forested banks of the Chattahoochee rose above either side of the swiftly moving river, dotted here and there with houses and buildings that seemed to rise out of the wilderness like an abandoned city. Tom glanced down at her, his green eyes shining in the light slanting through the wide window. "I wish we hadn't wasted all those years," he said.

She smiled and put her face up to be kissed. "Here's to new beginnings," she said.

• • •

Despite the change in locale, their lives followed the same routine they had established for themselves during the years in Charlotte. Sara rose early to head for the offices of Manning & Phillips with the often-vain hope that traffic along 400 would be light, and Tom rose and sat at his desk in his pajamas working on his dissertation or on what he called his "vain scribbling," which Sara was pretty sure was a novel. He had been offered a part-time teaching assistantship at Emory and was continuing to work on his dissertation, which he hoped to have completed the following spring.

Coming home in the evenings, she would look up and see the tree-lined rise that signaled the ascent to Roswell, and she would feel a little flutter of excitement in her stomach knowing that Tom was waiting for her, knowing that she was coming home to him. It was a feeling she never got over.

He was a good cook, and after dinner she would sit on his lap and muss his hair and when he tired of her teasing, he would tickle her or carry her up to bed.

Sometimes they might walk to the square, if the weather was fine, or even if it wasn't. They still enjoyed their walks in the rain. The storefronts and warehouses would be brightly lit, and they would sit in the middle of the square, beside the gazebo and the memorial plaque to Roswell King, and try to imagine what the place must have looked like when King first crossed the shallow ford at Vickery and gazed upon the thickly tangled wilderness. Often they would stop for a drink at the Public House, a restaurant and tavern on the square housed in one of the old cotton warehouses.

Gradually, their lives settled into a routine and they were happy, or at least Sara told herself they were. She worked too many long hours and Tom was worried, she knew, about defending his dissertation, but other than that, things were good. Sara spoke to Annie and Lola occasionally. She didn't speak to Mel at all for a while, and later only on the odd occasion when either one of them, feeling nostalgic, might pick up the phone and call. She followed Mel's burgeoning literary career with interest, and also with a secret, ironic feeling of pride. It was funny that of all the people she'd known, it was Mel who actually became a writer, the one she would have least expected to pen a novel, let alone four. She'd been in a bookstore recently and had picked up one of Mel's novels and she'd been surprised to find that it was good. Really good. She hadn't expected it. She was lying in bed late one night, reading *Big Sleazy* and laughing, and Tom said in a cool, indifferent voice, "Good book?" He was grading papers and had them strewn across the bed.

"Yes. Very."

"What's good about it?" He harbored, she knew, a secret desire to write novels that would be taught in future American lit classrooms and talked about in hushed voices by literary critics and writers' conference panelists.

"I don't know. It's—"

"Trite? Sentimental?"

"No. Fast and funny. It's not great literature but she tells a good story. Once I started it, I couldn't put it down."

He said nothing, but went back to grading papers. A few days later she couldn't find the book and she wondered if he'd taken it and was secretly reading it, although she could never quite bring herself to ask him.

One warm June evening, their neighbors, the Hatchers, invited Tom and Sara to join them for dinner. The four of them had cocktails, then walked the two blocks to the square for dinner. They were already a little tipsy. Mason liked his martinis dry with plenty of gin, and Tom held tightly to Sara's arm as they walked. It was a perfect summer evening. The moon was full, filling the street with a silvery light. Great banks of low-lying clouds blanketed the sky, and the air was heavy with the scent of jasmine and honeysuckle.

Sara walked beside her husband, glad for the steadying weight of his hand on her elbow, and feeling as if the ground was rolling beneath her feet like the deck of a ship. She usually didn't drink Mason's martinis, but tonight she'd had three, and she was paying the price. She stumbled once and fell against Tom, and he said, "Do I need to carry you?"

She giggled. "Would you?"

Behind them Mason said, "Newlyweds!" and Elizabeth said, "When was the last time you offered to carry me anywhere?"

"When was the last time you weighed one-twenty?"

"Bastard," Elizabeth said.

After that, Sara decided it might be a good idea if they didn't see too much of the Hatchers. Unhappiness was contagious, and she didn't want anyone or anything encroaching upon their carefully constructed little world. She and Tom had their careers, their colleagues, and their moonlit strolls through the square, and they didn't need anything else. They were young, they were happy, and they were in love, but there were times when

Sara, sitting on a bench watching the moon rise over the square like a phoenix, knew it couldn't last.

Having decided that partnership was more important than motherhood, at least for the foreseeable future, it was with a sense of disorientation and concern that Sara found herself, twenty months later, throwing away her birth control pills. She opened a bathroom drawer one morning and saw them there in their brightly colored case, and without a moment's deliberation, she picked them up and threw them in the trash. Later, she decided that it probably had something to do with the fact that she'd been on the pill for most of her twenties. She needed to give her body a break. She got a calendar and decided to use the rhythm method for a while.

Not that she told Tom any of this. They had never really talked seriously about having children. They had agreed to the idea, but they had never agreed on the specifics: how many? when? But now that the time had come when the subject should at least be broached, she found herself oddly hesitant.

Tom had successfully defended his dissertation in November and been awarded his Ph.D. Now he was planning a trip to England. He'd accepted a full-time teaching position at Emory but that wouldn't begin until the following fall, so he had plenty of time to plan their vacation. He went around the house whistling cheerfully and spent his time poring over glossy brochures and maps of England. Sara wasn't sure how she'd be able to pull herself away from the office for three weeks but she hadn't been able to tell him that either.

It was the first thing she had ever kept from him, at least since their marriage, and she wondered, in moments of quiet clarity, why she didn't tell him she had stopped taking the pill. He probably wouldn't have minded, or at least she didn't think he would, but she didn't want him questioning her decision. It was just easier this way. It was her body. And she didn't really want a child, she told herself, not when she was so close to making partner. Manning had hinted at it just last week over lunch, and Phillips had told her point-blank in December that if her billable hours stayed high, he saw no reason the offer wouldn't be forthcoming in the new year.

So why was she secretly jeopardizing it all now by risking a pregnancy?

She wondered if it was some kind of weird competition with Elizabeth

Hatcher. She saw her occasionally for coffee, although Tom had steadfastly refused to have any more contact with Mason. And Elizabeth was still desperately trying to get pregnant; she had been trying for years. *Don't wait too long,* she'd told Sara mournfully, *or your eggs will dry up.*

Sara had read somewhere that dogs kenneled together will go into heat at the same time. It was Mother Nature's way, she supposed, of ensuring the continuation of the species, this fierce competition over fecundity. And really, was that so surprising when competition was at the heart of everything? Competition for schools, for jobs, for partnerships. Competition for mates.

Sara faithfully marked her calendar and tried not to think about her eggs shriveling to leathery little bags.

In April, Sara and Tom attended the Atlanta Steeplechase. It was an annual tradition, advertised as *the Best Lawn Party in Georgia,* and people took it seriously. It was similar to tailgating at a prep school football game only with white tablecloths and sterling silver and people dressed up like those who attended the Kentucky Derby. Manning and Phillips always had a catered corporate tent on the backstretch, where they could easily watch infield festivities like the Ladies Hat Parade and the Jack Russell Terrier Races, as well as the thundering rush to the finish line of the five steeplechase races.

They had been to the steeplechase once before so they knew what to expect. It was a beautiful day, sunny and breezy with a clear blue sky stretching above the rolling hills. The landscape was dotted with colorful tents and long lines of automobiles glistening in the sun. There was an open bar at the Manning and Phillips tent. By midafternoon Sara had fallen asleep in her lawn chair, and Tom was standing at the finish line with a group of rowdy stalwarts, roaring at the contestants as they cleared the last hurdle and thundered past.

The firm had chartered a bus to take them home, and by the time they arrived back at their townhome that evening, Sara was beginning to sober up but Tom was more inebriated than she'd seen him in years. She put it down to his relief and celebration over the completion of his dissertation.

As she closed the door, he pulled her roughly against him and kissed her. His face was warm and smelled of cut grass and whiskey. He pulled her T-shirt over her head. "What are you doing?" she asked him drowsily.

She hadn't checked her calendar this morning but she was pretty sure she was still at the tail end of her fertile period. Give or take a few days.

He unzipped her skirt and pulled it down over her hips. "What do you think I'm doing?" he asked, kissing her and backing her across the room. He had taken off his shirt, and his shoulders were sunburned and covered by a light sprinkling of freckles. She loved his arms, the sturdy thickness of them, with their faint covering of auburn hair.

"Wait," she said. The dying sun pushed its way through the closed blinds, falling in narrow bands across the hardwood floor.

He picked her up and set her on the desk.

She couldn't let this go on. It wasn't fair to him with his dreams of England. It wasn't fair to her with her dreams of partnership. With a sudden fluid motion, he swept the top of the desk behind her. Paper clips and storage trays clattered to the floor.

She giggled suddenly. Apparently she wasn't as sober as she'd thought.

He grinned and slipped her bra off.

"Wait," she said. "I need to tell you something."

He touched her hair. He licked the little hollow at the base of her throat. Distantly, she could hear the sound of the river. She thought, *Maybe I read the calendar wrong.* She thought, *My eggs are probably too shriveled anyway.*

Five weeks later, when she told him, he took the news with characteristic calm. They were sitting in front of the opened French doors, watching the river run. Late-afternoon sun slanted across the surface of the water, turning the river a glinting sheet of blue. "When were you going to tell me you went off the pill?" he asked quietly.

"Don't be angry."

"I'm not angry, I'm just—confused."

Evening fell. Bats darted in the sky. Beyond the distant ridge a pale moon rose.

"I didn't really decide, I didn't think about it clearly, I just stopped taking it." She put her hand on her stomach. It felt tender. Her skin smelled different. Everything about her was different. "I kept a calendar. I thought we'd use the rhythm method, but it didn't work."

"Clearly."

"It worked up until the steeplechase," she said shortly.

He stood up and went to the opened doors, standing with his shoulder against the jamb and looking out. The night sounds were as rhythmic as a heartbeat. "Well, I guess I'm to blame for that," he said.

"No one's to blame," she said, rising swiftly and going to him. She laid a timid hand upon his shoulder, feeling the muscles tense and ripple beneath her fingers. "I don't know why I didn't tell you I had gone off the pill. Maybe I was afraid you'd say no. Maybe I was afraid that if we waited too long, I wouldn't be able to have a baby. I don't know. I guess I wasn't really thinking it through." She turned to go but he grabbed her hand and pulled her against him, folding his arms around her and resting his chin on her head.

"I'm getting used to it is all," he said. "It's a shock."

She pushed her face against his chest. "I want this baby."

His arms tightened around her. "I want it, too," he said.

Pregnancy was easier than she had expected. There was no morning sickness, no nausea. Except for the fact that she grew huge and her skin smelled strange, she might not have known she was pregnant. She was careful, at first, about her weight, but after the sixth month, she just didn't care anymore. Food tasted so great and she had so few pleasures now, besides eating and the occasional massage Tom gave her. He waited on her hand and foot. He brought her any food she craved, no matter what it was or when she wanted it. She was like a big swollen queen bee and he was her drone, busy and attentive to her every need.

The baby was due in January, and in October they signed up for a Lamaze class. All the other moms wore leotards and talked a lot about natural analgesics and amniotic sacs, and Sara felt like a fraud rolling around among them in her tent smock and stretch pants. Everyone was kind and cheerful, especially the moms who'd already gone through labor before, who were more than willing to share their graphic birth experiences with novices like Sara. She smiled politely and tried to steer the conversation around to something other than delivery. She didn't want to know the painful details. She figured the less she knew about the whole process, the better. She'd stopped reading her *Ready, Set, Deliver!* book after Chapter Seven ("Pelvic Pressure & Mucus Plugs!") because she didn't want to know what came next. It was this same logic that drove her to close her eyes and stick her fingers in her ears during the Lamaze birthing tape.

Tom was fascinated by the whole process. He treated her like an entomologist might treat some kind of rare molting caterpillar. "Wow," he would say, running his hand over her swollen belly, "how does it get so big? How do your hips know to stretch like that? Have your feet always had those little pads of fat?"

One night during her eighth month, she was lying in the bathtub reading *Ethan Frome*. Tom was standing at the bathroom mirror flossing his teeth. She had the book resting on her immense belly when suddenly, without warning, the baby kicked and the book went flying across the room.

"Oh, my God," Tom said, swinging around from the mirror, his expression a mixture of repulsion and awe. "Did you see that?"

Sara grimaced in pain as one small foot made its way slowly across the surface of her stretched skin. When the baby had finally rolled over, she sighed and pointed at the book. "Hand it to me, will you?" she asked wearily.

"It must have flown three feet," Tom said, shaking his head in amazement. He picked the book up and gave it back to her. "The kid's bound to be a punt kicker."

"Or a literary critic."

He squatted down beside the tub and ran his hand lightly over her belly.

"Don't touch my stomach like that. You'll just piss him off." She was rapidly losing her sense of wonderment at the whole process. Nine months was just too damn long, which was probably why women began to look *forward* to labor during the end of their term. Mother Nature knew what she was doing.

"How do you know it's a he?"

"Because the doctor said so."

"Doctors can be wrong. Sonograms can be wrong." Tom put both elbows along the edge of the tub and rested his chin on his hands. "I'm trying to picture who he'll look like," he said, looking down into the bathwater like he was gazing into a crystal ball. "I'm trying to see him as a baby, as a boy, as a young man."

Sara put her foot up and turned on the hot water with her toes. She had begun to realize just what a crapshoot genetics were. You never knew who you were going to get. You could be the best parents in the world and still wind up with a bundle of trouble. Ted Bundy's mother read him bedtime stories. Jeffrey Dahmer's mother made sure he didn't go outside without his mittens.

What was wrong with her? She sank down deeper into the steaming water. It was probably just pre-birth jitters. It was probably something every woman went through, something she would have learned if she'd managed to get past "Pelvic Pressure & Mucus Plugs!" Their son wouldn't be a serial killer. He would be small and sweet, and he would love his parents as unconditionally as they loved him.

Their son, she convinced herself, would be perfect.

And he was. Despite the fact that he had a cone head (he'd gotten stuck in the birth canal) and was covered with some kind of white chalky substance, despite the fact that he moved his frail little limbs like some kind of strange insect, he was perfect. He was theirs and he was perfect. The delivery room nurses laid him on Sara's chest, and she and Tom cuddled him and wept like babies.

She'd taken a six-week maternity leave and when the time came to go back to work, Sara was filled with anticipation and remorse. Anticipation because she enjoyed her job and missed it, and remorse because Adam was so small and helpless. The first time he slept the night, she awoke to a feeling of dread, sure he had died in the night. She rushed to the crib, only to find him sleeping peacefully. Her first day back at work she went along the halls greeting everyone, spoke to several clients on the phone, took a power lunch with the partners, then went into the bathroom and cried. Her guilt over leaving him was made easier by the fact that Tom's teaching schedule allowed him to be home with the baby most days. It was only Tuesdays and Thursdays when they needed to hire a nanny, and they quickly found an elderly widow, a retired schoolteacher who agreed, with Mary Poppins–like charm, to stay only until Adam began walking.

Tom absolutely adored his son. He was a wonderful father, as Sara had known he would be, and she returned home many evenings to find the two of them lying on a blanket on the floor, cooing and laughing at each other. He carried the baby in a sling against his chest while he did housework or graded papers, and he made Adam's baby food himself, mixing it in the Cuisinart and freezing the mix in ice trays for later use. On sunny afternoons they took walks to the square or lay on a blanket beside the river, watching the water run. It was a wonderful time, a time when the world seemed hopeful and bright with promise.

But there were other times when Sara, coming into the nursery at night and looking down at her sleeping child, would be overcome by a sudden overwhelming desire to crawl into the crib and cover him with her body.

He seemed so small and helpless and the world so dangerous. She worried over everything now. Abused and abandoned children, war, and the polluted environment all touched her in a way they had not done before, as if her awareness of the suffering in the world was made visible by her love for Adam.

She avoided Elizabeth Hatcher whenever she could. The poor woman hovered around the baby, constantly wanting to hold him, to feed him, to put him down for his nap.

"You two go out and let me babysit," she said desperately to Tom and Sara but they, of course, never even considered it.

In moments of quiet clarity, she thought about moving.

It would be easier, moving away and leaving all the drama of the Hatchers behind. And their townhome was three stories, which was not really good for a toddler, although Adam was not toddling yet; he was still crawling around like a fat grub. A one-level house would be better, maybe a fixer-upper in Sandy Springs with a large flat yard and access to good schools.

But Sara loved her old townhome with its brick walls and heart-pine floors and air of lives long past. And Sandy Springs was expensive. She needed to save the money in their bank account to buy into a partnership, on the slim chance that one would ever be offered.

And then one morning in September as she was getting ready for work, she heard a sound like a bowling ball rolling slowly down the stairs. She stopped applying her mascara to listen. In the split second before the rolling stopped, she realized it was the baby, falling down the stairs.

She screamed and ran out into the hallway. Leaning over the banister she could see Adam lying on his back on the first-floor landing, his face red, his mouth open in a soundless wail. Tom ran out of the kitchen. It was a Tuesday and he was dressed for work. He was shouting, "Oh, my God, oh, my God," and rushed down the stairs to the baby, but Sara could only stand there leaning over the railing, immobile with fear and grief.

Adam recovered his breath and began to howl. Tom picked him up and cradled him against his chest. "Where were you?" he shouted at Sara. "Why weren't you watching him?"

"I thought you were watching him!" She flew down the stairs. "My baby!" she cried. "My poor baby!"

They took him to the hospital but all the scans were negative. Babies are resilient, the doctors assured them, but Sara would not be comforted. There was a nagging sense of guilt that would not let her go, even years later, after his diagnosis, after the doctors had assured her that secondary autism can only be caused by an injury much greater than the one Adam had suffered rolling down the stairs, and that primary autism is present from birth.

No matter what they said, she couldn't let go of the guilt, the feeling that his affliction was somehow a punishment of her, something she was paying the price for at long last.

Chapter 29

~~~~~~~~~

After losing Lola at the marina, the trip to the Isle of Pines was uneventful. They followed the coastline, staying close to the barrier islands for Annie's sake, and fifteen minutes into the ride, she had relaxed like the rest of them. As long as she could see even a distant rim of land, she seemed fine. They sat up on the canopied flybridge, clustered around a table drinking pitchers of sweet tea while Captain Mike stood at the helm, steering the boat through the treacherous Frying Pan Shoals at the mouth of the Cape Fear River and out into open water. Hundreds of wrecks lay buried under these shoals, the debris of five hundred years of European and American naval traffic, but he seemed to know what he was doing. He stood with his legs spread slightly to take the shift and roll of the boat, his baseball hat turned backward, his eyes constantly scanning the horizon. He was built like a rugby player, solid and well muscled, and watching the way he handled the wheel, Mel felt a little tremor in the pit of her stomach.

"You can tell he loves this," she shouted at Lola, indicating Captain Mike's sturdy back.

"Yes." Lola pushed her wind-tossed hair behind one ear and nodded. "He's an old soul," she said in her singsong voice. "In another life he sailed with Stede Bonnet all along this coast. He knows every shoal and inlet between here and the Berry Islands."

Mel didn't know what to say to that so she said nothing. Looking at Captain Mike now, at the confident way he stood at the wheel, his sunstreaked hair fluttering against his deeply tanned neck, it wasn't too hard to imagine him as a buccaneer. Mel turned to Sara but she and Annie were deep in some private conversation, their heads close together, their voices low. They were fitted into the curve of the bench seat that circled the table like a horseshoe, and they seemed oblivious to anything else, to the sun sparkling off the whitecapped ocean, to the barrier islands with their wide beaches and dark rim of maritime forest. The *Miss Behavin'* churned past a charter boat anchored near an artificial reef, its cargo of scuba-diving tourists readying themselves for an afternoon dive. Two dolphins raced along the starboard side, slicing through the water like a pair of rodeo riders, before veering off toward open sea.

A few minutes later, April appeared on deck, carrying a tray of frozen margaritas. She set the tray down on the table in front of them.

"You read my mind," Mel said, reaching for a drink. Lola lifted one of the margaritas and offered it to April.

She took the glass, smiling, and said, "I thought I'd serve lunch once we get to the island."

Lola waved her hand lazily as if lunch was the last thing on her mind.

The girl moved off, her hips swaying gently to the subtle rocking of the boat. She was wearing a pair of short-shorts and a tiny T-shirt that showed her flat stomach. Her feet were bare. She stood next to Captain Mike with her hip resting against him, one arm looped casually over his shoulder. From time to time, she gave him her drink to sip. Mel couldn't hear what they were saying but they were obviously amused by something, chuckling and leaning their heads close together.

She was surprised to find herself suddenly jealous, which was odd, considering that she didn't even like Captain Mike. Not really anyway. She put it down to a week of drinking and inactivity bordering on boredom. Or maybe it was just loneliness.

As if reading her thoughts, Captain Mike turned his head and glanced behind him. He lifted one arm and pointed out the Isle of Pines, a long, low-lying barrier island that was visible now off the port bow. "Ten minutes," he shouted.

Annie stopped talking to Sara and stared at the distant island. "That place looks familiar."

"Maybe you knew it in another life," Mel said. She smirked and rolled her eyes at Sara, who smiled faintly but didn't say anything.

Lola didn't seem the least bit disturbed by Mel's skepticism. She stuck her finger in her glass and stirred the frozen mound. "We were sisters," she said, staring fondly at the pale green concoction.

Mel knew better than to ask the question but couldn't stop herself. "Who?" she asked. "Who were sisters?"

Lola twirled her finger in circles, indicating the four of them. "We were," she said. "Not *sister* sisters. The other kind. You know, nuns. In a seventeenth-century convent in Paris." She held her glass up and tapped the edges until the frozen mound collapsed into the middle.

Mel pursed her lips and gave her a patient stare. "Where do you get this crap, Lola?"

She pulled her feet up on the bench, folding her legs beneath her. "I did this thing called past-life hypnotic regression. Y'all should try it."

"I have enough trouble dealing with this life," Mel said, "much less dealing with one that happened hundreds of years ago."

"After the convent, I was a boy on the Kansas frontier whose parents died in an Indian attack," Lola said matter-of-factly. "And then I was an elderly woman who died at Treblinka."

No one said anything. Annie turned her head and stared at the distant shape of the Isle of Pines. Mel asked Lola, "What medication did you say you were taking?"

"I'm not taking any medication."

"Are you sure about that?"

Lola lifted her drink and sipped it. "Not now," she added in that enigmatic way she had of answering direct questions, like a child playing a game of twenty questions.

Mel felt a twinge of irritation. "Not now, as in 'Not while I'm drinking?' Or not now, as in 'Don't ask me now'?"

Lola giggled. Annie said warily, "The Bible doesn't say anything about reincarnation."

"Do you only believe what you read in the Bible?" Mel asked.

She didn't. Not anymore, anyway, but she had been raised to believe that the Bible was the inspired word of God, and her life had been a whole lot easier back when she still believed it. Now she found herself questioning everything. "I try to stay away from all that new age stuff."

"Reincarnation isn't exactly new age," Mel said. "It's one of the oldest known beliefs. Some people claim that it was a major tenet of the Christian religion up until the fifth ecumenical council in 553 A.D."

"I don't believe in reincarnation," Sara said. "Not rationally, anyway. But the concept of karma is pretty interesting. It makes a lot of sense if you think about it, the idea that we're all put here to learn from our mistakes, no matter how many lifetimes it takes. It's a whole lot more comforting than the Judeo-Christian belief that we're put on Earth with one life and one soul and if we screw up, we go to hell. A religion that has us believing in a loving God who watches over his flock. How does that explain abused children? How does that explain children dying of cancer?"

"That part bothers me, too," Annie said.

The sun had passed its zenith and was beginning its slow plummet toward the tree line. Mel crossed her legs on the bench seat, resting her drink in her lap. "Okay, Lola," she said. "So you're saying that if something bad happens to me, if I get run over by a bus or die in a car accident, it's because I was an SS guard at Buchenwald in another life? If something bad happens to me, *it's my fault?*"

Lola tilted her head as if contemplating this. "I don't think it's that simple," she said.

Sara stirred her drink and raised her glass. "Well, Lola is right about one thing," she said. "Y'all are my sisters. For better or for worse. I can say things to you that I couldn't say to anyone else." They all raised their glasses and clinked them together.

"Here's to girlfriends," Mel said. She smiled at Sara, then returned her attention to Lola. "Maybe if you'd said we were saloon girls during the California gold rush or Ziegfeld girls working on Broadway. But *nuns?* What could we possibly have learned as nuns?"

"No idea," Annie said.

"Don't ask me," Sara said.

"*Thaumaturgy,*" Lola said, holding her glass up so the sun shone through it like a prism. "Believing in miracles and loving each other. That's all there is."

• • •

They came through Rich Inlet and moored the yacht several hundred feet out, where the water was shallow and clear down to the sandy bottom. April served them lunch in the salon while Captain Mike got the dinghy ready. They could see the low flat outline of the Isle of Pines through the salon windows. It was a small island, only about five miles long, and had been sanctioned years ago as a bird sanctuary and turtle hatchery so there was no commercial development. It was all pristine wilderness and white sandy beaches. A few scattered fishing shacks still stood at the northern tip of the island but other than that, there were no signs of human habitation. The island looked very much like it had three hundred years earlier, when Blackbeard and Gentleman Stede Bonnet terrorized the coast aboard the *Queen Anne's Revenge*.

After lunch they hopped into the dinghy and Captain Mike motored them in to shore. The island rose like a mirage beneath a cloudless sky. Sandpipers scurried along the beach, watching them with bright beady eyes. A series of rolling dunes rimmed the beach, and beyond them, a dark ridge of maritime forest stretched into the bone-colored sky. As they approached the island they could see a pair of turtle tracks running along the beach and dunes like phantom tire tracks.

Captain Mike pulled the dinghy up on the beach and they climbed out. Waves lapped gently against the sand. The southern tip of the island faced the inlet and was somewhat sheltered, forming a slight cove. To the west stretched Middle Sound and to the east stretched the wild Atlantic. They walked up the beach and laid their towels on the sand. Sara and Lola went to look for shells, slowly following the gentle curve of the shoreline. Captain Mike put on a snorkeling mask and waded out into the water. A few minutes later, Mel joined him.

Annie reached into her beach bag and took out a tube of Vaseline, which she applied liberally to her lips. It was her one beauty secret, Vaseline. It kept her lips moist and wrinkle-free. In the winter months she applied it to her whole face. Her hair might be prematurely white and she might have flabby Jameson thighs, but she had the unlined skin of a teenager. You had to take the bad with the good.

She lay on her towel on the sand, resting her chin on a clenched fist and watching Captain Mike and Mel swim back and forth like a pair of ocean steamers. Captain Mike was always in front and Mel was always slightly behind, trying to keep up. Watching the two of them, Annie was glad, suddenly, that she was married and long past all that foolishness. *And married to a good man, too,* she thought. *A keeper.*

The afternoon was hot and muggy. The *Miss Behavin'* floated on the horizon like a toy boat. On her starboard side another yacht, slightly larger, passed slowly, its engines throbbing. Captain Mike stood up in the water and watched as the yacht motored out of the inlet and into the open sea. He had his mask pushed back on his head and he was holding something in his hands that he had plucked from the ocean floor. Mel stood beside him, peering down at it. She looked very pretty and very happy, standing there with Captain Mike. She was not a woman accustomed to rejection, and Annie guessed that she was having a hard time accepting Captain Mike's infatuation with April.

Still, you had to admire Mel. She had what the English like to call *pluck.* She wouldn't give in, not Mel, she wouldn't lie down and take it. She was competitive down to her last eyelash. It was that spirit of competition that kept her and Sara at odds; that and the unpleasantness that had passed between them all those years ago, that thing they never spoke of but was always there. The elephant in the room.

Farther down the beach she could see Lola and Sara making their slow progress along the sand. She smiled, thinking of Lola's strange word. *Thaumaturgy.* Annie had learned the word years ago in a Bible study class. It meant the art of working miracles.

A crab poked its head out of the sand and ran across in front of her with its comical, sideways motion. The blue sea shimmered, rising and falling gently beneath a line of gauzy clouds. Annie turned her head to the side and laid her cheek down on her arms.

Sara, of course, had her own cross to bear. They had spoken of it on the trip over, Annie listening quietly while Sara told her of the new program they had Adam on. She had visited Sara in Atlanta not long after Nicky was born, not long after Adam was first diagnosed with autism, and she had seen firsthand the devastation it had caused in Sara and Tom's lives, in their marriage. She had been there for Sara over the years, had tried to make herself available when she needed a friend to confide in, a shoulder to cry on. A mother herself, Annie had not been able to imagine anything worse than a damaged child, a child who could never be made whole no matter how many doctors he saw, no matter how many promising programs he underwent.

It was enough to make Annie's own tragedy pale in comparison.

• • •

Mel followed Captain Mike through the water like a remora trying desperately to latch on to a tiger shark. He was a good swimmer, and moved with smooth fluid strokes, but she had failed the Red Cross swimming test three times. The last time Leland, watching from the balcony, had left in disgust, refusing to ever pay for another swim lesson. It wasn't that she couldn't stay afloat; she could. But during times of stress or fatigue she had a tendency to relapse into a clumsy dog paddle. She did so now, following him like a feeble lapdog while below them a silvery ladyfish made its way lazily out to sea.

A lightning whelk moved slowly across the sandy bottom, and Captain Mike dove down and brought it up for Mel to see. They stood in chest-deep water and he pointed out the large muscular foot the whelk used to clamp down on its prey. Mel wished she had a similar appendage. She spent a few pointless minutes imagining herself attached to Captain Mike. "*Busycon perversum,*" he said, dropping it gently in the water, where it sank like a large stone.

Lola and Sara returned from their beachcombing trip, and Captain Mike went to join the three of them on the beach. He walked out of the water, the sun glistening on his wide shoulders, like a male version of Botticelli's Venus. He raised his arms and pushed his hair back off his face, and Mel thought that she'd been wrong the other night when she'd decided that he didn't look good with his hair slicked back. He walked up on the beach and stood over the three women, dripping water onto their brightly colored beach towels. Lola kicked sand at him and he leaned over her and shook his shaggy head like a dog. She screamed, giggled, jumped up, and ran a few feet down the beach.

Mel watched her with a sullen expression. The snorkeling mask pinched her face and she took it off, flinging it toward the shore. There was no doubt about it; she needed to get laid. It had been nearly three months, and she hadn't gone three months without sex since she was sixteen years old, except for the time she got sick, and then it had been nearly nine months, but that really didn't count. She needed to get laid before she went berserk. It shouldn't be this hard (it never had been before). Maybe she should just go right up to him and lay it on the table (so to speak). Maybe instead of trying to impress him, she should just tell him what she wanted so they could get on with it. She wanted sex. With him. Now.

He knelt in the sand and pulled a CD player out of a canvas bag. The Rolling Stones' "Sympathy for the Devil" rang out suddenly across the quiet cove.

Annie asked, "Do you have any Vince Gill?"

Lola said, "Turn it up!"

Mel did a slow backflip on the surface of the water so he could see her full bosom, her flat stomach, and her graceful hips, in case he had missed them earlier when she had stood so close to him that she was practically in his arms. As she surfaced, she slicked her hair back like a movie star, like Raquel Welch in *Fathom*.

He wasn't looking.

She floated on her back, then stuck one shapely leg straight up into the air, holding it there. It was a good leg, long and lean. Seriously, what man could resist a leg like that?

From the beach, Sara shouted suddenly with laughter. "What are you doing? Are you doing synchronized swimming? Look everyone, Mel's doing synchronized swimming!" He was looking now, but there was a grin on his face—not the effect Mel was going for.

Sara jumped up, slapping the sand off her bottom. "Come on, kids," she shouted, flailing her arms like a goofy schoolgirl, like one of those kooky girls from *Beach Blanket Bingo* or *How to Stuff a Wild Bikini*. "Let's go synchronized swimming!"

Lola and Annie, catching on, jumped up and ran into the water, giggling and squealing. Captain Mike grinned and turned the volume up on "Mother's Little Helper." The three of them lined up in the water and then swam on their backs in a straight line, lifting their legs into the air and twirling in unison. They swam back the other way, keeping time with the music.

Annie said, "Look at me, I'm Annette Funicello."

Lola said, "I'm Gidget. Hey, Moondoggie, go get me a beer."

Captain Mike grinned and tapped the side of his head with his palm. "Sorry, girls," he said. "The beer's on the boat."

Annie said, "Cramp!"

Sara said, "Ballet Leg! Fishtail! Catalina Rotation!"

Mel watched them glumly, refusing to join in their fun. She turned her back to them and stared out at the sea. Either she got laid soon, or someone was going to get hurt.

Chapter 30

~~~~~~~

Mel was flying to a book festival in Savannah when she decided to leave her first husband. She was twenty-nine, her fifth novel, *Cold Steal,* had just come out in hardcover, and she had accepted an invitation to speak at the Dolphin Beach Book Festival as a last-minute fill-in author, against her agent's wishes. Gabe seemed to think that her reading audience was located primarily in the Northeast, and that she was wasting her time attending book festivals south of the Mason-Dixon line. Mel was of the opinion that an audience was an audience, regardless of the location. A well-known author had developed a case of nerves and canceled at the last minute, and Mel had received an e-mail from a desperate festival coordinator looking for a "replacement author of equal *or greater* literary standing" (*i.e, an author with no advance publicity willing to prostitute herself for a few paltry book sales*).

"I'm your girl!" Mel e-mailed her back.

It was November (*Hurricane season,* Gabe noted archly), and Mel had been just as eager to get out of cold and dreary New York as the

Dolphin Beach Book Festival Replacement Committee had been to have her. Besides, it would give her some time to decide what to do about Richard.

Her marriage, which had effectively ended not long after the oceanside ceremony in Barbados, had limped along painfully for the last five years before reaching a state of total and irretrievable impairment. Richard, a masochist, had begun to hint desperately that children might be just the thing to get them going in the right direction and Mel, a realist, had just as vehemently refused to consider it. She knew firsthand the results of bringing children into an unhappy union, and she had no intention of making the same mistake her own parents had made. The sins of the father and all that.

In moments of quiet reflection she had to ask herself why she had stayed in the marriage as long as she had. Her answers were at first evasive, and later disturbing. She had stayed because she needed a quiet place to write. A place where she could work without constant daily distractions and worry over money.

It was pathetic, really. She was no more than a kept woman.

But now that she was making enough of an income on her own, she no longer needed to be kept. Poor Richard must find someone else. Someone with young ovaries and little imagination who could bear his Anglo-Saxon offspring like a dutiful wife should. The truth was, she'd been a wretched wife, and he would be better off without her. She was selfish and spoiled. She didn't want to give up her quiet, productive life in exchange for a life of dirty diapers, au pair girls, and burned dinners. She didn't want chaos. She had met other writers who tried to "have it all," women with distracted expressions and clothes that smelled of sour milk and Vicks Vapo-Rub. Women who attended conferences with cell phones strapped to their heads (*Sophia has a runny nose? Did you take her to the doctor? What color is the discharge? Is it clear or is it green?*) or who walked up and down bookstore aisles trying to calm frantic spouses (*MacKenzie has diarrhea? Did you take him to the doctor? Is the poopie brown or is it green?*). She had attended a conference recently with a dapper white-haired novelist in a tweed jacket, a professor at some prestigious back-east college, who had sat through a panel discussion called "The Angel and the Whore: Transcending Archetypal Symbolism in Dystopian Literature" with what appeared to be baby vomit on his lapel. He confessed to Mel later, over a double scotch and soda, that he'd been married before, a thirty-year union that had produced no children and ten novels. He had recently remarried a much younger woman who dropped three children in rapid succession, the result being that he, at sixty-five, now had three children under the age of four! And life was grand! (He hadn't written a word in five years but life was grand.) He stared pensively at a spot just beyond Mel's right shoulder, and she tried not to notice the vomit on his lapel. "I just *had* to know what I was missing," he said tenderly.

Premature death, she thought dismally. *A stroke at sixty-six. A coronary at sixty-seven.*

By the time she got off the plane in Savannah, Mel had decided. When she got back to New York, she'd start looking for an attorney.

The author of note she was replacing had been put up in style in a two-bedroom condo on Tybee Island. *So this is how they treat you when you sell eight million books,* Mel thought, walking through the luxurious place. The condo overlooked the Atlantic Ocean and was so grand that for a moment Mel contemplated calling Booker to come down and join her. But he was on a shoot in Chicago, interviewing students at Northwestern University for a documentary he was making on video game addicts.

"Is there such a thing as a video game addict?" she'd asked in surprise.

"Of course. It's quite common among the young." He was sitting on the sofa playing Mortal Kombat at the time, in a loft in Tribeca outfitted with pinball machines, a basketball hoop, and a video game collection that would surely qualify as every fifteen-year-old male's best wet dream.

Booker Ogar. Six feet four and blond as a Viking. In fact, he was a Viking; his parents had come from Naestved or some other ridiculous-sounding place. Mel had taken one look at him and fallen hard. She had met him five months before at a party she'd attended with Richard, one of those dreary West Village affairs popular with trendy young novelists, artists, and assorted hangers-on trying desperately to outdo one another in sheer outrageousness. At this particular party, one of the writers, a frail, disheveled young woman wearing a tutu, had done splits on a Porada coffee table while reciting the opening lines of Ginsberg's "Howl." Not to be outdone, a performance artist named Tool simulated defecating on a Chinese flag to protest Tiananmen Square, and afterward smeared his seminaked body with chocolate, inviting the spectators to "lick it off." Mel hated these parties. She hated the writers she met there, pretentious snobs who, when they found out she had a contract with a major publishing house, said things like, "Oh, really? So what exactly is it that you write about, dear?" As if being from the South and looking the way she looked, not to mention actually making a *living* as a writer, was somehow beneath them (when they were really just jealous). They were all graduates of the Columbia writing school, and they were like a high school clique, always discussing their latest "projects" in a breezy, affected manner (although it would seem that the New York City literary scene in 1989 was less about work and more about partying). They were always talking about the good old days of the Mudd Club and dear old (dead) Andy Warhol. They pretended to support one another but in actuality they were like terriers fighting over a bone, always gossiping about who was publishing (and who wasn't) and what kind of advances they were getting, watching jealously to see who was going "mainstream" and who wasn't. Mel had sickened of their company long ago, but it seemed that you couldn't go to a party in New York City without bumping into them.

On this particular evening in the West Village, Mel stationed herself behind a potted plant in the corner and proceeded to get very drunk. She was halfway there when Booker walked in. He was hard to miss; he stood head and shoulders above the crowd and he was wearing a gray cable-knit sweater and a pair of jeans, while most of the men were dressed in sport coats. Mel stared at him, all the while repeating to herself, *Look at me, look at me, look at me.* It was a game she liked to play with attractive men. She sent them telepathic messages and then waited for them to find her.

It took Booker about two minutes. A new record.

Later, he said to her, "Let's get out of here."

"I can't."

"Why not?"

"My husband wouldn't like it."

"We don't have to tell him."

She grinned. She was very drunk. She could see Richard across the room talking with some of his prep school buddies. They were talking stocks and bonds and the president's proposed cut on the capital gains tax. The older he got, the preppier Richard got. He was slowly metamorphosing into the perfect WASP. Not a cockroach, a wasp. She giggled, wondering what the Columbia crowd would make of that, what literary conclusions they would draw.

"What are you laughing at?"

"Nothing," she said. "Let's go."

• • •

Richard, of course, did not find it funny. When she finally managed to make it home the following day, he was waiting for her like an avenging prophet from the Old Testament. As their own relationship was predicated on infidelity, it did no good to deny that she'd slept with Booker. She didn't even try. She did promise, though, to attempt not to see him again, a promise that ultimately proved too difficult for her to keep. He was, after all, Booker. Sex with Richard, by comparison, was bland and uninspired. Booker was like no one else she'd ever fallen for. He didn't want to control her. He didn't want to be in charge. He was only three years younger than she but he had the temperament of a boy. An eternal golden boy, a Nordic Peter Pan. He pouted, he had temper tantrums, he watched cartoons on television and ate Captain Crunch for breakfast out of a plastic bowl decorated with Teenage Mutant Ninja Turtles. He was irresistible.

She and Richard moved into separate bedrooms in the brownstone and tried to work it out, but Mel was just going through the motions; her heart wasn't really in it. By the time she left New York for Savannah, she had already made up her mind.

Still, she wished she had done it differently. She had never been unfaithful to J.T., at least not while they were together, but she had been unfaithful to Phil and now Richard. She hoped she wasn't developing a pattern; cheat, love, cheat, leave. As she packed her suitcase for Savannah, she told herself this wouldn't happen again. She'd learned her lesson, and this time would be different.

Besides, Booker was the man of her dreams.

The Dolphin Beach Book Festival was held in an old cotton warehouse along the Savannah River. It was located in the Factors Walk, an area of tall brick warehouses crowding a cobblestoned quay, now a park, along the river. The area had once been a breeding ground for eighteenth-century pirates, prostitutes, stevedores, and stowaways, but in the urban renewal of the 1970s had been reborn as quaint shops, restaurants, and art galleries catering to the tourist crowd. The festival itself was held in an old brick warehouse that had been transformed by the local council into a regional arts center.

Mel gave a morning reading in one of the downstairs rooms to a shifting crowd of approximately thirty-five people, and afterward walked across Bay Street to the Pirates' House for lunch, returning to the arts center around two o'clock. She was scheduled for an afternoon panel session with a novelist who wrote crime thrillers and a woman who wrote, of all things, children's books about a magical rabbit named Pierre.

With any luck at all, she'd be able to make it through to happy hour.

She survived the panel session and then went back to the condo to lie down and rest. She was scheduled that evening for a cocktail party at a local country club, the last event of the festival, where the writers would be exhibited like a group of exotic beasts, and expected to mingle with the paying guests.

She called Booker at the number he'd left and got no answer. That was not unusual when he was working, but it left her feeling forlorn and anxious. She went to the kitchen, opened the bottle of red wine the festival people had so thoughtfully left, and poured herself a glass, taking it and the bottle out onto the balcony. She sat with her feet up on the railing, slowly drinking her wine and watching the dying rays of the sun turn the sea to gold. All along the distant horizon, the sky was washed in shades of rose and gray, and clouds stood in ridges like rows of grazing sheep.

Mel sipped her wine and tried not to worry about Booker. She didn't like leaving him alone for too long. He was a lightning rod for women; he couldn't help it, they flocked to him like cats around a milk bowl, even when she was with him. She couldn't imagine what it must be like when she wasn't there. Not that she blamed him, of course. He couldn't help it. He was just—Booker.

They sent a driver to pick her up, which was a good thing, considering that Mel was already pleasantly buzzed. The cocktail parties were always her least favorite events. It wasn't that she minded making conversation with a room full of strangers. It was just that she felt that they expected her to say something intelligent and witty, and after a while it just got to be too much of a burden, especially after a few cocktails (and after all, wasn't that the *point* of a cocktail party?). She found that after a few drinks she usually reverted to a Southern accent, which of course made people look at her as if she were stupid (especially New Yorkers), and she had a dry sense of humor that, when mixed with alcohol, became nearly combustible. Some people got her, and some didn't. Some people laughed, and some were deeply offended. The whole point of these affairs, of course, was to win new readers, not alienate old ones, so she was always a little nervous about saying the wrong thing.

The Dolphin Beach Book Festival cocktail party was being held at the Regatta Club on beautiful Skidaway Island. It was the usual setup, a room with expansive views overlooking a large body of water, long buffet tables laden with exotic food, an open bar (thank God), and waiters and waitresses in faux evening attire circulating to pick up empty glasses and discreetly supply full ones. The crowd at this affair was somewhat older, more the retirement set, an interesting mix of males and females and Old South aristocracy and Yankee transplants.

Mel set herself up at her favorite station (the bar). "Hello," she said, leaning over to read the bartender's nametag, "Todd."

He gave her a lazy smile. "What would you like, Pretty Lady?"

Nice. Todd had apparently missed the employee training film on sexual harassment in the workplace. "Let's start with a cactus banger, shall we, and then see what we work up to."

"I like your style."

"That means a lot to me, Todd."

"Tequila?"

"Patron Silver."

He smiled, setting a glass down on the bar. "So what's a pretty girl like you doing at one of these parties for old people?"

"I'm one of the writers."

"Oh." The smarmy look on his face disappeared and in its place slipped an expression of vacant professionalism. "Sorry. No offense, ma'am."

"None taken, Todd."

Just then the woman in charge, a tall, officious woman with an aristocratic accent, hurried up to Mel. "We're asking all the *owthas* to sit at the assigned tables, Miss *Bah-clay.*" She lifted her hands to indicate three long tables set up like barricades around the perimeter of the room.

It was the worst possible setup. The writers were herded behind tables, while the bibliophiles wandered up and down the interior of the room staring at them like they were mutants in a freak show. Mel was glad she had started drinking early.

She picked up her cactus banger, gazing morosely around the crowded room and letting her eyes wander over the captive writers, wondering if she would see anyone she knew. You could always tell the fiction writers from the nonfiction writers. The nonfiction writers were the extroverts, standing like barkers in a circus sideshow and calling to the large crowd that invariably thronged their table. The fiction writers, on the other hand, were the introverts. They sat mute, glumly staring into space as if imagining themselves anywhere but here.

Mel quickly spotted the fiction table. Three women sat in varying attitudes of repose. One was talking on a cell phone, one was staring at a spot on the tablecloth in front of her, and one appeared to be sleeping. Mel sighed and pointed with her glass. "I suppose I'm with them," she said.

The festival official looked aghast. "Oh, no, Miss *Bah-clay,* you took the *owtha* of note's place on the program. You're seated at the Poets' Table." Mel looked to where she was pointing, at a slightly raised dais at one end of the room where a man and two women sat gazing down at the crowd. *Dear God, the poets were even worse than the fiction writers.* They looked like the outcast table from high school, the one where all the suicides and visionaries sat, the kids who dressed in black and read Nietzsche during free period. One of the women looked like she might rise at any moment and open a vein, the other glared menacingly out at the crowd gathered in front of the nonfiction writers, and the man was reading aloud, to no one in particular, a rather depressing poem about dead leaves (from his own book, of course). Mel ordered another drink, and went to join them.

The female poets were rather uncommunicative but the male poet, Evan, was friendly enough. He was a pleasant-looking, gray-haired man in a turtleneck sweater. He was friendly, although he did ask Mel if she was a poet, and when she replied, *No, a novelist,* he looked at her like he would a smear of excrement on the bottom of his shoe. The three of them sat on one side of an empty chair and Mel sat on the other, with Evan closest to her. The empty chair was apparently reserved for the poet laureate of Georgia, who was a no-show and was rumored, according to one of the taciturn female poets, to have a "drinking problem." (*Me too!* Mel said, gaily lifting her glass.) After that, the female poets pretty much left her alone.

By the time she had finished her second cactus banger (named, no doubt, for the way her head would feel in the morning), Mel was beginning to enjoy herself. She stacked and restacked her novels in a series of intricate pyramids and began to call out to people hurrying by on their way to the nonfiction table, "Sir, you look like a man who knows his way around a crime scene," or "Madam, when was the last time you read a good romance novel about a serial killer?" In this fashion she managed to draw a pretty good crowd to the Poets' Table, which Evan, at least, seemed to appreciate. He even managed to sell a few of his slim volumes of poetry, and after a while had lapsed into an almost jovial mood. Mel signaled the waitress and ordered another cactus banger for her and one for Evan. She'd never yet met a poet who didn't drink, and Evan, as it turned out, was no exception.

"Ah, tequila," he said, lifting the drink Mel had ordered for him. "Nectar of the gods." It was a nectar Evan seemed all too familiar with, and before long he was ordering tequila shooters Mel had never even heard of, while the crowd of fascinated bibliophiles swirled around them and the lady in charge tried desperately to keep her *owthas* at the Poets' Table in line.

"Have you read any James Dickey?" Mel asked, lining up a couple of Mexican samurais in front of one of her dwindling book pyramids. She was only trying to make friendly conversation. The truth was, she hadn't read poetry since college, and the only poet she'd been able to think of in her inebriated state was Dickey.

Evan ordered another round of shooters. "Dickey!" he barked disdainfully. "That no-talent charlatan! That double-crossing imposter! I taught with Dickey at Vanderbilt, and I can tell you, that man's no poet."

Mel, a little surprised by his vehemence, said, "But *Deliverance*? That's a pretty good novel." She grinned and lifted her shot glass to the spinning crowd. "After all, it put Georgia on the map!" She tossed her drink back and set the glass down on the table.

"A good novelist, yes!" Evan thundered. "A good poet, no!"

Mel thought, *Hey, to each his own, Bud.* The cocktail waitress brought more Mexican samurai. The festival woman had warned her to cut them off thirty minutes ago but the waitress was working a double, and this was the most fun she'd had in ages. Who knew writers could be so entertaining?

"They say he was an airplane pilot," Mel said.

"Who says?"

"He does. I read it in an interview."

"Dickey's a liar, I tell you! The man's a lying chiseler. A fornicator, a hypocrite, a two-bit trickster! You can't trust a thing he says. You can't trust *him*." And with that Evan the Poet stood up and lurched off in search of a bathroom.

"Dickey slept with his wife," one of the other poets said to Mel by way of an explanation.

The crowd, drawn by the melodrama at the Poets' Table, had begun to desert the nonfiction writers in droves. The non-novelists stood on tiptoe, craning their necks to try to figure out what Mel's successful sales technique might be so they could steal it and use it at future book festivals. One of the poets argued bitterly with someone in the crowd over the mechanism of iambic pentameter. At the fiction table, the sole remaining writer put her head back and snored at the ceiling.

It was at moments like this that Mel had to remind herself that this was the life she had chosen. The failed love affairs, the children she would never have, the dull routine of a normal life, these had all been sacrifices on the altar of creative endeavor. Every decision she had ever made had brought her here, to this place, to this moment in time, a long line of choices and effects stretching back to that night in the darkened auditorium when she had listened to Pat Conroy speak and decided to become a writer.

Evan appeared sometime later, wedged between two burly book festival bouncers. He had misbuttoned his tweed sports coat and clamped his cap down at a jaunty angle on his gray curls. Mel could see the bottle of Casa Noble in his pocket.

"They're kicking us out!" he said, pointing with his thumb at one of the bouncers. "The drivers are here. Let's take this party back to my place!" The rest of the writers were being housed in a seedy downtown hotel. Mel hadn't had the heart to tell them about the two-bedroom condo on Tybee Island.

"I'll have to take a rain check," Mel said, wondering for the first time in several hours what Booker was doing. "I've got an early morning flight."

Someone turned the lights up and the club employees started breaking down the tables. Under the harsh overhead lights, the room looked suddenly stripped and forlorn. Mel got up, gathered her purse and coat, and stumbled out into the rainy night to look for her driver.

A month after returning to New York from the book festival, she moved out of the brownstone and in with Booker. Richard seemed to take her request for a divorce rather well, too well, really (Mel began to wonder if he might have something going on the side. Not that she would blame him if he did). They turned the gritty details over to their lawyers and began going through the process of obtaining a respectable New York divorce.

The change in living arrangements should have energized Mel but instead she found herself sinking into one of her depressive episodes (her

Black Slumps, she called them). Her love life was going fine; it was her career that had begun to stagnate. She had begun to find herself bogged
down in the sand trap that came with writing a series. Readers expected
the same thing every time they opened a Flynn Mendez novel. The novels
were gritty without being too disturbing, and there was always an element
of humor to offset the tragedy. Crime-solving in Manolo Blahniks. Kind
of a *Moonlighting* meets *Dirty Harry,* as the boys in the marketing department liked to describe her books.

But Mel was tired of writing the same thing every year. She'd been
watching a Discovery Channel show not too long after her divorce was
granted, and she'd come up with a great idea for a novel. And it would *not*
be a Flynn Mendez novel. Mel pitched the idea to her editor one day over
lunch at Felidia. It would be a thriller, the story of strange cattle mutilations occurring in Montana at the same time that a series of brutally mu-
tilated bodies are cropping up in New York, the presumed work of a serial
killer.

"Can you make it funny?" her editor asked.

This was a year after she'd left Richard and moved in with Booker. It
was during a period of continuing adjustments in her life, personally and
professionally, a midlife crisis coming twenty years too early. She and
Booker were talking about getting their own place but rent-controlled
apartments in New York City were hard to come by, so they made do at
Booker's Tribeca loft, which was really more like a college pad than a
grown-up's apartment. Mel had tried redecorating but Booker didn't like
his stuff touched; he liked the basketball goal where it had always been, he
liked the overstuffed La-Z-Boy recliners that doubled as a sofa positioned
in front of the big-screen TV, he liked the beanbag chairs that made it easy
to sprawl while playing video games scattered around the room like some
kind of exotic fungi. He had a fit when she threw out his Heather Lock-
lear posters (she let him keep the porn videos), and when she replaced his
water bed with a king-size box spring and mattress, he pouted for two
days. Mel realized then that she'd have to tread lightly; she'd have to replace one thing at a time and then wait for him to adjust before trying anything else.

It was a new experience for her, treading lightly. He was the only man
she'd ever done that with, the only man she'd ever tried *not* to upset. The
only man she spent all her time trying to please. To please Booker she
learned to cook, she learned to play poker, she learned to skydive. She wrote

scripts for his documentaries, she helped him organize his office, and she made calls to wealthy patrons who might finance his projects, using those few contacts, among the many she'd had while married to Richard, who still spoke to her after the divorce. She kept herself lean and attractive, and scoured lingerie catalogs in search of outfits she thought he might like.

Booker looked upon sex as a normal part of everyday life, like eating and sleeping, and since he was very good at it, and put a lot of time and effort into making sure Mel enjoyed it as much as he did, she didn't complain.

She made sure he ate well, made sure he took his vitamins, made sure he had clean underwear when he went for meetings with the studio execs. She organized poker nights with his friends and then stayed around to make sure they had enough to eat and drink.

In between taking care of Booker, she signed a contract to produce two more Flynn Mendez novels. And she began secretly working on her magnum opus her novel about the New York serial killer and the Montana cattle mutilations, tentatively titled *Dead Meat*.

All in all, her new life with Booker was not what she had imagined. It was not what she had thought she was leaving Richard for. It was exhausting. Especially in light of the fact that she was pretty sure he was cheating on her.

Not that he would ever admit it, of course. Booker was far too charming for that. He didn't like upsetting people. He liked everyone to be happy, and he didn't care what he had to do to ensure that they were: lie, cheat, steal. (Was it any coincidence that the charming serial killer in her new novel so closely resembled Booker?) She listened to him calmly lie to his producers about shooting schedules and postproduction delays, and she realized that Booker was a consummate liar, one of those people who can convince himself that something is true until it becomes, to him at least, *true*. One of those guys who could lie on an FBI polygraph test and pass with flying colors. So when she called a number that occurred with great regularity on his cell phone bill and a woman named Lucy answered, or when she went to surprise him at a shoot only to find that he wasn't shooting that day, Mel listened to his smooth assurances with a great deal of skepticism.

She married Booker (against the advice of several of her friends and her own good judgment) and over the next few years, she adjusted to her life with him (after all, one of them had to adjust). But over time she found that the little eccentricities she had once seen as adorable—his fickle nature, the boxes of Captain Crunch in the pantry, the all-night X-box tournaments with his friends—were gradually beginning to lose their charm.

Still, there was the matter of that dimple in his chin. And the sex. There was that.

Mel's mother died when she was thirty-three, the same year she married Booker, and she went back to Howard's Mill for the funeral. She didn't see Leland again for another five years, although she talked to him from time to time on the phone, usually when he'd been calling repeatedly, and she had no choice, finally, but to call him back.

He was looked after by a live-in nurse, a widow from Guadalajara named Mercedes who had come north to settle close to her son and his family. Mercedes had raised thirteen children, an occupation that served her well in caring for Leland Barclay, and she didn't take any shit from the old man. She understood English well enough but preferred not to use it, so over the years she and Leland developed their own language, a mishmash of words in both tongues. They relied more on tone of voice than actual language in communicating with each other.

"Goddammit, woman, I need a bath!" Leland would shout at her. "A *baño, comprendez, puta?*"

To which she would inevitably reply (with an obscene gesture), "Chinga tu madre!" which, roughly translated, meant "Bathe yourself, you old goat. You stinking, pus-filled son of a whore."

"I don't know why she stays with you," Mel said to him once.

"Well, Sister, why does anyone stay with someone who makes them miserable?"

"I don't know—why?"

"Money."

"It's not all about money," Mel said coldly.

"Spoken like someone who's always had plenty."

"I don't want your money. I don't even cash your checks anymore."

"Don't matter to me if you do or you don't," Leland said. "Everything I got is yours one day, whether you want it or not, Sister."

"I don't want it. Leave it to your favorite charity."

"You're my favorite charity."

"Leave it to Mercedes."

"Huh!" He snorted loudly. "I put that old *puta* in my will and I'll be dead by sundown."

"You should marry her, then. She's perfect for you."

"Now, Sister, don't be jealous. I loved your mama, in my own way."

"The same way you loved Junior?"

"A man does things he's ashamed of later on. We can't all be saints."

"That's a clever way of putting it."

"I might not have been the best daddy in the world, but I did the best I knew how to do."

"Well, that's all right then."

The summer she turned thirty-eight, she came home to Howard's Mill. She flew into Nashville and rented a car, coming in on the south side of town. It felt odd driving through the quiet streets where she had spent so much of her unhappy childhood. She drove past the country club, past the Dairy Freeze, past the Dixie Drive-In and the ramshackle high school where she had spent long hours counting down the days until she could get the hell out of this hayseed town. The high school was abandoned now in favor of the new county school built out from town. Someone had broken out most of the windows, and the darkened building stood back from the road in the middle of a weed-choked lot covered in kudzu. Everything looked smaller than she remembered, and dirty. The whole town seemed to be drying up, at least the older downtown section, where desolate storefronts advertised GOING OUT OF BUSINESS sales or optimistically proclaimed FOR LEASE. All the growth over the last few years had occurred out by the expressway, miles and miles of fast food chains and strip malls and gas stations that sprouted up around the exits like hemorrhoids. At night, the town looked like the Vegas Strip. Leland had sold the downtown car dealership years ago, and a modern new dealership had sprung up on the outskirts of town, complete with rows and rows of shiny new automobiles and signs that advertised FAST EDDIE'S AUTO! NOBODY WALKS, EVERYBODY RIDES! FAST EDDIE—THE WORKING MAN'S FRIEND!

She'd come home to see Leland because she'd been dreaming about graves. Every night. Not newly dug graves with their fresh mound of dirt, but ancient sunken burial spots covered in creepers and twisting vines. Her therapist said that the graves symbolized unfinished business and that it might be time to go home and confront Leland once and for all, but Mel thought that interpretation weak and decided to stop therapy instead. She had a problem with the direction the therapist was taking, not to mention her fixation on the so-called maternal aspects of her relationship with Booker. Mel was pretty sure the dreams would stop once the therapy stopped.

But they didn't stop. They got worse. They got so bad she couldn't sleep, she couldn't eat, she couldn't write. So, in desperation, she went home to do battle with Leland. She came home for the Mother of All Battles, the Armageddon of Dysfunctional Family Meltdowns. She hated to leave Booker home alone—there was no telling what he might get up to, but she had no choice. There was something she had to get off her chest.

Still when she saw the frail, diminished Leland she was unprepared for the effect it had on her. She had come home expecting to do battle with the bully of her youth, and instead she found a doddering old man. Leland, the rogue tyrant, had disappeared, and in his place was a thin, frail creature, a wispy little gnome of a man who looked like he might blow away in a heavy breeze. He was as small as a child now and walked with a cane, bent over at the waist and moving with the small mincing steps of a geisha. His hair was long and yellowed with age, and his big hairy ears sprouted on either side of his head like toadstools.

The sight of him compressed her heart like a vise. All the ugly things she had saved up to say, all the poison she had stored in her heart for thirty-eight years, stayed buried where they were. She could no more confront him than she could kick an old lame dog who showed up on her doorstep looking for a meal.

"Did you tell him how bad he fucked up your life?" Booker asked when she got home. "Did you beat him within an inch of his life?"

"Shut up, Booker." She'd made the mistake of telling him about her therapy dreams, a decision she now regretted.

"I knew you couldn't. I knew you couldn't bring yourself to do it." He sat in a recliner with a bowl of Cocoa Puffs resting on his lap, looking as fresh and rosy-cheeked as an English schoolboy. The older he got, the younger he looked. There was only three years' age difference between them, but Booker seemed to be regressing further and further into boyhood as she began the steep climb to forty. It was just a matter of time, Mel knew, before people started mistaking her for his mother.

"Why don't you stay out of it? It's none of your business."

"It's none of my business when you can't sleep at night? It's none of my business when you walk around the house all day in an old robe and a pair of ratty slippers?"

"Fuck off."

"You fuck off."

"Next time I'll send you. You're so eloquent. You're so good at cleaning up messes."

"Why would I want to go down there where everyone talks like Gomer Pyle?" He put his hand up like a traffic cop stopping traffic. "Sha-zam!" he said. "Ga-aw-lly." He laughed and dropped his hand.

Booker was one of those people who laughed at his own jokes even when they weren't funny.

"That's right. Why would I send you to do my talking for me when you can't even string a coherent sentence together?"

"Down where everybody talks like they've got marbles in their mouth. Down in the land of ignorant hillbillies."

Mel knew at that moment that her marriage was over.

Two months later she found a lump in her breast, and shortly after that, Booker left for good.

One word. Two syllables. Can anyone who's never heard the diagnosis *cancer* truly understand what it conjures? (Dread. Despair. Death.) Mel walked out of the surgeon's office feeling like a reprieved felon. (*You won't be executed today, but perhaps tomorrow, or maybe even the day after that. I really don't know. We'll just have to wait and see, won't we?*) Mortality is just a word until cancer. Every night you go to sleep aware of one more day of amnesty, and every morning you wake with fate hanging over your head like a noose. A trapdoor waiting to be sprung. A guillotine blade waiting to fall. A nightmare without end.

On the day Mel walked out of the surgeon's office, it was a bright, glorious spring day. The trees along Central Park were in full leaf. Traffic crowded the streets; plumes of exhaust disappeared against the pale blue sky. Everything was the same, and yet everything was different. Mel watched an old woman tottering along the street and she thought, *I'll never grow old.* She watched a young couple kissing in the park and she thought, *I'll never laugh again. I'll never love.* Despair settled over her like a thick, dank cloud. She couldn't breathe. She couldn't feel. As she walked she was thinking, *I can't live like this, I can't live like this.* It ran through her head like a mantra. By the time she reached her apartment, the mantra had changed. *I don't have to live like this, I don't have to live like this.*

It was her life. She could end it any way she chose.

Somehow that changed things. The idea that she could end her life if the despair became too much to bear caused a sudden shift in her perspective. It was odd, but the idea that she could step off a ledge or walk in front of a train or slip into a drug-induced coma if she so chose was strangely comforting. It gave her back a feeling of control over her life.

She told two close friends and then swore them to secrecy. She couldn't bear the idea of people looking at her with pitying eyes. She couldn't bear the thought of people whom she didn't like, or who didn't like her, being kind to her because of pity. She didn't want to see the fear in other people's eyes. She had her own despair to deal with; she didn't want to deal with theirs. She jettisoned all the negative people in her life, the depressives, the therapy addicts, the naysayers. She couldn't afford to have them around her anymore. It would take everything she had just to get well again.

"What are you going to tell Booker?" her friends asked her.

"The truth."

When she told him, he went into the bedroom and shut the door. Later he came out and his eyes were red and puffy. "What is it you want from me?" he said. "What is it you expect me to do?" She saw then that the tears had not been for her; they had been for himself.

"I want you to leave," she said. She hadn't decided until that moment but now that she'd said it, she knew it was true. She couldn't get well with him here. She couldn't take care of herself and Booker at the same time.

The doctors were guardedly optimistic. "It's early stage, and with the right treatment you have a ninety-five percent chance of making it five years," they said, as if they were granting her a boon. But then, in case her spirits should rise too high, they would add, "Of course, with breast cancer there are no guarantees. The literature is filled with cases of women diagnosed with Stage IV who live twenty years and women with Stage I who live nine months." They had been trained not to give hope. How much better to paint a bleak picture first, and then when things turned out to be not so dire after all, the patient would kiss their hands in gratitude.

By the time she'd finished treatment, Mel hated them all.

Gradually, she began to pull herself out of despair. She agreed to surgery to remove the lump, and afterward she agreed to chemotherapy, putting her head down and plodding through it like a dumb animal, saying I can do this. I can do this. But first she bought a wig (she refused the bald head and scarf that loudly proclaimed *Victim*) and then she had herself hypnotized to alleviate the hair loss and nausea. She ate a healthy diet and took large quantities of vitamins; she learned to meditate. She read every book she could find on miraculous healings and promising alternative therapies. She followed her doctors' orders but she supplemented them with whatever alternative therapies made sense to her. She learned to trust her intuition. (After all, the doctors could not guarantee success with their horrific treatments, so what did she have to lose?) Her hair, which had fallen out soon after the first chemotherapy treatment, began to regrow after the fourth. With her healthy diet, her constant exercise, and her afternoon naps, she began to feel better than she had in years. She didn't work, she didn't call friends, she didn't fritter her time away on meaningless pursuits. She spent all her time trying to get well.

When she called Leland and told him, he cried like a baby. Later, he said, "Don't you die up there with all those Yankee strangers. You come home to die, Sister."

She knew then that she wouldn't go home. And she wouldn't die either. She was strangely grateful to him, grateful for the anger he always roused in her, for her sudden determination to outlive him no matter what. She was glad now for his money, thankful that he'd pulled himself up from poverty and turned himself into a self-made millionaire. She had no health insurance, and he paid for everything, the doctors, the trips to Germany and Mexico.

She went to see a new therapist to help lighten her load of childhood anger and regret. She kept a dream journal. She paid close attention to her fourth-chakra issues. She meditated and tried to open her heart to love, trust, and compassion.

After her last chemo treatment, she went out with her friends to celebrate. *When do you start radiation?* they asked her.

I don't, she said. It had just occurred to her. She would do no more damage to her body. No scarred lungs, no late-blooming leukemia. Enough was enough. Quality of life was more important to her than quantity of life, although she knew most cancer patients didn't share her philosophy. And that was okay, too.

Her surgeon, when she told him her decision, wasn't happy.

"Well, if I'd known you weren't going to do radiation, I would have just taken the breast." His attitude was so condescending, so cavalier, as if her breast was his to do with as he pleased. He was blond, blue-eyed, the darling of the ward. But by then, she had had enough.

"Really?" she said coolly. "Well, how about if I just take your balls? Hmm? How about if I just cut them off? Would you like that?"

His eyes flashed anger (no one had ever spoken to him like that), then concern, and then fear (My God, she was crazy. She was capable of anything. Did no one screen these women?) as he turned and hurried out to find the nurse, leaving her chart behind on the table in his haste.

Mel watched him go. As the door closed behind him, she felt hope welling up inside her, swelling like a sail. She put her head back and laughed.

She knew then that she'd get well.

What else is there to say? Human beings are resilient; they can adapt to anything. Life returns in degrees, in increments, like the sun inching its way across a bare floor on a winter's day.

Mel continued meditating, she chanted and opened her heart to the Infinite, she walked in the park and drank her wheatgrass shakes and ate brown rice and seaweed until she could stand it no more. She went for her three-month checkup and then her six-month checkup, endured the X-rays, the scans, the gentle prodding of competent fingers. Her new doctor (a woman) patted her arm and said, "Whatever you're doing, keep up the good work."

Each visit was a milestone, a celebration. Six months cancer-free, one year, two years, and you give a deep sigh of relief. By five years, it's all begun to fade.

She thought often of Sara and Annie and Lola during these years, thought about calling them and letting them share her burden. She knew they'd do it gladly. But how to begin? They were no longer wide-eyed girls standing on the cusp of life. Their lives had gone in such different directions.

They had chosen motherhood and she had not. That, in itself, was not a barrier to friendship but it was an impediment, at least to Mel. They had their own busy lives, and she was gradually returning to hers. In moments of quiet reflection, she pondered the irony of their situations. She had rejected motherhood; yet while her friends had been happily growing fetuses, she had grown a tumor.

There was a book waiting to be written.

She went back to work, pulling the novel she had begun all those years ago, her magnum opus, out from underneath her bed. Her writing now had a new depth, a maturity, a quality of infused suffering that hadn't been there before her illness.

By seven years it was all a distant memory, a nightmare, something that had happened to someone else. She was who she was before; and yet, not quite. Never quite.

Chapter 31

~~~~~~~~~~~

By four o'clock they'd had enough of the sand and the sun and the synchronized swimming, and they headed back to the yacht. April made another batch of frozen margaritas and the four of them sat on the aft deck around a long table, watching as the sun fell slowly in the sky. Captain Mike put Jimmy Buffett on the stereo and went to help April in the galley. They could hear them from time to time in between tracks, laughing and talking.

"Is there anything more annoying?" Mel asked sullenly, lifting her drink.

"What?" Annie said, listening while Jimmy Buffett sang about changes in latitudes and changes in attitudes. She had never, until this very moment, understood what that song meant.

"Being stuck in an enclosed space with two people who can't keep their hands off each other."

"You wouldn't be complaining if it was you in the galley with Captain Mike."

"I told you. He's not my type."

"You told us, but no one believes you."

Mel glanced at her but didn't say anything. Nighthawks darted over the deserted beach like large exotic insects. The sun hung low over the horizon, catching in the branches of the distant trees, staining them crimson.

"Are you dating anyone right now?" Sara asked Mel.

"No." She stared at the bottom of her glass. "There was an editor I was seeing, but that didn't work out."

Lola asked, "Do you like being alone?" and Annie said, "Lola!" as if she'd said something inappropriate. Lola blushed, but before she could respond, Mel answered, "Not really. No."

"No one likes being alone," Sara said.

Mel looked at her. "What's that supposed to mean?"

"Nothing. I'm agreeing with you."

"Well, don't say it like that."

"Like what?"

"Like, *Oh, poor Mel, she's spent her life making shitty choices and now she's all alone.*"

"Look, Mel, no one's trying to make you feel bad about your choices. It's your life."

"That's right."

"Okay, forget it then."

"Fine."

"Fine."

Annie looked at Lola and rolled her eyes. Jimmy Buffett sang about Mother, Mother Ocean. Over in the corner, the elephant raised its trunk and trumpeted silently.

Annie went down to the forward stateroom to use the head, and when she came back up on deck, Sara and Lola were standing at the rail watching a school of skates swim by. "They remind me of underwater bats," Lola said, standing with her feet on the bottom rail and leaning over excitedly. Sunlight glinted off the lenses of her dark glasses.

"I think they're creepy," Sara said. "They look a lot like stingrays. Can they sting you?"

"No," Mel said. She was sitting at the table with her feet up on an empty chair. "They don't have stingers."

Lola crossed her arms on the railing and stared pensively at the black shapes gliding through the water. "They look like dark angels," she said. "Like avenging spirits." Sometimes Lola said the strangest things.

Annie joined them at the railing. They did look like bats gliding through the water, their black wings flapping. There were probably twenty of them swimming in circles between the boat and the shore, clearly visible against the sandy bottom, flitting through the water like wraiths.

"Once I was swimming and they came up to me and let me pet them," Lola said. Her skin was the color of honey. Her nose was covered by a sprinkling of freckles. Looking at her, Annie was reminded suddenly of Agnes Grace, the girl she had met while volunteering at the Baptist Home for Children. Agnes Grace would love the skates. She would love the beach. Annie was pretty sure the child had never been any farther than Bakertown but she would love the ocean and its exotic sea life.

Sara said, "If I was swimming and I looked down and saw those things, I'd probably have a heart attack." She pointed with her glass. "What was that?"

Annie looked where she was pointing. "What was what?"

"That dark shiny shape that just passed beneath the boat. And don't tell me it was a skate because it wasn't. It was long and narrow like a cigar."

"It might have been a barracuda," Lola said. "Did it have big teeth?" She grimaced, showing her teeth.

Mel got up and came over to the railing. "Maybe it was a shark."

"Okay," Sara said. "Now I'm getting chills."

"Don't be such a chickenshit," Mel said.

"I don't see you getting in the water."

"Well, I would if I wanted to."

"If it was a shark," Annie said, not wanting them to get started again, "it was a small one."

"Even small sharks have big teeth."

"There it is!" Lola said, pointing.

"Where?"

"There!" She stood up on her toes and leaned far over the railing. "It's a barracuda."

"Damn it, Lola, if you fall in I'm not going in after you."

Lola began jumping up and down. "See!" she said. Without warning, her glasses slid down her nose and plopped into the water. They sank slowly, weaving back and forth like a small frightened sea creature. "Oh, no," Lola said.

"I hope those weren't expensive. I have an extra pair of sunglasses in my purse," Annie said.

"They're not sunglasses," Lola said, staring blindly at the water. "They're real glasses."

"What do you mean, real glasses?"

"You know. Prescription. They turn dark in the sun, but they're not sunglasses."

They stood staring at her while, behind them, Jimmy Buffett sang about cheeseburgers in paradise. Mel said, "Are you still legally blind?"

Lola laughed and put her hands on the railing to steady herself. "Yes," she said.

"Do you want me to go down to the stateroom and get your other pair?"

Lola stopped laughing. "Other pair?" she said vaguely. She swiveled her head in Mel's direction. "The other pair's back in Birmingham."

Annie groaned. Mel stared at Lola. "Okay," she said patiently, as if she was speaking to an afflicted child. "What about your contacts?"

Lola bit her lower lip. Annie was reminded again of the child at the Baptist Home, Agnes Grace, after she'd done something wrong and been found out, and was trying to charm her way out of trouble. "My contacts are back at the beach house," Lola said. "But that's okay," she said, squinting and holding one hand out in front of her. "I'll be okay."

"What're we going to do?" Sara said to Mel. "We can't leave her wandering around the boat, not without a Seeing Eye dog, anyway, or a cane."

Lola giggled. "Seeing Eye dog," she said, "that's funny."

Mel stared despondently at the spot where the glasses had disappeared. "All right, well, one of us will have to go in after them. The water can't be much deeper than twenty feet."

"Are you crazy? There's a barracuda down there."

"So what? It won't hurt you."

"Fine. You go in then."

They both looked at Annie. "Count me out," she said, tapping the side of her head as if she were trying to dislodge something. "I have an inner ear problem. I can't dive much deeper than five feet."

Mel thought about it a moment, and then turned to face the galley doors. "Oh, Captain Mike!" she shouted. When he appeared in the doorway she crooked her finger, beckoning for him to come on deck. "We need you," she said sweetly.

It took him about twenty minutes of diving in thirty feet of water to find the glasses. When he surfaced, holding them above his head, they all cheered. He climbed aboard, and handed the glasses to Lola with a little flourish. She couldn't see a thing, of course, but Sara helped her grasp them and watched while she slid them on to her face.

"I can see! I can see!" Lola said, and for some reason they all laughed, more with relief than anything else because now they wouldn't have to motor home early. Everyone was happy again, resettling themselves in the deck chairs as the sun sank finally beyond the horizon and evening came on.

April came on deck carrying a T-shirt and a towel that she draped across Captain Mike's broad shoulders. He dried himself and snapped the towel at her playfully, and she squealed and ran back through the sliding doors into the galley. He was in a good mood. The closer it got to the end of the week, the more jovial he became. Mel wondered if it had anything to do with the fact that they'd all be leaving soon and he and April could get back to the private life they lived when no one was around.

"Join us," Mel said to him, lifting her margarita glass. She knew it was useless. He was in love with one woman, and nothing else mattered. J.T. had been like that.

"No," he said, his eyes reflecting the slate-blue color of the sea. "The captain of the ship has to keep his wits about him." His hair dripped steadily onto his clean T-shirt. It showed a shamrock and read, in big green letters across the front, WHO'S YOUR PADDY? "If you ladies don't need me, I think I'll go in and help April with supper." He stopped at the door and turned around again, grinning. A dimple appeared deep in his left cheek.

"Try not to drop anything else in the water until I get back," he said to Lola. "Try not to do anything stupid."

Mel knew suddenly what it was that she wanted. She wanted a man just like him. Someone she could have dinner with, bounce ideas off of, someone who would be there for her when the chips were down, when she was at her most unlovable, when she was old, sick, and out of print.

Jimmy Buffett posed the question "Why Don't We Get Drunk (and Screw)?" Twilight fell. Pewter-colored clouds massed in the sky, and a faint smattering of stars appeared on the horizon. The island was a dull glimmering shape now, a band of white beach bordered on one side by the black water and on the other by a dark fringe of forest.

Captain Mike came out to light the lanterns. "Dinner will be ready in twenty minutes," he said. He was whistling. Here on the water, he was very much a man in his element. A man tempered, but not broken, by adversity, Mel thought, noting his profile in the lamplight. She remembered the dead wife, the life he'd had to pack up and stow away like an old suitcase. J.T. Radford would look much the same, Mel imagined, trying suddenly to picture him as he must look today.

She finished her drink and set the glass down on the table, determined not to go down that road. Life was too short; it was useless to spend it wallowing in misery. She had learned that years ago.

It did no good to remember what she had once had, and lost.

They ate dinner on the aft deck, a wonderful meal of grilled ahi with an espresso glacé, while darkness closed around them like a curtain and ghost crabs scurried along the beach in the moonlight. Captain Mike and April joined them, and it was one big party (except that Captain Mike drank tea). He was charming and sweet, getting up to make them fresh drinks, and clearing the plates when they'd eaten their fill. Sometime during the long afternoon and evening he had acquired a certain swagger that suited him well. He had the jaunty, rolling gait of a man of the sea, and it wasn't too hard to imagine him as a pirate with a plumed hat and a cutlass strapped to his waist. He sat at one end of the table between Lola and April. Mel was pretty sure if she dropped her head beneath the tablecloth and looked, she'd find his hand plunged deep into April's girlish lap. He had the smug, self-satisfied look of a man who thinks he's being clever, secretly running his hand over his lover's thigh. Mel knew that look. She'd seen it often enough.

Lola laughed suddenly, her tinkling laugh like music, like coins jangling in a pocket. She stood up and knocked over a glass.

"Careful!" April called out, watching as she made her way to the galley door. "Do you need someone to go with you?"

"No."

"Are you sure?" Mel said.

"Why is the boat moving?" Lola said.

"The boat's not moving, silly."

Captain Mike stood up and went to help her.

Later, they moved up to the flybridge, where they had an unobstructed view of the stars. They sat at the horseshoe-shaped banquette with their drinks resting on the table in front of them. Behind them the dinghy rested in its cradle, covered by a bright blue tarpaulin. A yellow moon rose over the water. The great vault of the sky stretched above them, an endless dome of sparkling lights.

"Don't climb down these without me here to help," Captain Mike said, pointing to the steps to the aft deck. "They're too steep and you're too drunk." The deck lights illuminated the chiseled line of his jaw, the heavy browridge above the strong straight nose.

"Who're you calling drunk?" Mel said belligerently.

"If we call you, will you carry us down?" Lola asked, her sharp little laugh ringing out like a bell.

"Yes," he shouted, disappearing down the steps. They could hear April below, clearing up the supper dishes.

Mel had a sudden memory of J.T. the first night they met him, carrying her up the ridge in the moonlight while Sara stood waiting, her face rigid with anger and envy. "Do you remember the first time we met J.T.? That night at the bonfire?"

"No," Sara said flatly, lifting her glass.

"You didn't want to go," Mel said, shaking her head, her eyes shining in the lamplight.

A ship passed slowly out to sea, its lights twinkling in the darkness. Sara's expression was composed, polite. "How's your father?" she asked Mel. "How's Leland?"

"He's—old." The image of Leland as she'd last seen him filled Mel with a strange sadness. She sipped her drink and looked around the table at their faces, pale and lucid as the moon. Moonchildren. Moon girls.

"I remember your daddy," Lola said, wiping her upper lip with a dainty finger. "He was sweet."

"Sweet? Leland?" Mel looked at Sara, who smiled faintly. "You must be thinking of somebody else." She didn't want to talk about Leland any more than Sara wanted to talk about J.T. Leland was an old man; his days were numbered. It didn't seem right talking about him now. It didn't seem right blaming him. Even in her inebriated state she knew that. He probably thought he'd been a good husband and father. He'd provided financially for his family, made sure no one ever went hungry or without. His bullying had been his way of toughening them up for the hardships of life. Mel doubted he'd ever spent one minute wrestling with his conscience, wondering if he'd done the right thing by Juanita or Junior. He probably thought Junior had died of a congenital weakness of character. He probably thought Juanita had died of agoraphobia. Besides, he had one child who'd managed to survive childhood. Mel was his proof that he'd done things right.

"I don't think I ever met your dad," Annie said.

"You'd remember him if you had."

"It's great that you're a writer and you can write him off," Sara said. She frowned slightly and tilted her head, as if something had just occurred to her. "Is that where the saying comes from?"

Mel drank steadily. She set her glass down on the table and wiped the back of her mouth with one hand. "What are you rambling on about?"

"Your character. Flynn Mendez. She has a problem with male authority figures."

"So you have read my books!"

"I've read a few. Enough to know what I'm talking about. Enough to know that Flynn Mendez bears a striking resemblance to you. Every time she sticks a stiletto into a villain I imagine you metaphorically sticking a stiletto into Leland."

Mel snorted derisively and put her head back, striving to keep her tone indifferent. "It's fiction. It's all fiction. Besides, I let go of that shit with Leland years ago. That's what therapy's for."

She was a big talker. She wasn't fooling anyone; she could see it in their faces. What was it Leland used to say? *Big hat, no cattle. All suds, no beer.* She'd dreamed for years of confronting him, and then when the moment finally presented itself, she'd chickened out. How do you confront a dried-up husk of a man? A man who's cried over you and supported you through cancer. A man who was still there when all the others were gone. How do you confront a man like that, how do you tell him your trust issues, your broken relationships, your inability to love completely are all based on his piss-poor parenting skills?

The answer, of course, is that you don't. The time for confrontation was long past; Mel had been through enough therapy to know that.

All that was left now was forgiveness.

• • •

Later, Annie drank so much that she did her impersonation of Dolly Parton having sex with Porter Wagoner. (*Naw, Porter, you cain't put it there. What kind of girl do you think I am?*) Lola and Mel rolled around on the banquette thumping each other on the back. Sara laughed so hard she wet herself.

Captain Mike came up on the flybridge to check on them. "I was going to offer you girls another drink, but I think maybe you've had enough."

"Who are you, the Booze Nazi?" Mel took off her shoes and pitched them at him. One landed on the deck but the other one sailed over the railing into the water. "Now look what you made me do," she said.

He turned and called down to April to make a pot of coffee and bring it up.

"You know that's an urban legend," Mel said. "Coffee does not sober you up."

"Who says we have to sober up?" Annie said.

"Captain Mike."

"Just one more," Annie pleaded. "Come on, *Admiral* Mike, we're on vacation."

"Nice," Mel said.

"Shut up," Annie said. "I know what I'm doing."

He walked past them and over to the helm to check the instruments. He peered at the dark floating shape of the island. "I'm cutting you off for your own good."

Mel made a face at his wide back. She nudged Lola with her toe. "Hey, who's the employer here and who's the employee?" she asked in a loud voice.

He turned around and gave her a fierce look. "Who's the captain and who's the passenger?" he said. He kept his eyes on Mel long enough for her to know that he was serious. "It's late," he added, more reasonably, turning back around. "As soon as April brings the coffee, we'll shove off." He went back to checking his instruments and getting the yacht ready for departure. Behind his shoulder, the moon shone like a lantern. Edie Brickell & New Bohemians sang "What I Am."

Annie put her head back to look at the stars. The alcoholic haze in her head had settled down to a pleasant buzz, a feeling of light-headedness and euphoria. She wished she could feel this way always, as light and airy as a thistle floating on a breeze, weightless and lucid and empty of all emotion, even regret. Even guilt.

A pair of deer glided across the moonlit beach. Far off in the forest, a fox barked.

"This place is kind of creepy when the sun goes down," Sara said, looking at the shadowy island.

"You can feel the dead everywhere," Lola said, resting her cheek on her hand. In the moonlight, she had the beatific look of a martyred saint. "So lonely."

Sara touched her lightly on the arm, as if to reassure her.

"Sometimes I get sad," Lola said.

"We all do," Sara said.

"That's part of life."

"As long as you're not sad all the time."

"I'm not."

Mel sat up suddenly and pushed her coffee away. "It doesn't help that Briggs has you on all that medication."

Lola smiled sadly and stared at the moonlit beach. "He does it because he loves me."

"He has a funny way of showing it."

"He doesn't want me to feel my unhappiness," Lola said. "He doesn't want me to suffer. It's kind of like euthanasia, only slower."

Captain Mike flicked on the running lights. A wisp of melancholy floated on the warm night air, settling over the deck and its occupants.

"Slow euthanasia," Mel said. "That sounds like a tropical drink."

"Everything sounds like a drink to you."

"Let's make one up. What do you think? Vodka and absinthe? Rum and absinthe?"

"I'm pretty sure absinthe is illegal."

"Let's see if we can get some. I bet Captain Mike can get us some."

Captain Mike ran his fingers over the instrument panel, flicking switches and checking gauges. "Sorry girls, you'll have to get your own illegal substances," he said.

Lola's face in the moonlight was pale and raw, a wounded face, lost in painful memories. She seemed imbued with sadness, lit from within by a flickering, indistinct light. But then a strange thing happened. She put her head back and stared at the sky, and her face cleared and she was suddenly soft and pink-cheeked as a child, and you could see the woman Lola might have been had time and circumstance not conspired against her. "Look at all those stars," she said dreamily. "Look at that sky."

April brought their coffee, which was strong and heavy with warm, sweet cream. They sat in companionable silence, drinking and watching Captain Mike get the boat ready. The starry night stretched above them. A sudden gust of wind from the east brought with it the scent of rain. After a while, Sara stirred and said, "Do you know what I was afraid of when I agreed to come on this trip?"

"Alcohol poisoning?" Mel said.

"I was afraid I'd be bored." She picked up her coffee cup, and held it in front of her in both hands. "I was afraid after all these years apart, we wouldn't have anything to talk about. But the funny thing is, the minute I saw you all it felt like we were eighteen again. We're different, but the friendship's still there, it's intact, and it makes me feel—I don't know, safe. Y'all are the sisters I never had. I can tell you anything." She glanced around the table, suddenly shy. "There's nothing we can't talk about," she finished weakly.

Everyone was quiet. They stared at their coffee cups, too polite to disagree with her. Over in the corner, the elephant closed his eyes and went to sleep. There were some things no one was ready to talk about.

At least, not yet.

Chapter 32

~~~~~~~~

Annie was one of those women who went to pieces when her last child went off to college. She had spent twenty years arranging schedules, making sure everyone got to soccer practice and music lessons on time, making sure school deadlines were met and social activities were properly organized. Even up until the very last minute Carleton left for Duke she was busy organizing, making sure he had the right clothing, making sure he packed the proper necessities, making sure he didn't forget his toenail clippers or his asthma inhaler or his athlete's foot cream. When they dropped him off at the dorm the first time, she stayed and cleaned his room while Carleton and Mitchell went off to do some last-minute shopping. She made his bed and arranged his closet with a series of color-coded organizers; she packed his clothes neatly in his chest of drawers and made sure his desk was outfitted with the proper school supplies. She hung his Master P and Twiztid posters on the wall above his bed and his robe on a hanger behind the door. His slippers and bath supplies she placed discreetly beneath his bed.

When Carleton saw the room he said, "Mom, you know I have a room-mate, right?"

"Don't worry, I left plenty of room for his stuff."

"He'll think I'm a clean freak when he sees this room. He'll think I'm an obsessive-compulsive psychopath."

"No, he won't. He'll think you come from good people."

Mitchell, noting the color-coordinated closet, said, "Honey, I think the boy might have a point here," but Annie gave him "the look," the look every woman knows innately how to use, the one guaranteed to curdle milk or shrivel male testes with a single glance.

The first week after they dropped him off, Annie sat around the house listening to the clock tick. *Tick-tock* went her grandmother's antique man-tel clock. After a while she could hear it in her head like a metronome, like someone trying to beat their way out of her skull with a tiny hammer. *Tick-tock-tick-tock-tick-tock.*

She knew other women who'd gone through the same thing when their last child left home and they suddenly found themselves with too much time on their hands. Some went back to work, some went back to school, some started their own business or embarked on torrid love affairs with men not their husbands. The least imaginative among them got plastic surgery.

None of these things appealed to Annie. "Let's have another baby," she said to Mitchell one night over dinner. He had just stuck a piece of filet mignon into his mouth and was busy chewing, and as her words sank in, his eyes bulged and he seemed to be having trouble swallowing. Annie hoped she wasn't going to have to do the Heimlich maneuver. She knew how to use it on children—of course, you held them across your knees and pounded them on the back—but she couldn't imagine doing that to some-one of Mitchell's heft and build.

He opened and closed his mouth several times and then took a long drink of sweet tea (she made it now with artificial sweetener to keep his blood sugar from spiking but he hadn't seemed to notice). "Are you crazy?" he said finally.

Apparently so. She sighed and got up to go into the kitchen to polish the toaster. She could hear Mitchell chuckling to himself in the dining room.

The loss of her sons was made worse by a long period of spiritual malaise that Annie had been steadily undergoing. Her crisis of faith was not really a crisis; it was more a gradual evaporation, like milk seeping through cheesecloth. She preferred to think of it as a "questioning." It had begun many years ago and was based, at least in part, on a simple query made by four-year-old William. It was Christmas and they were readying a box for the needy, "for the poor little children who don't usually have a visit from Santa," and William looked up at her with his large blue eyes and asked innocently, "But, Mommy, why doesn't Santa bring the poor children toys? Aren't they good?" Looking down into his angelic face, Annie was struck dumb. She wrestled for a moment with the concepts of good and evil before replying simply, "Honey, Santa tries to bring each child one gift. It's the parents who bring all the others, and poor parents can't afford toys."

From that moment on Santa only brought her boys one gift each, and all the others were neatly wrapped with tags proclaiming *Merry Christmas From Mommy & Daddy.*

But William's question started her thinking, and it was just a short leap from Santa Claus to Jehovah. She found herself puzzling over a loving God who supposedly rewarded the good and punished the bad, because if you looked around, you could see that that wasn't true at all. *The meek shall inherit the earth,* but not in this lifetime, and in the meantime liars, fornicators, and thieves were rising to the highest echelons of public office, and good simple people who'd never broken a commandment their entire lives were struggling to pay their medical bills. Where was a loving God in all of that?

Reverend Reeves was an old-time fire-and-brimstone preacher, and he didn't take kindly to her queries. She could have found another denomination, of course, one that didn't mind its congregants asking questions relating to faith and fairness, but she had grown up in the Harvest Hollow Baptist Church, as had her parents and grandparents before her, and the church had provided a sort of framework, a scaffolding to build her entire life upon. She couldn't very well tear that scaffolding down unless she had something else to replace it with. And Mitchell had grown up in the church, too, and was comfortable there, as were the boys, who, with the benefit of a worldview shaped by *Sesame Street,* Barney the Purple Dinosaur, and *Thomas the Tank Engine,* seemed oblivious to the more apocalyptic aspects of Reverend Reeves's sermons.

From time to time Mitchell would ask her, "Honey, what's wrong?" And she would be tempted to tell him, to lay it all out for him in black and white. But to do that she would have to start at the beginning, she would have to go all the way back to that moment at the Mexican restaurant when she made the conscious decision to sleep with Paul Ballard, and thereby changed the course of her life forever. She would have had to use Mitchell as her confessor and try as hard as she might, she could not imagine herself being cowardly enough to do that.

It did no good to talk about forgiveness because the reality was, sin was sin. In moments of quiet contemplation, with the *tick-tock* banging in her head like a drum, Annie felt like Marie Antoinette on her way to the guillotine.

Annie had donated clothes and money to the Baptist Home for Children but she'd never actually volunteered to work there. The home was a kind of halfway house for children whose parents were incarcerated but who didn't want to give up custody or place their children in the dubious foster care system. It was located on approximately seventy acres of land south of Nashville, and included a pond, a recreation center, a chapel, and a series of cottages scattered throughout where children lived with houseparents and attended a local Christian school.

Annie had attended numerous fund-raisers for the home but had never actually set foot on the grounds. So when she got a call from Mildred Dodd asking her if she'd be willing to do some volunteer work on the campus, she was, for a moment, struck dumb. This was on a Tuesday afternoon not long after Carleton had first left for college. Annie was lying on a deck chair out by the pool reading one of her trashy novels.

"Hello," Mildred said finally. "Are you there?"

"Yes, I'm here," Annie said. "Sorry. When did you say you needed me?" It was one thing to send money and clothes, but something else entirely to have physical contact with the poor unfortunates who lived at the Baptist Home for Children. Annie wondered if, given her current fragile emotional state, that was such a good idea.

"Next Thursday. We need someone to volunteer in the afterschool care program. You know. Just help with homework, that sort of thing."

Annie said, "Homework?"

"These are elementary schoolchildren, so the homework is really no big deal."

"Thursday, did you say? Let me check my calendar." Annie put her hand over the receiver and sighed. She watched a calico cat prowl the outer edges of the wrought-iron fence dividing the back lawn from the north pasture. It must be one of Alan Jackson's cats; she'd never seen it before. Sparky, who was lying just underneath her chair, lifted his grizzled snout and growled. He had once been a fierce Jack Russell terrier, but over the years had suffered a series of strokes so that now his head sat at an odd angle on his shoulders, and his tongue protruded slightly to one side. He was nearly blind and deaf and incontinent, and he dragged one leg when he walked. Other than that, he was in pretty good shape. The vet predicted that with the proper (expensive) medication and perhaps a surgery or two (also expensive) Sparky would live at least another three or four years. Mitchell would have put him down long ago (*Damn, honey, that's just sad*) if Annie had not stubbornly refused to allow that. Sparky might be sad, but he was all she had left of the boys' childhoods.

She took her hand off the receiver. "I'm so sorry," she said. "I've checked my calendar, and Thursday won't work for me."

"How about Tuesday?"

Annie pretended to look. "No, I'm sorry, Tuesdays and Thursdays are pretty much booked. But thank you so much for thinking of me!" She had learned years ago how to graciously turn down a volunteer position. She'd had lots of practice.

Mildred Dodd, however, was wise to all the usual moves. "Well," she said archly, "I'm also in charge of the church thrift shop committee, and I note that you haven't worked a shift in quite a while, so let me see . . . how about the week of October second? Or the week of October sixteenth," she added smoothly.

Annie mentally calculated her proposal. One day at the Baptist Children's Home versus one week working at the church thrift shop. She had to hand it to Mildred; the woman was cunning. "Oh, wait just a moment," she said, pretending to check her calendar again. "I think I may have an opening after all. I can't work at the home this *coming* Thursday, but I can the *following* Thursday."

"Lovely!" Mildred said. "Check in at the administration cottage at two o'clock. That's the first building on your left, just inside the gates."

Annie clicked off the phone and tossed it on to the patio table. Sparky waited until the cat had disappeared and then dragged himself over to the fence to investigate. The metronome in her head went *tick-tock-tick-tock*.

Annie had never really liked Mildred Dodd, which was not very Christian, but true. Mildred had ruled the Women of God meetings with an iron fist for the last twenty years. It was Mildred who had organized Face the Truth Day, when rows and rows of little white crosses symbolizing aborted babies had been set up on the church lawn. Annie hadn't said anything at the planning meeting but when they pulled up in front of the church the following Sunday morning and she saw the rows and rows of little white crosses, she felt sick to her stomach. She put her hand to her waist and Mitchell said, "What? Are you sick?" and she said, "Yes, take me home."

Later, after he'd gone back to catch the late service, she'd sat out by the pool and cried. Clouds the color of babies' ears drifted across the wide blue sky and Annie thought of Mildred Dodd, and the more she thought of Mildred, the more hypocritical she seemed, at least to Annie. Mildred cared for the unborn more than she did for the already born. Here was a woman who, to Annie's knowledge, had never volunteered at a shelter for abused children, who'd never attended a class for unwed mothers or done anything to address inner-city poverty or the plight of single mothers everywhere trying to raise a family on minimum wages. Here was a woman who had never acted as a foster parent or offered to adopt a crack baby.

Instead she spent her days planting little white crosses on the church lawn, trying to make other people feel bad about decisions they'd had no choice but to make.

Glancing up at the exterior of her big house, at the lovely pool surrounded by banks of lamium and creeping phlox, and stands of rhododendron and azalea, Annie was suddenly ashamed of herself. Here she was with all the blessings in the world, a nice house, a loving husband, two healthy sons, complaining about having to spend an afternoon with a group of poor, unfortunate children. *Really, what was wrong with her?* When had she become so callous and hard-hearted? If she kept on this track, she'd become as bad as Mildred Dodd.

She called to Sparky and stood up to go into the house, determined not to think of this as an ordeal, something to be endured and hurried through as quickly as possible. She would think of it, instead, as a chance to spend time with some sweet and deserving children who simply needed help with their reading and multiplication tables.

The place was larger than she had expected, and as she pulled into the grounds she was amazed by the expanse of rolling tree-lined hills. She passed a pond bordered by a stone wall and farther on, a steep-roofed chapel. Ranch-style cottages were laid out along a series of narrow streets, so the place had the feel of a small English village. It was quaint and peaceful, and much nicer than Annie had expected. She followed the signs to the administration cottage.

Afterschool homework sessions were held in the recreation hall. Annie followed a pleasant, round-faced woman named Amanda down a narrow, winding stone path toward the hall. As they approached, they could hear the sound of children's voices growing louder. It sounded like a playground at recess.

"Oh, dear," Amanda said, hurrying her steps. "Oh, dear."

Annie followed behind her wondering what might be the trouble. She had expected a school run on the old-fashioned Christian principles of spare the rod, spoil the child, a place where order and civility were maintained at all costs, kind of like a Dickensian boarding school, only less harsh. So she was surprised when Amanda flung open the door on a scene of utter and complete chaos. Children were standing on tables and benches, and along the outskirts of the room, shouting and jostling one another like spectators at a dogfight. A harried-looking young teacher was trying to separate two children who were slugging it out in the middle of the room, rolling around on the floor and pummeling each other, a huge brightly colored mass of flailing fists and kicking feet.

Amanda, with a smooth move indicating much practice, put a large whistle to her lips and began to blow a series of sharp, loud blasts. Instantly, the spectator children lined up along the far wall. The young teacher managed to grab one of the children, a boy of maybe ten, and hauled him to his feet. His nose was bleeding and he had a cut on his upper lip. Amanda grabbed the other child, who turned out, to Annie's surprise, to be a girl. She was a lovely little thing, with skin the color of walnut shells and eyes so black you couldn't see the pupils. Despite her dirty T-shirt and uncombed hair, the child had the delicate face of an angel. Annie was instantly entranced.

"Agnes Grace, what has gotten into you?" Amanda asked, giving the girl's collar a little shake. "This is your third fight this week. What do you have to say for yourself?" Annie thought, *Agnes Grace. What a lovely name.*

Agnes Grace sniffed and wiped her top lip with a grimy finger. "That fucker started it," she said.

The other children sucked in their breath. Amanda said sharply, "Language!" Annie stood transfixed like a woman under a spell, trying to figure out if she'd heard the child right.

"Sorry, Matron," Agnes Grace said.

"She hit me first," the boy said, and began to sob.

"That's right, go ahead and cry, you big blubberpuss," Agnes Grace said.

"You started it."

"You called my mama a meth-head."

"Your mama is a meth-head."

Agnes Grace took a swing at him but Amanda held her tight. "All right, that's enough," she said. "Mrs. Stites, perhaps you can take Agnes Grace out to the pond and help her with her reading." Annie stood there looking at her dumbly. She wasn't sure she wanted to take Agnes Grace anywhere. She wasn't sure she wanted to be in the same room with Agnes Grace unless she'd been run through a metal detector and strapped into a straitjacket first. Agnes Grace shrugged out of Amanda's grasp, walked over to a table, and picked up a book. She walked to the door and looked at Annie over one shoulder. "Are you coming or not?" she asked.

Annie followed her to the pond. Once out of earshot of Amanda and the young teacher, Agnes Grace opened up about her life. Her mother, Dee, was in prison for stabbing her drug dealer in the back. He didn't die but he was "messed up," and that's why Dee was doing time. Agnes Grace was one of nine children.

"*Nine* children?" Annie asked, aghast.

"She's only thirty-six, and she's got nine kids and all her teeth," Agnes Grace said proudly. She walked beside Annie with a jaunty step, pulling the blooms off a mass of scarlet trumpet vine trailing along a fence, and crushing them in her tiny hands. Annie did her best to listen to Agnes Grace's life story without appearing too shocked, which was hard to do considering that the child had a vocabulary that would make a Juarez drug dealer blush. By the time they got to the pond, Annie felt like she'd been beaten about the head with a blunt object. Finally, she couldn't take it anymore.

She put her hand up and said, "Don't you know that young ladies aren't supposed to talk like that?"

"Who says?" Agnes Grace asked suspiciously.

"Everybody says. Parents, teachers, the president. God."

"Shit." Agnes Grace hooted derisively. She tilted her head and looked up at Annie. "Hon, how old are you?" she said.

"That's not a question you should ask a grown-up lady. How old are *you?*"

The child winked one eye slyly and said, "Old enough to know not to wet on an electric fence." She poked Annie in the ribs with a skinny elbow. "Get it?" she said.

Annie didn't know what was more disturbing, the child's language or the fact that she acted like a thirty-five-year-old stuck in an eight-year-old's body. (She was guessing about the age but she'd noted that on the inside of her book it read, AGNES GRACE SIBLEY—THIRD GRADE.) "Let's get started on our reading, shall we?" Annie said, sitting down on the edge of the stone wall.

"Hell's bells, woman, what's your hurry?" The girl skipped a stone sidearm across the placid pond.

"You have to read if you want to learn. You have to learn if you want to go to college and get a good job."

The girl did a couple of cartwheels and then came up in front of Annie and stood with her hands on her hips. "You got any kids?"

"Two. Two boys. They're grown now and in college. I used to read to them."

Agnes Grace winced to let Annie know that she wasn't falling for this. "Huh," she said. "Two? That's all you got?"

Annie resettled herself on the wall. "Two's all I ever needed."

"Hey, what's your name?"

"Mrs. Stites."

"Sucks for you," Agnes Grace said. Annie gave her a deadpan look and the child said, "No, really, what's your other name?"

"It's not proper for a child to call an adult by her first name."

"Shit, lady, you sure got a lot of rules."

"Rules are good. Without rules, civilization would crumble. And don't say, *shit;* it isn't nice."

"Hey, you got any candy on you?"

"No. I'll bring some next time."

"Yeah, sure," Agnes Grace said, scratching idly at her crotch. "I heard that before."

• • •

Annie was so shook up by her afternoon with Agnes Grace that she forgot to cook dinner. She went home and poured herself a glass of white wine, and she was still sitting at the breakfast bar in the dark, drinking, when Mitchell got home.

"What's the matter?" he said, when he saw her. "Are the boys okay?"

"The boys are fine," she said, rapping her knuckles repeatedly against a wooden column just to be sure. "I didn't feel like cooking is all."

"Okay." He'd never come home to a dark house and no dinner on the table, and he wondered if this might be a case of bad female hormones. He put his briefcase down on the counter, moving slowly and warily, like a man confronting a coiled snake. "No problemo. We can eat out. Let's go out to dinner, what do you say, Punkin'? Just the two of us for a romantic little dinner for two."

Annie lifted her glass. "Don't call me Punkin," she said.

Two hours and three chardonnays later, Annie had made up her mind. She did not need to feel guilty about not going back to the Baptist Children's Home. She had heard the clear challenge in the girl's voice, *Yeah, sure, I heard that before,* but she was under no obligation to respond. The girl was someone else's responsibility. She was someone else's problem. She was damaged goods, tainted irreparably by an insidious drug culture and a broken social system that spit out tens of thousands of hopeless children every year. Agnes Grace was a problem beyond Annie's ability to fix. She was a bright-eyed Lolita, a pornographer's dream. There was absolutely nothing Annie could do.

She went to bed that night, for the first time, without *tick-tock* ringing in her head. In its place was the drumming refrain, *Yeah-sure-yeah-sure-yeah-sure.* She finally managed to fall asleep around three o'clock, and dreamed she had a wart on the bottom of her foot, a plumy growth like a scarlet trumpet bloom that she couldn't get rid of, no matter how hard she tried. She tried burning it off, but it grew back. She tried cutting it off, but it reappeared even larger. Each attempt to uproot it only drove its roots deeper into her foot until they wound like a thorny vine up through her leg, growing inexorably and lethally toward her heart.

The next morning she called Mildred Dodd and volunteered to spend Tuesday and Thursday afternoons out at the Baptist Children's Home.

Agnes Grace wasn't really as bad as she appeared on first impression. Over the next eighteen months Annie got to know her better and discovered many admirable qualities in the girl's personality. Or maybe she just got used to her headstrong ways. Anyway, they developed a kind of friendship that grew into something deeper over the months they spent together. Annie began to look forward to her Tuesdays and Thursdays at the Baptist Children's Home, and after a while she set it up so that on Wednesdays she and Agnes Grace spent time together away from the home, shopping for school clothes, attending a museum, or (Agnes Grace's favorite thing) visiting the Nashville Zoo.

She had a way with animals. They seemed to bring out her gentler nature. When a nest of baby starlings was found in the chimney of one of the cottages, she took them home with her in a cardboard box and nursed them with an eyedropper. Abandoned by the mother and refused by the zoo, the baby birds were not given much chance to live. But Agnes Grace fed them a pureed insect concoction she made herself, and the birds not only lived, they thrived. They developed plump gray-feathered bodies and bright beady eyes. Annie would pull up some afternoons to find Agnes Grace sitting on the concrete stoop outside her cottage like a female St. Francis of Assisi, the birds resting on her outstretched arms or fluttering gaily around her head. When it came time for the birds to fly, Agnes Grace took each one out into the yard, and with gentle hands, threw it high into the sky, and watched as it sailed above the trees, circled twice around the yard, and then flew off forever.

Annie didn't tell Mitchell about Agnes Grace. He knew she spent afternoons volunteering out at the Baptist Children's Home, and he knew there was one child in particular, a little girl, that Annie spent a lot of time with. But Annie kept most of it to herself. Agnes Grace was her own pet project, Eliza Doolittle to Annie's Professor Higgins. She bought her new clothes, taught her how to speak correctly and how to use good table manners (*Eatin' regulations,* Agnes Grace called them), and encouraged her in her schoolwork. Agnes Grace was a voracious reader, although she'd had little enough to read before she came to the home. But Annie bought her a complete set of Nancy Drew and Hardy Boy mysteries, as well as the classics, *The Adventures of Tom Sawyer, Adventures of Huckleberry Finn,* and *Treasure Island. Black Beauty* was her favorite. When Agnes Grace read that book, it was the only time Annie had ever seen her cry.

Still, despite her improvements, Agnes Grace clung stubbornly to some of her old ways. She still cursed like a sailor, and she was prone to episodes of physical violence. (One of the big boys had stomped a toad and Agnes

Grace hit him in the head with a metal chair.) And she was clumsy, too. She was always breaking things, always knocking over iced tea glasses or dropping plates on the floor or leaning against chairs that toppled over. If there was a crash anywhere in the recreation hall everyone always said in unison "Agnes Grace!" Also she was stubborn and had a tendency to cling to her own opinions, even when she was wrong, an attitude that often landed her in the time-out chair.

Annie brought Agnes Grace over to the house several times to swim, but only when Mitchell wasn't home. Despite the girl's improvements, Annie still couldn't imagine introducing her to the naive Mitchell. Mitchell still labored under the old-fashioned impression that little girls were made of sugar and spice and everything nice; what would he think of Agnes Grace? She'd be likely to give him a stroke, or a massive coronary. Nor could she imagine introducing Agnes Grace to the boys when they were home from college. They'd been raised like princes; they'd grown up with debutantes and cotillion queens, and were unlikely to have much knowledge of girls like Agnes Grace (or at least Annie hoped they didn't; she hoped their expensive educations hadn't gone to waste).

No, the cultural differences between the girl and her own family were just too wide; bringing Agnes Grace into the bosom of the Stites family would be like introducing a pit bull pup into a family of poodles.

And then, two and a half years after Annie and Agnes Grace first established their odd but mutually satisfying friendship, everything changed.

They got word that Agnes Grace's mother, Dee, was getting out of prison. She'd been released early for "good behavior," which apparently, in prison, meant that she hadn't stabbed anyone with a homemade knife. She was being released to a halfway house, and expected to see the girls in a few weeks. Agnes Grace and her older sister, Loretta Lynn, set about making themselves ready. They were the only two Sibley children being housed at the Baptist Children's Home. Dee's children had arrived in two distinct shifts, with the first five being born between Dee's sixteenth and twenty-first birthdays. Thereafter occurred a five-year period of government-imposed birth control when Dee spent time in prison on a series of unrelated drug charges. When she got out, babies six through nine were born over a period of eight years. By the time Dee went to prison the second time, the older five children were either incarcerated themselves or trying to make it on their own, the youngest two were turned over to Dee's mother, and that left only Agnes Grace and Loretta Lynn, who wound up at the home.

Annie bought both of the girls new dresses for the occasion. She took them to the beauty parlor and had their hair cut and their nails done. The whole time Annie watched them excitedly getting ready for their mother's arrival, she had a slight queasy feeling in the pit of her stomach. A wobbly nauseous feeling, like morning sickness that lasted all day.

She sat out front with the girls on the concrete stoop, waiting for Dee. Annie had offered to pick her up and drive her to the home but Dee had asked instead for taxi fare, which Annie had dutifully sent. She was supposed to arrive by two o'clock.

It was a bright sunny day in late February. A cool breeze blew from the north but there was a hint of spring in the air. The trees were budding, and the forsythia along the edge of the yard had begun to sport green buds.

At two-fifteen, Agnes Grace said jovially, "Mama never could be nowhere on time."

At two-thirty, she said, "Remind me to buy her a wristwatch."

At three o'clock, she said, "Maybe they got lost." Loretta Lynn sat with her chin resting glumly on her knees. She was two years older, and she knew her mother better. She wasn't going to get excited until she saw the taxi pull in to the yard.

By now Annie's queasy feeling had turned to anguish and then to outrage. It was hard to imagine a mother abandoning her own children this way. (*But then, who was she to judge?*)

At three-thirty, Agnes Grace said, "I hope she wasn't in a car crash."

At four, she said, "Ain't this typical?"

At five, she said, "Well, what do you expect? She's nothing but a meth-head," and got up and stomped into the house. Loretta Lynn sighed and got up to go after her. From the door she turned to look at Annie.

"Hey, lady," she asked. "Can we keep the dresses?" and Annie said, "Sure, honey, of course you can," and wished now that she'd bought them complete wardrobes with rows and rows of matching shoes.

That night, Annie had a dream.

She'd found a baby in a basket floating in the rushes, like Moses, only this baby was a girl with ten sweet little fingers and toes, and a small, delicate face like a seashell. Annie reached down to pick the baby up but as she did, a sudden current plucked the basket and sent it floating toward the sea. Annie tried desperately to reach it, splashing through weeds that wrapped around her legs and pulled her down like hands. She struggled and cried out but each time they caught her more firmly. She awoke when the baby reached the sea, a tiny speck disappearing on the horizon.

SPRING OF
1982

Chapter 33

~~~~~~~~

Misery. That's what followed obsessive love. The two went hand in hand, as Annie soon discovered. Eight weeks after spreading her legs for Paul Ballard he began making excuses as to why he couldn't see her. He was good at it (he'd had plenty of experience), and in the beginning Annie didn't realize she was being given the brush-off. He was so charming when he called at the last minute to tell her he couldn't make it that she never suspected a thing. But as the weeks wore on she began to realize that it had been a week since she saw him last, then two weeks, and then when she did run into him on campus, he seemed preoccupied and told her he'd "have to call her later." Which he never did.

Her pride kept her from calling him, at least initially; but then misery got the best of her and she couldn't help herself. She left two messages with his secretary and he never returned either one.

It was April, and the campus was ripe with spring. Trees put forth their green-leaved finery, azaleas bloomed in riotous color, and the skies were blue and cloudless. Everywhere people and plants seemed infused with the renewal of life but Annie walked around like she was dead inside. A blight on the bright landscape, a black hole of misery that sucked everything around her into its vortex.

"Are you sick?" Mel asked, when she saw her moping around the house.

"Did you fail a test?" Sara asked her.

"Did I do something to upset you?" Lola asked her anxiously.

Annie responded with a sharp "No!" to each of them. "It's just been a crazy semester. I'm taking a lot of hours to try to finish up in May." Which really wasn't true. She was only taking nine hours, which left her a lot of time to lie around in her darkened bedroom thinking about Paul Ballard and feeling miserable.

It was her fault, of course. She had known from the beginning that she shouldn't fall in love with him; she had counseled herself to think of this as only a "fling," her last act of licentious freedom before settling down to marriage with Mitchell Stites. She had spent hours at the beginning of the relationship convincing herself that this was true. But sometime during the initial endorphin rush, the unthinkable had happened. Love had crept in like an oil slick, drenching her heart until it flopped around like a wounded seabird too swamped and bedraggled to fly.

Now there was nothing she could do. She couldn't see (she didn't want to see) Mitchell Stites, and she couldn't see (although she wanted to see) Paul Ballard. She was caught in a kind of lovers' purgatory, and she couldn't seem to find her way out. Lying on her bed and watching the sun slant through the closed venetian blinds, she thought (briefly and without any real compulsion) of throwing herself out a window. Bile rose suddenly in her throat, and a thick, viscous wave of nausea sent her running for the toilet.

And now, to make matters worse, she seemed to have picked up some kind of unshakable stomach flu.

It was Mel who first alerted her.

Annie was lying on her bed one evening not long after supper when Mel rapped on the door and stuck her head in. "Hey, sorry to bother you, but you don't happen to have an extra tampon, do you?"

Annie took her arm off her eyes and looked at Mel. "No, I'm out."

Mel grinned. "That's what we get for all having our periods at the same time. Bitches in heat." She closed the door and Annie could hear her knocking on Sara's door. It was a big joke, of course, the fact that their menses had become regulated over time. It had been the same when they lived together in the freshman dorm. But thinking about it now, on a warm spring evening in early April, Annie thought, *That's odd.* She couldn't remember the last time she'd bought tampons. In fact, she couldn't remember the last time she'd had her period.

She sat up suddenly, dizzy and sick with fear. She got up and went across the hall into the bathroom, locking the door behind her. She stood at the mirror, regarding herself carefully. She didn't look any different, except for the fact that she had dark circles under her eyes, and her skin was a sickly, pallid color. She took her T-shirt off, and her bra.

There was no doubt about it. Her boobs were definitely larger. And her nipples were huge and dark. *Oh, God,* she thought. *Oh, God, no.* She poked her belly gently with her thumb. It was tender. She slumped down on the toilet seat, jarring her teeth.

A few minutes later she put her T-shirt back on and walked to the all-night drugstore. There was no use panicking, until she knew the truth.

The truth was, she was pregnant. She took three separate home pregnancy tests and they all confirmed what Annie had known in her heart was true the minute she glimpsed her swollen breasts and enlarged nipples.

She went to the dresser and checked her supply of birth control pills. She'd run out in December and hadn't kept her appointment with the doctor to have them refilled. The thought that she needed to take care of that had nagged at her but she'd been too caught up in the excitement of falling for Professor Ballard to pay any attention. She'd been too intent on making herself available to him to think about anything else. Besides, he'd used a condom every time. She'd thought she was safe.

After she'd finished crying, she went into the bathroom to wash her face, and then locked her bedroom door behind her. She had to figure out what to do. She took a piece of paper out and stared at it a long time, trying to figure out how to diagram a solution to her problem. She remembered her cousin, Lucy, the black sheep of the family. She'd gotten pregnant and run off to Atlanta with her boyfriend, a drummer in a punk-rock band, and was rumored to have had an abortion. She was rumored to be living in sin with the punk-rock drummer in Decatur. No one had seen her in four years, not even her own mother. That was the kind of family Annie came from. *The wages of sin are death.*

She blew her nose and wrote down, *#1—Marry Mitchell Stites and raise* *the child as his own.* This would be the most logical solution although it would involve some fudging on her part because she hadn't actually slept with Mitchell since Thanksgiving and by her rough calculations, she was only two months gone.

But how could she do that to a fine upstanding boy like Mitchell Stites, a boy who loved and trusted her, who sang in the church choir and rose every day believing in the simple goodness and grace of God? How could she lie beside him every night knowing that proof of her infidelity, of her sin, lay just down the hallway in a wicker bassinet? How could she live with that gnawing away at her insides, year after year, swelling like a tumor?

Besides, she didn't love Mitchell anymore, and try as hard as she might, she couldn't imagine herself marrying him.

She wrote down *#2—Marry Professor Ballard.* After that, she wrote *Anne Louise Ballard. Annie Ballard. Paul and Anne Louise Ballard. Dr. and Mrs. Paul Ballard.*

There was no doubt about it. She was a sick puppy.

After that, she went around in a daze, trying to figure out what to do. She wanted to tell someone, but she couldn't tell Mel or Sara or Lola without telling her mother, too. And she couldn't bear the thought of telling her mother, she couldn't bear the thought of her mother's face crumpling in pain and disappointment. Annie had never in her entire life caused her mother shame, and she couldn't imagine laying this burden at her door now, at this time of her life.

That left only one choice. She would have to marry Paul Ballard.

Over the last few days the flights of fancy she had engaged in while writing her name as *Anne Louise Ballard* had begun to soar higher and higher. She was like a woman in a fever-induced delirium. She even managed to convince herself that once he heard the news, Paul Ballard would be *happy.* (Although what he would tell his shadowy wife and children she had yet to work out.) She imagined herself traipsing around campus in a long diaphanous dress, carrying the baby in a sling, the envy of all the freshman English girls. She and Paul would become a kind of campus myth; their May-December (well, May-October at least) romance sighed over by starry-eyed undergraduates. Bedford's very own version of Persephone and Hades.

Once she started on this tack, her mind ran round and round in circles so that after a while it was easy to convince herself that he had never truly meant for their relationship to end at all. Overburdened by work, he had simply been unable to call. Or perhaps he had become frightened of his feelings for her, and had decided to take a break to give himself time to regroup (oh, yes, that must be it!). Perhaps she had touched him in a way all his other conquests had not and he was simply giving her time to determine whether her feelings were as strong as his (how noble his silence seemed to her now).

By the end of the week she'd managed to work herself up into a frenzy of unrequited love, and when he didn't return her calls (silly goose!) she set out to waylay him on the department steps.

It was a beautiful evening. Nightjars fluttered against the twilit sky, and all along the campus masses of honeysuckle and ginger lilies were blooming. Annie sat down on the grass in front of Carter Hall to wait. She hadn't taken his class since last semester but she'd kept up with his schedule and knew he had an evening class on Thursdays that let out at 8:30. She plucked blades of grass from the warm earth and let them fall through her fingers. Behind her a knot of boys played Frisbee on the lawn. It felt odd looking up at the face of Carter Hall, the place where she'd spent so many happy days last semester. It had felt odd, too, when the semester had ended and she'd realized she wouldn't see him again in class, she wouldn't be able to hang around his office door waiting for his arrival like a student anxious to discuss an essay assignment. She'd picked up her grades (she'd made an A, of course) and hung around hoping he'd show up, but he didn't. Still, at the time, this hadn't seemed ominous. She'd felt like one chapter of her life was ending, and another was beginning.

And that's how she felt now, waiting for him to appear on this twilight evening so she could tell him her happy news. The shadows grew longer, and the air took on the slight damp chill of evening. The boys stopped playing Frisbee and went in to dinner. One of the doors swung open and several students bounded down the steps, laughing, followed by other students straggling out in ones and twos.

Annie stood up, wiping the back of her jeans with her hands. The rush of students trickled to one or two, and then stopped. Annie stood staring at the brightly lit double doors, willing him to appear.

She put her head back and stared at the sky. The lights of the campus twinkled merrily in the gathering gloom. She heard the doors open and she stepped forward, then stopped, hidden in the shadows of a magnolia tree.

Professor Ballard was standing beneath the dim glow of an overhead light, his arm around the shoulders of a tall blond girl. She was giggling loudly, and he leaned and put his hand on her mouth, then followed that with a long, deep kiss. He seemed entirely besotted with the girl, dangerously so, as he stood there kissing her on the steps of Carter Hall. Anyone could have seen them, and he didn't seem to care.

They came down the steps together, his arm still resting across her shoulders. He stopped again and kissed her, moaning, and when she tried to break away, laughing, he pulled her back. After a few minutes, they dropped their arms and walked on side by side without touching, very proper, a professor and his student deep in an academic discussion.

Annie stood watching in the darkness until they had disappeared from sight. Then she turned, and walked slowly home.

Chapter 34

~~~~~~~~~

Freedom! Was there a more beautiful word in the English language? Mel didn't think so. Now that she had only a month and a half left of school, she couldn't wait. She was leaving for New York City the day after graduation. She would use her graduation money (she'd already made arrangements to sell the car she knew Leland was buying her) and fly to New York to begin her new life. *(Dorothy Parker, here I come!)*

Sara and Annie seemed weighed down by sorrow at the thought of them all going their separate ways, but Mel couldn't wait. She couldn't wait to move to a place where no one knew her, where she could reinvent herself any way she saw fit. She would miss Sara, Annie, and Lola, of course. She and Sara had been friends for almost eighteen years, although the last couple of months, since Mel broke up with J.T. anyway, she had felt as if Sara was avoiding her. Giving Mel the cold shoulder, as though her loyalty lay not with Mel after all, but with J.T. And Annie, too, had seemed swamped by some kind of end-of-college depression. She spent most of her time alone in her darkened bedroom, refusing to talk to anyone. Twice Mel had thought she heard her sobbing in the night but when she checked, Annie was facedown on her bed. And then three days ago, in the middle of the night, Annie had decided to take the bus down to Atlanta to see a cousin she hadn't seen in years. Never mind that it was the middle of a school week, never mind that she had a paper due in her Indigenous Rituals class. Annie just got up and left, leaving a note on the kitchen table, telling them she'd be back in a few days and asking them to cover for her if her mother or Mitchell called.

And it wasn't just Annie who was behaving strangely. Lola had come in on Sunday night dragging a skinny boy named Lonnie behind her, and in a breathless voice had told them she was in love! With Lonnie Lumpkin! A high school dropout who sang in a heavy metal band and worked as a handyman at the school!

"Lonnie *Lumpkin?*" Mel said a couple of days later, still trying to talk Lola out of this foolishness. She, Sara, and Annie were sitting at the dining room table, finishing up a supper of spaghetti and meatballs. Lola leaned against the door frame, her eyes shining and her face flushed with excitement. She had just come from meeting Lonnie, where they'd put the finishing touches on their plan to elope the day after graduation. "A high-school *dropout?*" Mel said. "A *handyman?*"

"Yes!" Lola said. She looked very happy.

Sara and Mel exchanged long looks. Annie stared glumly at her plate. Mel put her fork down and folded her hands on the table, trying to appear calm and rational. "But Lola, how will you live?" she asked pleasantly.

Lola seemed perplexed by the question. Gradually, Mel's meaning dawned on her. "Oh," she said. "Lonnie can paint. He made almost five thousand dollars last year painting houses, and that was only part-time."

"Lola, five thousand dollars is not a lot of money to live on," Sara said.

"But it's enough," Lola said brightly. "And if you double it, that's ten thousand," she added, looking around as if daring anyone to doubt her math skills.

"Do you understand what you're saying?" Mel said. "Ten thousand dollars wouldn't even cover your tuition here at Bedford. Ten thousand dollars wouldn't cover your clothes or the expensive vacations you and Briggs are always taking."

"I can learn to"—Lola struggled with an unfamiliar word—"economize."

"What about Briggs?"

"I know, I know." Lola seemed genuinely distressed, her little hands fluttering around her face. "I don't want to hurt his feelings. But Briggs doesn't love me, not the way Lonnie does."

"He does love you, Lola. And he can support you, the way you're used to being supported."

"Oh, come on!" Annie said harshly, dropping her fork and looking up from her plate of spaghetti.

"Look," Mel said. "The dead speak."

"Fuck you, Mel."

Mel looked at her in surprise. She'd never heard Annie curse before. Even Lola and Sara seemed taken aback.

Annie's face seemed unusually pale. Dark circles ringed her eyes. "Why don't you just leave her alone? If she loves the guy and he loves her, that's all that matters."

"No, Annie, that's not all that matters, and you know it," Mel said. "Lola's been raised a certain way. She's used to certain things. Do you think she's going to be happy without them? No, all of you, stop looking at me like that. I'm just being honest." She picked her fork up and rapped it repeatedly against the table. Why was it that no one seemed to see it the way she did? Lola was a child; she needed someone to take care of her (the way Briggs did, the way her mother always had, the way Mel was now trying to do). With her cloud hair and beautiful face, Lola was a poster child for aristocratic inbreeding, a clear example of how generations of cousin marrying can breed out intelligence in favor of a docile nature and stunning good looks. Not that Lola was stupid; she just didn't have any common sense. She could be taken advantage of by any charlatan who stumbled across her path (and who's to say that this Lonnie wasn't trying to marry her for her money?). "What's your mother going to say, Lola? You know she'll cut you off without a penny."

"I'll work," Lola said, lifting her chin and regarding Mel coolly. "I'll teach school and Lonnie can paint houses. We won't have a lot of money, but we'll get by."

"I say go for it," Annie said morosely. "I say you only get one chance for happiness in life, so grab it with both hands and squeeze the shit out of it."

Everyone stared at Annie. She picked up her fork and went back to twirling noodles, and Mel could that see she hadn't eaten anything on her plate. Her arms were like toothpicks. When had she stopped eating?

Lola walked over to Annie and hugged her. Annie patted Lola's arm mechanically, still staring at her plate. When Lola straightened up, she said, "Y'all have to promise not to tell anyone about me and Lonnie. You can't say anything until after we've run off. I don't want my mother or Briggs to get wind of it because if they do, they'll find a way to stop us."

"You're of age," Sara said. "There's nothing they can do."

"You don't know my mother." Lola shook her head sadly. "You don't know Briggs."

"I'm only going to say one more thing and then I'll shut up," Mel said, and everyone groaned. She held up her hands to quiet them. "Lola, have you thought about this? If you marry him, you'll be Lonnie and Lola *Lumpkin*."

Lola giggled. "I've thought about that," she said.

"So what?" the intractable Annie said.

Sara said, "Could it be any worse than Mr. and Mrs. *Briggs* Furman?"

Three days later, Annie left in the middle of the night for Atlanta. Sara went back to hiding out in her room and avoiding Mel every chance she got. Lola walked around the house like she was walking on eggshells, like she was afraid her happiness might seep into Maureen and Briggs's dreams like an omen, a warning that their captive girl was about to slip through their fingers forever.

Mel had only seen J.T. twice since the fateful Howl at the Moon party. The first time had been across a crowded smoky barroom (she had left quickly with her date) and the second time was on campus. It was a rainy afternoon, gray-skied and foggy, and she'd stopped beneath the colonnade outside Dressler Hall to get out of the downpour. Students stood there in huddled groups, steam rising from their slickers, and as Mel glanced down the length of the curving porch she saw a hooded figure observing her. He was leaning against one of the columns, just beneath the overhang, and for a moment, not recognizing him, she smiled. He stared back in a decidedly unfriendly manner and it was then that she recognized him and turned around. She had still been clinging to the forlorn hope that they could be friends, but in that moment before she turned, she had seen his face and knew they could not. He hated her now, that much was clear. She stepped out into the rain and walked on to class. She felt sick, unsettled in her stomach and her resolve. She'd never had anyone hate her before, at least not someone she'd once loved. It made her question whether she'd made the right decision. It made her wonder if there was something wrong with her, some slight misfiring in the cerebral cortex, a missing genetic component that made her incapable of long-term commitments. It was that initial rush of love that she craved, like a compulsive gambler throwing out the first roll of the dice, all anticipation and adrenaline, hands trembling and skin damp.

Two days later it was the weekend and she had a date with Tyler Chandler. They'd been dating for a few weeks. Tyler was a funny guy, he had a great sense of humor, and he kept her laughing during movies, throughout drinks afterward, and all the way into bed. Sex was the only time he got serious. The sex was okay (most of the guys she dated now seemed to have read the same how-to manual), but it was the laughter she needed most. Later, he got up and went home and she had the whole bed to herself, which was wonderful. The whole dating scene was wonderful, no strings, no attachments, just dinner and a movie and if she was lucky, a few laughs. And if she wanted, a different guy in her bed every night (although oddly enough that part was less than satisfactory; it was funny that love seemed a necessary prerequisite to orgasm).

Despite her carefree attitude, there were times when she could feel J.T.'s hatred like a cold wind against her back. She had hoped he might move on, she had steeled herself to seeing him with other girls (he was, after all, a great-looking guy), but so far she hadn't heard that he was dating anyone else. (Okay, she had to admit, this made her vaguely happy.)

Still, J.T. didn't figure in to her future plans, and the sooner he accepted this and moved on with his life, the happier they'd both be.

Chapter 35

~~~~~~~~~

With graduation less than a week away, Lola found herself developing a nervous stomach. She couldn't eat, and she couldn't sleep either. She awoke every morning to a vague feeling of dread and apprehension, and an odd conviction that her time was almost up. It was probably no more than pre-wedding jitters, she told herself, no different from what brides everywhere felt just before they took that sacred walk down the aisle.

Their plan was simple. On Saturday afternoon she would walk across the stage and receive her diploma, and on Saturday evening, when everyone else was meeting at a downtown hotel for a graduation party, she and Lonnie would be on their way to Charlotte to get married. By the time Briggs and her mother figured out what she'd done, it would be too late. After Charlotte, they'd head to Atlanta. Atlanta was a big city, and they could stay lost for quite a while. Lola had a little money saved, not a lot but enough to get them started anyway. They could find an apartment and then they could both find jobs. It sounded so easy when Lonnie talked about it. Easy as pie. He made it sound like unemployed house painters ran off with daughters of former governors every day of the week. His confidence should have reassured her, but it did not.

After all, Lonnie was a simple boy. Simple and good. And he didn't know Briggs and Maureen.

She hadn't meant to tell her friends about Lonnie. She had kept him secret all these months but then, coming in one evening after a hurried rendezvous, she'd been so happy that she couldn't help herself. She brought him in with her. She had expected Mel to be a little more sympathetic. Mel, of all people, with her love of freedom, should have known something of how Lola felt being pledged, all these years, to Briggs. She had felt like a Hindu child bride being given away to a man she didn't know. Only in her case she wasn't Hindu, she wasn't a child, and she knew Briggs very well. Too well. Which was probably why she couldn't shake this overwhelming feeling of dread and apprehension that had barricaded itself inside her chest.

She had expected sympathy from Mel, but Mel hadn't been sympathetic at all, not that first night when Lola brought Lonnie home, or in the weeks that followed, when she hounded Lola for information, little bits that Lola gave up grudgingly: how long she'd known Lonnie, how he made her feel, how many children she'd planned for their future, how exactly they planned to pull off the elopement. Annie and Sara didn't ask any questions but Mel seemed to want to know everything. Lola figured she was gathering information for a future novel, now that she had decided to become a writer.

And it felt good, really, to have an ally in the house, a confidant. Sara kept to herself so much these days, closed up in her room, counting down the days until graduation. She'd already managed to find a job in Charlotte working as a paralegal in a law firm, and she was planning on moving immediately after graduation. And Annie; poor Annie was suffering from some kind of terrible unhappiness that kept her wandering the house at night like a lost soul. Once Lola had awakened to the sound of sobbing and when she went into Annie's room, she found her kneeling beside her bed with her face buried in her arms. When Lola knelt beside her and said, "Annie, what is it? Tell me what's wrong," Annie only sobbed louder and said, "I can't. I can't tell anyone ever." This had seemed unbearably sad to Lola because everyone needs a confessor. But try as as she might, Lola could not get Annie to unburden herself. She went around the house mute and anguished, and wouldn't talk to anyone.

Perhaps the dread Lola was feeling was simply the dregs of her room-mates' unhappiness. Lola tried to convince herself of this, as the long days wore on and graduation slowly approached.

It was a small thing, really, but Lola should have seen it as a warning. Years later, thinking back on all of this, she would be astounded at her own blindness, she would wonder that she had not immediately sensed danger when her mother showed up two days earlier than planned. This was on a Wednesday morning, and graduation was to be held on Saturday. Lola was sitting in the front room drinking a cup of coffee when the doorbell rang. Briggs pushed past her and said gruffly, "I'll get it." Over the past week he'd spent every night at her place—she'd hardly been able to get him to go home—which also should have tipped her off that something was wrong.

He swung open the door and Maureen stood there, dressed expensively in a white linen pantsuit. Lola was astonished to see her mother standing on her doorstep. Briggs didn't seem surprised at all.

He stepped aside for Maureen, and Lola said, "Mother, what are you doing here?"

"Hello, darling." (*Dah'lin,* her mother always said, in the somewhat affected accent of her youth. Once a Scotty, always a Scotty.) Maureen stepped into the room, letting her eyes wander over the cheap furniture, the stacks of books, and the magazines scattered everywhere. It killed her that her only daughter had chosen to leave the Delta Gamma House (without Maureen's knowledge, of course) in order to live in squalor. This was what came of sending a child to a liberal arts college in the middle of North Carolina. "I came a little early to do some shopping," she said, pulling herself in tightly so she didn't touch anything.

"Shopping?" Lola said vaguely. She didn't bother to rise and kiss her mother. The Rutherfords were not the kind of family that bestowed hugs and kisses freely.

"We thought you might like to do some shopping before graduation," Briggs said to Lola. "You know, maybe buy a dress for the graduation party." Maureen shot him a brittle look and he stopped talking. He was wearing a robe and a pair of blue slippers, and his face was swollen from lack of sleep.

Lola shook her head slowly. "I have a dress," she said.

"Well, then, we'll do something else," Maureen snapped. She raised her hands and motioned for Lola to get up. "Hurry up, you two." She included Briggs in her sharp gaze. "Go upstairs and get dressed and I'll take you to brunch."

Lola stood up. "Do you want me to wake the girls?"

"No. Just the three of us this time, darling. No one else. Just family."

Maureen took them to the hotel where she was staying, the only four-star hotel in town. It was called the Swan, and had been modeled after the Greenbrier. It had seen its heyday in the years preceding the War Between the States, and had fallen into disrepair in the first half of the twentieth century. During the 1940s a hotel conglomerate had purchased the place and pumped money into it, although it still maintained its air of seedy elegance, a hint of better days long gone. Guests were housed in rooms that boasted no television, and were expected to dress for dinner. It was the kind of place where Maureen was in her element.

This, too, was calculated, Lola would realize later. Maureen had carefully chosen the place for Lola's intervention, although very little intervening was done, at least on the surface; Maureen was more subtle than that. They ordered eggs Benedict and a pot of strong, rich coffee, and then Maureen began. She told Lola how proud her father would have been of her, graduating from college and moving into her place in society, just as the women in her family had done for generations. She painted a glowing picture of her future life with Briggs, the parties, the trips to Europe, the children (she knew just where to strike). She dabbed her eyes and spoke fondly of grandchildren and trust funds, of the benefits of never having to worry about money, of a life spent enjoying the finer things without the need for struggle. In Maureen's worldview, struggle was bad. Poverty was worse. She reminded Lola of her own privileged upbringing, of her illustrious family, of Briggs's own family connections, and the familial bonds they would forge by marrying. The Du Ponts and Rockefellers couldn't have given a more stirring tribute. By the time she finished, both Maureen and Briggs were misty-eyed but Lola sat staring apathetically at her plate.

Maureen put her hand to Lola's forehead. "Darling, what's wrong? You seem feverish."

Lola pulled away from her. "Nothing's wrong," she said. "I feel fine."

"Well, you don't look fine. Does she, Briggs?"

"I don't know," he said sullenly. "I don't know what's wrong with her."

"Nothing's wrong with me," Lola said coldly.

"I don't know," Maureen said, touching her cheek. "Your eyes seem feverish. Here, Briggs, feel her cheek."

"Oh, for God's sake, don't fuss, Maureen," he said.

Maureen raised her finger for the waiter and ordered another pot of coffee. Lola stared out at the window at a wide vista of lawn stretching down to an ornamental pond. She wondered what Lonnie was doing right now. She felt distant, removed from the other two at the table by her own secret happiness.

"There's flu in Birmingham," Maureen said to Lola. "It might be a good idea if you spent the next couple of days in bed. You don't want to be sick for graduation."

"I'm not staying in bed," Lola said evenly. "There's nothing wrong with me."

"Nothing a swift kick won't cure," Briggs said heavily.

Twin spots of color appeared on Lola's cheeks. She turned her head and looked at him.

Maureen stretched out her hands between them. "Children," she said. "Don't."

Briggs shook her hand free. "This isn't going to work," he said.

"I need to get back to the house," Lola said. "I've got some packing to do."

Briggs hooted derisively. "Packing?"

"Yes, packing. I've got some books to box up."

He looked at Maureen and tossed his napkin on the table. "I told you this wouldn't work." He stood up and Maureen said, "Where are you going?" but he didn't answer. They watched him stride across the crowded dining room.

Maureen put both hands on the table and leaned toward Lola. Her voice, when she spoke, was calm and low. "I don't understand you," she said.

The waiter brought the check. Maureen fumbled in her purse for her wallet, and Lola turned her face to the window. A pair of swans glided across the surface of the pond like boats in a carnival show. The sun, which had shone weakly all morning, slid behind a row of ragged clouds. Far off in the distance, a train whistle blew mournfully. Lola, watching the gliding swans, shivered suddenly and drew her sweater closer about her.

• • •

Lola and Lonnie had made arrangements to meet Thursday night at the duck pond. It was the last time they would see each other before Saturday afternoon. Lola had packed her boxes and left a note for Sara, along with some money to pay for putting the boxes in storage. She had packed her suitcases and hidden them in the laundry room. She would make some excuse to come back to the house to change clothes after graduation. She would tell Briggs to pick her up later. She'd left a note for him and one for her mother, too. Not that they would ever understand, of course, or forgive her, but it was something she had to do. Happiness didn't come around all that often (she knew that all too well) and you had to grab for any chance you got. Lonnie would be waiting for her at the corner on Saturday, and they would ride off like cowboys into the sunset, into their new life together.

But tonight he was late, which wasn't like him. Lola checked her watch again and looked at the sky. The sun had fallen behind the distant ridgetops. The sky was streaked with bands of red and yellow. Long shadows lay over the grass, and in the placid pond the trees were reflected like another world, like the gates to the underworld. A couple lay on a blanket in the grass, their heads close together. On a bench across the pond, a student sat reading.

Lola walked up to the road to see if she could see him. Maybe he'd had car trouble. The truck was old, and it was always breaking down, although Lonnie kept a tool kit in the back and knew how to use it. Maybe something had happened to his mother. Lola turned around and walked back down to the pond to wait. She sat down on a bench and stretched her legs in front of her. In another two days she would be Mrs. Lonnie Lumpkin. She trembled with joy at the thought. She would be Lola Lumpkin. Maybe they would name their children L names. *Louisa, Lewis, Laura, Lawrence. Lemuel, Lisa, Lula.* By the time the sky darkened she had a complete list ready. She stood up and walked around the pond, trying to keep warm. She hadn't seen Lonnie in three days, and all she could think about was his arms around her, his mouth on her mouth. She didn't care how long she had to wait to see him.

She would wait all night if she had to.

Chapter 36

~~~~~~~~

It was tragic. Sara could never look back on her college graduation without feeling an overwhelming sense of sadness and regret.

Two nights before they were set to graduate, Lola came home hysterical and crying that "Something happened to Lonnie!" They were supposed to meet that night at the duck pond and Lonnie had never shown up. Lola had hiked to a pay phone and called his mother, who told her Lonnie had left to meet her hours ago.

"I have to borrow your car!" Lola shouted at Mel, but she shook her head and said, "Lola, you need to calm down. You can't go anywhere as upset as you are. Why don't you sit down a minute and get hold of yourself and let us make a few phone calls?" They took her upstairs and had her lie down with a wet cloth across her eyes. Sara had never seen her so upset. When they went back downstairs, Sara said to Mel, "What do we do now?"

"Nothing," Mel said firmly. "We sit tight and wait."

Sara got up, went into the kitchen, and called the county hospital but no one matching Lonnie's description had been admitted. She felt, in some way, responsible for Lonnie. They had become allies, of a sort. The first time Lola brought Lonnie home, Sara had been shocked at her boldness. They had been walking in the woods (there were leaves in Lola's hair) and she'd decided on a whim that she just had to introduce him to her friends. That night. Which was insane because Lola shouldn't even be seen out with Lonnie, much less bring him home, where they were sure to be discovered. But you could see, looking at Lola, that she wasn't thinking clearly. She was crazy in love.

Mel, Sara, and Annie were sitting in the living room watching *Laugh-In* and trying not to show their shock and dismay over Lonnie. Lola took Lonnie into the kitchen. Mel was upset—she was all for breaking Lola and Lonnie up—but Sara and Annie wouldn't agree. They figured it was Lola's business who she loved, not theirs.

It was then that they heard a car door slam and Sara just had time to call out a warning to Lola in the kitchen before Briggs burst through the front door.

For a moment no one said anything. The canned laughter in the background rose and fell. Annie stirred and said to Briggs, "Have you ever heard of knocking?"

Briggs ignored her. His face was flushed with color, and he was breathing hard.

"Where's Lola?" he asked.

Before anyone could answer, Lonnie walked out of the kitchen.

"Who's he?" Briggs said, pointing a thick, hairy finger at Lonnie.

Lonnie moved forward but before he could take another step, Sara jumped up and grabbed his hand. "He's my boyfriend," Sara said to Briggs. "Lonnie."

They stood there staring at each other. The air in the room got heavy and thick. Sara tugged on Lonnie's hand and tried to lead him upstairs. At first he resisted, his eyes fixed on Briggs's face, but then he let her pull him up the stairs behind her.

Sara closed her bedroom door and locked it, and they sat on the bed for a while, talking in low voices. "I hope you and Lola have a plan," Sara said.

"We do. It's not one I like, but I'm trying to keep her happy. I'd just as soon tell him now and get it over with, but she says we have to wait."

"I can see how you two feel about each other, anyone can see it, but Briggs Furman is an asshole. You need to be careful."

"Yeah. That's what she says." He ran his hand wearily over his face, and

Sara could see suddenly what Lola saw in him. He had a gentle way about him. She could imagine him bringing home stray dogs or swerving to miss a turtle in the road. And he was cute, too, in a thin, boyish way, not like Briggs with his all-American quarterback good looks, but attractive. He had the smoldering intensity of a poet, a mixture of shyness and passion that women always found captivating.

They talked quietly together for a while and when Sara heard Lola's door click shut, she put her finger to her lips and rose, motioning for him to follow her. He stood for a moment in the hallway outside Lola's door and Sara had to tug hard on his hand to get him to move. The house below was dark. She let him out and locked the door behind him, watching through the glass as he walked off into the moonlight, his hands thrust deep into his pockets. He stopped once and looked up at the house, before turning and stepping into the shadows.

Behind her, Briggs said, "How come I've never met him?"

She jumped and swung around, her hand on her chest. He stood at the bottom of the stairs, a dark, menacing shape. "Goddamn it, Briggs, you scared the shit out of me."

"Why don't I know him?"

Her heart pounded in her chest. "He doesn't go to Bedford. He's a local boy."

"That's what I thought. A Tucker Town boy. You can do better."

"Well, you know Briggs, it's really none of your business who I date."

"It's my business if you bring him over here. I don't like strange men in the house."

Fear prickled her scalp. She wanted to go to bed but she didn't want to push past him to go up the stairs. She didn't want to put herself within distance of those long, powerful arms. Not that she thought he would hit her. It was more of an *implied* threat, a feeling of physical power barely restrained, a sense that here in this darkened room he could do whatever he wanted to her.

She forced herself to walk toward him as if nothing was wrong. "Good night, Briggs," she said.

He said nothing, and she pushed past him, and went up the stairs to bed.

Sara called the hospital again thirty minutes later to check on Lonnie, but no one matching his description had been admitted. At nine o'clock Maureen showed up. She asked for Lola and then went upstairs. When they came down a few minutes later, Lola's face was pale and swollen from crying but she appeared calm. "I have to go with my mother," she told them. "I'll be back in a little while." She followed Maureen outside to a long dark car that was parked at the curb. Maureen had apparently hired a driver. The whole thing seemed odd to Sara.

An hour later, Lonnie's mother called looking for Lola. She was crying. Lonnie had been in an accident. He was in the hospital, and she was on her way over there now. Sara hung up and gave the news to Mel and Annie.

"I'm going to the hospital," Sara said.

"I'm going with you," Annie said.

Mel was strangely quiet. She reached into her pocket, pulled out the keys to her car, and tossed them to Sara. On the ride over they were both silent, caught up in their own thoughts. Sara had a sick feeling in the pit of her stomach. She wondered if Lola and Maureen had been on their way to the hospital to see Lonnie, if they had somehow managed to get word early that he'd been injured.

But when she and Annie got to the hospital, Lola wasn't there. Lonnie's mother sat in the waiting room, surrounded by a small group of family and friends, her face swollen and tearstained. She told Sara and Annie what she knew. Lonnie's truck had been forced off the road and he'd been attacked. He had three broken ribs, a collapsed lung, and a skull fracture. He was in a medically induced coma, and no one could see him, but Sara did manage to catch a glimpse of him through the glass. His face, beneath the covering of bandages, was unrecognizable.

She and Annie sat through the night with Lonnie's mother, who kept crying and asking repeatedly, *Who would do such a thing to my boy?* a question that made Sara increasingly uncomfortable because as the night wore on and Lola failed to show, it didn't take a genius to figure out who was responsible.

Over the next few years, Sara gradually managed to piece together what had happened that night. Maureen had basically kidnapped Lola, although how she managed to entice Lola into the car remained unclear (perhaps she told her she had knowledge of Lonnie's whereabouts). The driver was a doctor Maureen had known since her days in the governor's mansion, and he had driven them to a very exclusive hospital in Virginia, the kind of place the general public doesn't know about, a four-star asylum where the privileged classes go to recover from drug addiction and nervous breakdowns. Lola was there for two months. She never made it to graduation (Briggs was also noticeably absent, allegedly doing charity work in Venezuela). One week after getting out of the hospital, Lola and Briggs were married in a small private ceremony in Dublin. Annie, Mel, and Sara weren't invited.

Lonnie eventually recovered, although he was in the hospital for nearly four months. Two weeks after getting out, he moved to Alaska to work on the pipeline with his uncle. What else was there for him? By then Lola had married Briggs and was on an extended European honeymoon. Lonnie's mother had unexpectedly come into some money and she moved to Panama City, where she bought a house on the beach near one of her sisters.

Sara lost track of Lonnie after that. Lola never mentioned him and Sara never asked. From time to time over the years, remembering that night they had spent in pleasant conversation in her bedroom, she would Google his name to see if anything came up, but nothing ever did.

Sara moved to Charlotte in June, and by November she'd decided to apply to law school. Her job as a paralegal entailed mostly real estate work, reviewing contracts and shopping center leases and attending closings, but she spent as much time as possible helping out in the litigation department. It was there that she thought she might eventually like to work. The firm was midsized, with a good mix of young partners and associates, so it felt more like a trendy boutique firm than a stodgy, old-fashioned one. In the evenings, she and a few of the staff would go out for drinks, and on the weekends she would go to parties or out to dinner with one of the vast number of eligible young men who seemed to congregate in Charlotte, the corporate banking center of the Southeast. Some nights she stayed home and watched movies on the VCR.

She wasn't lonely. She liked being in a place where no one knew her. She could reinvent herself anyway she chose, and she did, adopting a slightly more outgoing persona than the one she'd been born with. She still talked to Mel quite a bit (she'd gone up to visit her in July) and occasionally to Annie. She and the long-suffering Mitchell were scheduled to get married in September, and Sara and Mel were flying in as bridesmaids.

Once, not long after she moved to Charlotte, she had called Lola at the hospital and Lola, obviously out of it, had answered and said, "Sara? What happened?" But the next time she called, Maureen had answered the phone and in a wooden voice had claimed that Lola wasn't available. She was recovering from a nervous breakdown, and the doctors had decided it best that she not have any outside contact, at least not until she was well again. When she called Mel to tell her, Mel had said curtly, "What is it you think we can do? We can't drive to the hospital and kidnap her. She signed the papers."

"What makes you think she signed the papers?"

"Well," she said stiffly, "she would have to, wouldn't she? She's of legal age. They couldn't keep her against her will."

"I wouldn't put it past Maureen and Briggs to have figured out a way."

"Oh, come on, Sara! You're the one who should be writing novels."

After Lola returned from Europe, she called Sara several times. She had missed Annie's wedding, and seemed to feel a desperate need to reconnect with her college roommates. She and Briggs were living in Birmingham not too far from Lola's mother. The conversations were awkward and stilted because each time Lola sounded like she was heavily medicated. She was vague and jumped around from topic to topic, and Sara had a hard time following her.

Sara hadn't heard from J.T. Radford but as the cold winter days gave way to spring, she thought about him from time to time. The last time she'd seen him had been at graduation and he'd been standing under a chestnut tree talking to Mel. She'd had her head tilted away from him, a stony expression on her face, and he was pleading with her—you could see it in the stiff way he held his shoulders, in the desperate expression on his face—but you could also see she wasn't listening, she was already gone, too unattached and distant for him to ever win her back.

And then, in May, Sara ran into him in a bar in Southend. It was the same week she heard that she'd been accepted into law school, and she was out with some colleagues from work celebrating.

She was coming back from the bathroom when she heard a male voice behind her say, "Sara?"

And there he was, even better-looking than she remembered, more filled out than he had been when she saw him last. "What are you doing here?" she said, still trying to figure the odds of running into him in a bar in Charlotte.

He laughed and hugged her. "Probably the same thing you are."

"No," she said, stepping back. "I mean, what are you doing in Charlotte?"

"I live here. I teach at a boys' school out by Huntersville."

She shook her head, unable to believe that he lived here, where she'd decided to settle, where she'd decided to start over. Mel didn't know where he was. Or at least, she said she didn't. She'd told Sara she never talked to him anymore. "It's good to see you."

"It's good to see you, too," he said, smiling.

"Annie and Lola got married." She was rambling.

"Really? Who are the lucky guys?"

"Mitchell and Briggs."

"Well, that figures."

She was nervous suddenly that she would say the wrong thing. *Don't mention Mel,* she thought. "Do you ever talk to Mel?" she said.

He glanced behind her, his smile tightening. "No," he said.

Embarassed, she lifted her hand and pointed vaguely across the bar. "My friends are waiting for me."

He glanced at them over her shoulder. "I can see that." He put his hand out to her and she took it, awkwardly. "It's good to see you." She turned around to leave but he held on to her. "Sara?"

"Yes."

"I'd like to call you sometime. Maybe we can go out and have a drink and talk about the good old days."

She thought, *Don't do this.* She said, "My number's in the book."

Why had she told him that? Why had she said she'd go out with him when the last thing she wanted to do was hear him talk about Mel? (*The good old days.*) And why had she acted like a fucking robot when she saw him, like the old Sara, not like the new persona she had tried so carefully and meticulously to invent?

She spent the next week in a panic that he would call, jumping each time the phone rang. But by the middle of the second week, when she still hadn't heard from him, she'd begun to feel jilted, and by the end of the second week she'd decided that she wouldn't take his call even if it came.

But of course she did take it. "Sorry," he said. "My dad's been sick. I've been out of town."

He took her to a restaurant down on South Tryon. It was a beautiful evening, warm and balmy. A thin sliver of moon hung over the city, and the trees along the street had been strung with strings of white lights. They sat in a bricked courtyard drinking Coronas under the stars. J.T told her about his job teaching well-heeled prep school boys and she told him about her job as a paralegal, and how she'd been accepted into law school in the fall. Neither one mentioned Mel.

Afterward, they walked to Amos Music Hall. J.T. held her hand and she walked beside him feeling like an actress in a stage play. This couldn't be her. This couldn't be her life. Every time he touched her, she felt her heart flutter inside her chest like a flock of birds taking flight.

They danced until one o'clock in the morning, and then he took her home. Despite her body's traitorous reactions, she tried not to believe that this was anything more than a casual date. Two friends getting together after a long absence. She told herself she didn't care if she ever saw him again. She steeled herself not to feel anything for him. At the door, he kissed her.

"I'd like to see you again," he said.

"I can't," she said, feeling as if the ground had opened up and she was falling, floating like a feather. "I'm seeing someone."

"Oh, really? What's his name?"

She stood there for a moment, trying to think of someone, and when she couldn't, he grinned and kissed her again.

Their second date was to a movie, their third was a picnic, and their fourth was a pool party at one of the partner's houses. Sara hadn't really wanted to go, but she'd mentioned it to J.T. on the phone and he'd said, "Oh, come on, it'll be fun."

He stayed close to her side the whole evening except for when he went up to the bar to get their drinks. It was hard not to notice him. All the other men were dressed in polo shirts and madras plaid slacks, as if they'd been produced in the same bright, shiny factory, but he was dressed in jeans and flip-flops. When he went up to the bar, all the women from work flocked around her.

"Who in the world is that gorgeous guy?"

"Where have you been keeping him?"

"Does he have a brother?"

Across the yard, J.T. saw her and waved. She smiled and waved back.

Later, as the sun began to set and the party got more raucous, they went for a swim. The Beach Boys sang on the stereo. The water was cool and silky. Sara liked the feel of it against her skin. Someone turned the pool lights on and she dived and followed J.T. down to the deep end, where the shadows were longer. He surfaced under the diving board, putting his arms up to grab the board so that he hung there with his torso above the water. She surfaced beside him, clinging to the edge of the pool.

"You like most of these people, do you?" he asked.

"They're okay." She liked the way the muscles in his arms tensed as he held the board.

"What are you thinking?" he asked, and she blushed suddenly and said, "Nothing."

"Oh, I think you are." He let go of the board and slid into the water, moving toward her with the lower part of his face submerged. Water beaded and glistened in his hair. She turned and rested both elbows on the lip of the pool, letting her feet trail behind her. He slid up beside her and gently disengaged her from the side of the pool, pulling her into his arms. He put his knee up and she rested there like a child, her arms around his neck while he kissed her, slowly and deeply.

So far they hadn't slept together but Sara knew it was coming, not because he wanted it but because she did. Her desire was a hollow feeling beneath her heart. When he touched her she trembled as if she might break, because despite the boys she had dated in high school and the bad reputation she'd gained from running with Mel Barclay, despite the fact that she was pretty and modern and had dated a fair number of boys in college and out, she still felt inexperienced in the ways of love.

She had been saving herself all along, it would seem, for him.

It was a summer of perfect love. That's how she would remember it in the years to come. She had never been in love before, and now she was, and it was perfect. By the middle of July she had moved in with him. She kept her apartment, but it was more or less a storage facility now, a place where she kept furniture, and kitchen utensils, and out-of-season clothes. Her toothbrush, her cosmetics, her hair dryer she took to J.T.'s house along with some of her clothes. He never told her he loved her, but he made her happy and that was enough for her.

Or at least she told herself it was.

• • •

She was there with him the morning Mel called from New York. It was a cold, rainy day in early September. The phone rang and he answered it. She rolled over in bed, struggling toward consciousness, but by then he had already risen, the phone clutched in his hands. She heard his voice change, heard him say "Rough night," as he went into the bathroom and closed the door, and she knew he was talking to Mel.

When she asked him later who he was talking to he'd said, "Nobody," and when Mel called her at home, Sara had asked innocently, "How long since you spoke to J.T.?" and Mel had lied. She knew then that they still loved each other. It was only a matter of time before they reconciled. She had been a fool to think he could ever love her, to think he could ever love anyone but Mel.

She carried this knowledge around inside her until she couldn't bear the weight of it any longer. Then she sat down and wrote J.T. a note explaining why she couldn't see him again, and, packing up the few possessions she had kept at his house, she left the note on the bed, got into her car, and drove out of his life.

2005

Chapter 37

FRIDAY

Annie's attempt to keep her lips moist and youthful using Vaseline backfired big time. As it turned out, slathering her lips with petroleum jelly before undergoing five hours of ultraviolet light was akin to basting a roasting turkey with butter. She awoke to lips that were sunburned and swollen to twice their normal size.

"You look like a porn star," Mel said, when she saw her. Sara raised her eyebrows in alarm and Lola laughed and clamped her hand over her mouth. They were sitting on the porch drinking their coffee. It was late morning, and the sunlight falling across the back deck was so fierce it had driven them beneath the porch roof.

"You poor thing," Lola said. "Does it hurt?"

As a matter of fact, it did hurt. Annie did her best to sip her lukewarm coffee and finally gave up. They watched her with varying degrees of concern and amusement on their faces. "What?" she asked finally.

"It's just that you look so *different*," Sara said. "And in a strange way, attractive."

Annie thought so, too. She'd stood in front of the bathroom mirror turning her head back and forth. She'd always had thin lips as a girl, and they'd become wafer-thin as she aged. But now she looked like a different woman, someone she didn't recognize. The effect was both thrilling and terrifying.

"We're trying to decide what to do tonight," Mel said, pushing a chair out for Annie. "What about you, Kitten with a Whip? Any ideas?"

"Don't call me that." She wondered what Mitchell would say if he could see her now. She thought, for the first time in a long time, of the girl she had once been, small and slim and full of self-confidence. She would give anything if she could be that girl again, if she could go back and undo all the mistakes she'd made.

"Have you ever thought what your name would be if you were a porn star?" Lola asked dreamily.

"No, Lola, that's something I've never honestly thought about," Sara said.

"I'd be Luscious Lola."

"I'm kind of partial to Kitty LaFox," Mel said. "Or maybe Kandy Kleev-age."

"Y'all are disgusting."

Cicadas hummed in the trees. A sultry breeze blew from the sea, bringing with it the scent of fish and mudflats. Along the low cedar fence separating the house from the dunes, a riotous mass of wild grape grew.

"What are our options?" Annie asked. They all looked at her. "For tonight."

"It's our next to the last night on the island," Mel said. "Let's do something crazy."

"Somehow I knew you'd say that."

"We could take the boat across to Wilmington," Lola said. "There's this bar called the Pirate Shack."

"That sounds perfect," Mel said.

"It's usually pretty crowded, but I know the doorman, Dark Steven."

"Now, Lola, that doesn't sound very politically correct."

"No, silly, I call him Dark Steven because he's prone to depression. His aura's pretty dark."

Annie scratched irritably at her leg. She'd been listening to Lola's weird pronouncements all week and it was getting more and more frustrating. She sometimes felt like she was doing a field study of some strange, primitive person, someone who didn't speak her language. It was as if Lola was trying to tell them something, but she wasn't sure what. Annie liked things set forth in black and white, while Lola seemed to prefer the swirling colors of the rainbow. "Ridiculous," Annie said.

Lola stared at her sadly, as if she was reading Annie's aura and found it defective.

Annie put her leg down. "Let's go to the beach."

"I think you'd better keep your lips out of the sand today, Cherry Poppins," Mel said.

"Don't call me that," Annie said.

"She's right," Sara said. "Any more sun on those lips and they might explode."

"Y'all are real funny," Annie said. "You two should start a comedy routine." Why hadn't she ever considered collagen or Botox? she wondered, fingering her swollen lips. Maybe she could make herself over from head to foot, turn back the hands of time until she was once more a girl, shiny-new and full of promise.

"I think you look pretty," Lola said.

"Thanks." Annie touched her swollen lips gently. Unfortunately, it wasn't that simple. No matter what she did to her face, no matter how many surgical enhancements she underwent, she could never go back to being a girl. She could never be innocent again. Paul Ballard had seen to that. She had seen to that.

"I say we go over to the mainland and drink with the locals," Mel said.

"Why does everything you propose always involve alcohol?" Annie asked irritably. No matter how hard she tried, no matter how many lists she wrote, how many rules she followed, how many times she went to church, she couldn't get it back. How do you believe, in goodness and mercy, when you'd done what she'd done?

"Because we're on vacation, Little Oral Annie. You got any better ideas?"

Annie gave her a hard look. She wondered if she would have liked herself better if she'd gone off with Paul Ballard her senior year of college, if she'd stayed the spontaneous, devil-may-care girl she'd pretended to be for him. And what would Mel, Sara, and Lola say if they knew about Paul Ballard—would they use the same condescending manner they used with her now? Maybe she'd tell them just to see the looks on their faces. Just to teach them that you can't always judge a book by its cover. She fingered her swollen lips and imagined the words rolling around on her tongue like something cool and sweet.

But she couldn't tell them; she couldn't pull her finger out of the dyke because if she told them even one small thing the rest might come flooding out. Everything.

She pushed herself up suddenly and looked around the table. "I want to do something," she said. "Something I've never done before. That's what I wrote on my note. The one we put in the little box and buried under the deck. *Do something I've never done before.*"

"Hey, we need to dig those up," Mel said. She sipped her coffee and stretched her feet out on an empty chaise longue, watching Annie with an amused look. "So I'm curious, Annie. What's your idea of doing something you've never done before?"

"I know you think I'm just an old stick-in-the-mud, Mel, but I've done lots of wild and crazy things in my life. I've done all sorts of spontaneous things."

"Oh, really, Wendy Whoppers? Name one."

"Don't call me that." Annie gave her a severe look and then said, "Once I took the boys to school in my pajamas."

"Shocking!"

Sara frowned, running her finger along the rim of her coffee cup. "Did you actually get out of the car and go in or just drive there and let them out? Because I've done that a hundred times."

It was a stupid example. Annie didn't know why she'd used it. She could see that they weren't impressed. "I was wearing leopard-print pajamas and I got into a car accident and had to stand along the side of the road while everyone I knew drove slowly past. It was humiliating. It was the first and only time I ever wore leopard-print pajamas. Mitchell gave them to me for Christmas."

"Now that's funny," Mel said.

Annie didn't tell them that she was hit from behind by a guy in an old van hand-painted with strange quotes that read like Bible verses. It looked like a hippie van from the '60s, only instead of peace signs there were crude drawings of what appeared to be the devil, loading people into hell on the prongs of a pitchfork. The driver of the van was tall and thin with matted hair and a long beard. He wore a purple jumpsuit with "Save Jesus" emblazoned across the back. Not "Jesus Saves," but "Save Jesus." That should have been a tip-off to his mental state, Annie realized later. "Jesus

Saves" was comforting, whereas "Save Jesus" implied a bound and gagged Savior with a gun to his temple. Annie found the image disturbing.

What was more disturbing was the way the crazy guy looked at her as if he knew her. He stood there beside the strange van while she checked her car for damage. He lifted a crooked finger and pointed at her while behind his head a line of utility poles stood against the sky like crucifixes on Golgotha. "Blessed are those whose sins the Lord will never count against them," he said in a nasal, high-pitched voice.

Annie had stared at him uneasily, then shivered and climbed back into her car. Later, she tried not to take the whole incident as an omen. Moses at the burning bush. Saul on the road to Damascus.

"So you were spontaneous once and it didn't work out," Mel said. "You shouldn't give up. Wild and crazy didn't work the first time, so try it again."

Annie gave her a sullen look. "What do you have in mind?"

"Let's dye your hair."

Annie sighed. "Fine," she said.

Mel paused for a moment, as if she hadn't heard her clearly. Then she leaned forward and slapped the table. "Now you're talking."

"Are you sure?" Sara asked doubtfully.

"And I'll do your makeup," Lola said, clapping her hands in excitement.

Mel said, "When we're through with you, even your own mother won't recognize you."

"That's what I'm afraid of," Annie said.

"Hey, Lola, where'd you bury that box?"

Lola got up and walked around to the deck. While she was gone, Mel said, "So it's settled then? We'll stay in tonight, get drunk, and give Annie a makeover. Well, maybe not in that order."

"Definitely not in that order," Annie said.

When Lola came back a few minutes later she was carrying the box in her hands. It was covered in damp sand, and as she opened the lid, the little strips of paper fluttered gaily in the breeze. She picked one up and read it.

"This one says *Do something I've never done before*. Okay, we know who wrote that. This one says *Renew our friendship*." They looked at one another and grinned. Lola smiled shyly and held a strip above her head. "This one says *Smoke some weed*."

They all looked at Mel.

"I did not write that," she said.

"I did," Lola said.

Annie's eyes widened above her porn-star lips. Mel wagged one finger back and forth. "You're a very naughty girl, Luscious Lola."

"You're kidding," Sara said. "Right?"

"I never did it in college," Lola said, "and I always wanted to. At least once."

"I'm not doing something illegal just so you can relive the youth you never had," Sara said.

"That's not very generous of you," Mel said.

"Sorry. I didn't mean it like that."

"Where would we even get some? How do you go about getting it these days?"

Sara said, "Like I said, I'm not doing anything illegal."

"How about if we do it offshore? How about if we take the boat out into international waters?"

"I'm not boating two hundred miles out to sea to smoke a doobie."

"I'll take my chances with maritime law. It's bound to be less stringent."

Sara hooted. "Oh, so you're a lawyer now?"

"Stop being so paranoid. No one's going to catch us."

"I'll bet the Coast Guard hears that a lot."

The fact that Sara was so against it made it irresistible to Mel. She turned her head and looked at Lola. "Seriously, Lo, where can we get some?"

Lola tapped her nose with one finger. "Leave that to me," she said. She smiled mysteriously and picked up the last slip of paper. "This one says *Fuck Captain Mike.*"

"I wonder who wrote that."

Mel giggled.

Sara said flatly, "We all know that's not going to happen."

"Hey," Mel said. "A girl can dream."

Sara went with Mel to the store to pick up the Miss Clairol and on the way back they drove through the maritime forest. Sunlight filtered through the overhanging trees. Exotic birds sang in the greenery. From time to time they passed another cart, ambling along from the opposite direction, and Mel raised her hand and waved. Sara sat quietly beside her, looking out at the landscape.

"You're quiet this morning," Mel said. "Hungover?"

"I should be, after this week. But I'm not."

"Everything all right at home?"

Sara didn't want to talk about home. At least not with Mel. "Sure. Everything's fine." She stared at the distant marsh, flat and shimmering beneath the wide blue sky.

Mel picked up the box of Miss Clairol lying on the seat between them and said, "I wonder what got into Annie."

"Us probably. We always were a bad influence." Sara looked at her and grinned slowly, and Mel grinned back.

"I'd like to see her get a little outside herself," Mel said. "She's grown so rigid over the years."

"She was always rigid," Sara said.

"Was she? I don't remember."

"Well, maybe not so bad as now."

Tom had called while they were in the store buying the Miss Clairol and Sara had gone outside to take the call. He sounded tired. "Only two more days," he'd said, "and then you'll be home. We miss you." Something in the way he said *we* alerted her and she said quickly, "What's wrong?"

"Nothing."

"Something's wrong. I can hear it in your voice."

"We don't have to talk about it now. Enjoy the rest of your vacation. We'll talk about it when you get home."

Sometimes a marriage, even a good one, reaches a stalemate. They had been married for seventeen years, long enough to have accepted each other's faults, long enough for their relationship to have deepened into something else. She had always felt that her life with Tom was a series of stages; one ended and the next began on its heels. But then why suddenly did it feel as if they had stopped moving forward? Why did it feel sometimes as if they were treading the same dark water?

"I won't hang up until you tell me."

He sighed. "It's no big deal. Really."

"You let me be the judge of that." She dragged it out of him like she always did. Because she'd grown into a chronic worrier and no matter how small the problem she could turn it into something large and dismal. *His words.* He told her in a strained, clipped voice. Nicky had been stood up by her new boyfriend, who was already seeing another girl, and she was in mourning, refusing to eat. Adam had had a fit at school when he couldn't get the lid back on his glue bottle and Tom had been called in for a conference. Listening to his weary voice, she'd felt a chill fall over the sunny landscape. The sky seemed less brilliant now, marred by a series of distant clouds. No matter how many good things happened in her own life, it would never be enough. She would never be free from worrying about her children, not even when they were grown and she was an old, old woman.

"Let's make one stop," Mel said. They passed the lighthouse and without warning, she braked and swung into the narrow road leading to the museum. In the distance, through the screen of live oaks, they could see the glistening marsh. The post office, museum, and nondenominational church looked deserted. In the grassy clearing between the buildings, a mother sat watching her two children twirl in circles. At the edge of the marsh, the old lighthouse towered against the wide sky.

Mel pulled into the sandy parking area and parked.

"What are we doing here?" Sara asked, looking around the deserted square. The museum door opened and a young man walked out, studying a map. The children cried, "Daddy!" and ran to him.

Mel took the key out of the ignition. "It's our next to the last day on the island."

"So?"

"In another couple of days we'll be flying back to our real lives."

Sara rolled her shoulders and regarded Mel warily. "I'm not going up in that lighthouse," she said stiffly.

Mel shrugged. "I'm not asking you to." She leaned over and checked herself in the rearview mirror, smoothing her hair with her hands.

"You know I'm afraid of heights."

"You can tour the museum. I won't be long. It won't take me a minute to get to the top."

"That thing was built in 1802. It probably hasn't been repaired in two hundred years. It's stupid to go up there."

Mel grinned like an imbecile. "Stupid is as stupid does," she said.

"Forrest Gump wouldn't climb those stairs."

"He might."

"Well, he had an IQ of seventy-five, so go ahead, knock yourself out."

"You didn't used to be such a chickenshit."

"That's where you're wrong. I've always been a chickenshit."

"You used to be fearless. But that's okay. People change as they get older."

"That's right. They get smarter."

"Okay, I'm going." Mel stood up and walked off.

"Don't let go of the rail!" Sara shouted gaily. "Don't fall fifty feet to your death!" She watched as Mel pushed open the heavy wooden door and stepped inside. The young couple gathered their children and climbed back into their golf cart. High above the marsh a hawk circled endlessly. Sara sighed and looked at her feet.

After a minute, she got up and followed Mel.

Inside the lighthouse it was cool and damp. A faint odor of smoke and rotted wood hung in the air, and the stone floor smelled of wet earth. Mel sat on the stairs, waiting for her. She looked up and grinned when she saw Sara. "I knew you'd come," she said. Light slanted through the high windows and fell in wide swaths around her.

"If I fall, I blame you."

"Just remember, life is like a box of chocolates. You never know what you're going to get."

"Shut up and move so I can grab the rail."

The stairs were narrow and made of tabby. They seemed sturdy but the rickety wooden railing seemed less so. Sara found that by flattening her back against the wall as she climbed, she could see very little of the floor beneath her. Round and round they went, climbing slowly, Mel in front and Sara behind. She tried not to look down. She felt dizzy and sick to her stomach. Why had she let Mel talk her into this? Why, after all these years, was she still letting Mel push her into doing things she didn't want to do?

The brick wall, covered in whitewashed plaster, was cold against her back. The stairs were worn in the middle from the measured treads of ancient feet. Of long-dead climbers. She wondered what the children and Tom would say if they could see her now. They wouldn't believe it. Mom, the worrier, the one who saw danger in every situation, who warned constantly of broken bones, cavities, head injuries, and E. coli. Whose favorite refrain was, *Don't do that, don't touch that, don't eat that.*

When they got to the top, Mel laughed and said, "Doesn't this place remind you of that Hitchcock movie, *Vertigo*?" She stood at a narrow window, looking out.

Sara clung to the wall, trying not to look down. Once she'd been fearless and unafraid of life. What had happened to her? "*Vertigo*," she said. "Is that about the woman who assumes another woman's identity after she's killed by her husband?"

"That's right." Mel was standing above her, leaning precariously against the railing and peering down into the shadowy depths. "You know, I could throw you down this staircase and say it was an accident."

"Then you could assume my life."

Mel looked at her. She shook the railing slightly. "What makes you think I want your life?"

Sara shrank down on the steps, her back against the wall, her white-knuckled fingers clasping the railing. She tried to imagine Mel faithful to the same man for seventeen years, saddled with two children whose lives would always overshadow her own, but she couldn't. She tried to imagine herself living the life of a bohemian artist, unencumbered by loyalty and responsibility, but she couldn't. She and Mel had made their own choices. It was too late to start second-guessing it all now.

Mel gave her a curious look and stopped shaking the railing. She came slowly down the stairs, and, stepping over Sara, she stopped a couple of steps below her. "Here," she said. "Hold onto the wall with one hand and my shoulder with the other. I'll lead you down."

"I can't let go," Sara said.

"Yes, you can. Here." She pried Sara's hands gently off the railing, putting one against the wall and the other on her shoulder. "Face the wall. Look at the wall as we climb down."

"Go slowly."

"I will."

Mel led her carefully back down the staircase. It seemed to take an eternity, their footsteps echoing in the murky darkness. Bands of sunlight striped the plaster walls. When they reached the bottom, Sara sank down onto the steps, her head resting on her knees. She felt weak with relief, sweaty and light-headed, and curiously detached from her body.

Mel said, "I'm sorry. I shouldn't have made you do something like that."

Sara sat with her head on her knees, still fighting a feeling of dizziness. She was reminded suddenly of a long-ago trip she had taken with her family. It was not long after Adam's diagnosis and they were driving from Atlanta to North Carolina to visit Tom's parents. It was a gray and rainy day, approaching dusk. Outside the sky was dark and rain-swept but inside the car was cozy and dimly lit. The children were in the backseat, sleeping. Sara turned around to look at them. In sleep, Adam looked perfect, beautiful, a mirror image of Tom. She turned again to face the road, her mind caught up in its usual endless loop: Would Adam ever have a normal life?

Would he ever have a girlfriend, go to college, know the joys of fatherhood? All the little things we take for granted in our bustling, hurried lives. Overcome by a deep feeling of sadness, her eyes fixed on the yellow lines of the highway, she experienced a sudden profound shift in perception. It was like falling abruptly, like slipping between drops of rain. It was as if her emotions, attached to her thoughts, had suddenly let go. She was alone, floating free in a moment of perfect stillness. She thought, *This is what it feels like to die.*

It happened in less time than it took the car to hurtle past an abandoned house, in less time than it took the loop of negativity to start again in her head like an endless clang of straining winches and rusty gears. And yet for one profound moment she had glimpsed the possibility of a world without attachment, without pain, and she clung to that feeling as they hurtled through the darkness, weary travelers on an unknown road.

"Are you okay?" Mel asked, lightly touching her shoulder.

Sara stood up. Dust motes swirled in the slash of sunlight. "I need a drink," she said.

Everyone was stunned by Annie's transformation. Even Captain Mike did a double take when he saw her. They had worked on her all afternoon, and now she stood in the middle of the great room, waiting for the reveal. She was dressed in a low-cut blouse and a pair of white capri slacks that made her look slim and youthful. With her hair colored and her face made up, she looked ten years younger. Standing at the great room mirror admiring herself, Annie wished the snotty mothers in her sons' preschool class could see her now. She was pretty sure no one would call her Q-Tip.

"You look *fantastic*," Sara said.

"I told you hair color would make all the difference," Mel said.

"Just like Cinderella," Lola said, clapping her hands. She jumped up and down like a cheerleader.

Captain Mike was in the kitchen helping April with supper. He looked up at Lola's clapping, and smiled.

"What do you think, Captain Mike?" Mel asked, eyeing him boldly. "What do you think of our little Eliza Doolittle?"

He shook his head and grinned so deeply his dimply showed. "Wow," he said.

Under his close appraisal, Annie felt her face flush. She stared at herself in the mirror, smoothing her *Vixen Brown* hair with one hand, noting the way it brought out her eyes, the way it framed her face. Amazing how so simple a change could make such a big difference. She wondered what Mitchell would say.

"And that blouse, too," Mel said. "You have a nice figure. You should show some cleavage more often."

The blouse was Mel's, of course, and she had insisted that Annie wear it. It wasn't something Annie would have ever picked out for herself but somehow, with the new hair and lips and makeup, it worked. Standing in front of the long mirror, perusing the strange creature who peered back at her in the glass, she was amazed and oddly elated. She looked like a new woman.

"If you girls are ready, you should probably get going," Captain Mike said. It was after dinner, and he and April were in the kitchen finishing up the dishes. The women had decided to take a drive in the moonlight, on this, their last night on the island. Tomorrow they would spend the night on the yacht, moored in some magical place Lola had yet to show them, and the following morning Captain Mike would motor them over to the ferry landing so they could catch the limo to the airport.

The sun was setting as they set out on the golf cart. The sky was a deep purple, streaked with red, and the sea breeze was warm and steady. They took the maritime forest road. Mel drove with Lola in the front with her. Annie and Sara sat in the back.

Long shadows fell across the forest road. Crickets sang in the dense underbrush. Out in the tidal creeks skirting the marsh, a group of herons stood like old men on a street corner.

"What's the name of this place where we're going?" Mel asked Lola.

"Runaway Hill," Lola said.

"Why do they call it that?"

She shrugged. "I don't know." She was wearing a denim miniskirt, a white lace top, and a pair of strappy sandals, and she looked like a young girl. "I've been there lots of times!" she added.

"By yourself?"

Lola smiled faintly. "Sometimes," she said.

The climb up the ridge was a steep one, and Annie and Sara finally climbed off the back of the cart and walked up. The asphalt trail meandered up the side of the dune and ended in a small parking lot overlook-ing the sea. Halfway down the ridge on the other side, two dilapidated cot-tages stood, facing the sea.

"What are those?" Mel asked Lola, pointing. They sat on the cart in the gathering darkness, waiting for Sara and Annie to climb the ridge.

"The old caretakers' cottages. Back before the civil war the lighthouse keeper and his family lived there. Back before the island was developed."

It took Annie and Sara several minutes to reach the summit, and when they did, they threw themselves down onto the back of the golf cart.

"That was a climb," Sara said breathlessly. Evening was falling swiftly, the light glimmering along the dunes and the distant rim of beach. To the north and east stretched the wide Atlantic, an immense darkness along the horizon. To the south stretched a long expanse of deserted beach and windswept dunes. There were no lights except for the distant glimmer of the lighthouse, visible just above the tree line.

It was a lonely place. Annie shuddered, wishing now that she'd worn a sweater over Mel's flimsy blouse.

"Remember when we used to go to Myrtle Beach for spring break?" Sara asked.

"I remember," Mel said.

"It seems like only yesterday."

The four of them would load up the car with beer and beach towels and take turns driving from Bedford to Myrtle Beach. They'd gone their soph-omore year and Annie had been so embarrassed because Mitchell had fol-lowed her there, showing up at three o'clock in the morning at their hotel door with a cooler full of Pabst Blue Ribbon beer. It was a girls' trip, and boyfriends weren't supposed to come. Mel had told J.T. Radford he couldn't come and he'd gone off someplace else with a bunch of his bud-dies but Mitchell hadn't wanted male companionship; he'd wanted her. It was embarrassing hearing all the girls talk about how sweet and "crazy in love" Mitchell was. He didn't have any money, of course, so he'd spent the night sleeping on the floor of their hotel room. He made himself at home, and by the end of the week he was just one of the girls, laughing and drinking with the rest of them, letting them paint his fingernails and do his hair because that was Mitchell's way. He liked people and they liked him back. At the time it had pissed Annie off. She'd felt like there was something wrong with him, loving her the way he did. No one else's boyfriend was like that. Well, maybe J.T., but he pretty much did what Mel told him to do. If she'd told him to worship her from afar, he'd have done it. Annie could tell Mitchell to leave her alone and he'd just laugh and ask her what she wanted for dinner.

"Remember that time Mitchell showed up?" Mel said.

"That was the best trip."

"He was so much fun. I'm only sorry he wasn't there for all our trips."

"He drove all that way just to be with Annie," Lola said.

"Wait until he gets a look at her now," Sara said.

Annie smiled shyly. Listening to them talk, a funny thing happened. It started small, a pinpoint of emptiness in the pit of her stomach that swelled and grew slowly to a hollow feeling just beneath her breastbone. She thought at first it might be heartburn, before she recognized it for what it was. Homesickness. Loneliness. She missed Mitchell.

They were quiet for a moment, enjoying the view. There was no sound but the steady crashing of the surf and the low roar of the wind coming up the ridge.

Annie wondered what Mitchell was doing right now. Funny how you could become accustomed to the sound of one man's voice, the touch of one man's arms around your waist. She and Mitchell had known each other for thirty years. They had been through a lot. They'd built a business and raised two fine boys and suffered the death of a baby. A miscarriage, twenty-six weeks after Carleton's birth. Annie had felt like she could never be happy until she'd held a daughter in her arms but after the miscarriage she'd changed her mind. She'd been afraid then to try again, afraid the Lord was giving her a sign that she was, in some way, unworthy. Or at least that's how it had felt to her at the time, lost in her guilt and grief.

"I've had a lot of fun on this trip but I'm looking forward to going home," Sara said quietly.

"Yes," Annie said.

She pictured Mitchell slumped in front of the TV in his favorite recliner, his stockinged feet pointed at the screen, his one glass of red wine, carefully poured out and measured according to the doctor's instructions, resting on a side table. Things that had once annoyed her about Mitchell, seen now in the gentle light of missing him, seemed incredibly dear. His snoring, his dirty laundry left on the bathroom floor, his loud honks and gags as he cleared his throat every morning. In the movies, love was always loud and passionate; it was always unrelenting and tragic. She had had a taste of that kind of love with Paul Ballard. But there was a different kind too, a slow, quiet contentment that built gradually over time, a feeling based on trust and fortitude, on the shared experiences of raising children, on grief and hardship and joy. That was the love Annie felt for Mitchell. She had never, until this moment, realized it so clearly. She loved Mitchell, and yet she had come so incredibly close to losing him.

"We should do this again," Mel said.

"Every year," Sara said.

"Yes," Annie said.

She had come close to losing him through her own fault. Things that had seemed beyond her control at the time, situations that had caused her pain, had worked out for the best. Well, most of them had anyway; there were some things you could never explain or do over, you just had to accept them. Maybe that's what grace was. Maybe you had to reach a certain age before you could look back and see it at work in your life.

Annie put her head back and stared up at the starry sky. A bright yellow moon rose over the sea, bathing the ridge in a clear, luminous light. One thing was certain, though. When she got back to Nashville, she was introducing Mitchell to Agnes Grace.

A phone rang suddenly, startling them with its insistent chirping. Sara pulled her cell out of her purse and checked the display. "It's my husband," she said, rising.

"Talk about timely," Mel said.

Sara walked a little ways down the ridge. When she came back, a short while later, she was smiling.

"Does he miss you?" Annie asked, wondering if it was too late to call Mitchell.

Sara grinned. "Is the pope Catholic?" she said.

"How are Tom and the kids anyway?"

Mel groaned. "Haven't we talked enough about the husband and kids? Christ, that's all I've heard all week."

"He's fine," Sara said to Annie. "They're fine." She cut her eyes over to Mel and then back to Annie. "Thanks for asking."

Mel raised her hands apologetically. "It's not that I don't care," she said.

"It's just that I figure J.T. has his hands full, what with taking care of the kids while you're gone."

"Don't call him that," Sara said. "No one's called him that since college."

"Sorry, Mrs. Radford."

"His name is Tom," she said, shoving the phone back into her purse. "That's the name he goes by now."

Chapter 38

~~~~~~~~~

SATURDAY

Their last day at the beach dawned cloudy and rainy. Mel, packing her bags in her bedroom, was glad. It would be hard to leave paradise on a brilliant sun-drenched day. Rain seemed more conducive to her mood. Over on the dresser her cell phone was flashing its sad little light, warning of an unheeded call. She checked and was surprised to find a message from Leland.

"How you doing?" the message said. He sounded strange. Melancholy and strange. "I was just calling to see how you're doing."

Mel sensed that he wanted to chat, which was odd because she and Leland never called each other to chat. She hoped he wasn't on the verge of senile dementia, some latent mental illness that would drive him steadily and progressively back into his dismal childhood. Or hers. She had learned years ago that revenge was an unhealthy obsession. She had forgiven him, she had to, to get well, but the forgiveness was for her sake and not his own. Sooner or later Leland would have to wrestle with his own demons.

She pushed a button and erased the message. She'd call him tomorrow from the airport.

She finished packing and went downstairs to check on the others. They had planned to spend their last evening on the boat, but the rain would, no doubt, change all that.

She was surprised to find Captain Mike, Lola, and April in the kitchen laughing and talking, apparently unconcerned by the weather.

"The front's scheduled to move out by early afternoon," Captain Mike explained, "and we'll have smooth sailing from then on." He was loading fish into a cooler. April was loading kitchen supplies into a plastic tub. She glanced over her shoulder, giving Mel a wan smile. She seemed friendlier, more relaxed, as if she, too, realized that this trip was almost over and she was grateful for that.

"Well, I might be wrong but I don't think you'll get Annie out on a boat in rough seas," Mel said, sitting down at the breakfast bar to pour herself a cup of coffee.

Lola glanced at Mike but he smiled and closed the lid to the cooler. "You leave Annie to me," he said.

True to form, Annie refused to budge. They sat in the great room all morning watching the storm-tossed seas through the long windows. Mike tried to tell her the front would be moving out by midafternoon. Lola offered her Xanax, which she had somehow miraculously found. Finally Annie said, "I don't know why you're pushing this, Lola. You know how dangerous it can be out there in a storm. They don't call it the Graveyard of the Atlantic for nothing."

"I know," Lola said in a soothing voice. The hint of sadness that seemed to follow her had returned, settling around her narrow shoulders and delicate face. She seemed nervous; every time the phone rang she jumped, and Mel imagined how hard it must be for her, contemplating a return to Briggs. "But there's this hidden cove I really wanted you to see. I wanted all of you to see it by moonlight."

"What moonlight?" Annie asked in a wavering voice. "It's pitch-black out there."

Captain Mike stood at the window watching the rain, his hands clasped behind his back. "It'll clear," he said.

And then, as if following his command, it did clear. By three o'clock the gray clouds moved off and the sun peeked through, shimmering across the wet landscape. The sea continued to roll wildly, great foamy waves crashing against the beach, and Annie watched them anxiously. Lola went over and sat down next to her on the sofa. She put her arms around Annie.

"Don't worry," she said in her little-girl voice. "Captain Mike knows what he's doing. You'll be fine, I promise."

"I won't take it out into open sea while the water's rough," Mike said to Annie. "I'll keep to the coves and inlets."

"Oh, all right," she snapped. "I don't want to be the one ruining everyone else's fun."

"That hasn't stopped you before," Mel said.

"Bite me, Mel."

Sara laughed. Lola said mildly, "I just want it to be special. I want our last night together to be special."

True to his word, Captain Mike stuck to the coves and inlets. The women sat in the salon, sipping tall glasses of iced tea and watching the narrow islands pass beyond the long windows. They motored through the Carolina Beach Inlet and through Myrtle Grove Sound, past Masonboro Island and Wrightsville Beach. Dusk was falling as they passed the wide beach and tangled underbrush of the Isle of Pines, and continued north through Topsail Sound, anchoring finally in a sheltered cove off the northern tip of Lea Island. The water in the failing light was an oily gray color, and far out beyond Topsail Inlet the sea was a wide dark shape.

Mel leaned back and put her arm up across the back of the curved sofa. "Annie, are you still with us?"

Annie had taken Lola up on her offer of the Xanax. She'd taken half a tablet and sat now looking out at the distant shape of Lea Island with a dazed expression on her face. "It's strange," she said.

"What's strange?"

She turned her head slightly, trying to focus on Mel's face. "The way I feel. I mean, I know I'm in danger, I know the boat may capsize and we may all drown, but I don't really care."

"I know," Lola said brightly. "Isn't it great?"

"Don't get used to taking pharmaceuticals," Sara warned Annie, as if there might be a danger of this. "I see a lot of sad cases come through the court system."

"Speaking of pharmaceuticals," Mel said to Lola. "Were you able to score some weed?" Lola grinned and gave her a thumbs-up.

Sara said flatly, "I told y'all I'm not doing that."

"No one's twisting your arm."

"I mean it this time, Mel."

"I know you do, Sara. And it's okay."

"I'll do it," Annie said, waving her hand vaguely. "It's probably the last time I'll ever do it, so I'll do it for old time's sake."

"You're already under the influence. I think you should leave it at that," Sara said.

Annie stared at the rolling sea, her eyes narrowing slightly. "I only took half a tablet. And it's wearing off. In about two hours I'll need something to take the edge off."

Mel laughed. "Here's to taking the edge off," she said, lifting her glass of sweet tea. They all raised their glasses. Annie sipped her tea slowly, then set the glass down on the table. "We did what you wanted to do," she said, waving her finger at Sara. "Renew our friendship—we did that." She looked around the room as if daring anyone to dispute this, and no one did. "And I did something I've never done before. I dyed my hair. I let you dress me up like a tart. So now it's only fair that we do what Lola wanted to do, and smoke some weed."

Mel patted Annie's arm. "Easy there, Anne Louise. It doesn't have to be a group thing. Let's lighten up on the peer pressure, okay?"

Sara leaned back in her chair and crossed one leg over the other. "We still haven't done what Mel wanted to do either."

"You mean fuck Captain Mike?"

"That's right."

"Hey," Mel said. "The night's still young."

The weed was a gift from Captain Mike, some BC bud he'd picked up on a fishing trip to Canada. They sat out on the aft deck after dinner, smoking and enjoying the cool evening. The sky had cleared, and the moon shone like a lantern. Clouds of fireflies flickered in the darkness of Lea Island. Captain Mike and April cleared the table, carrying dishes into the galley. They left the women to their own devices (or vices), although as she was going in through the sliding doors, April gave them a smirk, the kind of look a cheeky teenage girl might give an octogenarian who shows up wearing a bikini on the beach. A look that said clearly, *Why don't you women act your age?*

Just wait, Mel thought dismally, watching the girl turn and step through the door. *Your time will come.*

She relit the doobie, which was professionally rolled and spoke volumes about Captain Mike's extracurricular activities. ("What," she'd said when he gave it to them, "no bong?") She passed it to Lola, who took a hit and passed it to Annie.

"Don't you just hate getting old?" Mel said. The moon peeked shyly from behind a screen of swiftly moving clouds. The water shone as smooth as glass.

"It sure beats the alternative," Annie said, exhaling.

"We're not old," Sara said, putting her feet up on one of the deck chairs. "Forty-five is not old." No one offered her a hit. Through the glass doors they could see Captain Mike and April, laughing and talking in the brightly lit galley.

"Well, we're not young either," Annie said.

"We're *experienced,*" Mel said.

"That's a nice way of putting it."

"In some ways I like it better now," Annie said. "I'm more settled than I was at twenty-two. The boys are grown, and it's just Mitchell and me now, and that's been a change, that's not been easy, but I'm starting to get used to it."

"So what are you and Mitchell going to do now that the kids are grown?" Mel asked. "Sell the big house and move to Boca Raton?"

"I'll never leave that house," Annie said. She and Mitchell had talked about traveling more, now that the business was going well and the boys were grown, but she was a homebody. She liked her nest.

"What about you, Lola, now that Henry's grown and soon to be a married man?" Sara asked.

Lola took a hit and lifted her chin, exhaling slowly. "Briggs wants to sell the place here and buy something in Aspen. He says he's tired of the beach."

"But what do *you* want to do?" Mel asked.

Lola shook her head, as if the thought hadn't occurred to her. "Hawaii sounds nice," she said. "Someplace tropical."

"What about you, Mel? Do you think you'll ever remarry?"

"No. I've learned my lesson. I'm not the marrying kind, I guess." It felt good to let go of that, finally. She had tried, and failed, at something she just wasn't cut out for. She had seen so clearly, as a young girl, the path her life must take, and despite the detours she'd taken along the way, despite wandering for so long in a desert of doubt and uncertainty, she saw clearly now that her youthful vision had been true. What was it Robert Frost had said, prattling on about two roads that diverged in a yellow wood? *I took the one less traveled by, and that has made all the difference.*

Captain Mike opened the sliding door and stuck his head out. "You girls okay?" he asked. Behind him, Pete Yorn sang on the sound system.

"Hey, turn that up," Mel said as he disappeared and a few minutes later the deck speakers came on. Mel smiled at him through the glass doors. She watched him duck his head and step through the salon door to the state-rooms. "Not that I wouldn't like a little male companionship in my life."

"Well, there's always the UPS guy."

"I'm sorry now that I told you about that." She stretched her legs out and put her feet up on the side of Sara's chair. "One thing's for certain," she said. "When I get back to New York I'm looking for a man just like Captain Mike. Someone with a little experience who knows how to look after himself. Someone who's good with his hands."

"Har," Annie said.

"You know what I mean. Someone who's smart and funny but handy around the house, too. The kind of guy who listens to public radio and works on his own car. Someone you'd feel safe with walking down Union Turnpike at three o'clock in the morning."

"You'll have to move south to find someone like that," Annie said. Lola smiled and passed her the joint. The moon disappeared behind a cloud. Far off in the distance a rumbling began, low and mournful as cannon fire.

Annie paused, holding the glowing joint in front of her. "Is that thunder?" she said.

"I don't believe all that crap about everyone having just one true soul mate," Mel said, still talking about her love life. "I mean, look at me. I've had four."

Sara looked at her quickly and said in a dubious tone, "Are you including Tom in that group?"

Mel took the joint from Annie and inhaled slowly. She put her head back and exhaled, staring at the moon as if she was weighing something she had to say, wanting to make sure she got it right. "If you're asking me if I had it to do all over again, would I break up with him, knowing what I know now? Probably not. He was perfect for me. But was I perfect for him? Could I have given him the things he wanted, a stable home life, children? Could I have made him happy? I don't think so. And he deserves to be happy. He deserves you, Sara."

Sara smiled faintly, her face coloring delicately. She moved and tucked her feet underneath her.

Mel passed the joint to Lola. "Since I'm getting everything off my chest, since I'm confessing, I just want you to know, I never really blamed you for what happened between you and J.T. Sorry, I mean Tom. I just felt left out when you two got married. It was hard, losing my two best friends at the same time. It made me really bitter for a while."

Annie said, "Your *two* best friends?"

Sara plucked at her sleeve. "And I felt guilty," she said, glancing at Mel and then down again at her sleeve. "I felt like I'd stolen something from you, which is ridiculous because you didn't want it. You didn't want him. You were already married to someone else."

"Yes." Mel nodded dully.

"I almost picked up the phone a million times to call you but over the years it just seemed to drag on. It just got more and more awkward."

"It felt like there was a wall between us. Something I couldn't get over."

"Which is crazy when you think about it."

"After all we've been through together."

"Yes."

The sky, where it met the sea, was a deep luminous green. Waves lapped gently against the side of the boat.

Lola stirred, giving them a dazzling smile. "See," she said. "Isn't this better?"

Mel pulled her knees up to her chest and stared at the distant horizon. "He wanted babies and I didn't. He wanted a settled life and I didn't. Anyone who's ever seen you two together knows you were meant for each other."

Sara gave her a grateful smile. "Thank you," she said quietly.

The boat rocked peacefully beneath them. Moonlight fell in a wide swath across the water. Lola leaned her cheek on the palm of her hand and said to Mel, "Your novels are your babies, if you think about it."

Mel smiled. *Funny, she never had.*

The distant rumbling had stopped but there was a smell of rain in the air. A sudden gust of wind blew out the candle on the table.

"It's not getting ready to storm, is it?" Annie asked, looking around at the others. She giggled suddenly. The BC bud was definitely beginning to take effect. The weed was stronger than anything they'd ever smoked in their youth.

"Let's play a game," Mel said. "Let's go around the table and say something about ourselves that no one else knows."

"No!" Annie put her fingers in her ears and began to hum.

"Haven't we already played this?" Lola asked.

"Okay," Mel said. "I'll go first." She took another hit and held it, tilting her head back to the green sky. She exhaled slowly and passed the joint to Annie. "Seven years ago I was diagnosed with breast cancer." She had meant to sound somber but her voice came out high and strained. Like Minnie Mouse. Like Minnie Mouse sucking on a helium balloon.

Annie sputtered all over the joint.

Lola sat there staring at Mel as if she hadn't heard her clearly.

Mel said, "I'm not kidding." Sara blinked, a look of studied concern settling over her features.

"Cancer!" Annie whooped and put her head back.

"Damn it, Annie, I'm serious."

"Oh, sure!"

"I had cancer, damn you," Mel said, fixing Annie with a severe look, but it was hopeless and she knew it, and then she, too, began to giggle.

Gallows humor. Under the influence of Xanax and BC bud, Annie had it in large measure. As, apparently, did Mel. When they had stopped snorting and punching each other on the arms, Sara got up and went to use the head. When she came back out on deck, her face was pale. She sat down at the table, not looking at Mel, not looking at anyone, her eyes fixed on the dark, slumbering shape of Lea Island. As the joint went by, she reached out and took it, inhaling deeply. "Okay, let's make a pact right now," Sara said tightly. "We never talk about this. Ever."

"What happens on the boat stays on the boat," Mel said, nodding gravely.

Looking at her, Annie sputtered and began to laugh again.

"I've got kids," Sara said, ignoring them. "I can't tell them to just say no to drugs and alcohol if Mommy isn't saying no."

"Sure you can," Annie said. "We all do it."

"But doesn't that make us hypocrites?"

"No. It makes us parents."

"That's right," Mel says. "Do as I say, not as I do. Don't ask, don't tell."

Annie and Lola thought that was very funny. "Don't ask, don't tell," Lola repeated like a Girl Scout. Sara waited for the THC to take effect. She waited for the joint to go around the circle several times before she was ready. Then she looked at Mel and asked, "Why?"

Mel stopped giggling. "Why what?" she said.

Annie, sobering suddenly, said, "Sorry about laughing about your cancer."

Mel said, "That's okay. It feels good to laugh."

Sara rapped her knuckles on the table to get Mel's attention. "Why didn't you tell us? Why did you try to get through all that on your own?"

Annie leaned over and relit the candle on the table. Lola watched her dreamily, letting the joint go out.

Mel shrugged and put her drink down. "It was early stage. I had a lumpectomy, followed by six rounds of chemo, and I've been fine ever since." She flicked the lighter and held it to the tip of the joint while Lola inhaled deeply.

"But how could you not tell us?" Sara said. "How could you go through that alone?"

Mel tossed the lighter on the table. She leaned forward on her elbows and put her head down, and when she looked up again her voice was calm and reasonable. "I didn't want people making a big deal out of it. I didn't want anyone to feel sorry for me. I knew it was something I could get through. You had your own lives to deal with."

"We'd have been there for you," Annie said.

"I know that. And I knew that if things got bad, I'd tell you." She took the joint from Lola and passed it to Sara. "It's just that when something like that happens, all of a sudden you feel doomed, like you're the only one in the world going through this run of bad luck. You see other people, bad people, shallow people, and you think, why did this happen to me? Why can't they get cancer? What did I do to deserve this? And all around you life goes on just like before. Everyone goes on with their own lives, and their lives seem so perfect."

"My life isn't perfect," Sara said mechanically. She sucked the joint and passed it on, narrowing her eyes as she exhaled. "My son has a mild form of autism. He goes to a special school. It's been the hardest thing in the world, worrying about a child and who will take care of him when I'm gone. When Tom is gone. It's nearly destroyed my marriage."

Another sudden gust of wind rattled the candle in its glass globe. The moon sailed slowly behind a covering of dark clouds. Lola leaned over and laid her hand on Sara's arm. "Is there any treatment?" she asked quietly.

"There are all kinds of treatments, many of them controversial. We've tried a lot of different things. Adam is highly functional but even so he doesn't do well in social situations. He doesn't have any friends, he doesn't get invited to spend the night. I go to the mall and I see teenage boys hanging out together and I think, Adam will never be one of those boys. It's hard."

Mel remembered the boy she'd seen in the airport all those years ago, his face fixed in a strange concentration as he navigated the crowd. She leaned over and put her hand on top of Lola's, giving Sara's arm a little tug. "I'm sorry," she said sincerely.

"Thanks," Sara said. She stared at Mel's hand. "I always wondered if it would have been different with you and Tom. If you two would have had normal kids."

"We wouldn't have had any kids at all," Mel said. "And that would have killed him. He always wanted a family."

Above them the broad shape of the dinghy rose from the flybridge, covered in its bright blue tarpaulin. Clouds scuttled across the moon.

Mel was quiet a moment, pulling her hand away. "I never told you this," she said, "but years ago I saw you in an airport. It was Christmas and I was coming back from a book tour. I saw Tom first—your daughter was sitting on his shoulders and your son was walking alongside—and the thing I noticed most about Tom was that he seemed so happy. I'm talking deep, life-affirming joy here. It was written all over his face. And I knew then that we could never have been happy together. All the fantasies I had carried over the years were just that, fantasies. They weren't real. They weren't what you and Tom have. What you and Tom and your children have."

Sara's face softened in gratitude. She looked like she was going to cry, and they could see her struggling to contain herself. "Thank you for telling me that," she said.

Mel leaned over and hugged her fiercely, and Sara hugged her back. The moon peeked from behind the clouds and shone brightly in the apple-green sky. Mel let her go. "I know it's a daily struggle. If you ever need to talk to anyone you can call me, or any of us."

"I know that." Sara ran her finger under her eyes. She smiled and looked around her circle of friends. "We're lucky that there are so many good doctors in Atlanta. Lately, we've been sending Adam to a neurologist who specializes in Lego therapy."

"Lego therapy?" Annie said. "You mean those little blocks that stick together?"

"Yes."

"My boys always loved those."

"This doctor has discovered that autistic children seem drawn to Legos. Adam's room is filled with them, all meticulously put together. Anyway, the doctor has formed play groups where he'll bring in several boys and engage them by using Lego sets. They'll make movies together, use the sets in imaginary games, interact in ways no one thought possible. So it's definitely a step in the right direction."

"Oh, Sara, that's wonderful," Lola said.

"I know things will work out," Annie said, trying to be hopeful. She'd known about Adam—Sara had been calling for years to confide in her—and she was glad things seemed to be going well. There had been so many hopeful beginnings, so many failed therapies. She felt another quick flush of gratitude for her sons, whole and healthy.

"What about you, Lola?" Mel asked, trying to change the subject, trying to take the pressure off Sara. "Do you have any secrets you'd like to share? Other than the fact that you like porn?"

Lola shook her head. "I don't," she said.

"Did you ever tell Henry about your wild and crazy youth?"

"Of course I did," Lola said. "I don't have any secrets from Henry." She frowned and sipped her iced tea. "Well, maybe one," she said, setting the glass down. She was quiet for a moment, staring at her hand as if it belonged to someone else. "I never told him about Lonnie."

No one wanted to talk about Lonnie. Mel got up and went into the galley to get another pitcher of tea. Captain Mike and April had disappeared, obviously heading down to the crew quarters for the night. She put "The Day I Forgot" on the CD player and came back out on the deck. The sea was calm and placid. A fish jumped, its scales glimmering in the moonlight. The storm seemed farther away now, the thunder more distant. Mel poured another round of sweet tea and sat down. She looked around the table at her friends, who sat staring pensively out at the water. "Shit, Annie," she said suddenly, "what'd you do with the joint?"

Startled, Annie looked around. "I must have dropped it."

They all got up and began to look.

"Don't think this gets you off the hook," Sara said to Annie. "You still have to tell us something about yourself that we don't know."

Annie looked surprised. Then she put her head back and laughed.

"What's so funny?" Mel asked.

"Everything."

"Tell us."

"I wish I could always feel like this."

"Don't we all," Sara said.

Annie told them about Professor Ballard. They sat around the table, smoking and listening, their faces pale and disbelieving in the candlelight. They were still listening ten minutes later when Captain Mike stuck his head out to check on them. "The sea has calmed," he said to Lola. "Do you still want me to take us offshore?"

Lola, who had been sitting with her chin in her hand, stirred and looked around the table. "I thought we'd take a moonlight cruise on our last night together. There's something I want to show you. It's not far," she added, looking at Annie as if she feared the trauma of an open sea cruise might be too much for her.

But Annie, in the middle of the tale of her doomed love affair with Paul Ballard, wasn't concerned. It was amazing how good it felt, finally telling someone. She felt purged, peaceful. Her back prickled, as if a great weight had been lifted from her shoulders. She didn't even wait for Captain Mike to leave before she began again.

They sat listening to her, expressions of grief and outrage on their faces. Annie was so elated and caught up in her story that she hardly noticed when Captain Mike fired up the engines and headed for open sea.

She hurried on, telling them everything.

They cruised for a while and then anchored a mile offshore. It was quiet here; there was no sound but the gentle lapping of the waves against the hull. Lola made Captain Mike turn off all the lights and they sat in the darkness, listening. The water, in the moonlight, was smooth and calm. Strange phosphorescent lights lit the depths, and sitting there it was easy to imagine how the Earth must have looked before time began. All along the mainland and the distant islands, lights twinkled, scattered outposts of civilization in the vast, quiet darkness.

"Does Mitchell know?" Mel asked suddenly, and everyone turned to peer at her in the dim light. The candle flickered in the center of the table, reflecting their somber, composed faces.

"No," Annie said quickly.

"You sly dog," Mel said.

"It's not really something I'm proud of, Mel. It's something that just happened."

"I know that, Annie. But it makes you more human, somehow."

"We all make mistakes," Sara agreed, not looking at anyone in particular.

Lola tapped her fingers against the candle's smoky globe. "I'm hungry," she said.

"I'm starving," Sara said.

"Do you have any junk food on this boat, Lola?"

"I'll see." She got up and went inside and a few minutes later all the lights came on in the galley. Lola stuck her head out the door. "How about a big plate of nachos?"

"You got any chocolate?" Mel asked.

"No chocolate, just nachos."

A short while later, she came out carrying a huge platter in her hands. She was wearing pajamas and her coke-bottom eyeglasses. "I thought Mel and I would sleep in the master stateroom and Annie and Sara in the VIP stateroom," she said, setting the plate down on the table. She scooted over and sat down next to Mel.

"I am getting kind of sleepy," Annie said.

"No one goes to bed before twelve," Mel warned. "This is our last night together. We have to make it last as long as possible. Although I'd like to go on record as saying that I think we should do this more often."

"I second that," Sara said, lifting her empty glass.

"Me, too," Annie said.

Lola pointed to the platter. "Shall I make more nachos?" she said.

They all went below to put on their pajamas and then came back up on deck to finish the nachos. After that, Lola made another plate and then heated up a frozen pizza she found in the freezer.

"Now I remember why I don't like smoking dope," Sara said. "I'll put on five pounds before I get home tomorrow."

Mel said, "It doesn't matter. Your husband will be glad to see you anyway."

Sara grinned. "You're probably right," she said.

A ship passed slowly along the horizon, its lights twinkling. Pete Yorn sang "Come Back Home" in the salon.

Mel had passed Captain Mike in the passageway and he'd smiled and said, *Cute pajamas.* She'd wondered for a moment if he was flirting with her, but then he said, *Good night,* and strode along the passageway to the crew quarters. She stood there watching him disappear, wondering what he would do if she followed him. She imagined herself standing outside his door, rapping lightly with her knuckles and then throwing herself into his arms when he appeared, sleepily, in the passageway.

What was it she always told herself just before beginning some particularly desperate enterprise? *This experience will make me a better writer.*

Maybe, after all, that was the best she could hope for.

Annie sat watching the moonlight shimmer on the water. The distant island was like a bowl overturned in the sea. She should have felt anxious, sitting here on a moonlit ocean far, far, from shore but instead she felt sleepy and content. And maybe even a little homesick. She wished that Mitchell was here.

Far off across the water the lights of Wilmington twinkled faintly. A radio tower blinked, its red beacon glowing dimly.

"Should I tell him?" Annie hesitated, staring at the distant lights. "Should I tell Mitchell?"

"About what?"

"About Professor Ballard."

Mel was quiet for a moment considering this. "Do you think it'll make him happy to know?" she asked carefully.

Annie shook her head. "No. It'll make him miserable. It'll ruin his life."

"Then you can't tell him," Sara said.

"There's your answer," Mel said.

Annie sat quietly, feeling the gentle rocking of the boat beneath her. *Forgiveness comes when you least expect it,* she thought, *dropping from the heavens like a cool rain.* She smiled faintly and said, "But it's okay now, isn't it? I've told you."

"Yes, you've told us," Lola said, touching Annie's hand. "You don't have to think about it anymore."

"You've been happy together for thirty years," Mel said. "Don't let anything spoil that."

It was then that Annie put her head down and began to cry.

They all cried for a while and then it was over. They wiped their faces, blew their noses, and looked at each other sheepishly. Mel got up and poured everyone another glass of tea, then she sat down again. She took a deep breath, pulling one knee up against her chest and resting her foot on the edge of her chair. "There's something I have to say," she said, and the others, sensing her gravity, steeled themselves for another revelation. She breathed again, more quietly this time, and turned to Lola. "I don't know how to begin," she said.

They waited patiently. Lola stirred the ice in her glass with a straw.

"Just say it," Annie said.

"Get it off your chest," Sara said.

Mel sighed heavily. She paused, avoiding Lola's eyes, and then said quickly, "Back in college. The night Briggs put Lonnie in the hospital." She hesitated again, but this time she met Lola's steady gaze. "It was me who told him about you and Lonnie."

No one said anything. Lightning flashed along the distant horizon.

Sara shook her head mutely. "I don't believe it," she said finally.

"How could you?" Annie said.

"I had no right," Mel said, and Lola dropped her chin to stare at the candle, a reticent expression on her face. "I was afraid you'd run off with Lonnie and be unhappy, and I didn't want that to happen, but I had no right. It was none of my business who you ran off with. It was your life, not mine."

Lola stared at the candle. "Did you tell my mother?"

"No. Briggs must have done that. Lola, I'm so sorry."

Sara stood up abruptly and walked over to the side of the boat. She put her hands on the railing and leaned out over the water as if she might jump. Annie chewed a mint leaf and stared solemnly at the moon.

"I didn't want to see you get hurt," Mel repeated slowly.

Lola took a deep breath. Her face, lit by the moon and the flickering candlelight, was calm but thoughtful. "It's all right," she said finally. "I know you did it for the right reasons."

"I was trying to protect you. But I shouldn't have done that. If I hadn't done it, you wouldn't have married Briggs and been so unhappy all these years."

"Hush," Lola said.

"I just wanted you to be happy."

"I know," Lola said. "Everyone wants me to be happy."

There was nothing else Mel could say. She sat back with her hands dropped carelessly in her lap. Lola's features, small and delicate, maintained their passive expression. The only sign of any inner agitation was a slight trembling of her chin.

She cleared her throat and leaned over, stretching her hands out across the table to Mel. "I forgive you," she said. "I know you did it with the best of intentions." She held on to Mel, then let her go, leaning back in her chair. "Besides, my mother would have hunted us down and had the marriage annulled, and I would've wound up married to Briggs anyway."

"But I didn't have to make it easy for them. I was your friend."

"You're still my friend," Lola said.

A sudden gust of wind blew the candle out. The sea was dark and still.

Mel said, "You know, I used to dream of rescuing you from that place your mother took you. That hospital. I used to dream of crashing in there like Sylvester Stallone and taking you out."

"Which is pretty funny," Sara said, "considering that you helped put her there."

"Don't," Lola said. "None of that matters anymore. This is all I want, the four of us right here, right now."

Annie leaned to relight the candle. There was a smell of rain in the air, subtle yet persistent, and she lifted her nose and sniffed. Sara came back to the circle and sat down. Mel smoothed her hair off her face and stared up at the bright moon. After a while, she said sleepily, "Can you believe the way this night's turned out?"

"I feel like I'm in therapy."

"You *are* in therapy."

"We're all in therapy."

"Here's to friendship," Annie said, lifting her glass and thinking how peaceful it all felt, the slumbering sea, the spreading moonlight. A bank of translucent clouds scuttled across the moon. It was impossible to believe in the randomness of life when looking at a sky like that.

"To friendship," they all said in unison, lifting their glasses.

The tension, which had been steadily growing between them all week, was gone. The elephant had tiptoed out on its huge feet. Annie drained her glass and set it down on the table. She felt better than she had in years, filled with an airy lightness of spirit. What was it Lola had said? *Thaumaturgy.* The working of miracles.

Mel leaned back expansively and opened her arms to the night sky. "See, Lola, you're the only one with nothing to confess. You're the only one who's never done anything rotten enough to ask for forgiveness."

Lola put her head back and laughed, a bright swelling laugh that made the others smile to hear it.

"Why are you laughing?" Mel asked.

"What's so funny?"

"If only it were that easy," Lola said.

Mel slept fitfully. She dreamed of a great cat resting on her chest and purring in her ear and she awoke to a distant puttering sound growing fainter, like the hum of an air conditioner or the slight clatter of bilge pumps. She looked at the clock. It was one-thirty. The room was shuttered, and dark and cold as a tomb. The bed was vast and covered in down. Mel quickly fell back to sleep and awoke later to a loud pounding on the door.

Captain Mike was standing in the dimly lit passageway. His face looked pale and worried. "I'm sorry to wake you," he said, "but there's another storm moving in. I think we should head back to the marina early." He looked past her. "Mrs. Furman?" he said. Mel turned around. The bed was empty. She went into the bathroom to check but that was empty, too. "She's not here," she said, still groggy with sleep, stepping into the hallway.

Sara's cabin door swung open. "Who's not here?" she asked, yawning.

"Where's Lola?"

Sara blinked. "I don't know," she said. "I thought she was with you."

Annie stood behind Sara, wrapping her robe tightly around her.

"Have you seen Lola?" Mel asked her.

Annie shook her head no. Captain Mike swore and pushed past Mel, heading for the stairs to the deck. They could hear him pounding up the stairs, running now. The wind had picked up, and the boat was shifting heavily in the waves. The women made their way up to the deck. All the lights were on in the salon and galley as they passed through and went out onto the aft deck. Captain Mike was leaning over the deck rail, calling frantically for Lola. They all began to call, leaning over the rail to peer into the dark rolling water. A few minutes later, Captain Mike ran up the stairs to the bridge, and they could hear him shouting into the radio.

Mel climbed the steps to the flybridge. The dinghy sat in its cradle, its seats glistening wetly in the moonlight. The instrument dial glowed dimly at the other end of the bridge. Captain Mike turned on the floodlight and slowly swept the dark rolling water in front of them. He shouted for Lola, his voice edging gradually toward panic. April came up on the bridge and said, "She's not in the engine room. She's not below." Mel turned and followed her back down to the aft deck.

The sky was growing light to the east. The mainland was a dim shape, shrouded in fog. Mel leaned over the railing, staring down into the pitching waves, fighting a rising sense of panic. She gripped the rail and shouted Lola's name.

It was then that she noticed Lola's eyeglasses, lying forlornly on the deck at her feet.

Chapter 39

~~~~~~~~~~

ENDINGS AND BEGINNINGS

The memorial service was to be held at the Episcopal church in Birmingham where Lola had been christened as a baby. Mel made arrangements to fly into Nashville and then drive down to Birmingham with Annie and Mitchell.

It was a beautiful day, warm and ripe with the promise of summer. The trees were green and leafy, and all along the roadside wildflowers bloomed. Mel had forgotten how pretty Tennessee was in late spring. She sat in the backseat watching the distant rim of blue hills that rose to the east, listening to Annie speculate endlessly about Lola's death.

"She may have gone up on the deck to get something and accidentally knocked her glasses off," Annie said over her shoulder to Mel, for maybe the fiftieth time. "You know how Lola was. And she was legally blind. Maybe she leaned down to pick up the glasses, lost her balance, and fell overboard." Mitchell patted Annie reassuringly on the shoulder, like the good husband that he was.

Mel stared out the window at the rolling landscape, trying not to imagine Lola, alone and nearly blind, stooping to pick up her glasses before pitching forward into the dark ocean. But that image was still preferable to the other one, that of Lola throwing herself purposefully over the railing. So far Mel was the only one to have imagined this scenario, at least to her knowledge. Annie had never mentioned it, nor had Sara in any of their late-evening conversations.

Outside the window the sunlight glinted off the limestone cliffs rising on either side of the expressway. Mel could see the holes the highway engineers had drilled to place the dynamite. In the front seat, Annie was still chattering away about someone named Agnes Grace, a child she'd met at some church orphanage. Annie's face was animated, and despite her obvious grief over Lola, she seemed happy. Mel was sure if she leaned over the seat she'd find Annie and Mitchell holding hands like teenagers.

She leaned her face on her palm and thought about her new novel, the one she'd begun to think about writing, the one she'd been incubating in her subconscious like a great, speckled egg. She was through with Flynn Mendez, at least for a while. She needed to try something else. She needed to recapture the excitement she'd felt that night in the darkened auditorium listening to Pat Conroy, that moment of epiphany when she'd felt like her whole life lay before her, and anything was possible if only she had the courage to try. Her agent told her it would be career suicide, but somehow it didn't feel that way. What was it the Native Americans said? *If you come to the edge of a tall cliff, jump.* Maybe that's what she needed to do to get her life back on track. To jump.

"What are you working on these days?" Annie asked politely.

Lola's body had never been found. Two pink slippers had washed up on Lea Island but that was all.

"Something new but nothing I'm willing to talk about yet."

Mel tried not to think about Lola, or the memorial service. She stared out the window at the green rolling landscape. It was hard to think about death on a day like this. As they came through the ridge cut, the glass towers of Nashville rose before her. She'd always liked Nashville, an artistic city with a small-town feel. Not like Howard's Mill, of course. Nothing like Howard's Mill. She sighed, thinking about her girlhood home.

"How's your daddy?" Annie asked, craning her head so she could see Mel.

"He's fine." He wasn't, of course. He was a mess. Leland was nearly blind, and he walked now with a walker. The long-suffering Mercedes had finally had enough and she'd left, and Mel had had to hire a long line of home-care nurses to come in and check on him. She could look down the road and see Leland's inevitable move to a nursing home. The last time she spoke to him, she'd tried to break it to him.

"Daddy, you can't stay by yourself."

Leland said, "Did you just call me Daddy?"

"Oh, my God, Leland, focus."

"Promise me you won't put me out to pasture," he said. "Promise me you won't put me in one of those old-folks' homes where the diaper-wetting bastards sit around waiting to die."

"They're not all like that. Some of them are nice."

It gave her a grim measure of satisfaction to know that she had the power to put him someplace he didn't want to go. Not that she would, of course, at least not anytime soon.

Outside the window, Nashville rose like the city of Oz. Mel rested her cheek against the glass and stared at the wide blue sky, wondering what death must feel like. She had cried herself empty but there were still moments when grief overcame her, rising up when she least expected it. When it became too much to bear, she called Sara.

She had spoken to J.T. several times since Lola's death, his voice cool and distant while he waited for Sara to pick up the phone. She didn't know if it was grief or anger that made him sound so detached but she'd dreamed of him afterward. And now this afternoon she would see him again for the first time in nine years.

She hoped he was bald and fat.

Annie rattled on about Agnes Grace, trying to fill the long silences. Mel had been morose and distant since they picked her up at the airport; she seemed to be taking Lola's death hard. They all were, really. It was a tragic event, the kind of thing they would never really get over.

Mitchell patted Annie reassuringly on the shoulder, and she gave him a bright little smile. He dropped his hand and reached over and took hers, and they drove for awhile like this, hand in hand, like a courting couple.

Something had happened to Annie out there on the island. Some shift in perception, an awareness dawning like a light on the horizon. Something potent and miraculous. She had gone out there the old Anne Louise Stites but she had returned a new woman. She had shed her skin like a snake, and that was why, despite Lola's death, despite the sadness of the occasion, she could still feel a deep and overwhelming sense of joy on this bright, sunlit day.

She squeezed his hand and Mitchell looked at her and grinned. He had been very sweet throughout this whole ordeal, flying down to be with her during the inquest, calling and making excuses as to why she couldn't be at various committee meetings, making sure no one bothered her while she was grieving. She had been a woman on a mission when she got back from North Carolina. She had wasted no time, driving out to the Baptist Home for Children to see Agnes Grace. She'd taken her a bag of seashells, a T-shirt that read BEACH BUNNY, and a book on turtles she'd picked up at the Whale Head Island Turtle Conservancy. Agnes Grace seemed happy to see her.

"Girl, where you been?" she asked, eagerly grabbing the gifts Annie had brought. "I thought you'd run off and left me."

"Now Agnes Grace, you know I told you I was meeting some friends for a week in North Carolina."

"Yeah. I forgot." She picked carefully through the shells. "How was it? Being with your friends, I mean."

"It was good." Annie smiled sadly and gently stroked the child's hair off her face. "It was really good." Agnes Grace had seen enough of death and hardship in her short life and Annie was determined not to burden her with more.

The next day she picked Agnes Grace up and took her to meet Mitchell. He was out by the pool, cleaning laurel leaves out of the water with a strainer, and Agnes Grace went right up to him and said, "Hey, what you doing?" Annie had told Mitchell about the child, of course, she had warned him, but Mitchell and Agnes Grace got on famously. They cleaned out the pool and then took a ride on the motorized Mule to see the farm and check out Alan Jackson's horses. When they got back, Agnes Grace was all excited.

"Mitchell says he'll get me a pony," she said, hopping from foot to foot. "For me to ride anytime I want."

Annie raised one eyebrow and looked at Mitchell, and he flushed and said, "Well, now honey, we got all that acreage just going to waste. And Agnes Grace can come out and ride and feed it and help muck out the barn."

"I can milk the goats, too!" Agnes Grace said, still hopping.

Annie said, "Goats?"

Mitchell took his cowboy hat off and wiped his brow with one arm. "Taking care of animals teaches a child responsibility. You know that, honey."

"That's right, taking care of animals teaches a child responsibility!" Agnes Grace shouted. Her face was red and streaked with sweat and dirt, and she looked happy, happier than Annie had ever seen her look.

"Well, I know that, but I think we might need to talk to the neighbors before we start buying goats."

Later that night, Annie lay in bed beside Mitchell and told him what she wanted, what she'd wanted from the very first time she met Agnes Grace, only she didn't know it then.

"Adoption's a pretty big decision," Mitchell said softly. "Even if her mama agrees to it, there's still the responsibility of raising a child at our age."

"Goodness, Mitchell, you make us sound like we're *old*. We're only in our mid-forties. And forty is the new thirty, in case you didn't know."

"Oh, is that right?" He leaned over and tickled her until she made him stop.

"We'll go slow," Annie said. "We'll introduce her to the boys and then we'll make a family decision, because once we invite her in, she's family. She'll be our little girl."

Mitchell put his hands behind his head and stared at the ceiling. "Well," he said. "She's a fine girl."

"Yes, she is."

Mitchell grinned, his teeth gleaming in the darkness. "And I can't wait to see how she shakes things up at that stuck-up private school you sent the boys to."

Annie giggled, thinking about that. *Q-Tip* was pretty tame compared to what future mothers would probably call her.

Outside her window, the green hills of Tennessee glided past. Annie hummed a little tune under her breath. She could never be a good mother to her lost children, but she could be a good mother to Agnes Grace. That would have to be enough.

"What time's the service?" Mel asked from the backseat.

"Two-thirty." Annie forced herself to stop thinking about the happy future and concentrate on the mournful present. Poor Lola. Poor Lola and

Lonnie. To have known, and lost, the love of a good man seemed tragic. It wasn't so much the life Lola had lost as much as it was the life she'd never lived that seemed so unbearably sad to Annie.

The night before the memorial service, Sara, Tom, and Nicky were sprawled on Tom and Sara's queen-size bed watching the latest Lego movie. Adam was down on the floor, building a Lego fortress.

"Okay, watch this," Tom said. Sara was lying on her side, spooned up against him. She looked up at him and smiled, putting her hand on his cheek. He hadn't shaved in days; the semester had ended this week, and his face was rough. She ran her fingers lightly over the stubble and he kissed them and said, "Look," pointing at the TV screen.

"Where's Adam?" Nicky said. "I don't see him." She was sprawled at the end of the bed on her stomach, her thin legs waving back and forth like windshield wipers. A plate of half-eaten pizza sat on the bed beside her. Caught by their measured movement, Sara stared at Nicky's legs. *Had they always been that thin?*

On the TV screen, a Lego tyrannosaurus, moved by two hands, attacked a city of Legos. "Roar," someone said in the background. Adam looked up. He stood, then sat on the edge of the bed. "That's me," he said, watching the screen. "The sound guy is me." They watched it until the end and then everyone clapped. Adam smiled and went back to playing with his Legos on the floor. Nicky folded her bird legs under her and rolled off the bed. "I'll be right back," she said, picking up the pizza plate.

"Are you going to the kitchen?" Sara tried not to stare at her arms and legs but she couldn't help herself. They were painfully thin; the child looked like she would blow away in a strong gust of wind.

Nicky put her hand on her hip and rolled her eyes. She sighed dramatically. "What do you want?" she asked.

"A glass of water."

"I'll have a beer," Tom said.

Nicky smiled at him. She didn't mind getting him a beer nearly as much as she minded getting her mother a glass of water. They heard her tripping down the hall and then her feet pattering down the back stairway to the kitchen.

"Follow her," Sara said, "and see if she goes into the bathroom."

"Stop it," Tom said. He leaned over and tapped Adam on the top of the head. "Hey, buddy, did you put together that space cruiser I got you?"

Adam didn't look at him but he said, "Yeah, do you want to see it?" He jumped up without waiting for his father to answer, and ran down the hallway to his bedroom to get it. Most teenage boys got excited by video games and iPods, but Adam got excited by a Lego space cruiser. Sara supposed she should be thankful that he got excited about *something*. She had to stop being so negative. She had to retrain herself to see things in a positive light. She thought again of that fleeting moment of perfect detachment that she had experienced on the long-ago road trip to North Carolina. She wanted to feel that way again. She wanted to stop worrying about her child, and the life he would never have. She wanted to build a new life with Tom, a better life than the one they had now, with its constant cycle of disappointment and hope. Surely they deserved better? Surely they were good people who deserved better?

"She's eating," Tom said, bringing her attention back to Nicky. "I saw her eat two helpings of the potatoes at dinner."

"But then she immediately runs to the bathroom. After every meal."

"So what are you suggesting—bulimia?"

"I don't know." Sara closed her eyes. "She's so thin."

"You were thin at her age."

"I know, I know." She opened her eyes and laid back on the pillows. "But I didn't grow up with the cult of perfection hanging over my head every minute of the day. We didn't start reading *Cosmopolitan* until college."

"Maybe we should just watch her for a few days."

"I've *been* watching her. I'm worried."

Tom ran his hand wearily over his face. "Can't we just worry about one child at a time?"

"I wish it were that simple." She rolled over on her side, facing him. "This isn't going to just go away."

"All right." He smiled faintly at her. He looked bone-tired, worn down by worry and fatigue. "I'll ask Dr. Eberhardt if he can recommend someone. It's probably a good idea if she talks to someone anyway, what with our constant focus on Adam. It must be hard for her."

She sat up on one elbow, fingering the buttons of his shirt, avoiding his gaze. "Are you ever sorry?" she asked.

"About what?"

"Me. The kids."

He leaned over and kissed her, running his hand lightly over the swell of her hip. "Never," he said.

Later, they all sat together on the bed, even Adam, and watched the tape one more time. There was a point where two Lego dinosaurs are fighting and then began to kiss and make up. They had seen the tape a dozen times but suddenly, without warning, Adam began laughing. He glanced over his shoulder at them and they were so startled, they began laughing, too. And in that brief moment of shared laughter, looking around at her family huddled together on the bed, Sara experienced a sudden unexpected happiness. A moment of sheer, startling joy. They laughed and played the scene over and laughed again, and looking around at their happy faces, Sara thought, *Maybe that's all there is, these small moments of unexpected joy. Maybe that's the best we can hope for.*

And for her, on this night at least, that was enough.

She took a long, hot bath and thought about Lola. The fact that she would never see her friend again, would never again witness the world through Lola's sweet, bright eyes seemed to her unbearably sad. She cried for a while, and when she was finished, she washed her face and lay back in the bath. She wondered if she'd be able to speak to Briggs at the service, to continue the pretense a little longer.

She climbed out of the tub and wrapped herself in a towel. She was glad Mel and Annie would be there tomorrow. She felt like she could get through anything if they were there. Tom came in and stood at the sink, brushing his teeth while she dressed.

"Are you nervous about seeing her again?" she asked, toweling her hair.

He rinsed his mouth and looked at her in the mirror. "Who?"

She smiled. "Mel."

"Not really. Why?"

"Well, she was your college sweetheart. She was the love of your life."

He pulled her roughly into his arms and kissed her, toothpaste still on his face. She laughed and he slapped her playfully on the rear end and kissed her again.

"You are the love of my life," he said.

Mel hadn't expected the church to be so big, but it was a good thing it was because there were several hundred people in attendance, among them many dignitaries, including the mayor and two state senators. Mel stood on her tiptoes scanning the crowd, looking for Sara and her family. They made their way slowly toward the front pews, Mel in front, followed by

Annie and Mitchell, still holding hands. Mel could see Lola's mother, Maureen, standing at the end of the aisle. She was greeting people as they came forward to find their seats, still a handsome woman at seventy, looking stoic and bitter, as if contemplating her lost child, her life's work, so finally and irrevocably beyond her control. Briggs stood beside her, his face rigid, expression fixed. He had aged overnight into an old man, slope-shouldered but fierce, like a crafty old bull waiting for the matador to wave the muleta. He said something to a young man sitting in a pew across the aisle and the young man turned to survey the crowd. *Henry,* Mel guessed. He looked so much like Lola that her heart lurched suddenly in her chest. Henry stared up at one of the stained-glass windows, looking strangely calm and peaceful.

April and Captain Mike were noticeably absent, not that Mel would have expected them at the memorial service. The inquest had been bad enough. Briggs had lost his temper and thrown himself at Captain Mike, who had manfully restrained himself even though you could see how badly he wanted to punch Briggs in the face. It had taken two large sheriff's deputies to haul Briggs away. He had been cursing Captain Mike the whole time. Briggs had to have someone else to blame for Lola's death. He couldn't blame himself.

In the aisle ahead of Mel, hidden by a screen of slow-moving mourners, Sara was nervously herding her family toward the front of the church. Nicky was in front, followed by Adam, and then Sara. Tom walked behind her, keeping his hand firmly pressed against the small of her back, steadying her. Sara prayed that Adam would be on his best behavior, that there would be no outbursts or inappropriate restlessness. She was nervous but she was proud, too, proud of their good looks and well-dressed appearance, of the way Nicky and Adam smiled and spoke politely as they navigated the crowd.

Nicky had found a pew at the front and she stopped, waiting for her parents. Beside her Adam fiddled with a Lego figure he had pulled from his pocket. Sara reached the pew and turned, and as she did, the crowd cleared and she saw Mel, looking tall and beautiful, coming up the aisle in front of Annie and Mitchell.

Sara lifted her hand and waved.

Mel saw Sara and hurried forward. Everyone was scrambling to find a seat; the music had begun, faint and mournful, Albinoni's "Adagio in G

Minor." Mel hugged Sara, closing her eyes, and when she opened them Sara was introducing her to Adam and Nicky, who smiled and took her hand politely. They were both tall and attractive; he looked like J.T. and she looked like Sara. They slid into the pew and Mel said, "They're beautiful."

Sara squeezed her hand. "Thanks," she said, her eyes bright. She slid in next to her children, and sat down.

"Hello, Mel."

"Hello, J.T."

He wasn't bald and fat, of course. He was as handsome as the day she had left him, only a bit more gray around the temples. A bit more weathered. There were lines at the corners of his eyes, deep grooves around his mouth. He smiled at her, briefly, and then glanced at his family, and Mel saw in that glance all the love and devotion he had once so foolishly wasted on her.

She looked away, turning her head to the crowded aisle. "Do you want to sit with your wife and children?"

"No, you go ahead and sit next to Sara. You two will need each other during the service."

Mel smiled sadly and pushed past him but he was already shaking hands with Mitchell. She heard his voice behind her and she realized it wasn't so much the man she loved as it was the memory of him, the idea of him, the idea of them together as they once were. Young, beautiful, fearless. He waited until Annie and Mitchell had sat down and then he slid in next to Mitchell, leaning briefly to catch Sara's eye before settling himself in the pew. He didn't look at Mel again. She knew then that her affection for him would gradually wane, that her dreams of him would become less and less frequent, would eventually fade like a sun-scorched photograph, and would finally cease altogether.

Because the reality was, and she knew this now, it wasn't about J.T. Radford at all.

Chapter 40

~~~~~~~~

LOLA

Six Months Later
Mayaguana, Bahamas

Dear Mel—

You once said I was the only one who had never done anything rotten enough to ask for forgiveness. After reading this, will you still feel that way?

I couldn't think of any other way to do this. My mother and Briggs were just too determined. They would have hounded us relentlessly, and we would never have had any peace. And peace is what I need. I don't know if this will work—there are never any guarantees in love—but I wanted a chance to try. I've lived half my life trying to please everyone else, and now I want a chance to please myself. I want a chance to be happy.

Mike says life is short and we must grab it with both hands while we can. He's a good man and a good captain. I love him. We spend our days fishing and lying in the sun. I've never known such happiness as I've known these last few months on this small boat.

I spent so many years not really living, just surviving. The drugs were to keep me from feeling. It was Mike who convinced me that I had to stop taking them, I had to grieve, to feel, if I was ever to get better. I know you were worried and I'm sorry. I had to pretend. I couldn't show that I'd changed. I couldn't do anything that might make Briggs suspicious.

Seeing all of you again made me realize how short life is, how important it is that we spend it with people we love, doing things that have meaning to us. Sara and Annie are lucky. Love can sustain you through anything, and I don't worry about them. And I don't worry about you either, Mel. You had the courage to strike out on your own, to live your life without regret, and I always admired that in you. You have your work, and that's all you ever needed. Well, not all, but most anyway.

Henry knows the truth, of course. And April. We couldn't have done it without dear April playing her part. And you can tell Sara and Annie, too. But no one else. Maybe I'll call you in a few months and we can all get together again. The islands here are beautiful—hundreds of little deserted cays and beaches with nothing but jasmine and flamingos and wild donkeys.

I am so happy. Forgive me.

Lola

Outside the window, the Manhattan skyline glowed against a wintry sky. Mel reread the letter several times. Then, grinning, she rose and went to call Sara.

ABOUT THE AUTHOR

~~~~~~~~~~~~~~~

CATHY HOLTON is the author of *Revenge of the Kudzu Debutantes* and *The Secret Lives of the Kudzu Debutantes*. She lives in Chattanooga, Tennessee.

ABOUT THE TYPE

This book was set in Garamond, a typeface originally designed by the Parisian typecutter Claude Garamond (1480–1561). This version of Garamond was modeled on a 1592 specimen sheet from the Egenolff-Berner foundry, which was produced from types assumed to have been brought to Frankfurt by the punchcutter Jacques Sabon.

Claude Garamond's distinguished romans and italics first appeared in *Opera Ciceronis* in 1543–44. The Garamond types are clear, open, and elegant.